W9-CBV-709

Praise for the novels of

LINDA LAEL MILLER

"A passionate love too long denied drives the action
in this multifaceted, emotionally rich reunion story
that overflows with breathtaking sexual chemistry."
—*Library Journal* on *McKettricks of Texas: Tate*

"As hot as the noontime desert."
—*Publishers Weekly* on *The Rustler*

"This story creates lasting memories of soul-searing
redemption and the belief in goodness and hope."
—*RT Book Reviews* on *The Rustler*

"Loaded with hot lead, steamy sex and surprising plot twists."
—*Publishers Weekly* on *A Wanted Man*

"Miller's prose is smart, and her tough Eastwoodian
cowboy cuts a sharp, unexpectedly funny figure in a
classroom full of rambunctious frontier kids."
—*Publishers Weekly* on *The Man from Stone Creek*

"[Miller] paints a brilliant portrait of the good,
the bad and the ugly, the lost and the lonely,
and the power of love to bring light into the
darkest of souls. This is western romance at its finest."
—*RT Book Reviews* on *The Man from Stone Creek*

"Sweet, homespun, and touched with angelic
Christmas magic, this holiday romance reprises characters
from Miller's popular McKettrick series and is a perfect
stocking stuffer for her fans."
—*Library Journal* on *A McKettrick Christmas*

"An engrossing, contemporary western romance."
—*Publishers Weekly* on *McKettrick's Pride* (starred review)

"Linda Lael Miller creates vibrant characters
and stories I defy you to forget."
—#1 *New York Times* bestselling author Debbie Macomber

Also available from

LINDA LAEL MILLER

and HQN Books

LINDA LAEL MILLER

THE CHRISTMAS BRIDES

HQN™

If you purchased this book without a cover you should be aware
that this book is stolen property. It was reported as "unsold and
destroyed" to the publisher, and neither the author nor the
publisher has received any payment for this "stripped book."

b116437650

2219283

ISBN-13: 978-0-373-77502-6

THE CHRISTMAS BRIDES   *377*

Copyright © 2010 by Harlequin Books S.A.

The publisher acknowledges the copyright holder
of the individual works as follows:

A McKETTRICK CHRISTMAS
Copyright © 2008 by Linda Lael Miller

A CREED COUNTRY CHRISTMAS
Copyright © 2009 by Linda Lael Miller

PLEASE RECYCLE

THIS PRODUCT IS RECYCLABLE

Recycling programs
for this product may
not exist in your area.

All rights reserved. Except for use in any review, the reproduction or
utilization of this work in whole or in part in any form by any electronic,
mechanical or other means, now known or hereafter invented, including
xerography, photocopying and recording, or in any information storage
or retrieval system, is forbidden without the written permission of the
publisher, Harlequin Enterprises Limited, 225 Duncan Mill Road,
Don Mills, Ontario M3B 3K9, Canada.

This is a work of fiction. Names, characters, places and incidents are
either the product of the author's imagination or are used fictitiously,
and any resemblance to actual persons, living or dead, business
establishments, events or locales is entirely coincidental.

This edition published by arrangement with Harlequin Books S.A.

For questions and comments about the quality of this book
please contact us at Customer_eCare@Harlequin.ca.

® and TM are trademarks of the publisher. Trademarks indicated with
® are registered in the United States Patent and Trademark Office, the
Canadian Trade Marks Office and in other countries.

www.HQNBooks.com

Printed in U.S.A.

CONTENTS

A McKETTRICK
CHRISTMAS

For all those people, everywhere, who make a loving space for pets in their hearts and their homes.

CHAPTER ONE

December 22, 1896

LIZZIE MCKETTRICK LEANED SLIGHTLY forward in her seat, as if to do so would make the train go faster. Home. She was going *home,* at long last, to the Triple M Ranch, to her large, rowdy family. After more than two years away, first attending Miss Ridgely's Institute of Deportment and Refinement for Young Women, then normal school, Lizzie was returning to the place and the people she loved—for good. She would arrive a day before she was expected, too, and surprise them all—her papa, her stepmother, Lorelei, her little brothers, John Henry, Gabriel, and Doss. She had presents for everyone, most sent ahead from San Francisco weeks ago, but a few especially precious ones secreted away in one of her three huge travel trunks.

Only her grandfather, Angus McKettrick, the patriarch of the sprawling clan, knew she'd be there that very evening. He'd be waiting, Lizzie thought happily, at the small train station in Indian Rock, probably at the reins of one of the big flat-bed sleighs used to carry feed to snowbound cattle on the range. She'd warned him, in her most recent letter, that she'd be bringing all her belongings with her, for this homecoming was permanent—not just a brief visit, like the last couple of Christmases.

Lizzie smiled a mischievous little smile. Even Angus, her closest confidant except for her parents, didn't know *all* the facts.

She glanced sideways at Whitley Carson, slumped against the sooty window in the seat next to hers, huddled under a blanket, sound asleep. His breath fogged the glass, and every so often, he stirred fitfully, grumbled something.

Alas, for all his sundry charms, Whitley was not an enthusiastic traveler. His complaints, over the three days since they'd boarded the first train in San Francisco, had been numerous.

The train was filthy.

There was no dining car.

The cigar smoke roiling overhead made him cough.

He was never going to be warm again.

And *what* in God's green earth had possessed the woman three rows behind them to undertake a journey of any significant distance with two rascally children and a fussy infant in tow?

Now the baby let out a pitiable squall.

Lizzie, used to babies because there were so many on the Triple M, was unruffled. Whitley's obvious annoyance troubled her. Although she planned to teach, married or not, she hoped for a houseful of children of her own someday—healthy, noisy, rambunctious ones, raised to be confident adults and freethinkers.

It was hard, in the moment, to square the Whitley she

was seeing now with the kind of father she had hoped he would be.

The man across the aisle from her laid down his newspaper, stood and stretched. He'd boarded the train several hours earlier, in Phoenix, carrying what looked like a doctor's bag, its leather sides cracked and scratched. His waistcoat was clean but threadbare, and he wore neither a hat nor a sidearm—the absence of both unusual in the still-wild Arizona Territory.

Although Lizzie expected Whitley to propose marriage once they were home with her family, she'd been stealing glances at the stranger ever since he entered the railroad car. There was something about him, beyond his patrician good looks, that constantly drew her attention.

His hair was dark, and rather too long, his eyes brown and intense, bespeaking formidable intelligence. Although he probably wasn't a great deal older than Lizzie, who would turn twenty on her next birthday, there was a maturity in his manner and countenance that intrigued her. It was as though he'd lived many other lives, in other times and places, and extracted wisdom from them all.

She heard him speak quietly to the harried mother, turned and felt a peculiar little clench in the secret regions of her heart when she saw him holding the child, bundled in a shabby patchwork quilt coming apart at the seams.

Whitley slumbered on, oblivious.

There were few other passengers in the car. A wan and painfully thin soldier in a blue army uniform, recuperating from some dire illness or injury, by the looks of him. A portly salesman who held what must have been his sample case on his lap, one hand clasping the handle, the other a smoldering cigar. He seemed to have an inexhaustible supply of the things, and he'd been puffing on them right along. An older couple, gray-haired and companionable, though they seldom spoke, accompanied by an exotic white bird in a splendid brass cage. Glorious blue feathers adorned its head, and when the cage wasn't covered in its red velvet drape, the bird chattered.

All of them, except for Whitley, of course, were strangers. And seeing Whitley in this new and disconcerting light made *him* seem like a stranger, too.

A fresh wave of homesickness washed over Lizzie. She longed to be among people she knew. Lorelei, her stepmother, would be baking incessantly these days, hiding packages and keeping secrets. Her father, Holt, would be locked away in his wood shop between ranch chores, building sleds and toy buckboards and dollhouses, some of which would be gifts to Lizzie's brothers and various cousins, though the majority were sure to find their way onto some of the poorer homesteads surrounding the Triple M.

There were always a lot of presents tucked into the branches of the family's tree and piled beneath it, and an abundance of savory food, too, but a McKettrick Christmas centered on giving to folks who didn't have so much. Lorelei, Lizzie herself, and all the aunts made rag dolls and cloth animals with stuffing inside, to be distributed at the community celebration at the church on Christmas Eve.

The stranger walked the aisle with the baby, bringing Lizzie's mind back to the here and now. He glanced down into her upturned face as he passed. He didn't actually smile—as little as she knew about him, she *had* figured out that he was both solemn and taciturn by nature—but something moved in his eyes.

Lizzie felt a flash of shame. *She* should have offered to spell the anxious mother three rows back. Already the child was settling down a little, cooing and drooling on the man's once-white shirt. If he minded that, he gave no indication of it.

Beyond the train windows, heavy flakes of snow swirled in the gathering twilight, and while Lizzie willed the train to pick up speed, it seemed to be slowing down instead.

She was just about to speak to the man, reach out for the baby, when a horrific roar, like a thousand separate thunderheads suddenly clashing together, erupted from every direction and from no direction at all. The car jerked violently, stopped with a shudder fit to fling the entire train off the tracks, tilted wildly to one side, then came right again with a sickening jolt.

The bird squawked in terror, wings making a frantic slapping sound.

Lizzie, nearly thrown from her seat, felt the clasp of a firm hand on her shoulder, looked up to see the stranger, still upright, the baby safe in the curve of his right arm. He'd managed somehow to stay on his feet, retain his hold on the child *and* keep Lizzie from slamming into the seat in front of her.

"Wh-what…?" she murmured, bewildered by shock.

"An avalanche, probably," the man replied calmly, as

though a massive snowslide was no more than he would have expected of a train ride through the rugged high country of the northern Arizona Territory.

Whitley, shaken awake, was as frightened as the bird. "Are we derailed?" he demanded.

The stranger ignored him. "Is anyone hurt?" he asked, of the company in general, patting the baby's back and bouncing it a little against his shoulder.

"My arm," the woman in back whimpered. "My arm—"

"Nobody panic," the man in the aisle said, shoving the baby into Lizzie's arms and turning to take the medical kit from the rack above his seat. He spoke quietly to the elderly couple; Lizzie saw them nod their heads. They were all right, then.

"Nobody panic!" the bird cawed. "Nobody panic!"

Despite the gravity of the situation, Lizzie had to smile at that.

Whitley rubbed his neck, eyeing the medical bag, after tossing a brief, disgruntled glare at the bird. "I think I'm hurt," he said. "You're a doctor, aren't you? I need laudanum."

"Laudanum!" the bird demanded.

"Hush, Woodrow," the old lady said. Her husband put the velvet drapery in place, covering the cage, and Woodrow quieted instantly.

The doctor's answer to Whitley was a clipped nod and, "Yes, I'm a physician. My name is Morgan Shane. I'll look you over once I've seen to Mrs. Halifax's arm."

The baby began to shriek in Lizzie's embrace, straining for its mother.

"Make him shut up," Whitley said. "I'm in pain."

"Shut up!" Woodrow mimicked, his call muted by the drapery. "I'm in pain!"

Lizzie paid Whitley no mind, got to her feet. "Dr. Shane?"

He was crouched in the aisle now, next to the baby's mother, gently examining her right arm. "Yes?" he said, a little snappishly, not looking away from what he was doing. The older children, a boy and a girl, huddled together in the inside seat, clinging to each other.

"The baby—the way he's crying—do you think he could be injured?"

"My baby is a girl," the woman said, between groans.

"She's just had a bad scare," Dr. Shane told Lizzie, speaking more charitably this time. "Like the rest of us."

"I think we's buried," the soldier exclaimed.

"Buried!" Woodrow agreed, with a rustle of feathers.

Sure enough, solid snow, laced with tree branches, dislodged stones and other debris, pressed against all the windows on one side of the car. On the other, Lizzie knew from previous journeys aboard the same train, a steep grade plummeted deep into the red rocks of the valley below.

"Just a bad sprain," Dr. Shane told Mrs. Halifax matter-of-factly. "I'll make you a sling, and if the pain gets to be too bad, I can give you a little medicine, but I'd rather not. You're nursing the baby, aren't you?"

Mrs. Halifax nodded, biting her lower lip. Lizzie realized with a start that the woman was probably close to her own age, perhaps even a year or two younger. She was thin to the point of emaciation, and her clothes were worn, faded from much washing, and although the children wore coats, frayed at the cuffs and hems and long since outgrown, she had none.

Lizzie thought with chagrin of the contents of her trunks. Woolen dresses. Shawls. The warm black coat with the royal blue velvet collar Lorelei had sent in honor of her graduation from normal school, so she'd be both comfortable and stylish on the trip home. She'd elected to save the costly garment for Sunday best.

She went back up the aisle, still carrying the baby, to where Whitley sat. "We need that blanket," she said.

Whitley scowled and hunched deeper into the soft folds. "I'm *injured*," he said. "I could be in shock."

Exasperated, Lizzie tapped one foot. "You are *not* injured," she replied. "But Mrs. Halifax is. Whitley, *give me that blanket.*"

Whitley only tightened his two-handed grasp, so that his knuckles went white, and shook his head stubbornly, and in that moment of stark and painful clarity, Lizzie knew she'd never marry Whitley Carson. Not even if he begged on bended knee, which was not very likely, but a satisfying fantasy, nonetheless.

"Here's mine, ma'am," the soldier called out from the back, offering a faded quilt ferreted from his oversize haversack.

The peddler, his cigar apparently snubbed out during the crash, but still in his mouth, opened his sample case. "I've got some dish towels, here," he told Dr. Shane. "Finest Egyptian cotton, hand-woven. One of them ought to do for a sling."

The doctor nodded, thanked the peddler, took the quilt from the soldier.

"If I could just get to my trunks," Lizzie fretted, settling the slightly quieter baby girl on a practiced hip. Between her younger brothers and her numerous cousins, she'd had a lot of practice looking after small children.

Dr. Shane, in the process of fashioning the fine Egyptian dish towel into a sling for Mrs. Halifax's arm, favored her with a disgusted glance. "This is no time to be worrying about your wardrobe," he said.

Stung, Lizzie flushed. She opened her mouth to explain why she wanted access to her baggage—for truly altruistic reasons—but pride stopped her.

"I'm in pain here!" Whitley complained, from the front of the car.

"I'm in pain here," Woodrow muttered, but he was settling down.

"Perhaps you should see to your husband," Dr. Shane said tersely, leveling a look at Lizzie as he straightened in the aisle.

More heat suffused Lizzie's cheeks. It was cold now, and getting colder; she could see her breath. "Whitley Carson," she said, "is most certainly *not* my husband."

A semblance of a smile danced in Dr. Shane's dark eyes, but never quite touched his mouth. "Well, then," he drawled, "you have more sense than I would have given you credit for, Miss…?"

"McKettrick," Lizzie said, begrudging him even her name, but unable to stop herself from giving it, just the same. "Lizzie McKettrick."

About to turn to the soldier, who might or might not

have been hurt, Dr. Shane paused, raised his eyebrows. He recognized the McKettrick name, she realized. He was bound for Indian Rock, the last stop on the route, or he would not have been on that particular train, and he might even have some business with her family.

A horrible thought struck her. Was someone sick? Her papa? Lorelei? Her grandfather? During her time away from home, letters had flown back and forth—Lizzie corresponded with most of her extended family, as well as Lorelei and her father—but maybe they'd been keeping something from her, waiting to break the bad news in person….

Dr. Shane frowned, reading her face, which must have drained of all color. He even took a step toward her, perhaps fearing she might drop the infant girl, now resting her small head on Lizzie's shoulder. The child's body trembled with small, residual hiccoughs from the weeping. "Are you all right, Miss McKettrick?"

Lizzie consciously stiffened her backbone, a trick her grandfather had taught her. *Keep your back straight and your shoulders, too, Lizzie-girl, especially when you're scared.*

"I'm fine," she said, stalwart.

Dr. Shane gave a ghost of a grin. "Good, because we're in for a rough patch, and I'm going to need help."

As the shock subsided, the seriousness of the situation struck Lizzie like a second avalanche.

"I have to check on the engineer and the conductor," Dr. Shane told her, stepping up close now, in order to pass her in the narrow aisle.

Lizzie nodded. "We'll be rescued," she said, as much

for her own benefit as Dr. Shane's. Whitley wasn't listening; he'd taken a flask from his pocket and begun to imbibe in anxious gulps. The peddler and the soldier were talking in quiet tones, while Mrs. Halifax and her children huddled together in the quilt. The elderly couple spoke to each other in comforting whispers, Woodrow's cage spanning from one of their laps to the other like a bridge. "When we don't arrive in Indian Rock on schedule, folks will come looking for us."

Her father. Her uncles. Every able-bodied man and boy in Indian Rock, probably. All of them would saddle horses, hitch up sleighs, follow the tracks until they found the stalled train.

"Have you looked out the window, Lizzie?" Dr. Shane asked, sotto voce, as he eased past her and the shivering child. "We're miles from anywhere. We have at least eighteen feet of snow on one side, and a sheer cliff on the other. I'm betting heavily on first impressions, but you strike me as a sensible, levelheaded girl, so I won't spare you the facts. We're in a lot of trouble—another snowslide could send us over the side. It would take an army to shovel us out, and one sick soldier does not an army make. We can't stay, and we can't leave. There's a full scale blizzard going on out there."

Lizzie swallowed, lifted her chin. Kept her backbone McKettrick straight. "I am not a girl," she said. "I'm nearly twenty, and I've earned a teaching certificate."

"*Twenty?*" the doctor teased dryly. "That old. And a schoolmarm in the bargain."

But Lizzie was again thinking of her family—her

papa, her grandfather, her uncles. "They'll come," she said, with absolute confidence. "No matter what."

"I hope you're right," Dr. Shane said with a sigh, tugging at the sleeves of his worn coat in a preparatory sort of way. "Whoever 'they' are, they'd better be fast, and capable of tunneling through a mountain of snow to get to us. It will be pitch-dark before anybody even realizes this train is overdue, and since delays aren't uncommon, especially in this kind of weather, the search won't begin until morning—if then."

"Where's that laudanum?" Whitley whined. His cheeks were bright against his pale face. If Lizzie hadn't known better, she'd have thought he was consumptive.

Dr. Shane patted his medical bag. "Right here," he answered. "And it won't mix with that whiskey you're swilling. I'd pace myself, if I were you."

Whitley looked for all the world like a pretty child, pouting. What, Lizzie wondered abstractly, had she ever seen in him? Where was the dashing charm he'd exhibited in San Francisco, where he'd scrawled his name across her dance card at every party? Written her poetic love letters. Brought her flowers.

"Aren't you even going to examine him?" Lizzie asked, after some inward elbowing to get by her new opinion of Whitley's character. Oddly, given present circumstances, she reflected on her earlier and somewhat blithe conviction that he would settle in Indian Rock after they were married, so that she could teach and be near her family. He'd seemed casually agreeable to the idea of setting up house far from his own kin, but now that she thought about it, he'd never actually committed to that or anything else. "He might truly be hurt, you know."

"He's fine," Dr. Shane replied curtly. Then, medical kit in hand, he moved up the aisle, toward the locomotive.

"What kind of doctor is he, anyhow?" Whitley grumbled.

"One who expects to be very busy, I think," Lizzie said, not looking at him but at the door Dr. Shane had just shouldered his way through. She knew the car ahead was empty, and the locomotive was just beyond. She felt a little chill, because there had been no sign of the conductor since before the avalanche. Wouldn't he have hurried back to the only occupied passenger car to see if there were any injuries, if he wasn't hurt himself? And what about the engineer?

Suddenly she knew she had to follow Dr. Shane. Had to know, for her own sanity, just how dire the situation truly was. She moved to hand the baby girl to Whitley, but he shrank back as if she'd offered him a hissing rattlesnake in a peck basket.

Miffed, Lizzie took the child back to Mrs. Halifax, placed her gently on the woman's lap, tucked the quilt into place again. The peddler and the soldier were seated together now, playing a card game of some sort on the top of the sample case. The old gentleman left Woodrow in his wife's care and stood. "Is there anything I can do?" he asked, of everyone in general.

Lizzie didn't answer, but simply gave the old man a grateful smile and headed for the locomotive.

"Where are you going?" Whitley asked peevishly, as she passed.

She didn't bother to reply.

A cold wind knifed through her as she stepped out of the passenger car, and she could barely see for the snow, coming down furiously now, arching over the top of the train in an ominous canopy. The next car lay on its side, the heavy iron coupling once linking it to its counterpart snapped cleanly in two.

Lizzie considered retreating, but in the end a desperate need to know the full scope of their predicament overrode common prudence. She climbed carefully to the ground, using the ice-coated ladder affixed to one end of the car, and stooped to peer inside the overturned car.

It was an eerie sight, with the seats jutting out sideways. She uttered a soft prayer of gratitude that no one had been riding in that part of the train and crawled inside. Clutching the edge of the open luggage rack to her left, she straightened and crossed the car by stepping from the side of one seat to the next.

Finally, she reached the other door and steeled herself to go through the whole ordeal of climbing to the ground and reentering all over again.

The locomotive was upright, however, and the snow was packed so tightly between the two cars that it made a solid path. Lizzie moved across, longing for her fancy new coat, and stepped inside the engine room.

Steam huffed forlornly from the disabled boiler.

The conductor lay on the floor, the engineer beside him.

Dr. Shane, crouching between them, looked up at Lizzie with such a confounded expression on his face that, had things not been at such a grave pass, she would have laughed.

"You *said* you might need my help," she pointed out.

Dr. Shane snapped his medical bag closed, stood. He looked so glum that Lizzie knew without asking that the two men on the floor of the locomotive were either dead or mortally wounded.

Tears burned in her eyes as she imagined their families, preparing for Yuletide celebrations, unaware, as yet, that their eagerly awaited loved ones would never return.

"It was quick," Dr. Shane said, standing in front of her now, placing a hand on her shoulder. "Did you know them?"

Lizzie shook her head, struggling to compose herself. Her grandfather's deep voice echoed in her mind.

Keep your backbone straight—

"Were they—were they lying there, side by side like that?" It was a strange question, she knew that, even as she asked. Perhaps she was still in shock, after all. "When you found them, I mean?"

"I moved them," the doctor answered, "once I knew they were both gone."

Lizzie nodded. Just the act of standing up straight and squaring her shoulders made her feel a little better.

A slight, grim smile lifted the corner of Dr. Shane's finely-shaped mouth. "These rescuers you're expecting," he said. "If they're anything like you, we might have some hope of surviving after all."

Lizzie's heart ached. What she wouldn't have given to be at home on the Triple M at that moment, with her family all around her. There would be a big, fragrant tree in the parlor at the main ranch house, shimmering with tinsel. Dear, familiar voices, talking, laughing, singing. "Of course we'll survive," she heard herself say. Then she looked at the dead men again, and a lump lodged in her throat, so she had to swallow and then ratchet her chin up another notch before she could go on. "Most of us, anyway. My papa, my uncles, even my grandfather—they'll all come, as soon as they get word that the train didn't arrive."

"All of them McKettricks, I suppose."

Lizzie nodded again, shivering now. The boiler wasn't putting out any heat at all. Most likely, the smoke stack was full of snow. "They'll get through. You wait and see. Nothing stops a McKettrick, especially when there's trouble."

"I believe you, Miss McKettrick," he said.

"You must call me Lizzie," she replied, without thinking. He had, though only once, and she needed the normality of her given name. Just the sound of it gave her strength.

"Lizzie, then," Dr. Shane answered. "If you'll call me Morgan."

"Morgan," she repeated, feeling bewildered again.

He went back to the bodies, gently removed the conductor's coat, then laid it over Lizzie's shoulders. She shuddered inside it, at once grateful and repulsed.

"Let's get back to the others," Morgan said quietly. "There's nothing more we can do here."

Their progress was slow and arduous, but when they returned to the other car, someone had lighted lanterns, and the place had a reassuring glow. Most of the passengers seemed to have regained their composure. Even Woodrow had ceased his fussing; he peered alertly through the bars of his cage, his snow-white feathers smooth.

Whitley had emptied his flask and either passed out or gone to sleep, snoring loudly, clinging possessively to his blanket even in a state of unconsciousness.

"I'd better take a look at him," Morgan said ruefully, stopping by Whitley's seat and opening his kit, pulling a stethoscope from inside. "My preliminary diagnosis is pampering by an overprotective mother or a bevy of fussy aunts or spinster sisters, complicated by a fond-ness for strong spirits. I've been wrong before, though." But not very often, he might have added, if his tone was anything to go by.

Lizzie could not decide whether she liked this man or not. He certainly wasn't one to remain on the sidelines in a crisis, which was a point in his favor, but there was a suggestion of impatient arrogance about him, too. Clearly, he did not suffer fools lightly.

She approached the Halifax family and found them still burrowed down in the faded quilt. The peddler had lighted another cigar, and the soldier was on his feet, trying to see out into the night. Darkness, snow and the reflected light of the lanterns on the window glass made it pretty much impossible, but Lizzie un-derstood his need to be doing something.

"Some Christmas this is going to be," he said, turning when Lizzie came to thank him for giving up his quilt to Mrs. Halifax and her little ones. "Nothing to eat, and it'll get colder and colder in here, you'll see."

"We'll need to keep our spirits up," Lizzie replied. "And expect the best." Lorelei said things generally turned out the way folks *expected* them to, Lizzie recalled, so it was important to maintain an optimistic state of mind.

"Reckon we ought to do both them things," the soldier said, his narrow, good-natured and plain face earnest as he regarded Lizzie. "But it wouldn't hurt to prepare for some rough times, either." He smiled, put out a hand. "John Brennan, private first class, United States Army," he said.

"Lizzie McKettrick," Lizzie replied, accepting the handshake. His palm and fingers felt dry and hot against her skin. Did he have a fever? "Do you live in Indian Rock, Mr. Brennan? I grew up on the Triple M, and I don't think I've ever seen you before."

"My wife's folks opened a mercantile there, six months ago. I was in an army hospital, back in Maryland, laid up with typhoid fever and the damage it done, for most of a year, so my Alice took our little boy and moved in with her mama and daddy to wait for my discharge." Sadness flickered in his eyes. "Reckon my boy's all het up about it bein' almost Christmas and all, and lookin' for me to walk through the front door any minute now."

Lizzie sat down in the aisle seat, and John Brennan lowered himself back into the one beside the window. Lorelei had written her about the new mercantile, pleased that they carried a selection of fine watercolors and good paper, among other luxuries, along with the usual coffee, dungarees, nails and tobacco products. "What's your boy's name?" she asked, "And how old is he?"

"He's called Tad, for his grandpappy," Mr. Brennan said proudly. "He turned four last Thursday. I was hoping to be home in time for the cake and candles, but my discharge papers didn't come through in time."

Lizzie smiled, thinking of her younger brothers. They'd be excited about Christmas, and probably watching the road for their big sister, even though they'd surely been told she'd arrive tomorrow. She consulted the watch pinned to her bodice; it was almost three o'clock. The train wasn't due in Indian Rock until six-fifteen.

She imagined her grandfather waiting impatiently in the small depot, right on time, hectoring the ticket clerk for news, ranting that in his day, everybody traveled by stagecoach, and by God, the coaches had been a hell of a lot more reliable than the railroad.

Shyly, John Brennan patted her hand. "I guess you've got home-folks waitin', too," he said.

Lizzie nodded. "Will you be working at the mercantile?" she asked, just to keep the conversation going. It was a lot less lonely that way. And a lot easier than thinking about the very real possibility of another avalanche, sending the whole train toppling over the cliff.

"Much as I'm able," Mr. Brennan replied. "Can't do any of the heavy work, loading and unloading freight wagons and such, but I've got me a head for figures. I can balance the books and keep track of the inventory."

"I'll be teaching at Indian Rock School when it reopens after New Year's," she said.

Mr. Brennan beamed. He was one of those homely people who turn handsome when they smile. "In a couple of years, you'll have my Tad in first grade," he said. "Me and Alice, we place great store by book learnin' and such. Never got much of it myself, as you can probably tell by listenin' to me talk, but I learnt some arithmetic in the army. Tad, now, he'll go to school and make something of himself."

Lizzie remembered how Mr. Brennan had given his quilt to Mrs. Halifax, even though he was obviously susceptible to the cold. He'd wasted during his confinement, so that his uniform hung on his frame, and plans to help out at the mercantile or no, he might be a semi-invalid for a long time.

"If Tad is anything like his father," she said, "he'll do just fine."

Brennan flushed with modest pleasure. Sobered when he glanced toward the front of the train, where Whitley was awake again and complaining to Dr. Shane, who looked as though he'd like to throttle him. "Is that your brother?" he asked.

"Just someone I knew in San Francisco," Lizzie said, suddenly sad. The Whitley she'd thought she'd known so well had been replaced by a petulant impostor. She grieved for the man she'd imagined him to be—the young engineer, with great plans to build dams and bridges, the cavalier suitor with the fetching smile.

Morgan left Whitley and came back down the aisle. "I'm going out and have a look around," he said, addressing John Brennan instead of Lizzie. "If I don't come back, don't come searching for me."

Lizzie stood up. "You can't go out there alone," she protested.

Morgan laid his hands on her shoulders and pressed her back into the hard, soot-blackened seat. "Mrs. Halifax might need you," he said. "Or the children. Or the old folks—the husband has a bluish tinge around his lips, and I'm worried about his heart." He paused, nodded toward Whitley. "God knows, that sniveling yahoo up there in the blanket won't be any help."

The peddler opened his sample case again, brought out a pint of whiskey, offered it to Morgan. "You may have need of this," he said. "It's mighty cold out there."

Morgan took the bottle, put it in the inside pocket of his coat. "Thanks."

"At least take one of the lanterns," Lizzie said, anxious wings fluttering in her stomach, as though she'd swallowed a miniature version of Woodrow.

"I'll do that," Morgan answered.

"Here's my hat," Mr. Brennan said, holding out his army cap. "It ain't much, but it's better than going bareheaded."

"I have a scarf," Lizzie fretted. "It's in my handbag—"

Morgan donned the cap. It looked incongruous indeed, with his worn-out suit, but it covered the tops of his ears. "I'll be fine," he insisted. He went back up the aisle, leaving his medical kit behind, and out through the door at the other end.

Lizzie watched for the glow of his lantern through the window, found it, lost track of it again. Her heart sank. Suppose he never came back? There were so many things that could happen out there in the frigid darkness, so full of the furious blizzard.

"I don't think your interest in the good doctor is entirely proper," a familiar voice said.

Lizzie looked up, mildly startled, and saw Whitley

standing unsteadily in the aisle, glowering down at her. His cheeks were flushed, his eyes glazed.

"Be quiet," she said.

"We have an understanding, you and I," Whitley reminded her.

"I quite understand *you,* Whitley," Lizzie retorted, "but I don't think the reverse is true. Unless you mean to make yourself useful in some way, I'd rather you left me alone."

Whitley was just forming his reply when the whole car shuddered again, listed slightly cliffward, and caught. The peddler shouted a curse. Mr. Brennan launched into the Lord's Prayer. Mrs. Halifax gave a soblike gasp, and her children shrieked in chorus. Woodrow squawked and sidestepped along his perch, and the elderly couple clung to each other.

"We're all right," Lizzie said, surprising herself by how serenely she spoke. Inside, she was terrified. "Nobody move."

"Seems to me," observed the peddler, having recovered a modicum of composure, "that we'd all better sit on the other side of the car."

"Good idea," Lizzie agreed.

Whitley took a seat very slowly, his face a ghastly white. Lizzie, the peddler, and John Brennan crossed the aisle carefully to settle in. So did the old folks and Woodrow.

Outside, the wind howled, and Lizzie thought she could feel the heartbeat of the looming mountain itself, ponderous and utterly impersonal.

Where was Morgan Shane?

Lost in the impenetrable snow? Buried under it?

Fallen into one of the treacherous crevasses for which the high country was well known?

Lizzie wanted to cry, but she knew it was an indulgence she couldn't afford. So she cleared her throat and began to sing, in a soft, tremulous voice, "'God rest ye merry gentlemen, let nothing you dismay…'"

Slowly, tentatively, the others joined in.

CHAPTER TWO

MORGAN HADN'T INTENDED TO wander far from the train—he'd meant to keep the lantern-light from the windows in view—but the storm was worse than he'd thought. Cursing himself for a fool, his own lantern having guttered and subsequently been tossed aside, he stood with the howling wind stinging his ears, bare hands shoved into the pockets of his inadequate coat. It was as though a veil had descended; he not only couldn't see the glow of the lamps, he couldn't see the train. All sense of direction deserted him—he might be a step from toppling over the rim of the cliff.

Be rational, he told himself. *Think.*

For the briefest moment the wind collapsed to a whisper, as though drawing another breath to blow again, and he heard a faint sound, a snatch of singing.

He pressed toward it, blinded by the pelting snow, blinked to clear his eyes and glimpsed the light shining through the train windows. Seconds later he collided hard against the side of the railroad car. Feeling his way along it, grateful even for the scorching cold of bare metal under his palms, he found the door.

Stiff-handed, he managed to open it and veritably *fall* inside. He dropped to his knees, steadied himself by grasping the arm rest of the nearest seat. His lungs burned, and the numbness began to recede from his hands and feet and face, leaving intense pain in its wake.

Frostbite? Suppose he lost his fingers? What good was a doctor and sometime surgeon without fingers?

He hauled himself to his feet and found himself face-to-face with a wide-eyed Lizzie McKettrick. He could have tumbled into the blue of those eyes; it seemed fathomless. She draped something around him—a blanket or a quilt or perhaps a cloak—and boldly burrowed into his coat pocket, brought out the pint the peddler had given him earlier.

Pulling the cork, she raised the bottle to his lips and commanded, "Drink this!"

He managed a couple of fiery swallows, waved away the bottle. His vision began to clear, and the thrumming in his ears abated a little. With a chuckle he ran a shaky forearm across his mouth. "If you have any kindness in your soul," he said laboriously, "you will not say 'I told you so.'"

"Very well," Lizzie replied briskly, "but I *did* tell you so, didn't I?"

He laughed. Not that anything was funny. He'd seen little on his foray into the blizzard, but he *had* confirmed a few of his worst suspicions. The car was off the tracks, and tipping with dangerous delicacy away from the mountainside. And *nobody*, McKettrick or not, was going to get through that weather.

If any of them survived, it would be a true miracle.

ONCE MORGAN STOPPED SHIVERING, Lizzie returned the quilt to Mrs. Halifax and went forward again to sit with him. Whitley glared at her as she passed his seat.

She'd gotten used to wearing the conductor's coat by then; even though it smelled of coal smoke and sweat, it was warm. She considered offering it to Morgan, but she knew he would refuse, so she didn't make the gesture.

"I heard you singing," Morgan said, somewhat distractedly, when she sat down beside him. "That's how I found my way back. I heard you singing."

Moved, Lizzie touched his hand tentatively, then covered it with her own. His skin felt like ice, and his clothes were damp. Once he dozed off, not that he was in any condition to stop her even then, she'd make her way back to the baggage car. Raid her trunks and crates, and Whitley's, too, for dry garments. And the freight car might contain food, matches, even blankets.

Lizzie's stomach rumbled. None of them had eaten since their brief stop in Flagstaff, hours before, and she'd picked at her leathery meat loaf and overcooked green beans. Left most of it behind. Now she would have devoured the sorry fare happily and ordered a cup of strong, steaming coffee.

Coffee.

Suddenly, she yearned for the stuff, generously laced with cream and sugar—and a good splash of brandy.

Morgan's fingers curled around hers, squeezed lightly. "Lizzie?"

"I was just thinking of hot coffee," she confessed, keeping her voice down, "and food. Do you suppose there might be food in the freight car?"

He grinned at her. "I watched you in the restaurant at the depot today," he said. "You barely touched your meat loaf special."

"You were watching me?" She found the idea at once disturbing and titillating.

"Hard not to," Morgan said. "You're a very good-looking woman, Lizzie. I did wonder, I confess, about your taste in traveling companions."

Lizzie felt color warm her cheeks, and for once, she welcomed it. Every other part of her was cold. "You seem to have formed a very immediate, and very poor, impression of Mr. Carson."

"I'm a good judge of character," he replied. "Mr. Carson doesn't seem to have one, as far as I've been able to discern."

"How could you possibly have reached such a conclusion merely by *looking* at him in a busy train depot?"

"He didn't pull back your chair for you when you sat down," Morgan went on, his tone just shy of smug. "And you paid the bill. It only took a glance to see those things—I saved the active looking for you."

"Mr. Carson," Lizzie said, mildly mortified, "is making this journey as my *guest*. That's why I paid for his meal. He is, I assure you, quite solvent."

"Planning to parade him past the McKettricks?" Morgan teased, after a capitulating grin. "I've only met one of them—Kade—a few weeks ago, in Tucson. He told me Indian Rock needed a doctor and offered me an office in the Arizona Hotel and plenty of patients if I'd come and set up a practice. Didn't strike me as the sort to be impressed by the likes of Mr. Carson."

All kinds of protests were brewing in Lizzie's bosom, but the mention of her uncle's name stopped her as surely as the avalanche had stopped the train. Though she wasn't about to admit it, Morgan's guess was probably correct. Kade, like all the other McKettrick men, judged people by their actions rather than their words. Whitley could talk fit to charm a mockingbird out of its tree, but he plainly wasn't much for pushing up his sleeves and *doing* something about a situation. There was no denying that.

"I'm afraid you're right," Lizzie conceded, bereft.

Morgan squeezed her hand again.

The wind lashed at the train from the side that wasn't snowbound, rocked it ominously back and forth. Lizzie spoke again, needing to fill the silence.

"Did you practice medicine in Tucson?" she asked.

Morgan shook his head. "Chicago," he said, and then went quiet again.

"Are you going to make me do all the talking?" Lizzie demanded after an interval, feeling fretful.

That smile tilted the corner of his mouth again. "I'm no orator, Lizzie."

"Just tell me something about yourself. Anything. I'm pretty scared right now, and if you don't hold up your end of the conversation, I'll probably prattle until your ears fall off."

He chuckled. It was a richly masculine sound. "All right," he said. "My name, as you already know, is Morgan Shane. I'm twenty-eight years old. I was born and raised in Chicago—no brothers or sisters. My father was a doctor, and that's why I became one. He studied in Berlin after graduating from Harvard, since, in his opinion, American medical schools were deplorable. So I went to Germany, too. I've never been married, though I came close once—her name was Rosalee. I practiced with my father until he died—probably would have stayed put, except for a falling-out with my mother. I decided to move west, and wound up in Tucson."

It was more information than Lizzie had dared hope for, and she felt her eyes widen. "What happened to Rosalee?" she asked, a little breathless, for she had a weakness for romance. Whenever she got the chance, she read love stories and sighed over the heroes. The woman must have died tragically, thereby breaking Morgan's heart and turning him into a wanderer, and perhaps the experience explained his terse way of speaking, too.

"She decided she'd rather be a doctor than a doctor's wife and went off to Berlin to study for a degree of her own. Or was it Vienna? I forget."

Lizzie's mouth fell open.

Morgan grinned again. "I'm teasing you, Lizzie. She eloped with a man who worked in the accounts receivable department at Sears and Roebuck."

She peered at him, skeptical.

He laughed. "Your turn," he said. "What do you plan to do with your life, Lizzie McKettrick?"

"I mean to teach in Indian Rock," Lizzie said, suddenly wishing she had a more interesting occupation to describe. A trapeze artist, perhaps, or a painter of stately portraits. A noble nurse, bravely battling all manner of dramatic diseases.

"Until you marry and start having babies."

Lizzie was rattled all over again. What *was* it about Morgan Shane that both nettled her and piqued her interest? "My uncle Jeb's wife is a teacher," she said defensively. "They have four children, and Chloe still holds classes in the country school house he built for her with his own hands." Jack and Ellen, living on the Triple M, would attend Chloe's classes, because the distance to town was too great to travel every day.

Morgan's eyes darkened a little as he assessed her, or seemed to. Maybe it was just a trick of the light. "How does Mr. Carson fit into all this?"

Lizzie sighed. Looked back over one shoulder to make sure Whitley wasn't eavesdropping. Instead he'd gone back to sleep. "I thought I wanted to marry him," she answered, in a whisper.

"Why?"

"Well, because it seemed like a good idea, I guess. I'm almost twenty. I'd like to start a family of my own."

"While continuing to teach?"

"Of course," Lizzie said. "I know what you think— that I'll have to choose one or the other. But I don't have to choose."

"Because you're a McKettrick?"

Again, Lizzie's cheeks warmed. "Yes," she said, quite tartly. "Because I'm a McKettrick." She huffed out a frustrated breath. "And because I'm strong and smart and I can do more than one thing well. No one would think of asking *you* when you'd give up being a doctor and start keeping house and mending stockings, if you decided to get married, would they?"

"That's different, Lizzie."

"No, it isn't."

He settled back against the seat, closed his eyes. "I think I'm going to like Indian Rock," he said. And then he went to sleep, leaving Lizzie even more confounded than before.

"I HAVE TO USE THE CHAMBER POT," a small voice whispered, startling Lizzie out of a restless doze. "And I can't find one."

Opening her eyes, Lizzie turned her head and saw the little Halifax girl standing in the aisle beside her. The last of the lanterns had gone out, and the car was frigid, but the blizzard had stopped, and a strangely beautiful bluish light seemed to rise from the glittering snow. Everyone else seemed to be asleep.

Recalling the spittoon she'd seen at the back of the car, Lizzie stood and took the child's chilly hand. "This way," she whispered.

The business completed, the little girl righted her calico skirts and said solemnly, "Thanks."

"You're welcome," Lizzie replied softly. She could have used a chamber pot herself, right about then, but she wasn't about to use the spittoon. She escorted the child back to her seat, tucked part of Mr. Brennan's quilt around her.

"We have to get home," the little girl said, her eyes big in the gloom. "St. Nicholas won't be able to find us out here in the wilderness, and Papa promised me I'd get a doll this year because I've been so good. When Mama had to tie a string to my tooth to pull it, I didn't even cry." She hooked a finger into one corner of her small mouth to show Lizzie the gap. "Schee?" she asked.

Lizzie's heart swelled into her throat. She looked with proper awe upon the vacant spot between two other teeth, shook her head. Wanting to gather the child into her arms and hold her tightly, she restrained herself. Children were skittish creatures. "I think *I* would have cried, if I had one of *my* teeth pulled," she said seriously.

She'd actually seen that particular extraction process several times, back on the ranch—it was a brutal business but tried and true. And usually quick.

"My papa works on the Triple M now," the little girl went on proudly. "He just got hired, and he's foreman, too. That means we get our own house to live in. It has a fireplace and a real floor, and Mama says we can hang up Papa's socks, if he has any clean ones, he's been batching so long, and St. Nicholas will put an orange in the toe. One for me, and one for Jack, and one for Nellie Anne."

Lizzie nodded, still choked up, but smiling gamely. "Your brother is Jack," she said, marking the names in her memory by repeating them aloud, "and the baby is Nellie Anne. What, then, is *your* name?"

The small shoulders straightened. "Ellen Margaret Halifax."

Lizzie put out a hand in belated introduction. "Since I'll be your teacher, you should probably call me Miss McKettrick," she said.

"Ellen," Mrs. Halifax called, in a sleepy whisper, "you'll freeze standing there in the aisle. Come get back under the quilt."

Ellen obeyed readily, and soon gave herself up to dreams. From the slight smile resting on her mouth, Lizzie suspected the child's imagination had carried her home to the foreman's house on the Triple M, where she was hanging up a much-darned stocking in anticipation of a rare treat—an orange.

Having once awakened, Lizzie found she could not go back to sleep.

The baggage and freight cars beckoned.

Morgan, the one person who might have stopped her from venturing out of the passenger car, slumbered on.

Resolutely, Lizzie buttoned up the conductor's coat, extracted a scarf from her hand luggage and tied it tightly under her chin, in order to protect her ears from a cold she knew would be merciless.

Once ready, she crept to the back of the car, struggled with the door, winced when it made a slight creaking sound. A quick glance back over one shoulder reassured her. None of the other passengers stirred.

The cold, as she had expected, bit into her flesh like millions of tiny teeth, but the snow had stopped coming down, and she could see clearly in the light of the moon. The car was still linked to the one behind it, and both remained upright.

Shivering on the tiny metal platform between the two cars, Lizzie risked a glance toward the cliff and was alarmed to see how close the one she'd just left had come to pitching over the edge.

Her heart pounded; for a moment she considered rushing back to awaken the others, herd them into the baggage car, which was, at least, still sitting on the tracks.

But would the second car be any safer?

It was too cold to stand there deliberating. She shoved open the next door. They would all be better able to deal with the crisis if she found food, blankets, *anything* to keep body and soul together until help arrived.

And help *would* arrive. Her father and uncles were probably on their way even then. The question was, would they get there before there was another snowslide, before everyone perished from the unrelenting cold?

Lizzie found her own three steamer trunks, each of them nearly large enough for her to stand up inside, stacked one on top of the other. A pang struck her. Papa had teased her mercilessly about traveling with so much luggage. *You'd never make it on a cattle drive,* he'd said.

God, how she missed Holt McKettrick in that moment. His strength, his common sense, his innate ability to deal ably with whatever adversity dared present itself.

Think, Lizzie, she told herself. *Fretting is useless.*

Chewing on her lower lip, she pondered. Of course the coat and her other woolen garments were in the red trunk, and it was on the bottom. If she dislodged the other two—which would be a Herculean feat in its own right, involving much climbing and a lot of pushing— would the inevitable jolts send the passenger car, so precariously tilted, plummeting to the bottom of the ravine?

She decided to proceed to the freight car and think about the trunks on the way back. It was very possible, after all, that orders of blankets and coats and stockings and—please, God, *food*—might be found there, originally destined for the mercantile in Indian Rock, thus alleviating the need to rummage through her trunks.

Getting into the freight car proved impossible—the door was frozen shut, and no amount of kicking, pounding and latch wrenching availed. She finally lowered herself to the ground, by means of another small ladder, and the snow came up under her skirts to soak through her woolen bloomers and sting her thighs. She was perilously close to the edge, too—one slip and she would slide helplessly down the steep bank.

At least the hard work of moving at all warmed her a bit. Clinging to the side of the car with both hands, she made her precarious way along it. Her feet gave way once, and only her numb grip on the iron edging at the base of the car kept her from tumbling to her death.

After what seemed like hours, she reached the rear of the freight car. Somewhere in the thinning darkness, a wolf howled, the sound echoing inside Lizzie, ancient and forlorn.

Buck up, she ordered herself. *Keep going.*

Behind the freight car was the caboose, painted a cheery red. And, glory be, a *chimney* jutted from its roof. Where there was a chimney, there was a stove, and where there was a stove—

Blessed warmth.

Forgoing the freight car for the time being, Lizzie decided to explore the caboose instead.

She had to wade through more snow, and nearly lost her footing again, but when she got to the door, it opened easily. She slipped inside, breathless, teeth chattering. Somewhere along the way, she'd lost her scarf, so her ears throbbed with cold, fit to fall right off her head.

There *was* a stove, a squat, pot-bellied one, hardly larger than the kettle Lorelei used for rendering lard at home. And on top of that stove, miraculously still in place after the jarring impact of the avalanche, stood a coffee pot. Peering inside a small cupboard near the stove, she saw a few precious provisions—a tin of coffee, a bag of sugar, a wedge of yellow cheese.

Lizzie gave a ranch-girl whoop, then slapped a hand over her mouth. Raised in the high country from the time she was twelve, she knew that when the snow was so deep, any sudden sound could bring most of the mountainside thundering down on top of them. She listened, too scared to breathe, for an ominous rumble overhead, but none came.

She assessed the long, benchlike seats lining the sides of the car. Room for everyone to lie down and sleep.

Yes, the caboose would do nicely.

She forced herself to go outside again—even the sight of that stove, cold as it was, had warmed her a little. The freight car proved as impenetrable from the rear door as from the first one Lizzie had tried, but she was much heartened, just the same. Morgan, Whitley and the peddler would be able to get inside.

She was making her way back along the side of the train, every step carefully considered, both hands grasping the side, when it happened.

Her feet slipped, her stomach gave a dull lurch, and she felt herself falling.

She slid a few feet, managed to catch hold of a tree root, the tree itself long gone. Fear sent the air whooshing from her lungs, as if she'd been struck in the solar plexus, and she knew her grip would not last long. She had almost no feeling in her hands, and her feet dangled in midair. She did not dare turn her head and look down.

"Help me!" she called out, in a voice that sounded laughably cheerful, given the circumstances.

Morgan's head appeared above her, a genie sprung from a lamp. "Hold on," he told her grimly, "and *do not* move."

She watched, blinking salty moisture from her eyes, as he unbuckled his belt, pulled it free of his trousers and fashioned a loop at one end. He lay down on his belly and tossed the looped end of the belt within reach.

"Listen to me, Lizzie," he said very quietly. "Take a few breaths before you reach for the belt. You can't afford to miss."

Lizzie didn't even nod, so tenuous was her hold on the root. She took the advised breaths, even closed her eyes for a moment, imagined herself standing on firm ground. Safe with Morgan.

If she could just get to Morgan....

"Ready?" he asked.

"Yes," she said. Still clinging to the root, which was already giving way, with one hand, she grasped the leather loop with the other. Morgan's strength seemed to surge along the length of it.

"I've got you, Lizzie," Morgan said. "Take hold with the other hand."

After another deep breath, she let go of the root.

Morgan pulled her up slowly, and very carefully. When she crested the bank, he hauled her into his arms and held her hard, both of them kneeling only inches from the lip of the cliff.

"Easy, now," he murmured, his breath warming her right ear. "No sudden moves."

Lizzie nodded slightly, her face buried in his shoulder, clinging to the fabric of his coat with both hands.

Morgan rose carefully to his feet, bringing Lizzie with him.

"The caboose," she said, trembling all over. "There's a stove in the caboose—and a c-coffeepot."

He took her there. Seated her none too gently on one

of the long seats. "What the *hell* were you thinking?" he demanded, moving to the stove, stuffing in kindling and old newspaper from the half-filled wood box, striking a match to start a blaze.

"I was looking for food...blankets—"

Morgan gave her a scathing look. Took the coffeepot off the stove and went out the rear door of the caboose. When he came back, Lizzie saw that he'd filled the pot with snow. He set it on the stove with an eloquent clunk. "You could have been killed!" he rasped, pale with fury.

"How did you know to...to come looking for me?"

"John Brennan woke me up. Said he'd seen you leave the car. At first, he thought he was dreaming, because nobody would do anything that stupid."

"*You* left the car," Lizzie reminded him. "What's the difference?"

"The *difference,* Lizzie McKettrick, is that you are a woman and I am a man. And don't you *dare* get up on a soapbox. If I hadn't come along when I did, you'd be at the bottom of that ravine by now. And it was the grace of—whoever—that we didn't *both* go over!"

He found a tin of coffee among the provisions, spooned some into the pot, right on top of the snow.

Lizzie realized that he'd put himself in no little danger to pull her to safety. "Thank you," she said, with a peculiar mixture of graciousness and chagrin.

"I'm not ready to say 'you're welcome,'" he snapped. "Leaving that car, especially alone, was a damnably foolish thing to do."

"If you expect an apology, Dr. Shane, you will be sorely disappointed. Someone had to do something."

The fire crackled merrily in the stove, and a little heat began to radiate into the frosty caboose. Morgan reached up to adjust the damper, still seething.

"Don't talk," he advised, sounding surly.

Lizzie straightened her spine. "Of course I'm going to talk," she told him pertly. "I have things to say. We need to bring everyone from the passenger car. It's safer here—and warmer."

"*We* aren't going to do anything. *You* are going to stay put, and *I* will go back for the others." He leveled a long look at her. "So help me God, Lizzie, if you set foot outside this caboose—"

She smiled, getting progressively warmer, catching the first delicious scent of brewing coffee. She'd probably imagined that part, she decided.

"Why, Dr. Shane," she mocked sweetly, batting her eyelashes, "I wouldn't *think* of disobeying a strong, capable man like you."

Suddenly he laughed. Some of the tension between them, until that moment tight as a rope with an obstreperous calf running full out at the other end, slackened.

It gave Lizzie an odd feeling, not unlike dangling over the side of a cliff with only a root to hold on to and the jaws of a ravine yawning below.

She blushed. Then her practical side reemerged. "I tried the door on the freight car," she said. "But I couldn't get in. If we're lucky, there might be food inside."

"Oh, we're lucky, all right," Morgan responded, his amusement fading as reality overtook him again. The sun was coming up, and Lizzie knew as well as he did that even its thin, wintry warmth might thaw some of the snow looming over their heads, set it to sliding again. "We're lucky we're alive." He studied her for a long moment. Then he snapped, "Wait here."

Frankly not brave enough to risk another plunge over the cliff-side, McKettrick or not, Lizzie waited. Waited when he left. Waited for the coffee to brew.

He brought the baby first.

Lizzie held little Nellie Anne and bit her lip, waiting.

Next came Jack, riding wide-eyed on Morgan's shoulders, his little hands clasped tightly under the doctor's chin.

After that, Mrs. Halifax. Her arm still in its sling, she fairly collapsed, once safely inside the caboose. Lizzie immediately got up to fill a coffee mug and hand it to the other woman. Mrs. Halifax trembled visibly as she drank, her two older children clutching at her skirts.

Whitley appeared, having made his own way, scowling. Still clutching his blanket, he looked even more like an overgrown child than before. When Mrs. Halifax gave him a turn with the cup, he added a generous dollop from his flask and glared at Lizzie while he drank. She'd seen him empty the vessel earlier; perhaps he had a spare bottle in his valise.

She did her best to ignore him, but it was hard, since he seemed determined to make his stormy presence felt.

The peddler arrived next, escorting the old woman, his jowls red with the cold. He'd brought his sample case, too, and he immediately produced a cup of his own, from the case, and poured a cup of coffee at the stove. "Hell of a Christmas," he boomed, to the company in general, understandably cheered by the warmth from the fire and probably dizzy with relief at having made the treacherous journey between cars unscathed. He gave the cup to the elderly lady, who took it with fluttery hands and quiet gratitude.

Finally, John Brennan came, on his feet but supported by Morgan. The old man accompanied them, carrying Woodrow's covered cage.

The peddler, after flashing a glance Whitley's way, conjured more cups from his sample case, shiny new mugs coated in blue enamel, and gave them to the newer arrivals.

"I'm starving," Whitley said petulantly. "Is there any food?"

"Starving!" Woodrow commented from his cage.

The grin Morgan turned on Whitley was anything but cordial. "I thought maybe we could count on you, hero that you are, to hike out with a rifle and bag some wild game," he said.

Whitley reddened, looked for a moment as though he might fling aside the coffee mug he was hogging and go for Morgan's throat. Apparently, he thought better of it, though, for he remained seated, taking up more than his share of room on the benchlike seat opposite Lizzie. Muttered something crude into his coffee.

Lizzie stood, approached Morgan. "I was thinking if we could find a way to—well, *unhook* this car from the next—"

"Stop thinking," Morgan interrupted. "It only gets you in trouble."

Lizzie felt as though she'd been slapped. "But—"

Morgan softened, but only slightly. Regarded her over the rim of his steaming coffee. "Lizzie," he said, more gently, "it's a question of weight. As shaky as our situation is, if we uncoupled the cars, we'd be *more* vulnerable, separated from the rest of the train, not less."

He was right, which only made his words harder for Lizzie to swallow. She averted her eyes, only to have her gaze land accidentally on Whitley. He was smirking at her.

She lifted her chin, turned away from both Whitley and Morgan, and set about helping Mrs. Halifax make a bed for the children, using John Brennan's quilt. That done, she turned to the elderly couple.

Their names were Zebulon and Marietta Thaddings, Lizzie soon learned; they lived in Phoenix, but Mrs. Thaddings's sister worked in Indian Rock, and they'd intended to surprise her with a holiday visit. Having no one to look after Woodrow in their absence, they'd brought him along.

"He's a good bird," Mrs. Thaddings said sweetly. "No trouble at all."

Lizzie smiled at that. "Perhaps I know your sister," she said.

Mrs. Thaddings beamed. "Perhaps you do," she agreed. "Her name is Clarinda Adams, and she runs a dressmaking business."

Lizzie felt a pitching sensation in the pit of her stomach. There was no dressmaker in Indian Rock, but there *was* a very exclusive "gentleman's club," and Miss Clarinda Adams ran it. Cowboys could not afford what was on offer in Miss Adams's notorious establishment, but prosperous ranchers, railroad executives and others of that ilk flocked to the place from miles around to drink imported brandy, play high-stakes poker and dandle saucy women on their knees.

Oh, Miss Adams was going to be surprised, all right, when the Thaddingses appeared on her doorstep, with a talking bird in tow. But the Thaddingses would be even more so.

Lizzie felt a flash of mingled pity and amusement. She patted Mrs. Thaddings's hand, still chilled from the perilous journey from one railroad car to another, and offered to refill her coffee cup.

Once they'd finished off the coffee and started a second pot to brewing, Morgan and the peddler set out to break into and raid the freight car.

As soon as they were gone, Whitley approached Lizzie, planted himself directly in front of her.

"If I die," he told her, "it will be *your fault*. If you hadn't insisted on bringing me into this wilderness to meet your family—"

Despite a dizzying sting—for there was truth in his words, as well as venom—Lizzie kept her backbone straight, her shoulders back and her chin high. "After staying alive," she said, with what dignity she could summon, "my biggest problem will be *explaining* you to my family."

With a snort of disgust, he turned on one heel and strode to the other side of the car.

And little Ellen tugged at the sleeve of the oversize conductor's coat Lizzie had been wearing since the day before. "Do you think St. Nicholas will know where we are?" she asked, her eyes huge with worry. "Jack's had a mean hankerin' for that orange ever since Mama told us we could hang up stockings this year."

"I'm absolutely certain St. Nicholas will know *precisely* where we are," Lizzie told Ellen, laying a hand on her shoulder. "But we'll be in Indian Rock by Christmas Eve, you'll see."

Would they? Ellen looked convinced. Lizzie, on the other hand, was beginning to have her doubts.

CHAPTER THREE

THE CABOOSE, although not much safer than the passenger car, was at least warm. When Morgan and the peddler returned from their foray, they brought four gray woolen blankets, as many tins of canned food, all large, and a box of crackers.

"There was a ham," the peddler blustered, red from the cold and loud with relief to be back within the range of the stove, "but the doc here said it was probably somebody's Christmas dinner, special-ordered, so we oughtn't to help ourselves to it."

Everyone nodded in agreement, including Ellen and Jack, her younger brother. Only Whitley looked unhappy about the decision.

There were no plates and no utensils. Morgan opened the tins with his pocket knife, and they all ate of the contents—peaches, tomatoes, pears and a pale-skinned chicken—forced to use their hands. When the meal was over, Morgan found an old bucket next to the stove and carried in more snow, to be melted on the stove, so they could wash up.

While it was a relief to Lizzie to assuage her hunger, she was still restless. It was December twenty-third. Her father and uncles must be well on their way to finding the stalled train. She yearned for their arrival, but she was afraid for them, too. The trip from Indian Rock would be a treacherous one, cold and slow and very hard going, most of the way. For the first time it occurred to her that a rescue attempt might not avert calamity but invite it instead. Her loved ones would be putting their lives at risk, venturing out under these conditions.

But venture they would. They were McKettricks, and thus constitutionally incapable of sitting on their hands when somebody—especially one of their own—needed help.

She closed her eyes for a moment, willed herself not to fall apart.

She thought of Christmas preparations going on at the Triple M. There were four different houses on the ranch, and the kitchens would be redolent with stove heat and the smells of good things baking in the ovens.

By now, having expected to meet her at the station in Indian Rock the night before, her grandfather would definitely have raised the alarm….

She started a little when Morgan sat down on the train seat beside her, offered her a cup of coffee. She'd drifted homeward, in her musings, and coming back to a stranded caboose and a lot of strangers was a painful wrench.

She saw that the others were all occupied: John Brennan sleeping with his chin on his chest, Ellen and Jack playing cards with the peddler, Whitley reading a book—he always carried one in the inside pocket of his coat—Mrs. Halifax modestly nursing baby Nellie Anne beneath the draped quilt. Mrs. Thaddings had freed Woodrow from his cage, and he sat obediently on her right shoulder, a well-behaved and very observant bird, occasionally nibbling a sunflower seed from his mistress's palm.

"Brennan," Morgan told Lizzie wearily, keeping his voice low, "is running a fever."

Lizzie was immediately alarmed. "Is it serious?"

"A fever is *always* serious, Lizzie. He probably took a chill between here and the other car, if not before. From the rattle in his chest, I'd say he's developing pneumonia."

"Dear God," Lizzie whispered, thinking of the little boy, Tad, waiting to welcome his father at their new home in Indian Rock.

"Giving up hope, Lizzie McKettrick?" Morgan asked, very quietly.

She sucked in a breath, shook her head. *"No,"* she said firmly.

Morgan smiled, squeezed her hand. "Good."

Lizzie had seen pneumonia before. While she'd never contracted the dreaded malady herself, she'd known it to snatch away a victim within days or even hours. Concepcion, her stepgrandmother, and Lorelei had often attended the sick around Indian Rock and in the bunkhouses on the Triple M, and Lizzie had kept many a vigil so the older women could rest. "I'll help," she said now, though she wondered where she was going to get the strength. She was young, and she was healthy, but her nerves felt raw, exposed—strained to the snapping point.

"I know," Morgan said, his voice a little gruff. "You would have made a fine nurse, Lizzie."

"I don't have the patience," she replied seriously, wringing her hands. They'd thawed by then, along with all her other extremities, but they ached, deep in the bone. "To be a nurse, I mean."

Morgan arched one dark eyebrow. "Teaching doesn't require patience?" he asked, smiling.

Lizzie found a small laugh hiding somewhere inside her, and allowed it to escape. It came out as a ragged chuckle. "I see your point," she admitted. She turned her head, saw Ellen and Jack enjoying their game with the peddler, and smiled. "I love children," she said softly. "I love the way their faces light up when they've been struggling with some concept and it suddenly comes clear to them. I love the way they laugh from deep down in their middles, the way they smell when they've been playing in summer grass, or rolling in snow—"

"Do you have brothers and sisters, Lizzie?"

"Brothers," she said. "All younger. John Henry—he's deaf and Papa and Lorelei adopted him after his folks were killed in Texas, in an Indian raid. Lorelei, that's my stepmother, sent away for some special books from back east, and taught him to talk with his hands. Then she taught the rest of us, too. Gabe and Doss learned it so fast."

"I'll bet you did, too," Morgan said. By the look in his eyes, Lizzie knew his remark wasn't intended as flattery. Unless she missed her guess, Dr. Morgan Shane had never flattered anyone in his life. "John Henry is a lucky little boy, to be a part of a family like yours."

"We've always thought it was the other way around," Lizzie said. "John Henry is so funny, and so smart. He can ride any horse on the ranch, draw them, too, so you think they'll just step right off the paper and prance around the room, and when he grows up, he means to be a telegraph operator."

"I'm looking forward to meeting him, along with the rest of the McKettricks," Morgan told her. His gaze had strayed to Whitley, narrowed, then swung back to Lizzie's face.

Something deep inside her leapt and pirouetted. Morgan wanted to meet her family. But of course it *wasn't* because he had any personal interest in her. Her uncle Kade had encouraged him to come to Indian Rock to practice medicine, and the McKettricks were leaders in the community. Naturally, as a newcomer to town, Morgan would seek to make their acquaintance. Her heart soaring only moments before, she now felt oddly deflated.

Morgan stood. "I'd better go outside again," he said. "See what I can round up in the way of fuel. What firewood we have isn't going to last long, but there's a fair supply of coal in the locomotive."

Lizzie hated the thought of Morgan braving the dangerous cold again, but she knew he had to do it, and she was equally certain that he wouldn't let her go in his stead. Still, she caught at his hand when he would have walked away, looked up into his face. "How can I help, Morgan?"

His free hand moved, lingered near her cheek, as though he might caress her. But the moment passed, and he did not touch her. "Maybe you could rig up some kind of bed for John, on one of these bench seats," he said quietly. "He used up most of his strength just getting here. He's going to need to lie down soon."

Lizzie nodded, grateful to have something practical to do.

Morgan left.

Lizzie sat a moment or so longer, then stood, straightening her spine vertebra by vertebra as she did. Fat flakes of snow drifted past the windows of the train, and the sky was darkening, even though it was only midday.

Papa, she thought. *Hurry. Please, hurry.*

Lizzie made up John Brennan's makeshift bed on one of the benches, as near to the stove as she could while still leaving room for her or Morgan to attend to him. He gave her a grateful look when she awakened him from an uncomfortable sleep and helped him across the car to his new resting place. Using two of the four blankets from the freight car as pillows, she tucked him in between the remaining pair. Laid a hand to his forehead.

His skin was hot as a skillet forgotten over a campfire.

"I could do with some water," he told Lizzie. "My canteen is in my haversack, but it's been empty for a while."

Lizzie nodded. "Dr. Shane brought in some snow a while ago. I'll see if it's melted yet."

"Thank you," Mr. Brennan said. And then he gave a wracking cough that almost bent him double.

"Is he contagious?" Whitley wanted to know. He stood at her elbow, his book dangling in one hand.

"I only wish he were," Lizzie answered coolly. "Then you might catch some of his good manners and his generosity."

"Don't you think we should stop bickering?" Whitley

retorted, surprising her. "After all, we're all in danger here, the way that sawbones tells it."

"Are you just realizing that, Whitley?" Lizzie asked. "And Dr. Shane is not a 'sawbones.' He's a *physician,* trained in Berlin."

"Well, huzzah for him," Whitley said bitterly. Apparently, his suggestion that they make peace had extended only as far as Lizzie herself. *He* was going to go right on being nasty. "I swear he's turned your head, Lizzie. You're smitten with him. And you don't know a damn thing about the man, except what he's told you."

"I know," Lizzie said moderately, "that when this train was struck by an avalanche, he didn't think of *himself* first."

Whitley's color flared. "Are you implying that I'm a coward?"

The peddler, Ellen and Jack looked up from their game.

John Brennan went right on coughing.

Woodrow, back in his cage, spouted, "Coward!"

"No," Lizzie replied thoughtfully. "I've watched you play polo, and you can be quite brave. Maybe 'reckless' would be a better term. But you are selfish, Whitley, and that is a trait I cannot abide."

He gripped her shoulders. Shook her slightly. "Now you can't 'abide' me?" he growled. "Why? Because you're a high-and-mighty McKettrick?"

A click sounded from somewhere in the car, distinctive and ominous.

Lizzie glanced past Whitley and saw that the peddler had pointed a small handgun in their direction.

"Unhand the lady, if you please," the man said mildly.

Ellen and Jack stared, their eyes enormous.

"Don't shoot," Lizzie said calmly.

Whitley's hands fell to his sides, but the look on his face was cocky. "So you're still fond of me?" he asked Lizzie.

"No," Lizzie replied, watching his obnoxious grin fade as the word sank in. "I'm not the least bit fond of you, Whitley. But a shot could start another avalanche."

Whitley reddened.

The peddler lowered the pistol, allowing it to rest on top of his sample case, under his hand.

"I'm catching the first train out of this godforsaken country!" Whitley said, shaking a finger under Lizzie's nose. "I should have known you'd turn out to be—to be *wild*."

Lizzie drew in her breath. "'Wild'? If you're trying to insult me, Whitley, you're going to have to do better than *that*." She jabbed at his chest with the tip of one index finger. "And kindly *do not* shake your finger at me!"

The peddler chuckled.

"Wild!" Woodrow called shrilly. "Wild!"

The door at the rear of the caboose opened, and Morgan came in, stomping snow off his boots. He carried several broken tree branches in his arms, laid them down near the stove to dry, so they could be burned later. His gaze came directly to Lizzie and Whitley.

"I'm leaving!" Whitley said, forcing the words between his teeth.

"That might be difficult," Lizzie pointed out dryly, "since we're *stranded*."

"I won't stay here and be insulted!"

"You'd rather go out there and die of exposure?"

"You think I'm a coward? I'm *selfish?* Well, I'll show you, Lizzie McKettrick. I'll follow the tracks until I come to a town and get help—since your highfalutin *family* hasn't shown up!"

"You can't do that," Morgan said, the voice of irritated moderation. "You wouldn't make it a mile, whether you followed the tracks or not. Anyhow, in case you haven't been listening, the tracks are *buried* under snow higher than the top of your head."

"Maybe you're afraid, *Dr.* Shane, but I'm not!" Whitley looked around, first to the peddler, then to poor John Brennan. "I think we should *all* go. It would be better than sitting around in this caboose, waiting to fall over the side of a mountain!"

Ellen raised a small hand, as though asking a question in class. "Are we going to fall over the mountain?" she asked. Jack nestled close against his sister's side, pale, and thrust a thumb into his mouth.

"You're frightening the children!" Lizzie said angrily.

Morgan raised both hands in a bid for peace. "We're *not* going to fall off the mountain," he told the little girl and Jack, his tone gentle. But when he turned to Whitley, his eyes blazed with temper. "If you want to be a damn fool, *Mr.* Carson, that's your business. But don't expect the rest of us to go along with you."

Little Jack began to cry, tears slipping silently down his face, his thumb still jammed deep into his mouth.

"Stop that," Ellen told him, trying without success to dislodge the thumb. "You're not a baby."

Whitley grabbed up his blanket, stormed across the car and flung it at Ellen and Jack. Then he banged out of the caboose, leaving the door ajar behind him.

Lizzie took a step in that direction.

Morgan closed the door. "He won't get far," he told her quietly.

"Come here to me, Jack," Mrs. Halifax said. She'd finished feeding and burping the baby, laid her gently on the seat beside her; Nellie Anne was asleep, reminding Lizzie of a cherub slumbering on a fluffy cloud.

Jack scrambled to his mother, crawled onto her lap.

Lizzie felt a pinch in her heart. She'd held her youngest brother, Doss, in just that way, when he was smaller and frightened by a thunderstorm or a bad dream.

"I have some goods in the freight car," the peddler said, tucking away the pistol, securing his case under the seat and rising. He buttoned his coat and went out.

Lizzie helped Ellen gather the scattered cards from their game. Mrs. Halifax rocked Jack in her lap, murmuring softly to him.

Morgan checked the fire, added wood.

"He'll be back," he told Lizzie, when their gazes collided.

He was referring to Whitley, of course, off on his fool's errand.

Lizzie nodded glumly and swallowed.

When the peddler returned, he was lugging a large wooden crate marked Private in large, stenciled letters. He set it down near the stove, with an air of mystery, and Ellen was immediately attracted. Even Jack slid down off his mother's lap to approach, no longer sucking his thumb.

"What's in there?" the little boy asked.

The peddler smiled. Patted the crate with one plump hand. Took a handkerchief from inside his coat and dabbed at his forehead. Remarkably, in that weather, he'd managed to work up a sweat. "Well, my boy," he said importantly, straightening, "I'm glad you asked that question. Can you read?"

Jack blinked. "No, sir," he said.

"I can," Ellen piped up, pointing to a label on the crate. "It says, 'Property of Mr. Nicholas Christian.'"

"That," the peddler said, "would be me. Nicholas Christian, at your service." He doffed his somewhat seedy bowler hat, pressed it to his chest and bowed. He turned to Jack. "You ask what's in this box? Well, I'll tell you. *Christmas*. That's what's in here."

"How can a whole day fit inside a box?" Ellen demanded, sounding at once skeptical and very hopeful.

"Why, child," said Nicholas Christian, "Christmas isn't merely a *day*. It comes in all sorts of forms."

Morgan, having poured a cup of coffee, watched the proceedings with interest. Mrs. Halifax looked troubled, but curious, too.

"Are you going to open it?" Jack wanted to know. He was practically breathless with excitement. Even John Brennan had stirred upon his sickbed to sit up and peer toward the crate.

"Of course I am," Mr. Christian said. "It would be unthinkably rude not to, after arousing your interest in such a way, wouldn't you say?"

Ellen and Jack nodded uncertainly.

"I'll need that poker," the peddler went on, addressing

Morgan now, since he was closest to the stove. "The lid of this box is nailed down, you know."

Morgan brought the poker.

Woodrow leaned forward on his perch.

The peddler wedged one end of it under the top of the crate and prized it up with a squeak of nails giving way. A layer of fresh wood shavings covered the contents, hiding them from view.

Lizzie, preoccupied with Whitley's announcement that he was going to follow the tracks to the nearest town, looked on distractedly.

Mr. Christian knelt next to the crate, rubbed his hands together, like a magician preparing to conjure a live rabbit or a white-winged dove from a hat, and reached inside.

He brought out a shining wooden box with gleaming brass hinges. Set it reverently on the floor. When he raised the lid, a tune began to play. "O little town of Bethlehem…"

Lizzie's throat tightened. The works of the music box were visible, through a layer of glass, and Jack and Ellen stared in fascination.

"Land," Ellen said. "I ain't—" she blushed, looked up at Lizzie "—I *haven't* never seen nothin' like this."

Lizzie offered no comment on the child's grammar.

"It belonged to my late wife, God rest her soul," Mr. Christian said and, for a moment, there were ghosts in his eyes. Leaving the music box to play, he plunged his hands into the crate again. Brought out a delicate china plate, chipped from long and reverent use, trimmed in gold and probably hand-painted. "There are eight of these," he said. "Spoons and forks and butter knives, too. We shall dine in splendor."

"What's 'dine'?" Jack asked.

Ellen elbowed him. "It means eating," she said.

"We ain't got nothin' to eat," Jack pointed out. By then, the crackers and cheese Lizzie had found in the cupboard were long gone, as were the canned foods pirated from the freight car.

"Oh, but we do," replied Mr. Christian. "We most certainly do."

The children's eyes all but popped.

"We have goose-liver pâté." He produced several small cans to prove it.

Woodrow squawked and spread his wings.

Jack wrinkled his nose. "Goose liver?"

Ellen nudged him again, harder this time. "Whatever patty is," she told him, "it's vittles for sure."

"Pah-tay," the peddler corrected, though not unkindly. "It is fine fare indeed." More cans came out of the box. A small ham. Crackers. Tea in a wooden container. And wonderful, rainbow-colored sugar in a pretty jar.

Lizzie's eyes stung a little, just watching as the feast was unveiled. Clearly, like the things stashed in her travel trunk, these treasures had been intended for someone in Indian Rock, awaiting Mr. Christian's arrival. A daughter? A son? Grandchildren?

"Of course, having recently enjoyed a fine repast," Mr. Christian said, addressing Ellen and Jack directly, but raising his voice just enough to carry to all corners of the caboose, "we'd do well to save all this for a while, wouldn't we?"

"I don't like liver," Jack announced, this time

managing to dodge the inevitable elbow from Ellen. "But I wouldn't mind havin' some of that pretty sugar."

Morgan chuckled, but Lizzie saw him glance anxiously in the direction of the windows.

"Later," Mr. Christian promised. "Let us savor the anticipation for a while."

Both children's brows furrowed in puzzlement. The peddler might have been speaking in a foreign language, using words like *repast* and *savor* and *anticipation*. Raised hardscrabble, though, they clearly understood the concept of *later*. Delay was a way of life with them, young as they were.

Lizzie moved closer to Morgan, spoke quietly, while the music box continued to play. "Whitley," she said, "is an exasperating fool. But we can't let him wander out there. He'll die."

Morgan sighed. "I was just thinking I'd better go and bring him back before he gets lost."

"I'm going, too. It's my fault he's here at all."

"You're needed here," Morgan replied reasonably, with a slight nod of his head toward John Brennan. "I can't be in two places at once, Lizzie."

"I wouldn't know what to do if Mr. Brennan had a medical crisis," Lizzie said. "But I *do* know how to follow railroad tracks."

Morgan rested his hands on Lizzie's shoulders, just lightly, but a confounding sensation rushed through her, almost an ache, stirring things up inside her. "You're too brave for your own good," he said. "Stay here. Get as much water down Brennan as you can. Make sure he stays warm, even if the fever makes him want to throw off his blankets."

"But what if he—?"

"What if he dies, Lizzie? I won't lie to you. He might. But then, so might all the rest of us, if we don't keep our heads."

"You're exhausted," Lizzie protested.

"If there's one thing a doctor learns, it's that exhaustion is a luxury. I can't afford to collapse, Lizzie, and believe me, I won't."

Wanting to cling to him, wanting to make him stay, even if she had to make a histrionic scene to do it, Lizzie forced herself to step back. To let go, not just physically, but emotionally, too. "All right," she said. "But if you're not back within an hour or two, I *will* come looking for you."

Morgan sighed again, but a tiny smile played at the corner of his mouth, and something at once soft and molten moved in his eyes. "I'll keep that in mind," he said. And then, after making only minimal preparations against the cold, he left the caboose.

Lizzie went immediately to the windows, watched him pass alongside the train. *Keep him safe,* she prayed silently. *Please, keep him safe. And Whitley, too.*

John Brennan began to cough. Lizzie fetched one of the cups, dashed outside to fill it with snow, set it on the stove. The chill bit deep into her flesh, gnawed at her bones.

Ellen and Jack whirled like figure skaters to the continuing serenade of the music box, Mr. Christian having demonstrated that it could play many different tunes, by virtue of small brass disks inserted into a tiny slot. Woodrow seemed to dance, inside his cage.

Mr. and Mrs. Thaddings took in the scene, smiling fondly.

"I'm burnin' up," Mr. Brennan told Lizzie, when she came to adjust his blankets. "I need to get outside. Roll myself in that snow—"

Lizzie shook her head. She had no medical training, nothing to offer but the soothing presence of a woman. "That's your fever talking, Mr. Brennan," she said. "Dr. Shane said to keep you warm."

"It's like I'm on fire," he said.

How, Lizzie wondered, did people stand being nurses and doctors? It was a sore trial to the spirit to look helplessly upon human suffering, able to do so little to relieve it. "There, now," she told him, near to weeping. "Rest. I'll fetch a cool cloth for your forehead."

"That would be a pure mercy," he rasped.

Lizzie took her favorite silk scarf from her valise, steeled herself to go outside yet again.

Mr. Thaddings stopped her. Took the scarf from her hands and made the journey himself, shivering when he returned.

The snow-dampened scarf proved a comfort to Mr. Brennan, though the heat of his flesh quickly defeated the purpose. Lizzie, on her knees beside the seat where he lay, turned her head and saw that Zebulon Thaddings had brought in a bucketful of snow. Gratefully, she repeated the process.

"It would be a favor if you'd call me by my given name," Mr. Brennan told her. His coughing had turned violent, and he seemed almost delirious, alternately shaking with chills and trying to throw off his covers. "I wouldn't feel so far from home thataways."

Lizzie blinked back another spate of hot tears. "You'll get home, John," she said, fairly choking out the words. "I promise you will."

A small hand came to rest on her shoulder. She looked around, saw Ellen standing beside her. "I could do that," the child said gently, referring to the repeated wetting, wringing and applying of the cloth to John's forehead. "So you could rest a spell. Have some of that tea Mr. Christmas made."

Lizzie's first instinct was to refuse—tending the sick was no task for a small child. On the other hand, the offer was a gift and oughtn't to be spurned. "Mr. Christmas?" she asked, bemused, distracted by worry. "Don't you mean Mr. Christian?"

Ellen smiled, took the cloth. Edged Lizzie aside. "Here, now, Mr. Brennan," the little girl said, sounding like a miniature adult. "You just listen, and I'll talk. Me and my ma and my brother Jack and my little sister, Nellie Anne, we're on our way to the Triple M Ranch—"

Lizzie got to her feet, turned to find Mr. Christian holding out a mug full of spice-fragrant tea, hot and strong and probably laced with the very expensive colored sugar.

Mr. Christmas. Maybe Ellen had gotten the peddler's name right after all.

CHAPTER FOUR

THE COLD WAS BRUTAL, the snow blinding. Morgan slogged through it, following the rails as best he could. It was in large part a guessing game, and he had to be careful to stay away from the bank on the left. That presented a challenge, since he couldn't be entirely certain where it was.

Carson, the damn fool, had left footprints, but they were filling in fast, and the man was clearly no relation to the famous scout with the same last name. Tracking him was more likely to lead Morgan to the bottom of the ravine than the nearest town.

Cursing under his breath—the wind buffeted it away every time he raised his head—Morgan kept going, ever mindful of the passing of time. If he took too long finding Carson and bringing him back, he knew Lizzie would make good on her threat to mount a one-woman search. John Brennan was too sick to stop her, let alone make the trek in her stead, and the peddler, well, he was a curious fellow, now guarding that sample case of his as if it contained the Holy Grail, now serving up goose-liver pâté and other delicacies on fancy china plates. He might keep Lizzie in the caboose, where she belonged, or send her out into the blizzard with his blessings. Morgan, by necessity an astute observer of the human animal, wasn't sure the man was completely sane.

Lizzie. In spite of his own situation, he smiled. What a hardheaded little firebrand she was—pretty. Smart as hell. Calm in a crisis that would have had many females—and males, too, to be fair—wringing their handkerchiefs and bewailing a cruel fate. He hadn't been joking when he'd said she'd make a good nurse.

Now, in the strange privacy of a high-country blizzard, he could admit something else, too—if only to himself. Lizzie McKettrick would make an even better doctor's wife than she would a nurse.

He felt something grind inside him, both painful and pleasant.

It was sheer idiocy to think of her in such intimate terms. They barely knew each other, after all, and she was set on teaching school, married or single. On top of that, she'd been fond enough of Whitley Carson to bring him home to her family during a sacred season. Her irritation with Carson would most likely fade, once they were all safe again. She'd forget the man's shortcomings soon enough, when the two of them were sipping punch beside a big Christmas tree in some grand McKettrick parlor.

The realization sobered Morgan. He felt something for Lizzie, though it was far too soon to know just what, but opening his time-hardened heart to her would be foolhardy. Rash. Until this trip, Morgan Shane had never done anything rash in his life. A week ago, even a few *days* ago, he wouldn't have considered taking the kind of stupid chance he was in the midst of right now, bumbling into the maw of a storm that might well swallow him whole.

Yes, he was a doctor, and a dedicated one. He was

a pragmatist's pragmatist, in a field where the most competent were bone skeptical. He believed that, upon reaching the age of reason, everyone was responsible for their own actions, and the resultant consequences. Therefore, if Whitley Carson was stupid enough to set off looking for help in the middle of a snowstorm, he had that right. From Morgan's perspective, his own duty, as a man and as a physician, lay with John Brennan, Mrs. Halifax and her children, the peddler, the Thaddingses, and Lizzie.

Hell, he even felt responsible for the bird.

So why was he out there in the snowstorm, when he knew better, knew the hopelessness of the task he'd undertaken?

The answer made him flinch inside.

Because of Lizzie. He was doing this for Lizzie. Whatever her present mood, she loved Carson. Bringing the man home to the bosom of her fabled clan was proof of that.

Flesh stinging, Morgan kept walking. His feet were numb, and so were his hands. His ears burned as though someone had laid hot pokers to them, and every breath felt like an inhalation of flame. He fumbled for the flask Nicholas Christian had given him earlier, managed to get the lid off, and took a swig, blessing the bracing warmth that surged through him with the first swallow.

He found Carson sprawled in the snow, just around a bend.

Was he dead?

Morgan's heartbeat quickened, and so did his half-frozen brain. He crouched beside the prone body, searched for and found a pulse.

Carson opened his eyes. "My leg," he scratched out. "I think I've broken my leg…slipped on the tracks… almost went over the side—"

Morgan confirmed the diagnosis with a few practiced motions of his hands, even though his wind-stung eyes had already offered the proof. He opened the flask again, with less difficulty this time, and held it to Carson's lips. "I'll get you back to the train," he said, leaning in close to be heard over the howl of the wind, "but it's going to hurt."

Carson swallowed, nodded. "I know," he rasped. He groaned when Morgan hoisted him to his one good foot, cried out when he tried to take a step.

Morgan sighed inwardly, crouched a little, and slung Carson over his right shoulder like a sack of grain. He remembered little of the walk back to the train—it was a matter of staying upright and putting one foot in front of the other. At some point, Carson must have passed out from the pain—he was limp, a dead weight, and several times Morgan had to fight to keep from going down.

When the train came in sight, Morgan offered a silent prayer of thanks, though it had been a long time since he'd been on speaking terms with God. The peddler, Mr. Christian, met him at the base of the steps leading up to the caboose. Stronger than Morgan would have guessed, the older man helped him get the patient inside.

Lizzie had concocted something on the stove—a soup or broth of some sort, from the savory aroma, but when she saw her unconscious beau, alarm flared in her eyes and she turned from the coffee can serving as an improvised kettle. "Is he…he's not—"

Morgan shook his head to put her mind at ease, but

didn't answer verbally until he and the peddler had laid their burden down on the bench seat opposite the place where John Brennan rested.

"His leg is broken," Morgan said grimly, rubbing his hands together in a mostly vain attempt to restore some circulation. He had a small supply of morphine in his bag, along with tincture of laudanum—he'd sent his other supplies ahead to Indian Rock after agreeing to set up a practice there. He could ease Carson's pain, but he dared not give him too much medicine, mainly because the damned fool had been tossing back copious amounts of whiskey since the avalanche. "I have to set the fracture," he added. "For that, I'll need some straight branches and strips of cloth to bind them to the leg."

Lizzie drew nearer, peering between Morgan and the peddler to stare, white-faced, at Carson. "Is he in pain?" she asked, her voice small.

No one answered.

"I'll see what I can find for splints," the peddler said.

Morgan replied with a grateful nod. He'd nearly frozen, hunting down and retrieving Carson. If he went out again too soon, he'd be of no use to anybody. "Stay near the train if you can," he told Christian. "And take care not to slip over the side."

The peddler promised to look out for himself and left. Mrs. Halifax and the children were sleeping, all of them wrapped up together in the quilt. Mr. and Mrs. Thaddings were snoozing, too, the sides of their heads touching, though Woodrow was wide-awake and very interested in the proceedings.

"When your friend regains consciousness, he'll be

in considerable pain," Morgan said, in belated answer to Lizzie's question. Her concern was only natural—anyone with a shred of compassion in their soul would be sympathetic to Carson's plight. Still, the intensity of her reaction, unspoken as it was, reconfirmed his previous insight—Lizzie might *think* she no longer loved Whitley Carson, but she was probably fooling herself.

She did something unexpected then—took Morgan's hands into her own, removed the gloves he'd borrowed from Christian earlier, chafed his bare, cold skin between warm palms. The act was simple, patently ordinary and yet sensual in a way that Morgan was quite unprepared to deal with. Heat surged through him, awakening nerves, rousing sensations in widely varying parts of his anatomy.

"I've made soup," Lizzie told him, indicating the coffee can on the stove, its contents bubbling cheerfully away. Morgan recalled the tinned ham from the peddler's crate and the dried beans from the freight car. "You'd better have some," she added. "It will warm you up."

She'd warmed him up plenty, but there was no proper way to explain that. Numb before, Morgan ached all over now, like someone thawing out after a bad case of frostbite. "Best get Mr. Carson ready for the splints," he said. "The more I can do before he wakes up, the better."

She nodded her understanding, but dipped a clean mug into the brew anyway, and brought the soup to Morgan. He took a sip, set the mug aside, shrugged out of his coat. Using scissors from his bag, he cut Carson's snow-soaked pant leg from hem to knee and ripped the fabric open to the man's midthigh. Lizzie neither flinched nor looked away.

Morgan had the brief and disturbing thought that Lizzie might not be unfamiliar with the sight of Carson's bare flesh. He shoved the idea aside—Lizzie McKettrick's private life was patently none of his business. He certainly had no claim on her.

"I've got a petticoat," she said.

The announcement startled Morgan. Meanwhile, Carson had begun to stir, writhing a little, tossing his head from side to side as, with consciousness, the pain returned. Morgan paused to glance at Lizzie.

She went pink. "To bind the splints," she explained.

Morgan nodded, trying not to smile at her embarrassment.

Lizzie stepped back, out of his sight. There followed a poignantly feminine rustle of fabric, and then she returned to present him with a garment of delicate ivory silk, frothing with lace. For one self-indulgent moment, Morgan held the petticoat in a tight fist, savoring the feel of it, the faint scent of lavender caught in its folds, then proceeded to rip the costly fabric into wide strips. In the interim, Lizzie fetched his bag without being asked.

Carson opened his eyes, gazed imploringly up at her. "I meant…" he whispered awkwardly, the words scratching like sandpaper on splintery wood. "I meant to find help, Lizzie…. I'm so sorry…the way I acted before…"

"Shh," she said. She sat down on the bench, carefully placed Carson's head on her lap, stroked his hair.

Morgan felt another flash of envy, a deep gouge of emotion, raw and bitter.

Christian returned with the requested tree branches, trimmed them handily with an ivory-handled pocket knife. The scent of pine sap lent the caboose an ironically festive air.

"This is going to hurt," Morgan warned Carson bluntly, gripping the man's ankle in both hands.

Carson bit his lower lip and nodded, preparing himself.

"Can't you give him something for the pain?" Lizzie interceded, looking up into Morgan's face with anxious eyes.

"Afterward," Morgan said. He didn't begrudge Carson a dose of morphine, but it was potent stuff, and the patient was in shock. If he happened to be sensitive to the drug, as many people were, the results could be disastrous. Better to administer a swallow of laudanum later. "It'll be over quickly."

"Do it," Carson said, and went up a little in Morgan's estimation. Perhaps he had some character after all.

Morgan closed his eyes; he had a sixth sense about bones and internal organs, something he'd never mentioned to a living soul, including his father, because there was no scientific explanation for it. He saw the break in his mind, as clearly as if he'd laid Carson's hide and muscle open with a scalpel. When he felt ready, he gave the leg a swift, practiced wrench.

Carson yelled.

But the fractured femur was back in alignment.

Quickly, deftly, and with all the gentleness he could manage—again, this was more for Lizzie's sake than

Carson's—Morgan set the splints in place and bound them firmly with the long strips of petticoat.

Taking a bottle of laudanum from his kit, Morgan pulled the cork and held it to Carson's mouth. "One sip," he said.

Sweating and pale, Carson raised himself up a little from Lizzie's lap and gulped down a mouthful of the bitter compound. The drug began taking effect almost immediately—Carson sighed, settled back, closed his eyes. Lizzie murmured sweet, senseless words to him, still smoothing his hair.

Morgan had set many broken limbs in his time, but this experience left him oddly enervated. He couldn't look at Lizzie as he put the vial of laudanum back in his kit, took out his stethoscope. There was something intensely private about the way she ministered to Carson, as tenderly as a mother with a child.

Or a wife with a husband.

Morgan turned away quickly, the stethoscope dangling from his neck, and crossed the railroad car to check Mr. Thaddings's heart, which thudded away at a blessedly normal rate, then moved on to examine John Brennan again.

"How are you feeling?" he asked the soldier gruffly. The question was a formality; the feverish glint in Brennan's eyes and the intermittent shivers that seemed to rattle his protruding skeleton provided answer enough.

Brennan's voice was a hoarse croak. "I heard that feller yell—"

"Broken leg," Morgan said. "Don't fret over it."

A racking cough tore itself from the man's chest.

When he'd recovered, following a series of wheezing gasps, Brennan reached out to clasp at Morgan's hand, pulled. Morgan leaned down.

Brennan rasped out a ragged whisper. "I got to stay alive long enough to see my boy again," he pleaded. "It's almost Christmas. I can't have Tad recalling, all his life, that his pa passed…." The words fell away as another spate of coughing ensued.

Morgan crouched alongside the bench seat, since there were no chairs in the caboose. He was not accustomed to smiling under the best of circumstances, so the gesture came a lot harder that day. Brennan had one foot dangling over an open grave, and unless some angel grabbed him by the coattails and held on tight, he was sure to topple in.

"You'll be all right," he said. "Don't think about dying, John. Think about *living*. Think about fishing with your son—about better times—" Much to his surprise, Morgan choked up. Had to stop talking and work hard at starting again. He couldn't remember the last time he'd lost control of his emotions—maybe he never had. *If you're going to be any damned use at all*, he heard his father say, *you've got to keep your head, no matter what's going on around you.*

"My wife," John said, laboring to utter every word, "makes a fine rum cake, every Christmas—starts it way down in the fall—"

"You suppose she baked one this year?" Morgan asked quietly, when he could speak.

John smiled. Managed a nod. As hard as talking was for him, he seemed comforted by the exchange. Probably he was clutching one end of the conversation for dear life, much as Lizzie had held on to Morgan's looped belt earlier, when she'd slipped in the snow. "She doubled the receipt," he ground out. "Just 'cause I was going to be home for Christmas."

Morgan noted the old-fashioned word *receipt*—his family's cook, Minerva, had used that term, too, in lieu of the more modern *recipe*—and then registered Brennan's use of the past tense. "You'll be there, John," he said.

Exhausted, John settled back, seemed to relax a little. His gaze drifted, caught on someone, and Morgan realized Lizzie was standing just behind him. She held a mug of steaming ham and bean soup and one of the peddler's fancy spoons.

Morgan straightened, glanced back at Carson, who seemed to be sleeping now, though fitfully. Sweat beaded the man's forehead and upper lip, and Morgan knew the pain was biting deep, despite the laudanum.

"I thought Mr. Brennan might require some sustenance," she said, her eyes big and troubled. She'd paled, and her luscious hair drooped as if it would throw off its pins at any moment and tumble down around her shoulders, falling to her waist.

Morgan nodded, stepped back out of the way.

Lizzie moved past him, her arm brushing his as she went by, and knelt alongside Brennan. "It would be better with onions," she said gamely, holding a spoonful of the brew to the patient's lips. "And salt, too." When he opened his mouth, she fed him.

"Them beans is sure bony," Brennan said. "I guess they ain't had time to cook through."

Lizzie gave a rueful little chuckle of agreement.

And Morgan watched, struck by some stray and nameless emotion.

It was a simple sight, a woman spooning soup into an invalid's mouth, but it stirred Morgan just the same. He wondered if Lizzie would fall apart when this was all over, or if she'd carry on. He was betting on the latter.

Of course, they'd have to be rescued first, and the worse the weather got, the more unlikely that seemed.

The thin soup soothed Brennan's cough. He accepted as much as he could and finally sank into a shallow rest.

Creeping shadows of twilight filled the car; another day was ending.

The peddler had engaged the children in a new game of cards. Carson, like Brennan, slept. Mrs. Halifax and the baby lay on the bench seat, bundled in the quilt, the woman staring trancelike into an uncertain future, the infant gnawing on one grubby little fist.

Madonna and Child, Morgan thought glumly.

He made his way to the far end of the car, sat down on the bench and tipped his head back against the window. Tons of snow pressed cold against it, seeped through flesh and bone to chill his marrow; he might have been sitting in the lap of the mountain itself. He closed his eyes; did not open them when he felt Lizzie take a seat beside him.

"Rest," he told her. "You must be worn-out."

"I can't," she said. He heard the slightest tremor in her voice. "I thought—I thought they'd be here by now."

Morgan opened his eyes, met Lizzie's gaze.

"Do you suppose something's happened to them? My papa and the others?"

He wanted to comfort her, even though he shared her concern for the delayed rescue party. If they'd set out at all, they probably hadn't made much progress. He took her hand, squeezed it, at a loss for something to say.

She smiled sadly, staring into some bright distance he couldn't see. "Tomorrow is Christmas Eve," she said, very quietly. "My brothers, Gabriel and Doss, always want to sleep in the barn on Christmas Eve, because our grandfather says the animals talk at midnight. Every year they carry blankets out there and make beds in the straw, determined to hear the milk cows and the horses chatting with each other. Every year they fall asleep hours before the clock strikes twelve, and Papa carries them back into the house, one by one, and Lorelei tucks them in. And every year, I think this will be the time they manage to stay awake, the year they stop believing."

Morgan longed to put an arm around Lizzie's shoulders and draw her close, but he didn't. Such gestures were Whitley Carson's prerogative, not his. "What about you?" he asked. "Did you sleep in the barn on Christmas Eve when you were little? Hoping to hear the animals talk?"

She started slightly, coming out of her reverie, turning to meet his eyes. Shook her head. "I was twelve when I came to live on the Triple M," she said.

She offered nothing more, and Morgan didn't pry, even though he wanted to know everything about her, things she didn't even know about herself.

"You've been a help, Lizzie," he told her. "With John Brennan and with Carson, too."

"I keep thinking about the conductor and the engineer—their families...."

"Don't," Morgan advised.

She studied him. "I heard what you told John Brennan—that he ought to think about fishing with his son, instead of…instead of dying—"

Morgan nodded, realized he was still holding Lizzie's hand, improper as that was. Drew some satisfaction from the fact that she hadn't pulled away.

"Do you believe it really makes a difference?" she went on, when she'd gathered her composure. "Thinking about good things, I mean?"

"Regardless of how things turn out," he replied, "thinking about good things feels better than worrying, wouldn't you say? So in that respect, yes, I'd say it makes a difference."

She pondered that, then looked so directly, and so deeply, into his eyes that he felt as though she'd found a peephole into the wall he'd constructed around his truest self. "What are *you* thinking about, then?" she wanted to know. "You must be worried, like all the rest of us."

He couldn't tell Lizzie the truth—that despite his best efforts, every few minutes he imagined how it would be, treating patients in Indian Rock, with her at his side. "I can't afford to worry," he said. "It isn't productive."

She wasn't going to let him off the hook; he could see that. Her blue eyes darkened with determination. "What was Christmas like for you, when you were a boy?"

Morgan found the question strangely unsettling. His father had been a doctor, his mother an heiress and a force of nature, especially socially. During the holiday season, they'd gone to, or given, parties every night. "Minerva—she was our cook—always roasted a hen."

Lizzie blinked. Waited. And finally, when certain that

nothing more was forthcoming, prodded, "That's all? Your cook roasted a chicken? No tree? No presents? No carols?"

"My mother wouldn't have considered dragging an evergreen into the house," Morgan admitted. "In her opinion, the practice was crass and vulgar—and besides, she didn't want pitch and birds' nests all over the rugs. Every Christmas morning, when I came to the breakfast table, I found a gift waiting on the seat of my chair. It was always a book, wrapped in brown paper and tied with string. As for carols—there was a church at the end of our street, and sometimes I opened a window so I could hear the singing."

"That sounds lonely," Lizzie observed.

His childhood Christmases had indeed been lonely, Morgan reflected. Which made December 25 just like the other 364 days of the year. For a moment he was a boy again, he and Minerva feasting solemnly in the kitchen of the mansion, just the two of them. His dedicated father was out making a house call, his mother sleeping off the effects of a merry evening passed among the strangers she preferred to him.

"If you hadn't mentioned a cook," Lizzie went on, when he didn't speak, "I would have thought you'd grown up in a hovel."

He smiled at that. His mother had regarded him as an inconvenience, albeit an easily overlooked one. She'd often rued the day she'd married a poor country doctor instead of a financier, like her late and sainted sire, and made no secret of her regret. Morgan's father had endured by staying away from home as much as possible, often taking his young son along on his rounds when he, Morgan, wasn't locked away in the third-floor nursery with some tutor. Those excursions had been happy ones for Morgan, and he'd seen enough suffering, visiting Elias Shane's patients, most of them in tenements and charity hospitals, to know there were worse fates than growing up with a spoiled, disinterested and very wealthy mother.

He'd had his father, to an extent.

He'd had Minerva. She'd been born a slave, Minerva had. To her, Lincoln's Emancipation Proclamation was as sacred as Scripture. She'd actually met the man she'd called "Father Abraham," after the fall of Richmond. She'd clutched at the sleeve of his coat, and he'd smiled at her. *Such sorrow in them gray, gray eyes,* she'd told Morgan, who never tired of the much-told tale. *Such sadness as you'd never credit one man could hold.*

Morgan withdrew from the memory. He'd have given a lot to hear that story just one more time.

Lizzie bit her lip. Took fresh notice of his threadbare clothes, then caught herself and flushed a fetching pink. "You're *not* poor," she concluded, then colored up even more.

He laughed, and damn, it felt good. "Oh, but I am, Lizzie McKettrick," he said. "Poor as a church mouse. Mother didn't mind so much when I went to Germany to study. She figured it would pass, and I'd come to my senses. When I came home and took up medicine in earnest, she disinherited me."

Lizzie's marvelous eyes widened again. "She did? But surely your father—"

"She showed him the door, too. She was furious

with him for encouraging me to become a doctor instead of overseeing the family fortune. Minerva opened a boarding house, and Dad and I moved in as her first tenants. We found a storefront, hung out a shingle and practiced together until Dad died of a heart attack."

Sorrow moved in Lizzie's face at the mention of his father's death. She swallowed. "What became of your mother?" she asked, sounding meek now, in the face of such drama.

"She sold the mansion and moved to Europe, to escape the shame."

"What shame?"

God bless her, Morgan thought, she was actually confused. "In Mother's circles," he said, "the practice of medicine—especially when most of the patients can't pay—is not a noble pursuit. She could have forgiven herself for marrying a doctor—youthful passions, lapses of judgment, all that—but when I decided to become a physician instead of taking over my grandfather's several banks, it was too much for her to bear."

"I'm sorry, Morgan," Lizzie said.

"It isn't as if we were close," Morgan said, touched by the sadness in Lizzie McKettrick's eyes as he had never been by Eliza Stanton Shane's indifference. "Mother and I, I mean."

"But, still—"

"I had my father. And Minerva."

Lizzie nodded, but she didn't look convinced. "My mother died when I was young. And even though I'm close to Lorelei—that's my stepmother—I still miss her a lot."

He couldn't help asking the question. It was out of his mouth before he could stop it. "Is money important to you, Lizzie?" He'd told her he was poor, and suddenly he needed to know if that mattered.

She glanced in Carson's direction, then looked straight into Morgan's eyes. "No," she said, with such alacrity that he believed her instantly. There was no guile in Lizzie McKettrick—only courage and sweetness, intelligence and, unless he missed his guess, a fiery temper.

He wanted to ask if Whitley Carson would be able to support her in the manner to which she was clearly accustomed, considering the fineness of her clothes and her recently acquired education, but he'd recovered his manners by then.

"Miss McKettrick?"

Both Lizzie and Morgan turned to see Ellen standing nearby, looking shy.

"Yes, Ellen?" Lizzie responded, smiling.

"I can't find a spittoon," Ellen said.

Lizzie chuckled at that. "We'll go outside," she replied.

"A spittoon?" Morgan echoed, puzzled.

"Never mind," Lizzie told him.

"I believe I'll go, too," Mrs. Halifax put in, rising awkwardly from her bed on the bench because of her injured arm, wrapping her shawl more closely around her shoulders.

Lizzie bundled Ellen up in the peddler's coat, readily volunteered, and the trio of females braved the snow and the freezing wind. The baby girl stayed behind, kicking her feet, waving small fists in the air, and cooing with sudden happiness. She'd spotted the cockatiel with the ridiculous name. What was it?

Oh, yes. Woodrow.

"I reckon we ought to be sparing with the kerosene," the peddler told Morgan, nodding toward the single lantern bravely pushing back the darkness. "Far as I could see when we checked the freight car, there isn't a whole lot left."

Morgan nodded, finding the prospect of the coming night a grim one. When the limited supply of firewood was gone, they could use coal from the bin in the locomotive, but even that wouldn't last more than a day or two.

The little boy, Jack, like Brennan and Carson, had fallen asleep.

The peddler spoke in a low voice, after making sure he wouldn't be overheard. "You think they'll find us in time?"

Morgan shoved a hand through his hair. "I don't know," he said honestly.

"You know anything about Miss Lizzie's people?"

Morgan frowned. "Not much. I met her uncle, Kade, down in Tucson."

"I've heard of Angus McKettrick," Christian confided, his gaze drifting briefly to Whitley Carson's prone and senseless form before swinging back to Morgan. "That's Miss Lizzie's grandpa. Tough as an army mule on spare rations, that old man. The McKettricks have money. They have land and cattle, too. But there's one thing that's more important to them than all that, from what I've been told, and that's kinfolks. They'll come, just like Miss Lizzie says they will. They'll come because she's here—you can be sure of that. I'm just hoping we'll all be alive and kicking when they show up."

Morgan had no answer for that. There were no guarantees, and plenty of dangers—starvation, for one. Exposure, for another. And the strong likelihood of a second, much more devastating, avalanche.

"You figure one of us ought to try hiking out of here?"

Morgan looked at Carson. "*He* didn't fare so well," he said.

"He's a greenhorn and we both know it," the peddler replied.

"How far do you think we are from Indian Rock?"

"We're closer to Stone Creek than Indian Rock," Christian said. "Tracks turn toward it about five miles back. It's another ten miles into Stone Creek from there. Probably twenty or more to Indian Rock from where we sit."

Morgan nodded. "If they're not here by morning," he said, "I'll try to get to Stone Creek."

"You're needed here, Doc," the peddler said. "I'm not as young as I used to be, but I've still got some grit and a good pair of legs. Know this country pretty well, too—and you don't."

Lizzie, Mrs. Halifax and Ellen returned, shivering. Lizzie struggled to shut the caboose door against a rising wind.

Morgan and the peddler let the subject drop.

They extinguished the lamp soon after that, ate ham and "bony" bean soup in the dark.

Everyone found a place to sleep.

And when Morgan opened his eyes the next morning,

at first light, he knew the snow had stopped. He sat up, looked around, found Lizzie first. She was still sleeping, sitting upright on the bench seat, bundled in a blanket. John Brennan hadn't wakened, and neither had Mrs. Halifax and her children. Whitley Carson, a book in his hands, stared across the car at him with an unreadable expression in his eyes.

"The peddler's gone," he told Morgan. "He left before dawn."

CHAPTER FIVE

LIZZIE DREAMED SHE WAS HOME, waking up in her own room, hearing the dear, familiar sounds of a ranch house morning: stove lids clattering downstairs in the kitchen; the murmur of familiar voices, planning the day. She smelled strong coffee brewing, and wood smoke, and the beeswax Lorelei used to polish the furniture.

Christmas Eve was special in the McKettrick household, but the chores still had to be done. The cattle and horses needed hay and water, the cows required milking, the wood waited to be chopped and carried in, and there were always eggs to be gathered from the henhouse. Behind the tightly closed doors of Papa's study, she knew, a giant evergreen tree stood in secret, shimmering with tinsel strands and happy secrets. The luscious scent of pine rose through the very floorboards to perfume the second floor.

Throughout the day, the uncles and aunts and cousins would come, by sleigh or, if the roads happened to be clear, by team and wagon and on horseback. There would be exchanges of food, small gifts, laughter and stories. In the evening, after attending church services in town, they would all gather at the main house, where Lizzie's grandfather Angus would read aloud, his voice deep and resonant, from the Gospel of Luke.

And there were in the same fields, shepherds, guarding their flocks by night...

Tears moistened Lizzie's lashes, because she knew she was dreaming. Knew she wasn't on the Triple M, where she belonged, but trapped in a stranded train on a high, treacherous ridge.

The smell of coffee was real, though. That heartened her. Gave her the strength to open her eyes.

Her hair must have looked a sight, that was her immediate thought, and she needed to go outside. Her gaze found Morgan first, like a compass needle swinging north. He stood near the stove, looking rumpled from sleep, pouring coffee into a mug.

He crossed to her, handed her the cup.

The small courtesy seemed profound to Lizzie, rather than mundane.

"Today," she said, "is Christmas Eve."

"So it is," Morgan agreed, smiling wanly.

Whitley, resting with his broken leg propped on the bench seat, caught her eye. "Good morning, Lizzie-bet," he said.

She gave a little nod of acknowledgment, embarrassed by the nickname, and sipped at her coffee. Evidently, Whitley's apology the day before had been a sincere one. He was on his best behavior. She discovered that she did not have an opinion on that, one way or the other.

"Where is Mr. Christian?" she asked Morgan, having scanned the company and noticed he was missing. The caboose was chilly, despite the efforts of the little stove. "Has he gone looking for firewood?"

A glance passed between Morgan and Whitley. Whitley raised both eyebrows, but didn't speak.

"He's on his way to Stone Creek," Morgan said, sounding resigned.

Lizzie sat up straighter, nearly spilling her coffee. "*Stone Creek?* That's miles from here—" She paused, confounded. "And you just *let him go?*"

Whitley finally deigned to contribute to the conversation. "He left before Dr. Shane woke up, Lizzie. And his mind was made up. Nobody could have stopped him."

Lizzie absorbed that. She thought of the tinkling music box and the tins of goose liver pâté and wondered if any of them would ever see Mr. Christian again.

"I'm going forward to the engine, for coal," Morgan said, taking up a bucket.

Lizzie thought of the conductor and engineer, lying frozen where they'd died. She thought of Mr. Christian, bravely making his way through snow that would be up to his waist in some places, over his head in others. The last, tattered joy of her Christmas dream faded away.

She simply nodded, and concentrated on drinking her coffee.

"Lizzie," Whitley said, when Morgan had gone, "come and sit here beside me."

The others were still sleeping. After a moment's hesitation, Lizzie crossed the caboose to join Whitley.

"Have you forgiven me?" Whitley asked, very quietly. His hazel eyes glowed with earnest affection; he really *was* a good person, Lizzie knew.

"I guess you were just scared," she said.

"I acted like a fool," Whitley told her.

Lizzie said nothing.

Shyly he took her hand. Squeezed it. "Now I've got to start the courtship all over again, don't I? I've botched things that badly."

"C-courtship?" Lizzie had looked forward to Whitley's proposal for months, dreamed of it, rehearsed the experience in her imagination, practiced her response. How many, many ways there were to say "yes." Now, something had changed, forever, and she knew it had far more to do with meeting Dr. Morgan Shane than anything Whitley had said or done since the avalanche. It wouldn't be fair, or kind, to pretend otherwise.

"Tell me I haven't lost you for good, Lizzie," Whitley said, tightening his grip on her hand as he read her face. "Please."

Just then, John Brennan began to cough so violently that Lizzie bolted off the seat and rushed across the caboose to help him sit up. The fit eased a little, but Lizzie felt desperately helpless, standing there patting the man's back while he struggled to breathe.

Whitley, meanwhile, got to his feet and stumped over to offer his flask. "It's just water," he said, when Lizzie looked at it askance, recalling all the whiskey he'd consumed from the vessel earlier.

She took the flask, opened it, held it to John's gray lips until he'd taken a few sips. After several tense moments, he seemed nominally better. Lizzie tested his forehead for fever, using the back of her hand as she'd seen Lorelei do so many times, and found it blazing hot.

Despair threatened Lizzie again. She swayed slightly on her feet, and Whitley caught hold of her arm just as Morgan returned, on a rush of cold wind, lugging a scuttle full of coal.

Time seemed to stop, just for a moment, as abruptly as the train had stopped when the avalanche struck.

Morgan carried the coal to the stove, crouched and tossed a few handfuls in on top of the last of the dry firewood.

Then the children woke up, and baby Nellie Anne began to wail for her breakfast. Whitley made his slow way back to the other side of the caboose, lowered himself onto the seat. Lizzie performed what ablutions she could, brushing her hair and pinning it up again, then grooming Ellen's hair, too. Mrs. Thaddings took Woodrow out of his cage so he could perch on her shoulder, ruffling his feathers and muttering bird prattle.

"Where's Mr. Christmas?" Jack asked, very seriously, as they all made a breakfast of leftover soup, crackers and goose liver pâté. Mrs. Halifax, clearly regaining her strength, had melted snow to wash her children's hands and faces, and they looked scrubbed and damp. "He said he'd teach me and Ellen to play five-card stud."

"He'll do no such thing," Mrs. Halifax said, but she smiled. Then she turned questioningly to Morgan. "Where *is* Mr. Christian?" she asked.

"He's making for Stone Creek," Whitley said, before Morgan could reply. "He should have stayed here."

Both Lizzie and Morgan gave him ironic looks—he'd broken his leg on a similar errand, after all—and he subsided, at least briefly.

Lizzie glanced at the windows overlooking the broad valley, hundreds of feet below the train's precarious perch on the mountainside. "At least the snow has stopped," she mused. "The traveling won't be any easier, but he'll be able to see where he's going."

Once the improvised meal was over, time seemed to crawl.

Mrs. Thaddings introduced Ellen and Jack to Woodrow, and they stared at him in fascination.

"If he was a homing pigeon," Ellen observed, bright child that she was, "he could go for help."

"We might have to eat him," Jack said solemnly, "if we run out of food."

Mr. Thaddings, who hadn't said much up until then, chuckled and shook his head. "He'd be pretty stringy," he told the boy.

"Stringy," Woodrow affirmed, spreading his wings and squawking once for emphasis.

Amused, Lizzie busied herself tending to John Brennan, while Morgan paced the center of the car and Mrs. Halifax discreetly nursed the baby, her back to everyone. Presently, when Woodrow retired to his cage for a nap, Jack and Ellen shyly approached Whitley, and sat themselves on either side of him.

He sighed, met Lizzie's gaze for a long moment, then flipped back to the front of the book he'd nearly finished, and began reading aloud. "'It was the best of times—'"

And so the morning passed.

At midafternoon, a knock sounded at the door of the caboose.

Hope surged in Lizzie's heart—her father and uncles had come at last—but even before she opened the door, she knew they wouldn't have bothered to knock. They'd have busted down the door to get in.

Mr. Christian stood on the small platform, frost in his eyebrows, his whiskers, his lashes. He clutched a very small pine tree in one hand and gazed into Lizzie's face without apparent recognition, more statue than man.

Morgan immediately moved her aside, took hold of the peddler by the arms, and pulled him in out of the cold.

"Tracks are blocked," Mr. Christian said woodenly, as Morgan took the tree from him and set it aside. "I had to turn back—"

Morgan began peeling off the man's coat, which appeared to be frozen and made a crackling sound as the fabric bent. Mr. Thaddings helped with the task, while Mrs. Thaddings rushed to fill a mug with coffee. Mr. Christian still seemed baffled, as though surprised to find himself where he was. Perhaps he wondered if he was in the caboose at all, or in the midst of some cold-induced reverie.

"Frostbite," Morgan said, examining the peddler's hands. "Lizzie, get me snow. Lots of snow."

Confounded, Lizzie obeyed just the same. She hurried out, filled the front of her skirt with as much snow as she could carry, returned to find that Morgan had settled Mr. Christian on the bench seat, as far from the stove as possible. She watched as Morgan took the snow she'd brought in, packed it around the peddler's hands and feet.

The process was repeated several more times, though when Mr. Thaddings saw that Lizzie's dress was wet, he took over the task, using the coal scuttle.

Mr. Christian lay on the train seat, shivering, wearing only his long johns by then, staring mutely up at the roof of the car. He still did not seem precisely certain where he was, or what was happening to him, and Lizzie counted that as a mercy. She was relieved when Morgan finally gave the poor man an injection of morphine and stopped packing his extremities in snow.

"The children," Mr. Christian murmured once. "The children ought to have some kind of Christmas."

Tears scalded Lizzie's eyes. She had to turn away, and while Morgan was monitoring the patient's heartbeat, she sneaked out of the car, unnoticed by everyone but Whitley.

He started to raise an alarm, but at one pleading glance from Lizzie, he changed his mind.

She made her way to the baggage car and, after some lugging and maneuvering, began opening trunks until she'd found what she sought. Her fine woolen coat, the paint set she'd brought all this way to give to John Henry, shawls and stockings. A pipe she'd bought for her father. A book for her grandfather. A pocket watch she'd intended to give to Whitley. Next, she looted Whitley's trunk, helped herself to his heavy overcoat, more stockings and warm underwear. When a tiny velvet box toppled from the pocket of the coat, Lizzie's heart nearly stopped.

She bent, picked up the box, opened it slowly. A shining diamond ring winked inside. More tears came; so Whitley *had* intended to propose marriage over the holidays. Lizzie tucked her old dreams inside that box with the ring, closed it, set it carefully back in Whitley's trunk.

When she'd taken a few moments to recover, she bundled the things she'd gathered into Whitley's coat and made her way outside again, along the side of the train, into the caboose.

Her return, like her departure, caused no particular stir.

She set her burden aside and went to stand in front of the stove, trying to dry the front of her dress. John Brennan was already down with pneumonia, Whitley's leg was in splints, Mrs. Halifax sported a sling, and now poor Mr. Christian was nearly dead of frostbite. It wouldn't do if she added to their problems by taking sick herself.

Everyone settled into sort of a stupor after that.

Lizzie, now dry, turned to gaze out the windows. The sun was setting, and there was no sign of an approaching rescue party. She drew a deep breath.

It was still Christmas Eve, whatever the circumstances, and Lizzie was determined to celebrate in some way.

Soon the sky was peppered with stars, each one shining as brightly as the diamond ring Whitley had meant to place on her finger. The snow glittered, deep and pristine, under those spilling stars, and the scent of the little pine tree Mr. Christian had somehow cut and brought back spiced the air.

Morgan looted the freight car again, and returned with a stack of new blankets and the spectacular Christmas ham they'd all agreed not to eat, just the day before. He fetched more coal and built up the fire, and they feasted—even John Brennan and Mr. Christian managed a few bites.

As the moon rose, spilling shimmering silver over the snow, Morgan stuck the trunk of the tiny tree between the slats of Mr. Christian's empty crate, and Whitley donated his watch chain for a decoration. Lizzie contributed several hair ribbons from her handbag, along with a small mirror that seemed to catch the starlight. Mrs. Thaddings contributed her ear bobs.

They sang, Lizzie starting first, Mrs. Halifax picking up the words next, her voice faltering, then John and Whitley and the children. Even Woodrow joined in.

"'O little town of Bethlehem, how still we see thee lie…'"

"We ain't gettin' our oranges," Jack announced stoically, as his mother tucked him and Ellen into the quilt bed, after many more carols had been sung. "There's no stockings to hang, and St. Nicholas won't find us way out here."

Ellen gazed at the little tree as though it were the most splendid thing she'd ever set eyes on. "It's Christmas, just the same," she said. "And that tree is right pretty. Mr. Christmas went to a lot of trouble to bring it back for us, too."

Jack sighed and closed his eyes.

Ellen gazed at the tree until she fell asleep.

Morgan moved back and forth between John Brennan and Mr. Christian. He'd given Whitley more laudanum after supper, when the pain in his injured leg had contorted his face and brought out a sheen of sweat across his forehead. Mr. and Mrs. Thaddings, having settled Woodrow down for the night, read from a worn Bible.

Watching them, Lizzie marveled at their calm acceptance. It seemed that, as long as they were together, they could face anything. She knew so little about the couple, and yet it would be obvious to anyone who looked that the marriage was a refuge for them both.

She wanted to be like them. To get old with someone, to live out an unfurling ribbon of years, as they had.

Presently, she turned to Morgan.

"I thought they'd come," Lizzie confided, very quietly. She was kneeling in front of the tree by then, breathing in the scent of it, remembering so many things. "I thought my family would come."

Morgan moved to sit cross-legged beside her. He said nothing at all, but simply listened.

A tear slipped down Lizzie's cheek. She dashed it away with the back of one hand. Straightened her spine.

"Maybe in the morning," she said.

"Maybe," Morgan agreed, gently gruff.

She got to her feet, retrieved the bundle she'd brought from the baggage car earlier. She folded Whitley's expensive overcoat neatly, placed it beneath the tree. John Henry's paint set went next, and then the pocket watch. Her beautiful velvet-collared coat found its way under the tree, too, and so did the pipe and the book and a few other things, as well.

She sat back on her heels when she'd finished arranging the gifts. Was surprised when Morgan reached out and took her hand.

"Lizzie McKettrick," he said, "you are something."

She bit her lower lip. Glanced in Whitley's direction to make certain he was asleep. He seemed to be, but he might have been "playing possum," to use one of her grandfather's favorite terms.

"He's going to ask me to marry him," she said, without intending to speak at all.

Morgan was silent for a long moment. Then he replied, "And you'll say yes."

She shook her head, unable to look directly at Morgan.

"Why not?" Morgan asked, his voice pitched low. It seemed intimate, their talking in the semidarkness, now that the lamp had been extinguished, the way her papa and Lorelei so often did, late at night, when they were alone in the kitchen, with the stove-fire banked low and the savory smell of supper still lingering in the air.

"Because it wouldn't be right," Lizzie said. "For Whitley or for me. He's a good man, Morgan. He really is. He deserves a wife who loves him."

Morgan didn't answer. Not right away, at least. "These are trying circumstances, Lizzie—for all of us. Don't make any hasty decisions. You'll have a long time to regret it if you make the wrong ones."

Again, Lizzie glanced in Whitley's direction, then down at her hands, knotted atop the fabric of her ruined skirts. "Maybe I'm not cut out to be married anyhow," she ventured. "Some people aren't, you know."

She felt his smile, rather than saw it. "It would be a waste, Lizzie, if you didn't marry. But I agree that you're better off single than tied to the wrong man."

"My pupils," Lizzie mused. "They'll be my children." Even as she said the words, a soft sorrow tugged at her heart. She so wanted babies of her own, sons and daughters, bringing the kind of rowdy, chaotic joy swelling the walls of the houses on the Triple M.

"Will they be enough, Lizzie?" Morgan asked, after a lengthy silence. "Your pupils, I mean?"

"I don't know," she answered sadly.

Morgan squeezed her hand again. "You have time, Lizzie. You're a beautiful woman. If you and Whitley can't come to terms, you'll surely meet someone else."

Lizzie feared she'd already met that "someone else," and he was Morgan. Normally a confident person, she suddenly felt out of her depth. The McKettricks were certainly prominent, and they were wealthy, but they lived in ranch houses, not mansions. Nobody dressed for dinner, or employed servants, or rode in fancy carriages, as Morgan's people surely had. She'd attended Miss Ridgley's, where she'd learned which fork to use with which course of a meal, how to embroider and entertain, and after that she'd gone to San Francisco Normal School. Morgan had studied medicine abroad. Estranged from his mother or not, he would be at home in high society, while Lizzie would be considered a frontier bumpkin at worst, one of the nouveaux riches at best.

"Lizzie?" Morgan prompted, when she didn't reply to his comment.

"I was just wondering why you'd want to live and work in a place like Indian Rock, instead of Chicago or New York or Philadelphia or Boston," she said. "Don't you miss…well…all the things there are to *do* in places like that?"

"Such as?"

"Concerts. Art museums. Stores so big you have to climb stairs to see everything they sell."

Morgan chuckled. "Do *you* miss concerts and museums and shopping, Lizzie?"

"No," she said. "San Francisco is beautiful—I really enjoyed being there. I made a lot of friends at school.

But there were times when I was so homesick, I wasn't sure I could stand it."

Morgan caressed her cheek with the backs of his knuckles, his touch so gentle that a hot shiver went through her. "I guess I'm homesick, too," he said, "but in a different way. The home I want is the one I never had—the one I'm hoping to find in Indian Rock."

Lizzie's throat thickened. It was only too easy to picture Morgan as a small child, having Christmas dinner in the kitchen of some yawning mausoleum of a house, with only the family cook for company. On the other hand, things would be different in Indian Rock—once word got around town that the new doctor didn't have a wife, the scheming and flirtations would begin. Meals would be cooked and brought to his door in baskets. He'd be invited to Sunday suppers, and unmarried women for miles around would suddenly develop delicate ailments requiring the immediate attention of the attractive new physician.

Thinking of it made Lizzie give a very unladylike snort.

In the moonlight, she saw Morgan's right eyebrow rise slightly, and a smile played at one corner of his mouth. "Now, what accounts for *that* reaction, Lizzie McKettrick?" he asked.

She loved it when he called her by her full name, though she could not have said why. But she was mightily embarrassed that she'd snorted in front of him, like an old horse nickering for oats. "You won't be single long," she said. "Once you get to Indian Rock, I mean."

She regretted the statement instantly; it revealed too much. Like a contentious colt, it had bolted from the place she contained such things and kicked up a fuss inside Lizzie.

Again, that crooked little smile from Morgan. "I think I'd like to be married," he mused, surprising her yet again; she'd *thought* she was getting used to his blunt way of speaking. "A lovely wife. A passel of children. It all sounds very good to me right now, but maybe I'm just being sentimental."

For some reason she could not define, Lizzie wanted to cry. And it wasn't because she was far from home on Christmas Eve, or because she knew she would have to turn down Whitley's proposal and he would be hurt and disappointed, or even because all their lives were in danger.

Not trusting herself to speak, or govern what she said if she made the attempt, Lizzie remained silent.

Morgan brushed her cheek with the tips of his fingers. "Get some sleep," he counseled. "Tomorrow's Christmas."

Tomorrow's Christmas. Lizzie found that hard to credit, even with the little tree and the presents so carefully arranged beneath it. She nodded, and she was about to get to her feet when, with no warning at all, Morgan suddenly caught her face between his hands and placed the lightest, sweetest kiss imaginable on her mouth.

A jolt shot through Lizzie; she might have captured liquid lightning in a metal cup, like fresh spring rain, and swigged it down. She knew Morgan felt her trembling before he lowered his hands from her face to take hers and help her to her feet.

"Good night, Lizzie McKettrick," he said gruffly. "And a happy Christmas."

She found a place to lie down on one of the long bench seats, never dreaming that she'd sleep. Her heart leaped and frolicked like a circus performer on a trampoline, and she could still feel Morgan's brief, innocent kiss tingling on her lips.

To distract herself from all the contradictory feelings Morgan had aroused in her, she imagined herself at home on the Triple M. She stood for a few moments in the familiar kitchen, lamp-lit and warm from the stove, and saw her papa and Lorelei sitting in their usual places at the table, though they did not seem to see her.

Mentally, she climbed the back stairway, made her way first to the room John Henry, Gabriel and Doss shared. They were all sound asleep in their beds, fair hair tousled on the pillows and flecked with hay from the customary Christmas Eve visit to the barn, and each one had hung a stocking from a hook on the wall, in anticipation of St. Nicholas's arrival. The stockings were still limp and empty—Lorelei would fill them later, when she was sure they wouldn't awaken. Rock candy. Toy whistles. Perhaps small wooden animals, hand carved by Papa, out in the wood shop.

The scene was achingly real to Lizzie—it made her eyes sting and her throat ache so fiercely that she put a hand to it. As she stared down at her brothers, drinking in the sight of them, John Henry opened his eyes, looked directly at her.

"Where are you?" he asked, using his hands to sign the words he couldn't speak.

Lizzie signed back. "I'll be home soon."

John Henry's small hands flew. "Promise?"

"Promise," Lizzie confirmed.

And then the vision faded, leaving Lizzie longing to find it again.

As she settled her nerves, she was aware of Morgan moving about the caboose, probably checking his various patients: Mrs. Halifax with her injured arm, Whitley with his broken leg, the peddler, Mr. Christian, who'd nearly gotten himself frozen to death, and last of all poor John Brennan, struggling with pneumonia.

And over them all loomed the mountain, ominously silent.

Finally Lizzie slept.

CHRISTMAS.

It had never meant so much to Morgan as it did that night. He wanted to give Lizzie everything—trinkets, the finest silks and laces, and beyond those things… his heart. For a brief fraction of a moment, he actually wished he'd granted his mother's wishes and become a banker, instead of a doctor.

Annoyed with himself, he shoved both hands through his hair, as he always did when he was frustrated—and that was often.

He concentrated on what he knew, taking care of the sick and injured, knowing full well that sleep would elude him.

John Brennan seemed marginally better.

Mrs. Halifax would be fine, once she'd gotten some real rest.

Mr. Thaddings was resting quietly, the bluish color gone from his lips.

Even Christian, the peddler, who had come danger-ously close to dying, appeared to be rallying somewhat. He might lose a few toes, but otherwise, he'd probably be his old self soon.

Whitley Carson's leg would mend; he was young,

healthy and strong. Unless he was the biggest fool who ever lived, he'd pursue Lizzie until she accepted his proposal, married him and bore his children. Maybe he was smart enough to know that a woman like Lizzie McKettrick came along about as often as the proverbial blue moon, and maybe he wasn't.

Morgan hoped devoutly for the latter.

If they got out of this situation alive, Morgan decided, and if Lizzie *didn't* change her mind about marrying Whitley, by some miracle, he would court her himself.

Did he love her?

He didn't know. He certainly admired her, respected her and, God knew, *wanted* her, and not just physically. She'd opened some whole new region in his soul, an actual landscape, golden with light. Should Lizzie refuse his suit, as she well might, he'd have that magical place to retreat into, for the rest of his life, and he'd find some sad solace there.

He shook his head. Such thoughts were utterly foreign to his nature. He was a realist; did not have a fanciful bone in his body. He was a doctor, not a poet. And yet Lizzie had changed him, and he knew the alteration was permanent.

The coffee was cold, and full of grounds, but he poured some anyway, and lifted it to his lips. Moved to the window side of the car to look out over the blue-white night. He sipped, pondering the irony of meeting Lizzie in this peculiar time and place.

And before he'd swallowed a second sip of coffee, he heard the deep, growling rumble overhead.

CHAPTER SIX

THE CABOOSE SHOOK VIOLENTLY, rousing Lizzie instantly from a shallow sleep. She sat bolt upright, the startled shouts of the others echoing in her ears, her heart in her throat, and waited for the railroad car to go tumbling over the side of the cliff.

It didn't.

There was a second great shudder, and then... stillness.

Was this what it was like to die?

She looked around, but the darkness was as densely black as India ink. She might have been at the bottom of a coal mine at midnight, for all she could see.

"Morgan?" she called softly.

"I'm here," he assured her, from somewhere close by.

"What happened?" asked one of the children.

"How come it's so dark?" inquired the other, the words scrambling over those of the other child.

"Dark!" Woodrow fretted loudly. "Dark!"

"There's been another avalanche," Morgan said matter-of-factly, over Woodrow's continuing rant. "The snow must be blocking the windows, but we're still on the tracks, I think."

"Did the Christmas tree get ruint?" Lizzie identified the voice as Ellen's.

"Never mind the Christmas tree," Whitley said, sounding testy and shaken. "And will somebody shut that bird up?"

"Will somebody shut that bird up?" Woodrow repeated.

"How long will the air last?" John Brennan asked.

"I don't know," Morgan asked. "Everybody stay put. I'll see if I can get the door open to have a look. Maybe we can dig our way out."

"We could smother in here," Whitley said.

"Hush," Lizzie snapped. "We're not going to smother!"

"Stringy bird!" Woodrow prattled on. "Don't eat the bird!"

The baby began to cry, first tentatively, then with a full-lunged wail.

Mrs. Halifax sang to the infant, her soft voice quavering.

Mrs. Thaddings spoke tenderly to Woodrow.

A match was struck, lamplight flared, feeble against the terrible darkness. Morgan stood holding the lantern, a man woven of shadows. The incongruous thought came to Lizzie that he needed a shave.

Snow covered the windows on both sides of the car now, and it was clear that Morgan had been unable to force the door open. They were effectively buried alive.

Remarkably, the forlorn little Christmas tree still stood, the gifts undisturbed beneath it.

"Look!" Ellen cried, nudging a blinking Jack and pointing to the spectacle. "St. Nicholas came!"

Lizzie's gaze locked with Morgan's. Something unspoken passed between them, and Morgan nodded.

Lizzie worked up a cheerful smile. "And there are presents for everyone," she said, making her way to the tree. She took her prized coat up first, handed it to Mrs. Halifax. "For you," she said. She gave John Henry's paint set to Ellen and Jack, and Whitley's hand-tailored overcoat went to John Brennan, the pipe she'd bought for her father to Mr. Christian. Whitley got the book, and Morgan the pocket watch. She gave Mr. and Mrs. Thaddings a small box of hand-dipped chocolates from a shop in San Francisco, specially chosen for Lorelei.

"What about you?" Ellen asked, staring first at the paint set and then at Lizzie. "Isn't there something for you, Miss Lizzie?"

For the first time since he'd returned to the railroad car, clutching that little tree, Mr. Christian spoke a coherent sentence. "Why, St. Nicholas meant the music box for Lizzie," he said weakly.

Ellen relaxed, much to Lizzie's relief, and set to examining the paints and brushes and special paper she and Jack were to share. She wouldn't accept the music box, of course, as generous as Mr. Christian was to offer it—it had belonged to his late wife, after all. It was an heirloom.

They couldn't build a fire, for fear the chimney was covered by a deep layer of snow, and the chill set in pretty quickly. If they were going to die, Lizzie decided, they would die in good spirits.

She squared her shoulders and lifted her chin, but before she could speak, she heard the first, faint clank, and then another.

"Listen!" she said, shushing everyone.

Another clank, and then another—metal, striking metal. Shovels? Distant and faint, perhaps up the line of cars a ways, toward the engine.

"They're here," Lizzie whispered. "They're here!"

Everyone looked up, as though expecting their rescuers to descend through the roof.

Time seemed to stop.

Clank, clank, clank.

And then—some minutes later—footsteps on the metal roof of the caboose, a muffled voice.

Her papa's voice.

"Lizzie!" Holt McKettrick called.

"In here, Papa!" Lizzie cried, on a joyous sob. "In the caboose!"

She heard him speak to the others—her uncles and perhaps even her grandfather. The clanking commenced in earnest then, and the voices became clearer.

"Lizzie?" Her papa again. "Hold on, sweetheart."

The door Morgan had been unable to open earlier jostled on its hinges, then creaked with an ear-splitting squeal. Holt McKettrick gave a wrench from outside, and then he was there, filling the chasm.

Big. Strong. So handsome he made Lizzie's heart swell with pride and gladness. Holt McKettrick would have moved heaven and earth, if he had to, for his daughter, for a train full of strangers.

Lizzie flew to him.

He scooped her up into his arms, clean off her feet, and kissed her hard on top of the head. She felt the warmth of his tears in her hair. "Thank God," he murmured. *"Thank God."*

She clung, crying freely now, not even trying to hold

back the sobs of joy rising from the very core of her being. "Papa...Papa!"

"Hush," Holt said gruffly. "You're all right now, girl."

Behind him, she saw her uncles enter—Rafe then Kade then Jeb. Then another man, someone Lizzie didn't recognize.

"Pa!" Ellen and Jack screamed in unison, rushing to be enfolded in the tall, lean cowboy's waiting arms. Over their heads he exchanged a look of reverent gratitude with Mrs. Halifax, who was holding the baby so tightly that it struggled in her embrace. Tears slipped down her face.

Lizzie finally recovered a modicum of composure when Holt set her back on her feet. She gulped, looking up at him. "I knew you'd come," she said.

Holt grinned. "Of course we came," he replied. "We couldn't have had Christmas without our Lizzie."

"S-some of the others are hurt," Lizzie said, remembering suddenly, feeling some chagrin that, in her excitement, she'd forgotten them.

Her uncles were already assessing the situation.

"We'd better get out of here quick, Holt," Rafe said, with an upward glance. He was a big man, burly and dark-haired, his eyes the intense blue of a chambray work shirt.

Kade, meanwhile, greeted Morgan with a handshake. "Hell of a welcome to Indian Rock," he said, as Lizzie drank in the sight of him—well built, with chestnut hair and a quiet manner. He gave her a wink.

Morgan looked solemn—and completely exhausted.

"The engineer and the conductor didn't make it," he told Kade. "They're in the locomotive."

Kade nodded grimly. "We'll have to come back for them later," he said. "Along with any trunks or the like. Rafe's right. We'd best get while the getting is good."

After that, things happened fast, and Lizzie experienced it all through a numbing haze, shimmering silvery at the edges. They'd brought a large, flat-bed sleigh, as Lizzie had expected they would, piled with loose straw and drawn by four gigantic plow horses. There were blankets and bear hides, too, to keep the travelers warm, and flasks filled with strong spirits. Farther along the tracks, her father told her, half the hands from the Triple M waited, having set up camp the night before, when they'd all had to stop because of the darkness and the weather.

Lizzie was bundled, like a child, in quilts she recognized from home, and her uncle Jeb, the youngest McKettrick brother, fair-haired and agile, carried her to the sleigh. She settled into a sort of dizzy stupor, the sweet scent of the fresh straw lulling her further.

"You're safe now, Lizzie-bet," Jeb told her, his azure eyes glistening suspiciously. "Pa kicked up some kind of fuss when we wouldn't let him come along to find you. Too hard on his heart, Concepcion said. We had to hogtie him and throw him in jail, and we could still hear him bellowing five miles out of town."

Lizzie smiled at the image of her proud grandfather behind bars. He'd be prowling like a caged mountain lion, furious that they'd left him behind. "There'll be the devil to pay when you let him out," she warned.

Jeb chuckled, ran the sleeve of his wool-lined leather

coat across his eyes. "We're counting on you to put in a good word for us," he said, tucking straw in around her before turning to go back and help bring out the others.

When they had all been rescued, and placed securely on the back of the heavy sled, Holt took the reins and shouted to the team. Kade and Jeb rode mules, as did Mr. Halifax.

The going was slow, the snow being so deep, and it was precarious. Lizzie drifted in and out of her hazy reverie, aware of Whitley nearby, and Morgan at a little distance.

Considerable time passed before they reached the camp Holt had mentioned. Cowboys greeted them with hot coffee and good cheer, and they lingered awhile, in a broad, snowy clearing under a copse of bare-limbed oak trees, safe from the possibility of another avalanche.

It was past nightfall when they reached Indian Rock.

A soft snow was falling, church bells rang, and it seemed the whole town had turned out to greet the Christmas travelers. Lorelei rushed to Lizzie, knelt on the bed of the sleigh, and pulled her into her arms.

"Lizzie," she whispered, over and over again. "Oh, Lizzie!"

Next, Lizzie saw her grandfather, tall and fierce-faced, his thick white hair askew because he'd been thrusting his fingers through it. His gaze swept over his sons, daring any one of them to interfere, then he gathered Lizzie right up and carried her inside the Arizona Hotel.

The lobby was blessedly warm, and alight with glowing lamps.

There were people everywhere.

"Lizzie-bet," Angus McKettrick said, "you like to scared me to death when your train didn't turn up on time."

Lizzie rested her head against his strong shoulder. "I'm sorry, Grampa," she said. Then she looked up into his face. "I reckon you're pretty mad at Papa and Kade and Rafe and Jeb," she ventured. "For locking you up, I mean."

"I'll have their hides for it," Angus vowed, and though his voice was rough as sandpaper, Lizzie heard the tenderness in it. He loved his four sons deeply, and probably understood that they'd only been trying to protect him by throwing him in the hoosegow. "Right now, Lizzie-girl, all I care about is that you're safe. Soon as you've rested up, we'll all head home to the Triple M."

"I guess I missed Christmas," Lizzie said.

Angus carried her up the stairs and into a waiting room. He laid her gently on the bed, and stepped back to let Lorelei attend to her. Only then did he reply, "You didn't miss Christmas. We held it for you."

"Leave us alone, Angus," Lorelei said quietly. "I need to get Lizzie out of these wet, cold clothes and into something warm and dry."

Angus clenched his jaw, then inclined his head to Lizzie in reluctant farewell before leaving the room and closing the door softly behind him.

"What happened out there?" Lorelei asked, as she deftly undid the buttons on Lizzie's shoes.

"There was an avalanche," Lizzie said. The warmth of the room made her skin burn, and she wondered, briefly, if she'd been frostbitten. If she'd lose fingers and toes or maybe an ear. Tears scalded her eyes. She was *alive,* that was what mattered. And she was home—or almost home. "I didn't let myself think for one moment that Papa and the others wouldn't come for us." Her conscience stirred. "Well," she added, "maybe there were a *few* moments—"

Lorelei smiled gently, continuing to peel away Lizzie's clothes, then dressing her again in a long flannel nightgown. "You were McKettrick tough," Lorelei said, when she'd pulled the bedcovers up to Lizzie's chin. "We're all very proud of you, Lizzie."

"The others—Morgan, Whitley...the children...?"

"They're all being taken care of, sweetheart. Don't worry."

Lizzie closed her eyes, sighed. "I hope I'm not dreaming," she said "You're really here, aren't you, Lorelei? You and Papa and Grampa—?"

"Rest, Lizzie," Lorelei said, with tears in her voice. "It's not a dream. You're back home in Indian Rock, with your family around you."

She recalled the Thaddingses and how they expected to find Miss Clarinda Adams running a dressmaker's shop, not a high-toned brothel. Would Miss Adams take them in, Mr. and Mrs. Thaddings and Woodrow? Or would they refuse, in their inevitable shock, to accept hospitality from the town madam?

Where would they go, either way? Lizzie knew very little about them, but she had discerned that they weren't rich.

"There's an older couple—they have a bird—they think Clarinda Adams makes dresses for a living—"

Lorelei smiled, patting Lizzie's hand. "Clarinda's

moved on," she said. "Married one of her clients and high-tailed it back east three months ago."

"But Mr. and Mrs. Thaddings—they expected to stay with her…."

"Everyone will be taken care of, Lizzie, so stop worrying. Right now, you need to rest."

"There's a bird—"

"Hush," Lorelei said, kissing Lizzie's forehead. "I'll make sure the Thaddingses *and* their bird find lodging."

Lizzie sighed again and slept.

MORGAN ASSESSED his new quarters. The town had built on to the hotel, providing him with a small office and examination room and living space behind that. The place was well furnished and well supplied. He found coffee on the shelf above the small stove and put some on to brew.

His bed was within kicking distance, narrow and made up with clean blankets, obviously secondhand. There was a bathtub, too, a great, incongruous thing served by a complicated system of exposed pipes, equally close, and with a copper hot water tank attached to the wall above it.

He smiled to himself. If only his mother could see him now.

Morgan lit the gas jet under the boiler on the hot water tank—it would take a while to heat—and put coffee on to brew while he waited. Finally he filled the tub with water, steaming gloriously. His clothes and other belongings were still on the train, out there on the mountainside, but thanks to the McKettricks, he'd been provided with a change of clothes, shaving gear, soap and a tall bottle of whiskey.

After he poured coffee into a chipped cup, also donated no doubt, and then added a generous dollop of whiskey for good measure, he stripped and lowered himself into the tub.

The bath was bliss, and so was the whiskey-laced coffee. But the best thing was knowing Lizzie was all right, safe upstairs, being cared for by her stepmother.

John Brennan's family had been right there to greet him as soon as they arrived, and two of the townsmen had carried him, blanket-wrapped and half-delirious, toward the mercantile. If John made it through the night, Morgan figured he'd have a good chance of surviving.

Whitley Carson was resting in one of the hotel rooms, as were the Halifaxes, the Thaddingses and Woodrow.

Morgan hadn't seen where the peddler was taken, but he assumed he'd been gathered up, too, by kinfolks or friends. For the time being, Morgan could allow himself to simply be a very relieved, very tired man, not a doctor.

He finished the coffee and soaked until the water began to cool, then hastily shaved, scrubbed and got out of the tub. Dressed in his borrowed clothes, he headed for the lobby. The place was so crowded he'd have sworn somebody was throwing a party.

After a few moments, he realized his first impression had been right. The entire town seemed to be present, hoisting a glass, celebrating that the lost had been found. Kade caught his eye and beckoned, and Morgan followed him through the cheerful throng into the hotel dining room.

"Figured you'd be hungry for hot food," McKettrick said.

Morgan *was* hungry, though he hadn't realized it until that moment. His stomach grumbled loudly, and he sat down at one of the tables next to the window, looking out at the Christmas-card snowfall.

A waitress appeared, and Kade, seated across from him, ordered for them both. There was no one else in the dining room.

"Thanks," Morgan said.

McKettrick raised one eyebrow, but didn't speak.

"For coming for us," Morgan clarified. "Lizzie said you would. I don't think she ever doubted it—but I wasn't so sure."

Kade smiled fondly at the mention of Lizzie's name. "If there's one of us missing from the supper table," he said, "the rest will turn the whole countryside on its top to find them."

"It must be nice to be part of a family like that," Morgan said, without really meaning to. He didn't feel sorry for himself, and he didn't want to give the impression that he did.

"It has its finer moments," Kade answered mildly. "I take it you don't come from a big outfit like ours?"

"There's just me," Morgan replied. "That peddler—Mr. Christian—did somebody come to meet him?"

Kade frowned. "Who?"

The waitress returned with hot bread, a butter dish and two cups of coffee, all balanced on a tray.

Morgan didn't answer until she'd gone again.

"Mr. Christian. An older man, a peddler with a sample case."

Kade shook his head. "I don't recall anybody fitting that description," he said. "There was you and Lizzie, the Halifaxes, the soldier, an elderly pair with a bird and the yahoo with the broken leg."

Morgan started to rise from his chair, certain the old peddler must have been left behind by mistake. Or maybe he'd fallen off the sleigh, somewhere along the way, and nobody had noticed—

"Sit down," Kade said. "We got everybody off that train. Everybody who was still alive, anyway."

Morgan sank back into his chair, befuddled. "But there has to be some kind of mistake. There was an old man—ask Lizzie—ask any of the others—"

"I'll do that, if it makes you happy," Kade allowed. "But we got everybody there was to get."

The food came. Fried chicken, mashed potatoes swimming in gravy, green beans cooked with onions and bacon. It was a feast, and Morgan was so desperately hungry that he practically dove into his plate. He was done-in, he told himself. Not thinking straight. In the morning, after a good night's sleep, he'd make sense of the matter of Mr. Christmas, as the children had called him.

THEY'D LIGHTED THE CANDLES on the tree for him, and made him up a nice bed on the settee, there in the fine apartments above the mercantile, and his wife and boy were staying close, while the in-laws hovered in the distance. There was good food cooking, and a fire blazing on the hearth, and John Brennan figured he'd died for sure and gone straight to heaven.

"ST. NICHOLAS *DID TOO* COME," Jack told his smilingly skeptical father. "He brought a paint set for Ellen and me."

"Did he now?" Ben Halifax asked his son. Mama, Ellen and the baby were all sleeping, cozied up in the same hotel bed. Ben and Jack would share the other, and, in the morning, if the weather was good and everybody was up to the trip, they'd all head out to the Triple M, where they'd be staying on, not just passing through. "I guess he must have been in two places at once, then, because he filled some stockings out at the ranch, too."

Jack widened his eyes. He'd had supper, and he knew he ought to be in bed asleep, like his mama and sisters, but he was just plain too excited. "But me and Ellen wasn't there to hang any stockings," he argued.

"I hung them up for you," his father said. "And darned if I didn't wake up this morning and find those old work socks just a-bulging with presents."

Jack blinked, wonderstruck. "I guess if anybody could be in two places at once," he said with certainty, "it would be St. Nicholas who done it."

Ben laughed, ruffled the boy's hair. His eyes glistened, and if Jack hadn't known better, he'd have bet his pa was crying. "It's Christmas," Ben said, his voice sounding all scrapey and rough. "The time when miracles happen."

"What's a miracle?" Jack asked, puzzled.

"It's having you and your ma and your sisters right here with me, where you belong," Ben answered. Then he did something Jack couldn't remember him ever doing before. He lifted Jack onto his lap, held him real tight, and kissed him on top of the head. "Yesiree, that's all the miracle I need."

ZEBULON THADDINGS BENT TO strike a match to the fire laid in the hearth of the sumptuously decorated parlor. The lamps all had painted globes, the rugs were foreign, the furniture plentiful and fussy, and there were naked people cavorting in the paintings on the walls.

"Your sister has done well, for a dressmaker," he told Marietta, who was gazing about with an expression of troubled wonder on her dear face. In point of fact, he hadn't wanted to make this journey in the first place, since he'd known all along, even if his wife hadn't, how Clarinda had been able to afford the fine jewelry and exquisite clothing she'd worn when she visited them in Phoenix. There simply hadn't been any other possible explanation.

Zebulon had lost his job running an Indian school, and with it, of course, the minuscule salary and the tiny house provided for the headmaster and his wife. They were destitute. The plain and difficult truth was that they had hoped Clarinda would take them in, along with Woodrow, not just welcome them for a holiday visit.

They'd had nowhere else to go, and Zebulon had used the last few dollars he had, to pay for their train fare to Indian Rock.

Now they were basically squatting in Clarinda's grand house. God only knew where they would go next, but for the time being, at least, they had a roof over their heads, a bed to sleep in, and a pantry stocked with foodstuffs.

Woodrow, provided with a fresh supply of birdseed

by a kindly shopkeeper, sat in his shiny cage, looking around.

"Why are all these people…naked?" Marietta fretted, wringing her hands a little as she took in the large and scandalous painting above the fireplace. Bare-fleshed men and women lay about a forest, some of them intertwined, eating grapes, sipping from elaborate chalices and generally looking swoony.

"Naked!" Woodrow exclaimed. "Naked as a jaybird!"

Woodrow mostly repeated the words of others, but occasionally, like now, he added commentary of his own from his past repertoire. Zebulon had to smile.

Crossing to Marietta, the Turkish rug soft beneath the thin soles of his shoes, he embraced his wife. She'd been a true helpmeet over the years, never complaining about their near penury, never voicing her great disappointment that they hadn't been blessed with children of their own.

"Dearest," he said, after clearing his throat. "About Clarinda—"

Marietta looked up at him, tears gleaming in her gentle eyes. "She isn't a dressmaker, is she?"

Zebulon shook his head. "No," he answered.

"What are we going to do, Zebulon?"

Zebulon's own eyes burned. He blinked rapidly. "I don't know," he said.

"Perhaps Clarinda intends to return soon," Marietta speculated hopefully, brightening a little.

"Perhaps," Zebulon agreed, though doubtful.

"Hadn't we better send her a wire or write a letter? Someone in Indian Rock must have her address."

The scent of cigar smoke lingered in the air.

Clarinda's possessions were all around, giving the strange impression that she'd merely left the room, not the territory.

"You ought to lie down and rest awhile, dear," Zebulon told Marietta. "I'll brew a nice pot of tea."

Marietta hesitated, then nodded. Gently raised, and a preacher's daughter into the bargain, she hadn't quite accepted the obvious—that her spirited younger sister ran a house of ill repute. She settled herself on the long, plush sofa facing the fireplace, and Zebulon covered her tenderly with a knitted afghan.

"Tea!" Woodrow chirped, as Zebulon left the room, headed for the massive kitchen. "Tea for two!"

WHEN LIZZIE OPENED HER EYES, the room was full of snow-gleam, and her young brothers were standing next to her bed. Well, at least, John Henry was standing—Doss and Gabriel were jumping up and down on the foot of the mattress, shouting, "Wake up! Wake up!"

Lizzie laughed, used her elbows to push herself upright. After fluffing her pillows, she leaned back against them.

Lorelei appeared and whisked the younger boys away, both of them protesting vigorously. Was Lizzie going to sleep all day long? Wouldn't they *ever* get to go home and open their Christmas presents?

John Henry stayed behind, regarding Lizzie with solemn, thoughtful eyes.

She ruffled his hair.

"I saw you in our room," John Henry signed. "On Christmas Eve."

A shock went through Lizzie as she remembered her

imagined visit home. "I was still on the train on Christmas Eve," she signed back.

John Henry shook his head, repeated, the motions of his small, deft hands insistent, "I *saw* you, Lizzie," he reiterated. "You were wearing a man's coat and your hair was all mussed up. You said not to worry, because you were coming home soon."

Lizzie blinked. Something tightened in her throat, making it impossible to speak.

The door of the hotel room opened, and her father came in. He sent John Henry downstairs to have breakfast with his brothers, and the child scampered to obey, but not before he cast one last, knowing look back at Lizzie.

Holt dragged a chair up alongside the bed. "Feeling better?" he asked.

Lizzie nodded.

"Lorelei's bringing up a tray. All your favorites. Sausage, hotcakes with lots of syrup, and tea."

He offered Lizzie his hand, and she took it. After swallowing, she managed to speak. "Morgan," she said. "Is he...is he all right?"

"He's fine," Holt answered with a slight frown. "I guess I figured you'd be more interested in the other one. According to young Mr. Carson, he means to set about claiming your hand in marriage, first chance he gets. Already asked for my permission to propose."

Lizzie's emotions must have shown clearly on her face, because her father's frown deepened. "What did you say?" she asked, almost in a whisper.

"I told him you were nineteen years old, and if you want to marry him, that's all right by me." Holt shifted in the hotel chair, which seemed almost too spindly to support his powerful frame. "Should I have said something different, Lizzie?"

A tear slipped down Lizzie's cheek. "I don't love Whitley, Papa. I thought I did—oh, I *really* thought I did—but when everything happened up there on the mountain—"

Holt leaned forward, folded his arms, rested them on his knees as he regarded his daughter. "It's the doctor you love, then," he said. "Morgan Shane."

"I wouldn't say I love him," Lizzie replied slowly, after some thought. "I don't know *what* I feel. He's strong and he's good and when people were hurt and sick, he forgot about himself and did what had to be done. On the other hand, he makes me so angry sometimes—"

Holt smiled. "I see. I assume Mr. Carson didn't comport himself in the same way?"

"No," Lizzie said. "But I suppose I could overlook that, if I wanted to. It's just that, when I met Morgan, everything changed."

"Well then, when the proposal comes, you'll have to turn it down."

"Couldn't you just—withdraw your permission? Tell Whitley you've changed your mind and he can't propose to me after all?"

Her father chuckled, shook his head. "It isn't like you to take the coward's way out," he said. "You brought that young fella all the way up here from California, intending to show him off to all of us and, I suspect, hoping he'd give you an engagement ring. You'll have to tell him the truth, Lizzie. However he might have behaved on that train, he deserves that much."

Lizzie sighed heavily and sank back onto her pillows. "You're right," she said dolefully.

Holt laughed. "It's nice to hear you admit that," he said, as Lorelei came in with the promised tray, and despite the prospect of refusing Whitley Carson's suit, Lizzie ate with a good appetite. She expected to remember that particular meal for the rest of her natural life, it was so delicious.

When her father had gone—there had been a thaw, and he, Rafe, Kade and Jeb were heading out to the ranch to feed livestock—Lorelei had a bathtub brought to the room and filled bucket by bucket with gloriously hot water. After breakfast, a bath and a shampoo, Lizzie felt fully recovered from her ordeal. She dressed in clothes Lorelei had purchased for her at the mercantile, a green woollen dress with lace at the collar, lovely sheer stockings and fashionable high-button shoes.

"You mustn't overdo," Lorelei fretted. Usually a practical person, today Lizzie's stepmother seemed almost fragile. The shadows under her eyes indicated that she'd worried a great deal over the past few days, and gotten little or no sleep.

"Lorelei," Lizzie said, placing her hands on her stepmother's pale cheeks, "I'm home. I'm *fine*. You said it yourself—I'm McKettrick tough."

"I was so frightened," Lorelei confessed, with an uncharacteristic sniffle.

The two women embraced, clung tightly.

"I want to look in on the others," Lizzie said, when they'd drawn apart. "Morgan—Dr. Shane—first. Then

Whitley and Mr. and Mrs. Thaddings and the Halifaxes
and John Brennan and Mr. Christian—"

Lorelei frowned. "Mr. Christian? I recall the other
names—and I met Dr. Shane last night. But no one
mentioned a Mr. Christian."

"You must have seen him," Lizzie insisted. "He was
very ill—with frostbite—and he would have needed
tending. I'll ask Morgan."

Lorelei still seemed puzzled. "Perhaps I'm mistaken," she said doubtfully. Lorelei McKettrick was
rarely mistaken about anything, and everyone knew
it. She paused, rallied a little. "I'd better round up
your brothers. They must have finished breakfast by
now, and my guess is, they'll be up to mischief pretty
soon."

Lizzie and Lorelei went down the stairs together and
parted in the lobby. Lizzie immediately noticed Whitley
sitting alone in a leather chair, his injured leg propped
on an ottoman, gazing out at the snowy street beyond
the window. He looked almost forlorn.

Procrastinating, Lizzie decided resolutely, would only
make matters worse. She approached, cleared her throat
softly when Whitley didn't notice her right away.

When he did, his face lit up and he started to rise.

"Please," Lizzie said. "Don't get up."

He sank back into his chair, gestured goodnaturedly
at the plaster cast replacing the improvised splint
Morgan had applied onboard the stranded train. "Modern
medicine," he said. "I'll be walking properly within six
weeks."

"That's wonderful," Lizzie said, wringing her hands

a little, then quickly tucking them behind her back. "I'm…I'm so sorry, Whitley."

"For what?" he asked.

"Getting you into all this," Lizzie answered, flustered. "Inviting you here— You wouldn't have broken your leg if I hadn't, or nearly perished in an avalanche—"

Whitley's smile faded, and he tried to stand again.

To keep him in his chair, Lizzie drew up a second ottoman and perched on it, facing him.

"Lizzie?" he prompted when she didn't say anything right away. She, affectionately known on the Triple M as "chatterbox," couldn't seem to find words.

"I saw the ring," she said. "When I took your good overcoat out of your trunk to put under the Christmas tree for John Brennan."

"Ah," Whitley said, still unsmiling. "The ring. It belonged to my grandmother, you know. I had it reset, before we left San Francisco."

Pain flashed through Lizzie. For a moment, she actually considered accepting Whitley's ring, going through with the wedding, just to keep from dashing his hopes. Reason soon prevailed—she'd do him far greater harm if she trapped him in a loveless marriage. "It's very beautiful," she said sadly.

Whitley's face filled with eagerness and hope. "Will you marry me, Lizzie? I know this isn't the most romantic proposal, and I don't even have the ring to put on your finger, since it's still in my trunk and none of our things have been recovered from the train yet, but I've already spoken to your father—"

"Whitley," Lizzie said, almost moaning the name, *"stop."*

"Lizzie—"

"No," she whispered raggedly. "Please. I can't marry you, Whitley. I don't…I don't love you."

"You'll *learn* to love me—"

Lizzie shook her head.

Whitley reddened. "It's Shane, isn't it? He's stolen you away from me, turned your head, acting like a hero on the train—"

Again Lizzie shook her head. Then she couldn't bear it any longer, and she got to her feet and turned to flee, only to collide hard with Morgan.

CHAPTER SEVEN

MORGAN GRIPPED LIZZIE'S SHOULDERS gently and steadied her. Spoke her name in a worried rasp. Behind her, Lizzie heard Whitley shoving to his feet, and his anger struck her back like a flood of something hot and dark.

"What can he give you?" Whitley demanded furiously. "Tell me what *Dr.* Morgan Shane can give you that I can't!"

Mortified, Lizzie gazed helplessly up into Morgan's concerned face. She saw a muscle twitch in his strong jawline, and his gaze sliced past her to Whitley.

His expression strained—he was clearly trying to rein in his temper—Morgan pressed Lizzie into a nearby chair and turned on Whitley.

"What the *hell* is going on here?" he growled.

Awash in misery and abject humiliation, Lizzie sat up very straight and breathed deeply. She had not turned down Whitley's proposal precisely because of her feelings for Morgan, though they had certainly been part of her reasoning. Now Morgan would think she'd set her cap for him, refused Whitley so she could pursue Indian Rock's handsome new doctor instead.

In fact, she hadn't decided anything of the kind. Yes, she was drawn to Morgan, profoundly so, but it was far too soon to know if the attraction would last. And how in the *world* was she going to look him directly in the eye, after a scene like this?

"You took advantage!" Whitley shouted at Morgan, every word ricocheting off Lizzie's most tender places like a stone flung hard and true to its mark.

"Sit down, before you fall over," Morgan replied, his voice ominously calm. "And may I remind you that this is a public place?"

Lizzie couldn't look at either of them. Indeed, it was all she could do not to cover her face with both hands in absolute mortification.

"What can you give her, Shane?" Whitley persisted, sputtering now. "Tell me that! A name? A respectable home? Money?" He paused, gathering his forces to go on. "*My* family has a mansion on Nob Hill and a place in San Francisco society. Our name—"

Out of the corner of her eye, Lizzie saw her grand-father striding toward them, from the direction of the hotel dining room. "Lizzie *has* a name—a fine one," Angus boomed. "It's McKettrick. And she'll never lack for money or a 'respectable home,' either!"

Lizzie risked a glance at Morgan and saw that he looked confounded and not a little angry. He must have felt her gaze, because he returned it, though only briefly, a sharp, cutting edge.

"It is my understanding," he said coolly, ignoring Angus and Lizzie, too, "that Miss McKettrick intends to teach school, rather than marry. If she's spurned you, Carson, you have my sympathies, but her decision has nothing to do with me. And if you want your nose broken as well as your leg, just keep raving like a lunatic. I'll be happy to oblige."

At last, drawing some quiet strength from her grand-father's presence, Lizzie managed to look directly, and steadily, at Whitley and Morgan. They were standing dangerously close to each other, their hands clenched into fists at their sides, their eyes blazing.

"Reminds me of a couple of bucks facing off in rutting season," Angus observed, looking and sounding amused, now that he knew what the ruckus was about, and that his granddaughter was in no physical danger.

Lizzie blushed so hard her cheeks ached. "Whitley misunderstood," she told Morgan, after swallowing hard. "When I told him I couldn't accept his proposal, he jumped to the conclusion that…that something was happening between you and me."

"Imagine that," Morgan said, his tone scathing.

Inside, where no one could see, Lizzie flinched. Outside, she wore her fierce McKettrick pride like an inflexible garment. "Imagine that indeed," she retorted, as a frown took shape on Angus's face. "It just so happens that I'm not the least bit interested in *either* of you."

With that, she made for the doorway leading onto the street.

As she left, she heard mutters from both Whitley and Morgan, and a low burst of laughter from her grandfather.

AT LEAST LIZZIE WASN'T going to marry Carson, Morgan reflected, while he willed himself to simmer down. His pride stung, he'd retreated to his office, and once there, he took a fresh look around.

Carson was right. Morgan couldn't offer Lizzie

a mansion, or a name more prominent than the one she already had. God knew, he didn't have money, either.

Saddened, Morgan went on through the office and into his living quarters—the stove, the bulky bathtub, the too-narrow bed. He couldn't imagine Lizzie living happily in such a place—though the bed had a certain delicious potential—when she was used to big ranch houses, fancy schools, the best of everything.

He heard the office door open, shoved a hand through his hair and went to see if he had a patient. He found Angus McKettrick looming in the examining room, which must have seemed hardly larger than a tobacco tin to a man of his size and stature. White-haired and wise-eyed, McKettrick studied Morgan.

"Where there's smoke," he said, in that portentous voice of his, "there's bound to be fire."

Morgan studied him, at a loss for a response.

"Our Lizzie-bet," Angus went on, after indulging in a crooked little smile and folding arms the size of tree trunks, "is too much woman for most men."

Morgan felt his neck heat up. "Lizzie's independent-minded, all right," he agreed evenly. "But if you're here because you think I wrecked her marriage plans with Mr. Nob Hill out there, I didn't."

"Oh, I believe you did," Angus said complacently. "You just don't seem to *know* it."

Something inside Morgan soared, then dived straight back to hard ground, landing with shattering impact. "You heard Lizzie," he said, when he was fairly certain he could speak rationally. "She's not interested in Carson *or* me."

"So she says," Angus drawled. "I don't think Lizzie knows what's going on here any more than you do."

"Look around you," Morgan bit out, waving one hand for emphasis. "This is what I have to offer your granddaughter."

"Not much to it," Angus agreed, his tone dry, his eyes twinkling. "But I think there's something to *you*, Dr. Shane. You've got some gumption and grit, the way I hear it, and Lizzie's cut from the same kind of cloth. She'd climb straight up the velvet draperies, penned up in some fancy house in San Francisco. She's a country girl, and something of a tomboy. She sits a horse as well as any of us, and she can shoot, too. Before you go deciding you don't have what she needs, you might want to spend a little time finding out just what that is."

The old man's words nettled Morgan and, at the same time, gave him hope. "What makes you think I'm interested in Lizzie?" he asked.

Angus merely chuckled. Shook his head.

And, having said his piece, he turned and left Morgan's office, the door standing wide open behind him.

LIZZIE STORMED TOWARD nothing in particular, delighting in the bracing chill of the winter air as she left the Arizona Hotel, the familiar sights and sounds surrounding her, the hustle and bustle of wagons, buckboards and buggies weaving through the snowy street. Furious tears scalded her cheeks, and she wiped them away with a dash of one hand, walking faster and then faster still.

When she found herself in front of the mercantile, its wide display window cheerfully festooned with bright ribbon and evergreen boughs, she stopped, drew a deep breath and went inside.

The scent of Christmas assailed her—a tall pine stood in the center of the general store, bedecked with costly German ornaments, shining and new. Brightly wrapped gifts, probably empty, encircled the base of the tree.

A woman in her early thirties rounded the counter, smiling. She wore a practical dress of lightweight gray woolen, and her blond hair, pinned into a loose chignon at her nape, escaped in wisps around her delicate face. Her eyes were a shining blue, and they smiled at Lizzie a fraction of a moment before her bow-shaped mouth followed suit.

"Aren't they lovely?" the woman asked, apparently referring to the blown-glass balls and angels and St. Nicholases shimmering on the fragrant tree.

Lizzie nodded. She had not come into the mercantile to admire the merchandise, but to inquire after John Brennan. When she'd last seen him, he'd been desperately ill. "Mrs. Brennan?" she asked.

The woman nodded. Approached Lizzie and put out a hand. "Call me Alice," she said. "You must be Lizzie McKettrick. John told me how kind you were to him."

Lizzie swallowed. "Is he—is he better?"

Alice Brennan smiled. She was as pretty, and as fragile, as the most delicate of the tree ornaments. "He's holding on," she said, worry flickering in her eyes. "Would you like to see him?"

"I wouldn't want to disturb his rest," Lizzie said.

"I think he'd welcome a visit from you," Alice replied, turning slightly, beckoning for Lizzie to follow her.

Lizzie did follow, at once reluctant to impose on the

Brennans and eager to see John and measure his progress with her own eyes.

There were stairs at the back of the large store, behind cloth curtains. Alice led the way up, with Lizzie a few steps behind.

The family living quarters above were spare, by comparison to downstairs, where every shelf and surface was stuffed with merchandise of various kinds, but a large iron cookstove chortled out heat in one corner, and there was a smaller Christmas tree on a table in front of the windows overlooking the street.

John Brennan lay, cosseted in blankets, on a settee. He smiled wanly when he saw Alice.

"I've brought you a visitor," Alice told her husband.

A little boy, undoubtedly Tad, sat on the floor near the settee, playing with a carved wooden horse. He looked up at Lizzie with benign curiosity, then went back to galloping the toy horse across a plain of pillows.

John beamed when he saw Lizzie; he'd been lying prone when she came in, and now he tried to sit up, but he was weak, and failed in the effort. Alice bent to kiss his forehead, smooth his hair back, murmur something to him. Then she stepped back and, with a gesture of one hand, offered Lizzie a seat in a sturdy wing-back chair nearby.

Lizzie sat, feeling like an intruder.

"You said I'd get home to Alice and the boy," John said, his eyes shining, "and here I am."

Lizzie only smiled, blinked back tears. John Brennan was home, but he was still a very sick man, obviously, and hardly out of danger. Had he survived the ordeal on the train, and the rigorous journey to Indian Rock by horse-drawn sleigh, only to succumb to pneumonia after all?

"I reckon if you say I'll get well," John labored to add, "that will happen, too. There's something real special about you, Lizzie McKettrick."

Lizzie's throat ached. "You'll get well," she said, more because she *wanted* to believe than because she did. Alas, there was no magic in her, as John seemed to think. She was an ordinary woman. "You've got little Tad to raise, and Alice and her folks will need your help running the store."

John nodded, relaxed a little, as though Lizzie had given him some vital gift by saying what he needed to hear. "You seem to be holding up all right," he said, the words rattling up out of his thin chest.

"I'll be fine," she said, and she knew that was true, at least. She'd hurt Whitley, and alienated Morgan in the process, but she still had her family, her friends, her teaching certificate, her future. John Brennan might not be that lucky.

"The others?" John asked.

She told him what she could about their fellow passengers—Whitley, the Halifaxes, Morgan. Mr. and Mrs. Thaddings, who were staying, according to Lorelei, in Clarinda Adams's house. She spoke of everyone except Mr. Christian; for some reason, she was hesitant to mention him.

"That's good," he said, and Lizzie saw that he could barely keep his eyes open. She'd stayed too long—it was past time for her to be on her way.

"Is there anything I can do to help?" she asked Alice, at the top of the stairs.

"Just pray," Alice said. "And come back to visit when you can. It heartens John, receiving company."

Lizzie nodded.

There had been no sign of Alice's parents, who actually owned the mercantile, according to what John had told her on the train. She'd meet them later, she was sure, since Indian Rock was a small town and she'd be trading at the store regularly, once she moved into the little room behind the schoolhouse.

Outside again, Lizzie decided she wasn't ready to go back to the hotel. Lorelei would insist that she lie down again, and even if she managed to avoid Morgan and Whitley as she passed through the lobby, she would still be painfully aware of their presence.

She pulled her cloak, provided by Lorelei, more tightly around her, raised the hood to protect her ears from the clear but bitter cold and proceeded along the sidewalk, again with no particular destination in mind. She wasn't headed *toward* anything, she realized uncomfortably, but *away* from Whitley's anger and Morgan's terse dismissal.

She went to the schoolhouse, a red-painted framework building with a tiny bell tower and quarters in back, for the teacher. Her aunt Chloe, Jeb's wife, had once taught here, and made her home in the little room behind the classroom.

All the doors were locked, but she stood on tiptoe to peer in a window at what would be her home directly after New Year's, when she took up her duties. There was a little stove, an iron bedstead, a table and chair and not much else. She'd looked so forward to teaching school, earning her own money, paltry though her salary was, shaping the lives of children in small but important ways.

Now it seemed a lonely prospect, as empty as those cheery packages under the Christmas tree in the mercantile.

She sighed and turned from the window and was startled to find Mr. Christian standing directly behind her. He looked particularly hearty, showing no signs of frostbite or exhaustion. In fact, there seemed to be a faint glow to his skin, and his eyes shone with well-being.

He touched the brim of his bowler hat. Smiled.

Lizzie felt something warm inside her, despite the unrelenting cold. "I'm so glad to see you," she said. "No one seems to remember—"

"No one seems to remember what?" Christian asked kindly. He wore a very fine overcoat, one Lizzie hadn't seen before, and his hands bulged in the deep pockets.

"Well," Lizzie said, groping a little, *"you."*

Mr. Christian smiled again. "Dr. Shane remembers," he said. "And the children will, too. Little Ellen and Jack will remember—always."

The oddness of the remark struck Lizzie, but she was so pleased to see that her friend had recovered that she paid little mind to it. "I've just been to visit John Brennan," she said. "I'm afraid—"

Mr. Christian cut her off with a kindly shake of his head. "He'll recover," he said with certainty.

Lizzie frowned, puzzled. "How can you be so sure?"

"Call it a Christmas miracle," Mr. Christian said.

A little thrill tripped down Lizzie's spine. The

freezing air seemed charged somehow, as though electricity had gathered around the two of them, silent, a small, invisible tornado. "I'd like to introduce you to my stepmother, Lorelei," she said, after a moment in which her heart seemed to snag on something sharp.

"Because she doesn't believe I exist?" Mr. Christian asked, his smile muted now, and full of quiet amusement.

Lizzie sighed. "Not *only* that," she protested. "Lorelei probably knows your family and—"

"I have no family, Lizzie. Not the kind you mean, anyway."

"But you said—"

Again, the faint and mysterious smile came. The glow Lizzie had noticed before intensified a little. And it came to her that Mr. Christian simply could not have recovered so completely in such a short time. Had he... died? Was she seeing his ghost? She'd heard of things like that, of course, but never given them serious consideration before that moment.

"Who are you?" she heard herself ask, in a near whisper.

He didn't answer.

Lizzie reached out, meaning to clutch at his sleeve, a way of insisting that he reply, but grab though she might, she couldn't seem to catch hold of him. It was the strangest sensation—he was *there,* not transparent as she imagined a spirit might be, but a real person, one of reality and substance. Without moving at all, he still managed to evade her touch.

"Who are you?" she repeated, more forcefully this time.

"That's not important," he said quietly. Then he pointed to someone or something just past Lizzie's left shoulder. "Look there," he added. "There's your young man, coming to make things up. Give him every opportunity, Lizzie. He's the one."

Lizzie turned to look, saw Morgan vaulting over the schoolyard fence, starting toward her. She turned again, with another question for Mr. Christian teetering on the tip of her tongue, but he was gone.

Simply *gone*.

Startled, her heart pounding, Lizzie swept the large yard, but there was no sign of Mr. Christian. She hurried to look behind the building, but he wasn't there, either. Nor was he behind the outhouse or the little shed meant to house a horse or a milk cow.

"Lizzie?"

She whirled.

Morgan stood at her side. "What's the matter?" he asked, frowning.

"Mr. Christian," she sputtered. "He was just here— surely you must have seen him—"

Morgan frowned. "I didn't see anybody but you," he said, taking her arm. "Are you all right?"

She was shaking. She felt like laughing—and like crying. Like dancing, and like collapsing in a heap in the powdery snow.

The snow.

She searched the ground—Mr. Christian would have left footprints in the snow, just as she had. But there were no tracks, other than her own and Morgan's.

She sagged against Morgan, stunned, and his arms

tightened around her. "Lizzie!" There was a plea in his voice. *Be all right,* it said.

"I…I must be seeing things—" She gulped in a breath, shook her head. "No. I *did* see Mr. Christmas— *Mr. Christian*—he was right here. We spoke…he told me—"

"Lizzie," Morgan repeated, gripping her upper arms now, looking deep into her eyes. "Stop chattering and *breathe.*"

"He was here!"

Morgan led her around to the front of the school-house, sat her down on the side of the porch, where the snow had melted away, took a seat beside her. "I believe you," he said, holding her hand. She felt his innate strength, strength of mind and spirit and body, flowing into her, buoying her up. Sustaining her. "Lizzie, *I believe you.*"

She let her head rest against his shoulder, not caring who saw her and Morgan, sitting close together on the schoolhouse porch, holding hands, even though it was highly improper.

For a long while, neither of them spoke. Lizzie was willing her heartbeat to return to normal, and Morgan seemed content just to be there with her.

Finally, though, he broke the silence. "You're really not going to marry Carson?" he asked, looking as sheepish as he sounded.

"I'm really not going to marry Whitley," Lizzie confirmed. Her heart started beating fast again.

"He was right," Morgan went on, after heaving a resigned sigh. He gazed off toward the distant mountain, where they'd been stranded together, nearly buried under tons of snow. "About all the things he said earlier, back at the hotel, I mean. I can't offer you what he can. No position in society. No mansion. No money to speak of."

Lizzie blinked, studied him. "Morgan Shane," she said, "*look* at me."

He obeyed, grinned sadly.

"What are you saying?" she asked.

He hesitated for what seemed to Lizzie an excruciatingly long time. Then, with another sigh, he answered her question with one of his own. "Can you imagine yourself being courted by a penniless country doctor with no prospects to speak of?"

Lizzie's breath caught. She considered the matter for all of two seconds. "Yes," she said. "I can imagine that very well."

He enclosed the hand he'd been holding in both his own, looked straight into Lizzie's soul. "I know it will take time. There's a lot we don't know about each other. You've got classes to teach, and I'll be building a medical practice. But if you'll have me, Lizzie McKettrick, I'll be your husband by this time next year."

"D-do you love me?" Lizzie asked, color flaring in her cheeks at the audacity of her question.

"I'm pretty sure I do," Morgan replied, with a saucy grin. "Do you love me?"

"I certainly feel *something*," Lizzie said, blissfully bewildered. "But I'm not sure I trust myself. After all, I thought I loved Whitley. All I could think about, before we left San Francisco—" *before I met you* "—was whether he'd propose to me over Christmas or not."

Morgan chuckled.

"I guess it proves something my grandfather always says," Lizzie went on. "Be careful what you wish for, because you might damn well get it."

This time Morgan laughed out loud. "Amen," he said.

Lizzie turned thoughtful. "I'd want to go right on teaching school, even if we got married," she warned.

"And I'll want children," Morgan said.

A great joy swelled inside Lizzie, one she could barely contain. "At least four," she agreed. "Two girls and two boys."

Morgan's eyes gleamed. "The room behind my office might get a little crowded," he told her.

"We'll think of something," Lizzie said.

"The hardest part will be waiting," Morgan told her, leaning in a little, lowering his voice. "To get those babies started, I mean."

Lizzie blushed, well aware of his meaning. She'd never been intimate with a man, not even Whitley, though she'd allowed him to kiss her a few times, but she craved *this* man, this "penniless country doctor," with her entire being. She wondered if she could endure a whole year of such wanting.

Reading her expression, Morgan chuckled again, rested his forehead against hers. "I'm about to kiss you, Lizzie McKettrick," he said. "Like I've wanted to kiss you from the moment I first laid eyes on you. And if the whole town of Indian Rock sees me do that, so be it."

Lizzie swallowed, tilted her head upward, ready for his kiss. Longing for it. And feeling utterly scandalized by the ferocity of her own desire.

He laid his mouth to hers, gently at first, then with

a hunger to match and even exceed her own. His lips felt deliciously warm, despite the frigid weather, and wonderfully soft. She trembled as the kiss deepened, caught fire inside when his tongue found hers. It was a foretaste of things to come, things that could only happen when they were married, but she felt it in her most feminine parts, as surely as if he'd laid her down on that schoolhouse porch and taken her outright, made her his own.

She moaned.

Morgan's soft laugh echoed in her mouth.

He knew. He *knew* what she was thinking, what she was feeling.

Lizzie's face felt as hot as the blood singing through her veins.

"Oh, my goodness," she gasped, when the kiss was over.

"Only the beginning," Morgan promised gruffly, twisting a loose tendril of her hair gently around one finger.

"Hush," she said helplessly.

He let go of her face, which he'd been holding between his hands while he kissed her, while he *possessed* her, and put a slight but eloquent distance between them. "I'd better get back to the hotel," he said. "I'm expecting some patients, now that I've figuratively hung out my shingle."

"I'll go with you," Lizzie said, not because she particularly wanted to return to the hotel, where she would be treated like an invalid, albeit a cherished one, but because she couldn't be parted from Morgan.

Not yet. Not after what had just happened between them—whatever it was.

As Lizzie had expected, word had gotten around that the new doctor was young, handsome and eligible. Three women, all of them known to Lizzie and notoriously single, awaited him, in varying stages of feigned illness.

She had the silliest urge to shoo them away, like so many hens fluttering around a rooster. Fortunately, she recovered her good sense in time, and simply smiled.

Whitley had left the lobby, perhaps retreating to his nearby room, and Lizzie was relieved by that. She'd be glad when he left Indian Rock, but she knew it might be a while before the train ran again, and the roads were all but impassable.

Suddenly hungry, she made her way through the empty dining room to the kitchen, and found Lorelei there, chatting with the Chinese cook.

"There you are," Lorelei said, in a tone of good-natured scolding. "Your cheeks are flushed. Have you taken a chill?"

Lizzie still felt the tingle of Morgan's kiss on her mouth, and things had melted inside her, so that she was a little unsteady on her feet. She sank into a rocking chair near the stove, smiling foolishly. "No," she said. "I haven't taken a chill. But I'm famished."

The cook dished up a bowl of beef stew dolloped with dumplings and handed it to Lizzie where she sat, along with a spoon, then left.

Lorelei drew up a second chair.

"Something very strange happened to me today,"

Lizzie confided, without really intending to, between bites of savory stew.

"I saw you come in with Dr. Shane," Lorelei said, with a gentle but knowing smile. "Lizzie McKettrick, I do believe you've fallen in love."

Perhaps she *had* fallen in love, Lizzie thought. Time would tell.

"Lizzie?" Lorelei prompted, when Lizzie didn't confirm or deny her stepmother's assertion.

"He's going to court me," she said. "Do you think Papa will object?"

"No," Lorelei responded, watching Lizzie very closely. "Would it matter if he did?"

Lizzie laughed. "No," she said. "I don't think it would."

Lorelei smiled, her eyes glistening with happy tears. "It's love, all right. When I met your father, I figured we were all wrong for each other, and I wanted to be with him so badly that I couldn't think straight."

"Something else happened," Lizzie went on, because there was very little she didn't share with her stepmother. Quietly, carefully, she told Lorelei about her encounter with Mr. Christian, at the schoolyard, leaving nothing out.

"Good heavens," Lorelei said, when the tale was told. Then she reached out and tested Lizzie's forehead for fever. Finding her flesh cool, she frowned and managed to look relieved at one and the same time.

"You believe me, don't you?" Lizzie asked shyly.

"If you say you saw this Mr. Christian," Lorelei said, without hesitation, "then you saw him. You are no flibbertigibbet, Lizzie McKettrick."

"But how could he have just—just *disappeared* that way?"

"I don't have the faintest idea," Lorelei answered. Then she rose from her chair. "Finish your stew. I'll be back in a few minutes, and we'll have tea."

Lizzie nodded and her stepmother hurried out of the kitchen, only to be replaced by Angus. He helped himself to a cup of coffee from the pot on the stove and stood watching Lizzie curiously, as though she'd changed in some fundamental way.

And perhaps she had.

"You did a fine job after that avalanche," he told her. "Looking after folks. Trying to keep their spirits up."

"Thank you," Lizzie said. Hers was an independent spirit, but she valued her grandfather's opinion of her, along with those of Lorelei and, of course, her papa.

He sipped his coffee. "You're all right, aren't you, Lizzie-girl? You seem—well—different."

"It's possible I'm in love," she said.

Angus smiled, lifted his coffee cup as if in a toast. "I'll drink to that," he replied, just as Lorelei returned to the kitchen, carrying a Bible.

Lizzie set aside her bowl of stew, and Lorelei practically shoved the Good Book under her nose.

"Read this," she ordered, pointing to a passage in Hebrews, thirteenth chapter, second verse:

"Be not forgetful to entertain strangers; for thereby some have entertained angels unawares."

CHAPTER EIGHT

"MR. CHRISTIAN MAKES AN UNLIKELY ANGEL," Lizzie told Morgan, standing in his examining room, several hours after Lorelei had shown her the Bible verse in the hotel kitchen. "Don't you think?"

Morgan pulled his stethoscope from around his neck and set it aside. "Not having made the acquaintance of all that many angels," he replied, "I couldn't say."

"He played cards with the children," Lizzie said, groping for reasons why Mr. Christian could not be a part of the heavenly host. "He pulled a gun on Whitley once, and he gave you *whiskey* when you went out into the blizzard—"

"Positively demonic," Morgan teased. "I guess I missed the part where he drew a gun."

"You were outside," Lizzie answered.

"Why would a peddler feel compelled to threaten Carson with a gun, annoying though he is?"

Lizzie shook off the question. "I'm *trying* to make some sense of what happened, Morgan," Lizzie protested, "and you are not helping."

He grinned. "Some things just don't make sense, Lizzie McKettrick," he said. "Like why every unmarried woman in Indian Rock seems to have developed some fetching and very melodramatic malady."

Lizzie laughed, though she wasn't amused. "No

mystery to that," she answered. "You're an eligible bachelor, after all."

He moved closer to her, rested his hands on her shoulders. "Oh, but I'm *not* eligible," he said, his low voice setting things aquiver inside Lizzie. "I'm definitely taken."

He was about to kiss her again, but the office door crashed open with a terrible bang, and both of them turned to see Doss, Lizzie's seven-year-old brother, standing on the threshold.

"Pa's back!" he shouted exuberantly. "The roads are clear, and after church, we can go home and have Christmas!" He paused, his small face screwed into a puzzled frown. "Were you *smooching?*" he demanded, looking suspicious.

Lizzie laughed, and so did Morgan.

"No," Lizzie said.

"Yes," Morgan replied, at the same moment.

"You'd better get married, then," Doss decided. "You're not supposed to kiss people if you're not married to them."

"Is that right?" Morgan asked, approaching Doss and ruffling his thick blond hair.

"I bet it says so in the Bible," Doss insisted solemnly.

"Do we have a budding preacher in our midst?" Morgan asked Lizzie, his eyes full of warm laughter.

Lizzie giggled. "Doss? Perish the thought. He's more imp than angel."

At the word *angel,* a little silence fell. Lizzie thought of Mr. Christian, of course, and the insoluble mystery he represented.

"We had to wait to have Christmas," Doss complained. "There are a whole *bunch* of packages under our tree at home, and some of them are mine. And now we have to sit through *church,* too."

Lizzie's attention was on Morgan. "Will you come with us?" she asked. "To celebrate a McKettrick Christmas, I mean?"

Morgan looked reluctant. "I'd be intruding," he said.

"That man with the broken leg is going," Doss put in, relentlessly helpful.

Morgan merely spread his hands to Lizzie, as if to say *I told you so.*

"You belong with us," Lizzie said, not to be put off. It would be awkward, celebrating their delayed Christmas with both Whitley and Morgan present, but that was unavoidable. To leave Whitley alone at the hotel while everyone else enjoyed roast goose and eggnog was simply not the McKettrick way.

In the end Morgan relented.

Pastor Reynolds held a Christmas Eve service at sunset, and the whole town attended. Candles were lit, carols were sung, a gentle sermon was preached. After the closing prayer, gifts were given out to all the children, and Lizzie recognized her father's handiwork, made in his woodshop, and the cloth dolls and animals Lorelei and the aunts had sewn. Every child received a present.

Mr. and Mrs. Thaddings watched fondly, and somewhat wistfully, Lizzie thought, as Ellen Halifax showed off the doll she'd wanted so much. Jack received a stick horse with a yarn mane, and galloped up and down the aisle, despite his mother's protests. John and Alice Brennan were there, too, with Alice's parents and little Tad, who seemed fascinated with his toy buckboard.

Lizzie approached the Thaddingses. She knew Pastor Reynolds had wired Clarinda Adams on their behalf, hoping she'd allow them to stay on until she either returned or sold the house, but there hadn't been time for an answer.

Mrs. Thaddings embraced her. "You look well, Lizzie," she said.

"I'm happy to be home," Lizzie replied. Whitley, standing nearby, letting his crutches support his weight, looked despondent. She wondered if he'd ever considered staying on in Indian Rock, or if he'd always intended to insist they live in San Francisco, after they were married.

She would probably never know, she decided. And it didn't matter.

"We'd better get back and see to Woodrow, dear," Mr. Thaddings told his wife, taking a gentle hold on her elbow. "Before this snow gets too deep."

Lizzie wasn't about to let the Thaddingses walk home, and quickly conscripted her goodnatured uncle Jeb to drive them in his buggy.

Later, when the McKettrick clan left Indian Rock for the Triple M, Morgan was with them, seated next to Lizzie in the back of her father's wagon. Whitley, alternately scowling and looking bleak, rode in the other. The snow, so threatening on the mountain, fell like a blessed benediction all around them, soothing and soft, almost magical.

The first sight of the main ranch house brought tears to Lizzie's eyes. She'd thought, before the rescue, that she might never see the home place again, never warm herself before one of the fires, dream in a rocking chair while a summer rain pattered at the roof. But there it was, sturdy and dearly familiar, its roof laced with snow, its windows alight with a golden glow.

Dogs barked a merry greeting, and small cousins, as well as aunts and uncles, poured from wagons and buckboards, their voices a happy buzz in the wintry darkness.

Lizzie stood still, after Morgan helped her down from the wagon, taking it all in. Hiding things in her heart.

Inside her grandfather's house, a giant tree winked with tinsel. Piles of packages stood beneath it, some simply wrapped in brown paper or newsprint, others bedecked in pretty cloth and tied with shimmering ribbons.

Concepcion, her grandfather's wife, must have been cooking for days. The house was redolent with the aromas Lizzie had yearned for on the stranded train—freshly baked bread, savory roast goose, spices like cinnamon and nutmeg. Lizzie breathed deeply of the love and happiness surrounding her on all sides.

The children were excited, of course, all the more so because, for them, Christmas was just plain late. At Holt's suggestion, they were allowed to empty their bulging St. Nicholas stockings and open their packages.

Chaos reigned while dolls and games and brightly colored shirts and dresses were unwrapped. Lizzie watched the whole scene in a daze of gratitude and love for her large, boisterous family. Morgan stood nearby, enjoying the melee, while Whitley slumped in a leather chair next to the fireplace, wearing an expression that said, "Bah, humbug."

If she hadn't known it before, Lizzie would have known then that Whitley simply didn't belong with this rowdy crew. Morgan, on the other hand, had soon taken off his coat, pushed up his sleeves and knelt on the floor to help Doss assemble a miniature ranch house from a toy set of interlocking logs.

A nudge from her father distracted Lizzie, and she started when she saw what he was holding in his hands—Mr. Christian's music box, the one he'd given her on Christmas Eve, aboard the train.

She blinked. Surely they'd left it behind, along with most of their other possessions, to be collected later.

"The tag says it's for you," Holt said, looking puzzled. Clearly, he didn't recall seeing the music box before.

Lizzie's hands trembled as she accepted the box. A strain of "O Little Town of Bethlehem" tinkled from its depths, so ethereal that she was sure, in the moment after, that she'd imagined it.

She found a chair—not easy since the house was bulging with McKettricks—and sank into it, stricken speechless.

Whitley, as it happened, already occupied the chair next to hers. He frowned, eyeing the music box resting in Lizzie's lap like some sacred object to be guarded at all costs.

"That's pretty," he said, with a grudging note to his voice. "Did Shane give it to you?"

Lizzie shook her head, made herself meet Whitley's gaze. "Don't you remember, Whitley?" she asked, referring to Christmas Eve on the train, when they'd *all* seen the music box, listened with sad delight to its chiming tunes.

"Remember what?" Whitley asked. He wasn't pretending, Lizzie knew. He honestly didn't recall either the music box *or* Mr. Christian.

"Never mind," Lizzie said.

Dinner was announced, and Whitley got up, reaching for his crutches, and stumped off toward the dining room. Most of the children had fallen asleep on piles of crumpled wrapping paper, and the adults had all gone to eat.

All except Morgan, and Lizzie herself, that is.

"Hungry?" Morgan asked, extending a hand to Lizzie.

She set the music box aside, on the sturdy table next to her chair, and took Morgan's hand. "Starved," she said.

Instead of escorting her into the dining room, where everyone else had gathered—their voices were like a muted symphony of laughter and happy conversation, sweet to Lizzie's ears—Morgan drew her close. Held her as though they were about to swirl into the flow of a waltz.

"If what I'm feeling right now isn't love," Morgan said, his lips nearly touching Lizzie's, "then there's something even *better* than love."

Lizzie's throat constricted. She whispered his name, and he would have kissed her, she supposed, if a third party hadn't made his presence known with a clearing of the throat.

"Time for that later," Angus said, grinning. "Supper's on the table."

BY NEW YEAR'S, the tracks had been cleared and the trains were running again. Lizzie waited on the platform, alongside Whitley, the sole traveler leaving Indian Rock that day.

A cold, dry wind blew, stinging Lizzie's ears, and she felt as miserable as Whitley looked.

You'll meet someone else.

That was what she wanted to say, but it seemed presumptuous, under the circumstances. Whitley's feelings were private ones, and she had no real way of knowing what they were.

"You're sure about this?" he asked quietly, as the train rounded the bend in the near distance, whistle blowing, white steam chuffing from the smokestack against a brittle blue sky. "We could have a good life together, Lizzie."

Lizzie blinked back tears. Yes, she supposed they *could* have a good life together, she and Whitley, good enough, anyway. But she wanted more than "good enough," for herself and Morgan—and for Whitley. "You belong in San Francisco," she told him gently. "And I belong right here, in Indian Rock."

Whitley surprised her with a sad, tender smile. "I hate to admit it," he said, "but you're probably right. Be happy, Lizzie."

The train was nearly at the platform now, and so loud that Lizzie would have had to shout to be heard over the din. So she stood on tiptoe and planted a brief, chaste kiss on Whitley's mouth.

Metal brakes squealed as the train came to a full stop.

Whitley stared into Lizzie's eyes for a long moment, saying a silent fare-thee-well, then he turned, deft on his crutches, to leave. She watched until he'd boarded the train, then turned and walked slowly away.

In the morning, her first day of teaching would commence. She headed for the schoolhouse, where her father and her uncle Jeb were unloading some of her things from the back of a buckboard.

Jeb nodded to her and smiled before lugging her rocking chair inside, but Holt came to Lizzie and slipped an arm around her shoulders. Kissed her lightly on the forehead.

"Goodbyes can be hard," he said, knowing she'd just come from the train depot, "even when it's for the best."

Lizzie nodded, choked up. "I was so sure—"

Holt chuckled. "Of course you were sure," he said. "You're a McKettrick, and McKettricks are sure of everything."

"What if I'm wrong about Morgan?" she asked, looking up into her father's face. "I don't think I could stand to say goodbye to him."

"Don't borrow trouble, Lizzie-bet," Holt smiled. "You've got a year of courting ahead of you. And my guess is, at the end of that time, you'll know for sure, one way or the other."

She nodded, swallowed, and rested her forehead against Holt's shoulder.

Later, when she'd explored her classroom, with its blackboard and potbellied stove and long, low-slung tables, for what must have been the hundredth time, she went into her living quarters.

Her father and uncle had gone, and her personal belongings were all around, in boxes and crates and travel trunks. Her books, her most serviceable dresses, a pretty china lamp from her bedroom at the ranch, the little writing desk her grandfather had given her as a Christmas gift.

Lorelei had packed quilts and sheets and fluffy

pillows, meant to make the stark little room more home-like, and before they'd gone, her father and uncle had built a nice fire in the stove.

Lizzie searched until she found the music box, set it in the middle of the table, and sat down to admire it. And to wonder.

Truly, as the bard had so famously said, there *were* more things in heaven and earth than this world dreams of.

A light knock at her door brought Lizzie out of her musings, and she went to open it, found Morgan standing on the small porch facing the side yard. His hands stuffed into the pockets of his worn coat, he favored her with a shy smile.

"I know it isn't proper, but—"

"Come in," Lizzie said, catching him by the sleeve and literally pulling him over the threshold.

Inside, Morgan made such a comical effort not to notice the bed, which dominated the tiny room, that Lizzie laughed.

"I can't stay," Morgan said, making no move to leave.

"People will talk," Lizzie agreed, still amused.

His gaze strayed past her, to the music box. "This was quite a Christmas, wasn't it?" he asked.

"Quite a Christmas indeed," Lizzie said, watching as he approached the table, sorted through the stack of little brass disks containing various tunes, and slid one into the side of the music box. He wound the key, and the strains of a waltz tinkled in the air, delicate as tiny icicles dropping from the eaves of a house.

Morgan turned to Lizzie, holding out his arms, and she moved into his embrace, and they danced.

They danced until the music stopped, and then they went on dancing, in the tremulous silence that followed, around the table, past the rocking chair and the bed. Around and around and around they went, the doctor and the schoolmarm, waltzing to the beat of each other's hearts.

CHAPTER NINE

December 20, 1897

"MISS MCKETTRICK?" lisped a small voice.

Lizzie looked up from the papers she'd been grading at her desk and smiled to see Tad Brennan standing there. Barely five, he was still too young to attend school, but he often showed up when classes were over for the day, to show Lizzie his "homework."

"Tad," she greeted him, cheered by his exuberant desire to learn. In the year Lizzie had been teaching, he'd mastered his alphabet and elementary arithmetic, with a lot of help from his father. By the time he officially enrolled in the fall, he'd probably be ready to skip the first grade.

"Mama says you're getting married to Dr. Shane soon," Tad said miserably.

"Well, yes," Lizzie said, resisting an urge to ruffle his hair. She knew her little brothers hated that gesture. "Dr. Shane and I *are* getting married, the day before Christmas. You're invited to the ceremony, and so are your parents and grandparents."

Tad's eyes were suddenly brilliant with tears. "That means we'll have a new teacher," he said. "And I wanted *you*."

Lizzie pushed her chair back from her desk and held out her arms to Tad. Reluctantly he allowed her to take him onto her lap. Like her brothers, he regarded himself as a big boy now, and lap sitting was suspect. "I'll be your teacher, Tad," she said gently. "The only difference will be, you'll call me Mrs. Shane instead of Miss McKettrick."

The child looked at her with mingled confusion and hope. "But aren't you going to have babies?"

Lizzie felt her cheeks warm a little. She and Morgan had done their best to wait, but one balmy night last June, the waiting had proved to be too much for both of them. They'd made love, in the deep grass of a pasture on the Triple M, and since then, they'd been together every chance they got.

"I'm sure I'll have babies," she said. "Eventually."

"Mama says women with babies have to stay home and take care of them," Tad told her solemnly.

"Does she?" Lizzie asked gently.

Tad nodded.

"Tell you what," Lizzie said, after giving him a little hug. "I promise, baby or no baby, to be here when you start first grade. Fair enough?"

Tad beamed. Nodded. Scrambled down off Lizzie's lap just as the door of the schoolhouse sprang open.

The scent of fresh evergreen filled the small room, and then Morgan was there, in the chasm, lugging a tree so large that Lizzie could only see his boots. The school's Christmas party was scheduled for the next afternoon; Lizzie and her students, fourteen children of widely varying ages, would spend the morning decorating with paper chains and bits of shiny paper garnered for the purpose.

"Miss McKettrick promised to be my teacher in first grade," Tad told Morgan seriously, "*even* if she's got a baby."

Morgan's dark eyes glinted with humor and no little passion. Late the night before, he'd knocked on Lizzie's door, and she'd let him in. He'd stayed until just before dawn, leaving Lizzie melting in the schoolteacher's bed.

"I just saw your pa," he told the child, letting the baby remark pass. "He's wanting you to help him carry in wood."

Tad said a hasty goodbye to Lizzie and hurried out. John Brennan had come a long way in the year since they'd all been stranded together in a train on the mountainside, but his health was still somewhat fragile and he counted on his son to assist him with the chores.

"Did you really meet up with John?" Lizzie asked, suspicious.

Morgan grinned, leaned the tree against the far wall and crossed the room to bend over her chair and kiss her soundly. Electricity raced along her veins and danced in her nerve endings. "I could have," he said. "Walked right past the mercantile on my way here."

Lizzie laughed, though the kiss had set her afire, as Morgan Shane's kisses always did. "You're a shameless scoundrel," she said, giving his chest a little push with both palms precisely because she wanted to pull him close instead.

"We're invited to supper at the Thaddingses'," Morgan replied, still grinning. He could turn her from a schoolmarm to a hussy within five minutes if he wanted to, and he was making sure she understood that. "They have news."

Lizzie stood up, once Morgan gave her room to do so, and began neatening the things on her desk. "News? What kind of news?"

Morgan stood behind her, pulled her back against him. She felt his desire and wondered if he'd step inside with her, after walking her back from supper at the Thaddingses', and seduce her in the little room in back. "I don't know," he murmured, his breath warm against her temple. "I guess that's why it will come as—well—*news.*"

His hands cupped her breasts, warm and strong and infinitely gentle.

"Dr. Morgan Shane," Lizzie sputtered, "this is a *schoolroom.*"

He chuckled. "So it is. I'd take you to bed and have you thoroughly, Miss McKettrick, but I saw your father and one of your uncles coming out of the Cattleman's Bank a little while ago, and my guess is, they're on their way here right now."

With a little cry, Lizzie jumped away from Morgan. Smoothed her hair and her skirts.

Sure enough, a wagon rolled clamorously up outside in the very next moment. She heard her father call out a greeting to someone passing by.

Lizzie put her hands to her cheeks, hoping to cool them. One look at her, in her present state of arousal, and her father would know what she'd been up to with Morgan. If he hadn't guessed already.

Morgan perched on the edge of her desk, folded his arms and grinned at her discomfort. "Damn," he said, "you're almost as beautiful when you want to make love as just afterward, when you make those little sighing sounds."

"Morgan!"

He laughed.

The schoolhouse door opened, and Holt McKettrick came in, dressed for winter in woolen trousers, a heavy shirt and a long coat lined in sheep's wool. His gaze moving from Morgan to Lizzie, he grinned a little.

"Lorelei sent some things in for the new house," he said. "Rafe and I will unload them over there, unless you'd rather keep them here until after the wedding."

"There would be better," Lizzie said.

Over Morgan's protests, when their engagement had become official on Lizzie's twentieth birthday in early August, her grandfather had purchased a little plot of land at the edge of town, and now a small white cottage with green-shuttered windows awaited their occupancy. Angus, Holt, the uncles and Morgan had built the place with their own hands and, little by little, it had been furnished, with one notable exception: a bed.

When Lizzie had commented on the oversight the week before, while they sat in the ranch house kitchen sewing dolls to be given away at church on Christmas Eve, her stepmother had smiled and said only, "I was your age once."

Morgan, whistling merrily under his breath, gave the evergreen a little shake, causing its scent to perfume the schoolhouse, and nodded a greeting to Holt.

"We'll be going, then," Holt said, with a note of bemused humor in his voice. His McKettrick-blue eyes twinkled. "Lorelei and the other womenfolk are wanting to fuss with your wedding dress a little more, so you'd best pay a visit to the ranch in the next day or two."

Lizzie nodded. "I'll be there," she promised.

Her papa kissed her cheek, glanced Morgan's way again and left.

As soon as Holt had gone, Morgan kissed Lizzie, too, though in an entirely different way, asked her to meet him at Clarinda Adams's place at six, and took his leave as well.

"COMPANY!" Woodrow squawked, from inside the once-notorious Clarinda Adams house. "Company!"

Morgan smiled down at Lizzie, who stood with her cloak pulled close around her, shivering a little. The ground was blanketed with pristine white snow, and it glittered in the glow from the gas-powered streetlight on the corner. Curlicues of frost adorned the front windows. "That bird takes himself pretty seriously," Morgan observed.

"Hurry up!" Woodrow crowed. "Hurry up! No time like the present! Hurry up!"

Lizzie chuckled. The Thaddingses had become dear friends to her and to Morgan—and so had Woodrow. Once, Mr. Thaddings had even brought the bird to the schoolhouse, and the children had been fascinated by his ability to repeat everything they said to him.

The door opened, and Zebulon stood on the threshold. He wore a red silk smoking jacket, probably left behind by one of Clarinda's clients, and held a pipe in one hand. "Come in," he said. "Come in."

"Come in!" Woodrow echoed.

Gratefully, Lizzie preceded Morgan into the warm house. Once, according to local legend, there had been paintings of naked people on the walls, but they were long gone.

Woodrow hopped on his perch. "Lizzie's here!" he cried jubilantly. "Lizzie's here!"

She laughed and, as Morgan closed the front door behind them, Woodrow flew across the entry way to land on Lizzie's shoulder.

"Lizzie's pretty," the bird went on. "Lizzie's pretty!"

"Smart bird," Morgan said, amused.

Woodrow tugged at one of the tiny combs holding Lizzie's abundance of hair in a schoolmarmish do.

"Flatterer," Zebulon scolded Woodrow affectionately. Then, to Lizzie and Morgan, he confided, "He's been after that comb all along."

Lizzie laughed again. Stroked Woodrow's top feathers with a light finger. "When are you coming back to school?" she asked him.

"Woodrow to school!" he crowed. "See the pretty birdie!"

"He'll keep this up for hours if we let him," Zebulon said, turning to lead the way into the main parlor.

Just as they reached that resplendent room, Mrs. Thaddings—Marietta, to Lizzie—entered from the dining room, carrying a tray in both hands. She was gray and frail, but Lizzie had long since stopped thinking of Marietta Thaddings as elderly. She was an active member of Indian Rock society, such as it was, hosting card clubs and giving recitations from her vast store of memorized poetry. She was the soul of kindness, and Lizzie loved her like a grandmother.

"Come, sit down by the fire," Marietta said. "I've brewed a nice pot of tea, and supper is almost ready."

Lizzie sat.

Morgan took the tray from Marietta's hands and

placed it on the low table between the settee and several chairs drawn up close to the fire. Although Morgan was always polite, his solicitude worried Lizzie a little. He was, after all, Marietta's doctor as well as her friend. Was her health failing?

Marietta's eager smile belied the idea. She sat, and Woodrow flew to perch in the back of her chair.

"We've heard from Clarinda," she announced.

Lizzie braced herself. Was the legendary Miss Adams about to return to Indian Rock, and upset the proverbial apple cart? During her absence, the Thaddingses had served as caretakers of sorts. If Clarinda returned, she would almost certainly reestablish her business.

Morgan's hand landed lightly on Lizzie's shoulder, steadying her. There was so little she could hide from him; he sensed every change of mood.

"Lizzie's been a little nervous lately," he said. "What with the wedding coming up in a few days and all."

Zebulon and Marietta beamed. "So it is," Zebulon said. "Christmas Eve, after the church service the two of you will be married."

"It's so romantic," Marietta sighed sweetly.

"Let's tell them our news," Zebulon said, after giving his wife a long, adoring look.

"Clarinda has decided not to come back to Indian Rock," Marietta told them. "She hired us as permanent caretakers, and we can do what we want with the place. Turn it into a hospital or a boarding house." She paused, and she and Zebulon exchanged a glance. "Or a sort of school."

Lizzie's eyes stung with happy tears.

"We'll need to do something," Zebulon hurried to contribute. "To make ends meet, I mean, and the

Territory is willing to pay us a stipend if we'll take in Indian children. The ones with no place else to go."

"You wouldn't feel we were—infringing or anything, would you, Lizzie?" Marietta asked, gently anxious.

"Infringing?" Lizzie repeated, confused. "I think it's wonderful."

Both Zebulon and Marietta sighed with relief.

"Are you up to it?" Morgan asked them, ever the practical one. "Kids are a lot of work."

Zebulon's eyes shone. "We never had children of our own, as you know, and we love them so. We'll be fine." He turned to Lizzie, looking worried again. "It will mean more pupils for you," he said. "The schoolhouse will probably have to be expanded. Usually, these little ones have been shuffled from place to place, and they're the ones without a family to take them in. They might get up to some mischief."

"After the wedding," Morgan said diplomatically, "Lizzie won't need the teacher's quarters anymore. If the town council agrees, it would be easy enough to knock out a wall and add a few desks."

Both Zebulon and Marietta looked relieved.

When it came time to serve supper, Lizzie followed Marietta back to the kitchen to help in whatever way she could.

"What's it like to live here?" she asked, because curiosity was her besetting sin and she hadn't stopped herself in time.

Marietta looked gently scandalized. "Early on, several confused gentlemen came to the door," she admitted, cheeks pink. "For a while, there, we got at least one caller every time the train stopped at the depot."

"I shouldn't have asked," Lizzie said.

"It's natural to wonder," Marietta assured her. "And Lord knows, I've done *my* share of wondering. Clarinda and I were raised in a decent, God-fearing home. My sister was always spirited, that's true, but I certainly never *dreamed* she'd grow up to run a…a *brothel*."

Marietta took a roast from the oven and placed it carefully on a platter. Lizzie picked up a bowl brimming with fluffy mashed potatoes, answering, "People are full of surprises."

"Whatever she's done in the past, it's kind of Clarinda to let Zebulon and me live here. Heaven only knows what we'd have done if she hadn't given us shelter. Why, she even wired the people at the mercantile, instructing them to let us buy whatever we needed on her account."

When the four of them were seated in the massive dining room, huddled together at one end, Zebulon offered grace. After the amen, they all ate in earnest. Woodrow remained in the parlor, squawking away.

"It hardly seems possible," Zebulon said, "that a whole year has gone by since we all met."

Morgan gave Lizzie a sidelong glance. "It seems like a long time to some of us," he said.

Lizzie elbowed him and smiled at Zebulon. "When will the children arrive?"

It was Marietta who answered. "Right after New Year's," she said. "We'll have a lot to do, Zebulon and I, to get ready."

"I can promise a whole crowd of McKettrick women to help out," Lizzie told her, with absolute confidence that it was so.

After supper, Lizzie and Marietta attended to the dishes while Zebulon, Morgan and Woodrow talked politics in the parlor.

A fresh snowfall had begun when Lizzie and Morgan left the Thaddingses' house. Instead of heading for the schoolhouse, Morgan steered Lizzie toward their cottage on the outskirts of town.

To Lizzie's surprise, lights glowed in the windows, and the tiny front room was warm when they stepped inside. They visited the house often, separately and together—Lizzie liked to imagine what it would be like, living there with Morgan, and she suspected the reverse was true, too.

The plank floors gleamed with varnish, the scent of it still sharp in the air. Two wing-backed chairs faced the small brick fireplace, and lace curtains, sewn by her stepmother and aunts, graced the many-paned windows. A hooked rug, Concepcion's handiwork, added a splash of cheery color to the room.

Dreaming, Lizzie moved on to the kitchen, with its brand-new cookstove, its stocked shelves. There was a table with four chairs; her father had built it himself, in his wood shop on the ranch.

In addition to the parlor and kitchen, there was a little bathroom with all the latest in plumbing. A bedroom stood on either side—the smaller one empty, the larger one furnished with a bureau and a wardrobe, donated by Lizzie's grandfather, but no bed.

"Where are we going to sleep?" Lizzie asked.

Morgan laughed and drew her into his arms. Kissed the tip of her nose. "I'm not planning on doing all that much sleeping," he said. "Not on our wedding night, at least."

Lizzie's cheeks burned with both anticipation and embarrassment. "Be practical," she said. "We need a bed. Shouldn't we order one at the mercantile?"

Morgan held her close, and then closer still. "Stop worrying," he said. "Things always turn out for the best, don't they? Look at Zebulon and Marietta—at John Brennan—and us."

Lizzie rested her forehead against Morgan's shoulder, content to be there, wrapped in his strong embrace. Things *had* turned out for the best—the Halifaxes were living happily on the Triple M, Ellen and Jack attending Chloe's school, rather than her own, because the ranch was a long way out of town. Whitley had written recently to say that he'd met the woman he wanted to marry; they'd met at a party following a polo match. Morgan's practice was thriving, though he earned next to nothing, and Lizzie loved teaching school.

"Do you ever think about Mr. Christian?" she asked.

Morgan stroked her hair. "Sometimes," he said. "Especially with Christmas coming on. Mostly, though, Lizzie McKettrick, I think about you."

She tilted her head back to look up into his face. "I love you, Dr. Morgan Shane," she said.

He kissed her, with a hungry tenderness, then forced himself to step back. They had been intimate, but never in the cottage. They were saving that.

"And I love you," he said, after catching his breath. "Does it bother you, Lizzie, to take my name? You won't be a McKettrick anymore, after we're married."

"I'll *always* be a McKettrick," Lizzie told him. "No matter what name I go by. I'll also be your wife, Morgan. I'll be Lizzie Shane."

He grinned, his hands resting lightly on her shoulders. His eyes glistened, and when he spoke, his voice came out sounding hoarse. "You're the best thing that ever happened to me," he said. "I never once thought—"

Lizzie stroked his cheek with gentle fingers still chilled from being outside in the snowy cold. "Hush," she told him. "Stop talking and kiss me again."

THE MAIN RANCH HOUSE seemed about to burst at the corners, the morning of Christmas Eve, as Lizzie stood obediently on a milk stool in Angus and Concepcion's bedroom upstairs, feeling resplendent in her lacy wedding dress, while Lorelei and the aunts, Emmeline, Mandy and Chloe, pinned and stitched and chattered.

Katie, the child born late in life to Angus and Concepcion, now eleven-going-on-forty, as Lorelei liked to say, sat on the side of her parents' bed, watching the proceedings. With her dark hair and deep-blue eyes, Katie was exquisitely beautiful, although she hadn't realized it yet.

"When I get married," she said, her gaze sweeping over Lizzie's dress, "*I'm* not going to change my name. I'm still going to be Katie McKettrick, forever and ever, no matter what."

"You won't be getting married for a while yet," Chloe told her. Married to Lizzie's uncle Jeb, Chloe was a beauty herself, with copper-colored hair and bright, intelligent eyes. She taught all the children on and around the ranch in the little schoolhouse Jeb had built for her as a wedding present. "By then, you might have changed your mind about taking your husband's name."

Stubbornly, Katie folded her arms. "No, I won't," she said.

"You're just like your father," Concepcion told her daughter, entering the room and closing the door quickly behind her, so none of the men would get a glimpse of Lizzie in her dress. "Katie, Katie, quite contrary."

Lizzie smiled. "You'll make a very lovely bride," she told the little girl.

Katie beamed. "You look so pretty," she told Lizzie. "Like a fairy queen."

Lizzie thanked her, and the pinning and stitching went on. Finally, though, the sewing was done, and she was able to step behind the changing screen, shed the sumptuous dress and get back into her everyday garb. That day, it was a light-blue woolen frock with prim black piping and a high collar that tickled her under the chin.

Ducking around the screen again, she was surprised to see that though Concepcion, Lorelei and the aunts had gone, Katie remained.

Lizzie sat down on the bed beside her and draped an arm around Katie's shoulders. Although Katie was much younger, she was actually Lizzie's aunt, a half sister to Holt, Rafe, Jeb and Kade.

"All right," Lizzie said gently, "what's bothering you, Katie-did?"

Tears brimmed in Katie's eyes. "You're getting married," she said. "Everything is going to be different now."

"Not so different," Lizzie replied. "I'll still be your niece."

Katie giggled at that, and sniffled. "I missed you so much when you went away to San Francisco," she whispered.

Lizzie hugged her. "And I missed you. But I'm home now, and I'm staying."

"You're getting *married*," Katie repeated insistently.

"You're going to be Lizzie Shane, not Lizzie McKettrick. What if Morgan decides he doesn't like living in Indian Rock and takes you somewhere far away?"

"That isn't going to happen," Lizzie said.

"How can you be so sure? When a woman gets married, the man's the boss from then on. You have to do what he says."

Lizzie smiled. "Now, where would you have gotten such an idea, Katie McKettrick?" she teased. "Does your mama do what your papa tells her? Do any of your sisters-in-law take orders from your brothers?"

Katie brightened. "No," she said.

"Morgan and I have talked all this through, Katie. We're staying right in Indian Rock, for good. He'll do his doctoring, and I'll teach school."

"Will you have babies?"

The question made Lizzie squirm a little. She'd checked the calendar that morning, for a perfectly ordinary reason, and realized something important. "I certainly hope so," she said carefully.

Katie wrapped both arms around Lizzie and squeezed hard. "The little kids think St. Nicholas is coming on Christmas Eve," she confided. "But I'm big now, and I know it's Papa and Mama who fill my stocking and put presents under the tree."

"Do you, now?" Lizzie countered mysteriously, thinking of Nicholas Christian—Mr. Christmas, as the Halifax children had called him.

"You're all grown up," Katie said. "You don't believe in St. Nicholas."

"Maybe not precisely," Lizzie replied, "but I certainly believe in miracles."

"What kind of miracles?" Katie wanted to know.

Young as she was, she had a tenaciously skeptical mind.

"I think angels visit earth, disguised as ordinary human beings, for one thing."

"Why would they do that?"

"Maybe to help us be strong and keep going when we're discouraged."

"Have you ever been discouraged, Lizzie?"

"Yes," Lizzie answered. "Last Christmas, when Morgan and I and all the rest of us were trapped aboard that train, up in the high country, I wondered if we'd make it home. I kept my chin up, but I was worried."

"You knew Papa and Holt and Rafe and Kade and Jeb would come get you," Katie insisted.

Lizzie nodded.

"Then why were you scared?"

"It was cold, and folks were sick and injured, and I was far away from all of you. There had been an avalanche, and one avalanche often leads to another."

"And an angel came? Did it have wings?"

Lizzie laughed. "No wings," she said. "Just a sample case and a flask of whiskey. He went out into the blizzard, though, and came back with a Christmas tree."

Katie wrinkled her nose, clearly disappointed. "That doesn't sound like any angel I've ever heard of," she replied. "They're supposed to fly, and have wings and halos—"

"Sometimes they have bowler hats and overcoats instead," Lizzie said. "I know I met an angel, Katie McKettrick, a real, live angel, and you're not going to change my mind."

"How did you *know?*" Katie wondered, intrigued in spite of herself. "That he was an angel, I mean?"

Lizzie glanced from side to side, even though they were alone in the room. "He disappeared," she said. "I was talking to him last year, around this time, in the schoolyard in town. I turned away for a moment, and when I looked back, he was gone."

Katie's wondrous eyes widened. "Are you joshing me, Lizzie?" she demanded. "I'm not a little kid anymore, you know."

Lizzie chuckled. "I'm telling you the truth," she said, holding up one hand, oath-giving style. "And you know what else? He didn't leave any footprints in the snow. Mine were there, and so were Morgan's, but it was as if Mr. Christmas hadn't been there at all."

Katie let out a long breath.

Lizzie gave her young aunt another squeeze. "The point of all this, Katie-did," she said, "is that it's important to believe in things, even when you're all grown up."

"I still don't believe in St. Nicholas," Katie said staunchly.

A knock sounded at the bedroom door, and Concepcion stuck her head in. "We're all leaving for town early," she announced. "Angus says the way this snow is coming down, we might be in for another Christmas blizzard."

CHAPTER TEN

THE WIND RATTLED THE WALLS and windows of that sturdy little church, and as Holt McKettrick waited to walk his daughter up the aisle, following the Christmas Eve service, he thought about miracles. A year before, he'd come closer to losing Lizzie for good than he was willing to admit, even to himself. Now, here she stood, at his side, almost unbearably lovely in her wedding dress.

His little girl. About to be married.

Married.

She'd been twelve when she'd come to live with him—before that, he hadn't even known she existed. For a brief, poignant moment, he yearned for those lost years—Lizzie, learning to walk and talk. Wearing bows in her hair. Coming to him with skinned knees, disappointments and little-girl secrets.

But if there was one thing he'd learned in his life, it was that there was no sense in regretting the past. The *present,* that was what was important. It was all any of them really had.

The children in the congregation were restless, having sat through the service—it was Christmas Eve, after all—and the adults were eager. A low murmur rose from the crowd, and then a small voice rang out like a bell.

"Is it over yet?"

Doss, his and Lorelei's youngest.

The wedding guests laughed, and Holt joined in. Relaxed a little when his gaze connected with Lorelei's. She favored him with a smile and nodded slightly.

Holt nodded back. *I love you,* he told her silently.

And she nodded again.

Holt shifted his attention to the bridegroom.

The man standing up there at the altar, straight-backed and bright-eyed, was the *right* man for Lizzie, Holt was convinced of that. He suspected they'd jumped the gun a little, Lizzie and Morgan, and if Morgan hadn't been exactly who he was, Holt would have horsewhipped him for it.

They were young, as Lorelei had reminded him, when he'd told her he thought the bride and groom had been practicing up for the wedding night ahead of time, and they were in love.

He warmed at the memory of Lorelei's smile. "Remember how it was with us?" she'd asked. In truth, that part of their relationship hadn't changed. They had children and a home together now, so they couldn't be quite as spontaneous as they'd once been, but the passion between them was as fiery as ever.

The organist struck the first note of the wedding march.

"Ready?" Holt asked his daughter, his voice coming out gruff since there was a lump the size of Texas in his throat.

"Ready," Lizzie assured him gently, squeezing his arm. "I love you, Papa."

Tears scalded Holt's eyes. "I love you right back, Lizzie-bet," he replied.

And they started toward the front of the church, where Morgan and Preacher Reynolds waited. The crowd blurred around Holt, and he wondered if Lizzie sensed that they were stepping out of an old world and into a brand-new one. Things would be different after tonight.

SHE WAS SO BEAUTIFUL, Morgan thought, as he watched Lizzie gliding toward him on her father's arm, a vision in her spectacular home-sewn dress. There was love in every stitch and fold of that gown and in every tiny crystal bead glittering on the bodice. Though he wasn't a fanciful man, Morgan knew in that moment that one day he and Lizzie would have a daughter, and she, too, would wear this dress. He'd know how Holt felt, when that day came. At the moment, he could only guess.

Finally Lizzie stood beside him.

His head felt light, and he braced his knees. Damn, but he was lucky. Luckier than he'd ever dreamed he could be.

"Who giveth this woman in marriage?" the preacher asked, raising his voice to be heard over the blizzard raging outside.

"Lorelei and I do," Holt answered gravely. He kissed the top of Lizzie's head and went to sit beside Lorelei in the front pew, along with Angus and Concepcion.

Morgan smiled to himself. Earlier in the evening, Angus had informed him, in no uncertain terms, that if he ever did anything to hurt Lizzie, he'd get a hiding for it.

The holy words were said, the vows exchanged.

And then the preacher pronounced Lizzie and Morgan man and wife.

"You may kiss the bride," Reynolds said.

His hands shaking a little—the hands that were so steady holding a scalpel or binding a wound—Morgan raised Lizzie's veil and gazed down into her upturned face, wonderstruck. She glowed, as though a light were burning inside her.

He kissed her, not hungrily, as he would later that night, when they were alone in the cottage, but reverently. A sacred charge passed between them, as though they had not only been joined on earth, but in heaven, too, and for all of time and eternity.

The organ thundered again, a joyous, triumphant sound, bouncing off the walls of that frontier church, and again a child's voice piped above the joyous chaos.

"It's over!"

Morgan laughed along with everybody else, but he was thinking, *It isn't over. Oh, no. This is only the start.*

THE RECEPTION WAS HELD IN the lobby of the Arizona Hotel, where a giant Christmas tree loomed over the proceedings, glittering with tinsel and blown-glass balls, presents piled high beneath it. Knowing the family wouldn't be able to get back to the ranch after the wedding, because of the storm, Lizzie's grandfather had had everything loaded onto hay sleds and brought to town. Most of the McKettricks would be staying at the hotel, while the overflow spent the night with the Thaddingses.

Lizzie, dazed with happiness, ate cake and posed for the photographer, with Morgan beside her. There were piles of wedding gifts: homemade quilts, preserves, embroidered dish towels and pillowcases. She was hugged, kissed, congratulated and teased.

A band played, and she danced with her father first, then her grandfather, then each of her uncles in turn. By the time Morgan claimed *his* dance, Lizzie was winded.

When the time finally came for her and Morgan to take their leave, Lizzie was both relieved and quivery with nervous anticipation. She was Morgan's *wife,* now. And she had a gift for him that couldn't be wrapped in pretty paper and tied with a shimmery ribbon.

How would he respond when she told him?

A horse-drawn sleigh awaited the bride and groom in the snowy street outside. Lizzie left her veil in Lorelei's care, and they hastened toward the sleigh, Morgan bundling Lizzie quickly in thick blankets before huddling in beside her. Looking through the blinding flurries of white, she saw a figure hunched at the reins and wondered which of her uncles was driving.

The sleigh carried them swiftly through the night.

Lamps burned in the cottage windows when they arrived, glowing golden through the storm.

Morgan helped Lizzie down from the sleigh, swept her up into his arms, and carried her up the path to the front door. Looking back over her new husband's shoulder, Lizzie caught the briefest glimpse of the driver as he lifted his hat, and recognized Mr. Christmas. She started to call out to him, but the blizzard intensified and horse, sleigh and driver disappeared in a great, glittering swirl of snow.

And then they were inside, over the threshold.

Someone had decorated a small Christmas tree, and

placed it on a table in front of the window. Lizzie nearly knocked it over, rushing to look outside, hoping to see her unlikely angel again.

The wind had stopped, and the snow fell softly now, slowly, big, fluffy flakes of it, blanketing the street in peace.

"Lizzie, what is it?" Morgan asked, standing behind her, wrapping his arms around her waist and drawing her back against him.

"I thought I saw—"

"What?"

She sighed, turned to Morgan, smiled up at him. "I thought I saw an angel," she said.

Morgan smiled, kissed her forehead. "It's Christmas Eve. There might be an angel or two around."

Lizzie swallowed, thinking that if she loved this man even a little bit more, she'd burst with the pure, elemental force of it. She paused, smiled. "I have a Christmas gift for you, Morgan," she told him, very quietly.

He glanced down at the packages under the little tree, raised an eyebrow in question.

She took his hand, pressed it lightly to her lower abdomen. "A baby," she said. "We're going to have a baby."

Morgan's face was a study in startled delight. "When, Lizzie?"

"July, I think," she replied, feeling shy. And much relieved. A part of her hadn't been sure Morgan would be pleased, since they were so newly married and had yet to establish a home together.

Gently, Morgan untied the laces of her cloak, slid it off her shoulders, laid it aside. "July," he repeated.

"There'll be some gossip," she warned. "I'm the schoolmarm, after all."

Morgan chuckled, his eyes alight with love. "You know what they say. The first baby can come anytime, the rest take nine months."

Lizzie was too happy to worry about gossip. She wasn't the first pregnant bride in Indian Rock, or in the McKettrick family, and she wouldn't be the last. "You're really glad, then?" She had to ask. "You don't wish we'd had more time?"

"I wouldn't change anything, Lizzie. Not anything at all."

She sniffled. "I love you so much it scares me, Dr. Morgan Shane."

He kissed her, lightly, the way he'd done in front of the altar earlier that night, when the preacher pronounced them man and wife. "And I love you, Mrs. Shane."

She laughed, and they drew apart, and Lizzie glanced at the little tree and the packages beneath it. "Did you do this?" she asked.

Morgan shook his head. "I thought you did," he replied.

"It must have been Lorelei, or the aunts," Lizzie said, pleasantly puzzled. She picked up one of the packages and recognized her stepmother's handwriting. "To Morgan," the tag read. "Open it," she urged.

Morgan's expression showed clearly that he had other things in mind than opening Christmas presents, but he took the parcel and unwrapped it just the same. Inside was an exquisitely made toy locomotive, of shining black metal—a reminder of how he and Lizzie had met.

He smiled, admiring it. "Open yours," he said.

Lizzie reached for the second parcel, gently tore away the ribbon and brightly colored paper. Lorelei had given her a baby's christening gown, frothy with lace, and a tiny bonnet to match.

"They *knew*," she marveled.

Morgan's grin was mischievous. "Maybe we were too obvious," he said.

Lizzie's cheeks warmed.

Morgan laughed and curved a finger under her chin. "Lizzie," he said, "Holt and Lorelei aren't exactly doddering old folks. They're in love, too, remember?"

She smiled. Nodded. "I'd like to change out of this dress," she said.

Morgan's eyes smoldered. "You do that," he replied gruffly. "I'll build up the fire a little."

Lizzie nodded and headed for the bedroom, stopping on the threshold to gasp. "Morgan!" she called.

He joined her.

A beautiful bed stood in the place that had been so noticeably vacant before, the headboard intricately carved with the image of a great, leafy oak, spreading its branches alongside a flowing creek. Birds soared against a cloud-strewn sky, and both their names had been carved into the trunk of the tree, inside a heart. Lizzie + Morgan.

Lizzie drew in her breath. This was her father's wedding gift, to her and to Morgan. It was more than a piece of furniture, more than an heirloom that would be passed down for generations. It was his *blessing,* on them and on their marriage.

"Lizzie McKettrick Shane," Morgan said, leaning

to kiss the side of her neck, "you come from quite a family."

She nodded, moved closer to the bed, stroked the fine woodwork with the tips of her fingers, marveling at the time, thought and love that had gone into such a creation. "And now you're part of it," she told Morgan. "You and our baby and all the other babies that will come along later."

Morgan lingered in the doorway, framed there, looking so handsome in his new suit, specially bought for the wedding, that Lizzie etched the moment into her memory, to keep forever. *Her husband.* Even when she was an old, old lady, creaky-boned and wrinkled, she knew she would recall every detail of the way he looked that night.

"I'll see to the fire," he said, after a long, long time.

Lizzie nodded, shyly now. Waited until Morgan had stepped away from the door before taking a lacy nightgown from the trunk containing her trousseau and changing into it. She folded her wedding gown carefully, placed it in a box set aside for the purpose. She took down her hair and brushed it in front of the vanity mirror until it shone.

Morgan had never seen her with her hair down.

Warmth filled the cottage and, one by one, the lamps in the parlor went out. Lizzie waited, her heart racing a little.

Morgan filled the bedroom doorway again, a man-shaped shadow, rimmed in faint, wintry light. The sweet silence of the snow outside seemed to muffle all sound. They might have been alone in the world that Christmas

Eve, she and Morgan, two wanderers who'd somehow found their way to each other after long and difficult journeys.

Morgan whispered her name, came toward her.

She slipped into his arms.

They'd looked forward to making love on their wedding night, both of them. Now, by tacit agreement, they waited, savoring every nuance of being together.

Morgan threaded his hands through Lizzie's hair.

She felt beautiful.

"To think," Morgan said quietly, "that I almost didn't get on that train last Christmas."

"Don't think," Lizzie teased. He'd said the same thing to her, once, while they were stranded on the mountainside.

He chuckled, and kissed her with restrained passion. Eagerness and wanting sang through Lizzie, but she was willing to wait. There was no hurry: she and Morgan were married now, after all. They would make love countless times in the days, weeks, months and years ahead.

They'd already conceived a child, and Lizzie knew something of the pleasures awaiting her, but tonight was special. It was their first time as husband and wife.

Her breath caught, and her heartbeat quickened as Morgan caressed her, touching her lightly in all the places she loved to be touched, all the places she *needed* to be touched.

She gave herself up to him, completely, joyously, with little gasps and sighs as he pleasured her, slowly. Ever so slowly, and with such expertise that Lizzie wished that night would never end.

She was transported, in the bed with the tree carved into the headboard. She died there, and was reborn, a new woman, even stronger than before. She gasped and whimpered and sobbed out Morgan's name, clinging to him with everything she had, riding wave after wave of sacred satisfaction.

Hours passed before they slept, sated and spent, arms and legs entwined.

Lizzie awakened first, to the cold, snowy light of a clear Christmas morning. The fire had gone out during the night, but she was warm, through and through, snuggled close to Morgan under a heavy layer of quilts.

He stirred beside her, opened his eyes. "I'd better get the fire going," he said, his voice sleepy.

"Not yet," Lizzie whispered, burrowing closer to him.

"We'll freeze," he said.

Lizzie laughed and shook her head. "I don't think so," she answered, nibbling mischievously at his neck.

He rolled on top of her, his elbows pressed into the mattress on either side. "Have I married a hussy?" he asked.

"Most definitely," Lizzie answered, beaming. "And you thought I was only a schoolmarm."

Morgan laughed, and the sound was beautiful to Lizzie, and in the distance the church bells pealed, ringing in Christmas.

* * * * *

A CREED COUNTRY
CHRISTMAS

For Jean Woofter
With love and gratitude

CHAPTER ONE

THE INTERIOR OF WILLAND'S Mercantile, redolent of saddle leather and wood smoke, seemed to recede as Juliana Mitchell stood at the counter, holding her breath.

The letter had *finally* arrived.

The letter Juliana had waited for, prayed for, repeatedly inquired after—at considerable cost to her pride—and, paradoxically, dreaded.

Her heart hitched painfully as she accepted the envelope from the storekeeper's outstretched hand; the handwriting, a slanted scrawl penned in black ink, was definitely her brother Clay's. The postmark read Denver.

In the distance, the snow-muffled shrill of a train whistle announced the imminent arrival of the four o'clock from Missoula, which passed through town only once a week, bound for points south.

Juliana was keenly aware of the four children still in her charge, waiting just inside the door of a place where they knew they were patently unwelcome. She turned away from the counter—and the storekeeper's disapproving gaze—to fumble with the circle of red wax bearing Clay's imposing seal.

Please, God, she prayed silently. *Please.*

After drawing a deep breath and releasing it slowly, Juliana bit her lower lip, took out the single sheet folded inside.

Her heart, heretofore wedged into her throat, plummeted to the soles of her practical shoes. Her vision blurred.

Her brother hadn't enclosed the desperately needed funds she'd asked for—money that was rightfully her own, a part of the legacy her grandmother had left her. She could not purchase train tickets for herself and her charges, and the Indian School, their home and hers for the past two years, was no longer government property. The small but sturdy building had been sold to a neighboring farmer, and he planned to stable cows inside it.

Now the plank floor seemed to buckle slightly under Juliana's feet. The heat from the potbellied stove in the center of the store, so welcome only a few minutes before when she and the children had come in out of the blustery cold, all of them dappled with fat flakes of snow, threatened to smother Juliana now.

The little bell over the door jingled, indicating the arrival of another customer, but Juliana did not look up from the page in her hand. The words swam before her, making no more sense to her fitful mind than ancient Hebrew would have done.

A brief, frenzied hope stirred within Juliana. Perhaps all was not lost, perhaps Clay, not trusting the postal service, had *wired* the money she needed. It might be waiting for her, at that very moment, just down the street at the telegraph office.

Her eyes stung with the swift and sobering realization that she was grasping at straws. She blinked and forced herself to read what her older brother and legal guardian had written.

My Dear Sister,
I trust this letter will find you well.
Nora, the children and I are all in robust health. Your niece and nephew constantly inquire as to your whereabouts, as do certain other parties.
I regret that I cannot in good conscience remit the funds you have requested, for reasons that should be obvious to you....

Juliana crumpled the sheet of expensive vellum, nearly ill with disappointment and the helpless frustration that generally resulted from any dealings with her brother, direct or indirect.

"Are you all right, miss?" a male voice asked, strong and quiet.

Startled, Juliana looked up, saw a tall man standing directly in front of her. His eyes and hair were dark, the round brim of his hat and the shoulders of his long coat dusted with snow.

Waiting politely for her answer, he took off his hat. Hung it from the post of a wooden chair, smiled.

"I'm Lincoln Creed," he said, gruffly kind, pulling off a leather glove before extending his hand.

Juliana hesitated, offered her own hand in return. She knew the name, of course—the Creeds owned the largest cattle ranch in that part of the state, and the *Still-*

water Springs Courier, too. Although Juliana had had encounters with Weston, the brother who ran the newspaper, and briefly met the Widow Creed, the matriarch of the family, she'd never crossed paths with Lincoln.

"Juliana Mitchell," she said, with the proper balance of reticence and politeness. She'd been gently raised, after all. A hundred years ago—*a thousand*—she'd called one of the finest mansions in Denver home. She'd worn imported silks and velvets and fashionable hats, ridden in carriages with liveried drivers and even footmen.

Remembering made her faintly ashamed.

All that, of course, had been before her fall from social grace.

Before Clay, as administrator of their grandmother's estate, had all but disinherited her.

Mr. Creed dropped his gaze to the letter. "Bad news?" he asked, with an unsettling note of discernment. He might have had Indian blood himself, with his high cheekbones and raven-black hair.

The train whistle gave another triumphant squeal. It had pulled into the rickety little depot at the edge of town, right on schedule. Passengers would alight, others would board. Mail and freight would be loaded and unloaded. And then the engine would chug out of the station, the line of cars rattling behind it.

A full week would pass before another train came through.

In the meantime, Juliana and the children would have no choice but to throw themselves upon the uncertain mercies of the townspeople. In a larger community, she might have turned to a church for assistance, but there weren't any in Stillwater Springs. The faithful met sporadically, in the one-room schoolhouse where only white students were allowed when the circuit preacher came through.

Juliana swallowed, wanting to cry, and determined that she wouldn't. "I'm afraid it *is* bad news," she admitted in belated answer to Mr. Creed's question.

He took a gentle hold on her elbow, escorted her to one of the empty wooden chairs over by the potbellied stove. Sat her down. "Did somebody die?" he asked.

Numb with distraction, Juliana shook her head.

What in the world was she going to do now? Without money, she could not purchase train tickets for herself and the children, or even arrange for temporary lodgings of some sort.

Mr. Creed inclined his head toward the children lined up in front of the display window, with its spindly but glittering Christmas tree. They'd turned their backs now, to look at the decorations and the elaborate toys tucked into the branches and arranged attractively underneath.

"I guess you must be the teacher from out at the Indian School," he said.

Mr. Willand, the mercantile's proprietor, interrupted with a *harrumph* sound.

Juliana ached as she watched the children. The storekeeper was keeping a close eye on them, too. Like so many people, he reasoned that simply because they were Indians, they were sure to steal, afforded the slightest opportunity. "Yes," she replied, practiced at ignoring such attitudes, if not resigned to them. "Or, at least, I *was*. The school is closed now."

Lincoln Creed nodded after skewering Mr. Willand with a glare. "I was sorry to hear it," he told her.

"No letters came since you were in here last week, Lincoln," Willand broke in, with some satisfaction. The very atmosphere of that store, overheated and close, seemed to bristle with mutual dislike. "Reckon you can wait around and see if there were any on today's train, but my guess is you wasted your money, putting all those advertisements in all them newspapers."

"Everyone is sorry, Mr. Creed," Juliana said quietly. "But no one seems inclined to help."

Momentarily distracted by Mr. Willand's remark, Lincoln didn't respond immediately. When he did, his voice was nearly drowned out by the scream of the train whistle.

Juliana stood up, remembered anew that her situation was hopeless, and sat down again, hard, all the strength gone from her knees. Perhaps she'd used it up, walking the two miles into town from the school, with every one of her worldly possessions tucked into a single worn-out satchel. Each of the children had carried a small bundle, too, leaving them on the sidewalk outside the door of the mercantile with Juliana's bag.

"There's a storm coming, Miss—er—Mitchell," Lincoln Creed said. "It's cold and getting colder, and it'll be dark soon. I didn't see a rig outside, so I figure you must have walked to town. I've got my team and buckboard outside, and I'd be glad to give you and those kids a ride to wherever you're headed."

Tears welled in Juliana's eyes, shaming her, and her throat tightened painfully. Wherever she was headed? *Nowhere* was where she was headed.

Stillwater Springs had a hotel and several boarding houses, but even if she'd had the wherewithal to pay for a room and meals, most likely none of them would have accepted the children, anyway.

They'd hurried so, trying to get to Stillwater Springs before the train left, Juliana desperately counting on the funds from Clay even against her better judgment, but there had been delays. Little Daisy falling and skinning one knee, a huge band of sheep crossing the road and blocking their way, the limp that plagued twelve-year-old Theresa, with her twisted foot.

Lincoln broke into her thoughts. "Miss Mitchell?" he prompted.

Mr. Willand slammed something down hard on the counter, causing Juliana to start. "Don't you touch none of that merchandise!" he shouted, and Joseph, the eldest of Juliana's pupils at fourteen, pulled his hand back from the display window. "Damn thievin' Injuns—"

Poor Joseph looked crestfallen. Theresa, his sister, trembled, while the two littlest children, Billy-Moses, who was four, and Daisy, three, rushed to Juliana and clung to her skirts in fear.

"The boy wasn't doing any harm, Fred," Lincoln told the storekeeper evenly, rising slowly out of his chair. "No need to raise your voice, or accuse him, either."

Mr. Willand reddened. "You have a grocery order?" he asked, glowering at Lincoln Creed.

"Just came by to see if I had mail," Lincoln said, with a shake of his head. "Couldn't get here before now, what with the hard weather coming on." He paused, turned to Juliana. "Best we get you to wherever it is you're going," he said.

"We don't have anyplace to go, mister," Joseph said, still standing near the display window, but careful to keep his hands visible at his sides. Since he rarely spoke, especially to strangers, Juliana was startled.

And as desperate as she was, the words chafed her pride.

Lincoln frowned, obviously confused. "What?"

"They might take us in over at the Diamond Buckle Saloon," Theresa said, lifting her chin. "If we work for our keep."

Lincoln stared at the girl, confounded. "The Diamond Buckle…?"

Juliana didn't trust herself to speak without breaking down completely. If she did not remain strong, the children would have no hope at all.

"Mr. Weston Creed said he'd teach me to set type," Joseph reminded Juliana. "Bet I could sleep in the back room at the newspaper, and I don't need much to eat. You wouldn't have to fret about me, Miss Mitchell." He glanced worriedly at his sister, swallowed hard. He was old enough to understand the dangers a place like the Diamond Buckle might harbor for a young girl, even if Theresa wasn't.

Lincoln raised both hands, palms out, in a bid for silence.

Everyone stared at him, including Juliana, who had pulled little Daisy onto her lap.

"All of you," Lincoln said, addressing the children, "gather up whatever things you've got and get into the back of my buckboard. You'll find some blankets there—wrap up warm, because it's three miles to the ranch house and there's an icy wind blowing in from the northwest."

Juliana stood, gently displacing Daisy, careful to keep the child close against her side. "Mr. Creed, we couldn't accept…" Her voice fell away, and mortification burned in her cheeks.

"Seems to me," Lincoln said, "you don't have much of a choice. I'm offering you and these children a place to stay, Miss Mitchell. Just till you can figure out what to do next."

"You'd let these savages set foot under the same roof with your little Gracie?" Mr. Willand blustered, incensed. He'd crossed the otherwise-empty store, shouldered Joseph aside to peer into the display window and make sure nothing was missing.

The air pulsed again.

Lincoln took a step toward the storekeeper.

By instinct, Juliana grasped Mr. Creed's arm to stop him. Even through the heavy fabric of his coat, she could feel that his muscles were steely with tension—he was barely containing his temper. "The children are used to remarks like that," she said quietly, anxious to keep the peace. "They know they aren't savages."

"Get into the wagon," Lincoln said. He didn't pull free of Juliana's touch, nor did he look away from Mr. Willand's crimson face. "All of you."

The children looked to Juliana, their dark, luminous eyes liquid with wary question.

She nodded, silently giving her permission.

Almost as one, they scrambled for the door, causing the bell to clamor merrily overhead. Even Daisy, clinging until a moment before, peeled away from Juliana's side.

After pulling her cloak more closely around her and raising the hood against the cold wind, Juliana followed.

LINCOLN WATCHED THEM GO. He'd hung his hat on one of the spindle-backed wooden chairs next to the stove earlier, and he reached for it. "There's enough grief and sorrow in this world," he told the storekeeper, "without folks like you adding to it."

Willand was undaunted, though Lincoln noticed he stayed well behind the counter, within bolting distance of the back door. "We'll see what *Mrs.* Creed says, when you turn up on her doorstep with a tribe of Injuns—"

Lincoln shoved his hat down on top of his head with a little more force than the effort required. His wife, Beth, had died two years before, of a fever, so Willand was referring to his mother. Cora Creed would indeed have been surprised to find five extra people seated around her supper table that night—if Lincoln hadn't left her with enough bags to fill a freight car at the train depot before stopping by the mercantile. She was headed for Phoenix, where she liked to winter with her kinfolks, the Dawsons.

"I'll be back tomorrow if I get the chance," he said, starting for the door. With that storm coming and cattle to feed, he couldn't be sure. "To see if any letters came in on today's train."

Willand glanced at the big regulator clock on the wall behind him. "My boy's gone to the depot, like always, and he'll be here with the mail bag any minute now," he said grudgingly. "Might as well wait."

Lincoln went to the window, looked past his own reflection in the darkening glass—God, he hated the shortness of winter days—to see Miss Mitchell settling her unlikely brood in the bed of his wagon. Something warmed inside him, shifted. The slightest smile tilted one corner of his mouth.

He'd been advertising for a governess for his seven-year-old daughter, Gracie, and a housekeeper for the both of them for nearly a year; failing either of those, he'd settle for a wife, and because he knew he'd never love another woman the way he'd loved Beth, he wasn't too choosey in his requirements.

Juliana Mitchell, with her womanly figure, indigo-blue eyes and those tendrils of coppery hair peeking out from under her worn bonnet, was clearly dedicated to her profession, since she'd stayed to look after those children even now that the Indian School had closed down. A lot of schoolmarms wouldn't have done that.

This spoke well for her character, and when it came to looks, she was a better bargain than anyone all those advertisements might have scared up.

Glancing down at the display, with all the toys Wil-land was hoping to sell before Christmas, Lincoln's gaze fell on the corner of a metal box, tucked at an odd angle under the bunting beneath the tree. He reached for the item, drew it out, saw that it was a set of watercolor paints, similar to one Gracie had at home.

Was this what the boy had been looking at when Willand pitched a fit?

For reasons he couldn't have explained, Lincoln was sure it was.

He held the long, flat tin up for Willand to see, before tucking it into the inside pocket of his coat. "Put this on my bill," he said.

Willand grumbled, but a sale was a sale. He finally nodded.

Lincoln raised his collar against the cold and left the mercantile for the wooden sidewalk beyond.

The kids were settled in the back of the wagon, all but the oldest boy snuggled in the rough woolen blankets Lincoln always carried in winter. Juliana Mitchell waited primly on the seat, straight-spined, chin high, trying not to shiver in that thin cloak of hers.

Buttoning his coat as he left the store, Lincoln unbuttoned it again before climbing up into the box beside her. Snowflakes drifted slowly from a gray sky as he took up the reins, released the brake lever. The streets of the town were nearly deserted—folks were getting ready for the storm, feeling its approach in their bones, just as Lincoln did.

Knowing her pride would make her balk if he took off his coat and put it around her, he pulled his right arm out of the sleeve and drew her to his side instead, closing the garment around her.

She stiffened, then went still, in what he guessed was resignation.

It bruised something inside Lincoln, realizing how many things Juliana Mitchell had probably had to resign herself to over the course of her life.

He set the team in motion, kept his gaze on the snowy road ahead, winding toward home. By the time they reached the ranch, it would be dark out, but the horses knew their way.

Meanwhile, Juliana Mitchell felt warm and soft against him. He'd forgotten what it was like to protect a woman, shield her against his side, and the remembrance was painful, like frostbitten flesh beginning to thaw.

Beth had been gone awhile, and though he wasn't proud of it, in the last six months or so he'd turned to loose women for comfort a time or two, over in Choteau or in Missoula.

The quickening he felt now was different, of course. Though anybody could see she was down on her luck, it was equally obvious that Juliana Mitchell was a lady. Breeding was a thing even shabby clothes couldn't hide—especially from a rancher used to raising fine cattle and horses.

Minutes later, as they jostled over the road in the buckboard, Juliana relaxed against Lincoln, and it came to him, with a flash of amusement, that she was asleep. Plainly, she was exhausted. From the way her face had fallen as she'd read that letter, which she'd finally wadded up and stuffed into the pocket of her cloak with an expression of heartbroken disgust in her eyes, she'd suffered some bitter disappointment.

All he knew for sure was that nobody had died, since he'd asked her that right off.

Lincoln tried to imagine what kind of news might have thrown her like that, even though he knew it was none of his business.

Maybe she'd planned to marry the man who'd written that letter, and he'd spurned her for another.

Lincoln frowned, aware of the woman's softness and warmth in every part of his lonesome body. What kind of damned fool would do that?

His shoulder began to ache, since his arm was curved around Juliana at a somewhat awkward angle, but he didn't care. He'd have driven right past the ranch, just so she could go on resting against him like that for a little while longer, if he hadn't been a practical man.

The wind picked up, and the snow came down harder and faster, and when he looked back at the kids, they were sitting stoically in their places, bundled in their blankets.

The best part of an hour had passed when the lights of the ranch house finally came into view, glowing dim and golden in the snow-swept darkness.

Lincoln's heartbeat picked up a little, the way it always did when he rounded that last bend in the road and saw home waiting up ahead.

Home.

He'd been born in the rambling, one-story log house, with its stone chimneys, the third son of Josiah and Cora Creed. Micah, the firstborn, had long since left the ranch, started a place of his own down in Colorado. Weston, the next in line, lived in town, in rooms above the Diamond Buckle Saloon, and published the *Courier*—when he was sober enough to run the presses.

Two years younger than Wes, Lincoln had left home only to attend college in Boston and apprentice himself to a lawyer—Beth's father. As soon as he was qualified to practice, Lincoln had married Beth, brought her home to Stillwater Springs Ranch and loved her with all the passion a man could feel for a woman.

She'd taken to life on a remote Montana ranch with amazing acuity for a city girl, and if she'd missed Boston, she'd never once let on. She'd given him Gracie, and they'd been happy.

Now she rested in the small, sad cemetery beyond the apple orchard, like Josiah, and the fourth Creed brother, Dawson.

Dawson. Sometimes it was harder to think about him and the way he'd died, than to recall Beth succumbing to that fever.

Juliana straightened against Lincoln's side, yawned. If the darkness hadn't hidden her face, the brim of her bonnet would have, but he sensed that she was embarrassed by the lapse.

"We're almost home," he said, just loudly enough for her to hear.

She didn't answer, but sat up a little straighter, wanting to pull away, but confined by his arm and the cloth of his coat.

When they reached the gate with its overarching sign, Lincoln moved to get down, but the Indian boy, Joseph, was faster. He worked the latch, swung the gate wide, and Lincoln drove the buckboard through.

His father and Tom Dancingstar had cut and planed the timber for that sign, chiseled the letters into it, and then laboriously deepened them with pokers heated in the homemade forge they'd used for horseshoeing.

Lincoln never saw the words without a feeling of quiet gratification and pride.

Stillwater Springs Ranch.

He held the team while the boy shut the gate, then scrambled back into the wagon. The horses were eager to get to the barn, where hay and water and warm stalls awaited them.

Tom was there to help unhitch the team when Lincoln drove through the wide doorway and under the sturdy barn roof. Part Lakota Sioux, part Cherokee and part devil by his own accounting, Tom had worked on the ranch from the beginning. He'd named himself, claiming no white tongue could manage the handle he'd been given at birth.

He smiled when he saw Juliana, and she smiled back.

Clearly, they were acquainted.

Was he, Lincoln wondered, the only yahoo in the countryside who'd never met the teacher from the Indian School?

"Take the kids inside the house," Lincoln told Juliana, and it struck him that rather than the strangers they were, they might have been married for years, the two of them, all these children their own. "Tom and I will be in as soon as we've finished here."

He paused to lift the two smaller children out of the wagon; sleepy-eyed, still wrapped in their blankets, they stumbled a little, befuddled to find themselves in a barn lit by lanterns, surrounded by horses and Jenny Lind, the milk cow.

"I'll tend to the horses," Tom told him. "There's a kettle of stew warming on the stove, and Gracie's been watching the road for you since sunset."

Thinking of his gold-haired, blue-eyed daughter, Lincoln smiled. Smarter than three judges and as many juries put together, Gracie tended toward fretfulness. Losing her mother when she was only five caused her to worry about him whenever he was out of her sight.

With a ranch the size of his to run, he was away from the house a lot, accustomed to leaving the child in the care of his now-absent mother, or Rose-of-Sharon Gainer, the cumbersomely pregnant young wife of one of the ranch hands.

The older boy's gaze had fastened on Tom.

"Can I stay here and help?" he asked.

"May I," Juliana corrected with a smile. "Yes, Joseph, you may."

With that, she leaned down, weary as she was, and lifted the littlest girl into her arms. Lincoln bent to hoist up the smaller boy.

"This is Daisy," Juliana told him. "That's Billy-Moses you're holding." The girl who'd spoken of working for her keep at the Diamond Buckle ducked her head shyly, stood a little closer to her teacher. "And this is Theresa," she finished.

Leaving Tom and Joseph to put the team up for the night, Lincoln shed his coat at the entrance to the barn, draped it over Juliana's shoulders. It dragged on the snowy ground, and she smiled wanly at that, hiking the garment up with her free arm, closing it around both herself and Daisy.

They entered the house by the side door, stepping into the warmth, the aroma of Tom's venison stew and the light of several lanterns. Gracie, rocking in the chair near the cookstove and pretending she hadn't been waiting impatiently for Lincoln's return, went absolutely still when she saw that he wasn't alone.

Her cornflower-blue eyes widened, and her mouth made a perfect O.

Daisy and Billy-Moses stared back at her, probably as amazed as she was.

"Gracie," Lincoln said unnecessarily. "We have company."

Gracie had recovered by then; she fairly leaped out of the rocking chair. Looking up at Juliana, she asked, "Did you answer one of my papa's advertisements? Are you going to be a governess, a housekeeper or a wife?"

Lincoln winced.

Understandably, Juliana seemed taken aback. Like Gracie, though, she turned out to be pretty resilient. The only sign that the child's question had caught her off guard was the faint tinge of pink beneath her cheekbones, and that might have been from the cold.

"I'm Miss Mitchell," she said kindly. "These are my pupils—Daisy, Billy-Moses and Theresa. There's Joseph, as well—he's out in the barn helping Mr. Dancingstar look after the horses."

"Then you're a *governess!*" Gracie cried jubilantly. Young as she was, she could already read, and because Lincoln wouldn't allow her to travel back and forth to school in Stillwater Springs, she was convinced that lifelong ignorance would be her lot.

"Gracie," Lincoln said, setting Billy-Moses on his feet. "Miss Mitchell is a guest. She didn't answer any advertisements."

Gracie looked profoundly disappointed, but only for a moment. Like most Creeds, when she set her mind on something, she did not give up easily.

For the next little while, they were all busy with supper.

Tom and Joseph came in from the barn, pumped water at the sink to wash up and joined them at the table, while Gracie, who had already eaten, rushed about fetching bread and butter and ladling milk from the big covered crock stored on the back step.

His daughter wanted to make Miss Mitchell feel welcome, Lincoln thought with a smile, so she'd stay and teach her all she wanted to know—and that was considerable. She hadn't asked for a doll for Christmas, or a spinning top, like a lot of little girls would have done.

Oh, no. Gracie wanted a dictionary.

Wes often joked that by the time his niece was old enough to make the trip to town on her own, she'd be half again too smart for school and ready to take over the *Courier* so he could spend the rest of his life smoking cigars and playing poker.

As far as Lincoln could tell, his brother did little else but smoke cigars and play poker—not counting, of course, the whiskey-swilling and his long-standing and wholly scandalous love affair with Kate Winthrop, who happened to own the Diamond Buckle.

Gracie adored her uncle Weston—and Kate.

Casting a surreptitious glance in Juliana's direction whenever he could during supper, Lincoln saw that she could barely keep her eyes open. As soon as the meal was over, he showed her to his mother's spacious room. She and Daisy and Billy-Moses could share the big feather bed.

Joseph bunked in with Tom, who slept in a small chamber behind the kitchen stove, having given up his cabin out by the bunkhouse to Ben Gainer and his wife. Theresa was to sleep with Gracie.

Lincoln's young daughter, however, was not in bed. Wide-awake, she sat at the table with Lincoln, watching as he drank lukewarm coffee, left over from earlier in the day.

"Go to bed, Gracie," he told her.

Tom lingered by the stove, also drinking coffee. He smiled when Gracie didn't move.

"I couldn't possibly sleep," she said seriously. "I am entirely too excited."

Lincoln sighed. She was knee-high to a fence post, but sometimes she talked like someone her grandmother's age. "It's still five days until Christmas," he reminded her. "Too soon to be all het up over presents and such."

"I'm not excited about *Christmas*," Gracie said, with the exaggerated patience she might have shown the village idiot. Stillwater Springs boasted its share of those. "You're going to marry Miss Mitchell, and I'll have Billy-Moses and Daisy to play with—"

Tom chuckled into his coffee cup.

Lincoln sighed again and settled back in his chair. Although he'd thought about hitching up with the schoolteacher, he'd probably been hasty. "Gracie, Miss Mitchell isn't here to marry me. She was stranded in town because the Indian School closed down, so I brought her and the kids home—"

"Will I still have to call her 'Miss Mitchell' after you get married to her? She'd be 'Mrs. Creed' then, wouldn't she? It would be really silly for me to go around saying 'Mrs. Creed' all the time—"

"Gracie."

"What?"

"Go to bed."

"I told you, I'm too excited."

"And *I* told *you* to go to bed."

"Oh, for heaven's sake," Gracie protested, disgruntled.

But she got out of her chair at the table, said goodnight to Tom and stood on tiptoe to kiss Lincoln on the cheek.

His heart melted like a honeycomb under a hot sun when she did that. Her blue eyes, so like Beth's, sparkled as she looked up at him, then turned solemn.

"Be nice to Miss Mitchell, Papa," she instructed solemnly. "Stand up when she comes into a room, and pull her chair back for her. We want her to like it here and stay."

Lincoln's throat constricted, and his eyes burned. He couldn't have answered to save his hide from a hot brand.

"You'll come and hear my prayers?" Gracie asked, the way she did every night.

The prayers varied slightly, but certain parts were always the same.

Please keep my papa safe, and Tom, too. I'd like a dog of my very own, one that will fetch, and I want to go to school, so I don't grow up to be stupid....

Lincoln nodded his assent. Though it was a request he never refused, Gracie always asked.

Once she left the room, Tom set his cup in the sink, folded his arms. "According to young Joseph," he said, "he and his sister have folks in North Dakota—an aunt and a grandfather. Soon as he can save enough money, he means to head for home and take Theresa with him."

Lincoln felt a lot older than his thirty-five years as he raised himself from his chair, began turning down lamp wicks, one by one. Tom, in the meantime, banked the fire in the cookstove.

They were usual, these long gaps in their conversations. Right or wrong, Lincoln had always been closer to Tom than to his own father—Josiah Creed had been a hard man in many ways. Neither Lincoln nor Wes had mourned him overmuch—they left that to Micah, the eldest, and their mother.

"Did the boy happen to say how he and the girl wound up in a school outside of Stillwater Springs, Montana?"

Tom straightened, his profile grim in the last of the lantern light. "The government decided he and his sister would be better off if they learned white ways," he said. "Took them off the reservation in North Dakota a couple of years ago, and they were in several different 'institutions' before their luck changed. They haven't seen their people since the day they left Dakota, though Juliana helped him write a letter to them six months back, and they got an answer." Tom paused, swallowed visibly. His voice sounded hoarse. "The folks at home want them back, Lincoln."

Lincoln stood in the relative darkness for a few moments, reflecting. "I'll send them, then," he said after a long time. "Put them on the train when it comes through next week."

Tom didn't answer immediately, and when he did, the

whole Trail of Tears echoed in his voice. "They're just kids. They oughtn't to make a trip like that alone."

Another lengthy silence rested comfortably between the two men. Then Lincoln said, "You want to go with them."

"Somebody ought to," Tom replied. "Make sure they get there all right. Might be that things have changed since that letter came."

Lincoln absorbed that, finally nodded. "What about the little ones?" he asked without looking at his friend. "Daisy and Billy-Moses?"

"They're orphans," Tom said, and sadness settled over the darkened room like a weight. "Reckon Miss Mitchell planned on keeping them until she could find them a home."

Lincoln sighed inwardly. *Until she could find them a home.* As if those near-babies were stray puppies or kittens.

With another nod, this one sorrowful, he turned away.

It was time to turn in; morning would come early.

But damned if he'd sleep a wink between the plight of four innocent children and the knowledge that Juliana Mitchell was lying on the other side of the wall.

CHAPTER TWO

THE MATTRESS FELT LIKE A CLOUD, tufted and stuffed with feathers from angels' wings, beneath Juliana's weary frame, but sleep eluded her. Daisy slumbered innocently at her right side, sucking one tiny thumb, while Billy-Moses snuggled close on the left, clinging to her flannel nightgown—the cloth was still chilled from being rolled up in her satchel, out in the weather most of the day.

Juliana listened as the sturdy house settled around her, her body still stiff with tension, that being its long-established habit, heard a plank creaking here, a roof timber there. She caught the sound of a door opening and closing just down the corridor, pictured Lincoln Creed passing into his room, or bending over little Gracie's bed to tuck her in and bid her good-night. Would he spare a kind word for Theresa, who was sharing Gracie's room, and so hungry for affection, or reserve all his attention for his little daughter?

Gracie was a charming child, as lovely as a doll come to life, with those thickly lashed eyes, golden ringlets brushing her shoulders and the pink-tinged porcelain perfection of her skin. Privileged by comparison to most children, not to mention the four in Juliana's own charge, Gracie was precocious, but if she was spoiled, there had been no sign of it yet. She'd greeted the new arrivals at

Stillwater Springs Ranch with frank curiosity, yes, but then she'd ladled milk into mugs for them, even served it at the table.

Juliana's heart pinched. Gracie had a strong, loving father, a home, robust good health. But behind those more obvious blessings lurked a certain lonely resignation uncommon in one so young. Gracie had lost her mother at a very early age, and no one understood the sorrows of that more than Juliana herself—she'd been six years old when her own had succumbed to consumption. Juliana's father, outraged by grief, torn asunder by it, had dumped both his offspring on their maternal grandmother's doorstep barely two weeks after his wife's funeral and, over the next few years, delivered himself up to dissolution and debauchery.

Clay, nine at the time of their mother's passing, had changed from a lighthearted, mischievous boy to a solemn-faced man, seemingly overnight. In a very real way, Juliana had lost him, in addition to both her parents.

Victoria Marston, their grandmother, already a widow when her only daughter had died, dressed in mourning until her own death a decade later, but she had loved Juliana and Clay tirelessly nonetheless. Grandmama had given them every advantage—tutors, music lessons, finishing school for Juliana, who had immediately changed the course of her study to train as a schoolteacher upon the discovery that "finishing" involved learning to make small talk with men, the proper way to pour tea and a lot of walking about with a book balanced on top of her head. There had been college in San Francisco for Clay, even a Grand Tour.

Juliana had stayed behind in Denver, living at home

with Grandmama, attending classes every day and letting her doting grandmother believe she was being thoroughly "finished," impatiently waiting for her life to begin.

For all the things she would have changed, she appreciated her blessings, too; she'd been well-cared-for, beautifully clothed and educated beyond the level most young women attained. Yet, there was still a childlike yearning inside Juliana, a longing for her beautiful, laughing mama. The singular and often poignant ache was mostly manageable—except when she was discouraged, and that had been often, of late.

After graduating from Normal School—her grandmother had died of a heart condition only weeks before Juliana accepted her certificate—she'd begun her career with high hopes, pushed up her sleeves and flung herself into the fray, undaunted at first by her brother's cold disapproval. He'd wanted her to marry his business partner, John Holden, and because he controlled their grandmother's large estate, Clay had had the power to disinherit her. On the day she'd given back John's engagement ring and accepted her first teaching assignment at a school for Indian boys in a small Colorado town a day's train ride from Denver, he'd done that, for all practical intents and purposes.

Juliana had been left with nothing but the few modest clothes and personal belongings she'd packed for the journey. Clay had gone so far as to ban her from the family home, saying she could return when she "came to her senses."

To Clay, "coming to her senses" meant consigning herself to a loveless marriage to a widower more than twenty years her senior, a man with two daughters close to Juliana's own age.

Mean daughters, who went out of their way to be snide, and saw their future stepmother as an interloper bent on claiming their late mother's jewelry, as well as her home and husband.

Remembering, Juliana bit down on her lower lip, and her eyes smarted a little. She might have been content with John, if not happy, had it not been for Eleanor and Eugenie. He was gentle, well-read, and she'd felt safe with him.

In a flash of insight and dismay, Juliana had realized she was looking for a father, not a husband. She'd explained to John, and though he'd been disappointed, he'd understood. He'd even been gracious enough to wish her well.

Clay, by contrast, had been furious; his otherwise handsome features had turned to stone the day she'd told him about the broken engagement.

In the six years since, he'd softened a little—probably because his wife, Nora, had lobbied steadily on Juliana's behalf—writing regularly, even inviting Juliana home for visits and offering to ship the clothing and books she'd left behind, but when it came to her inheritance, he'd never relented.

Even when John Holden had died suddenly, a year before, permanently disqualifying himself as a possible husband for the sister Clay had once adored and protected, teased and laughed with, he had not given ground. After months of working up her courage, she'd written to ask for a modest bank draft, since her salary was small, less than the allowance her grandmother had given her as a girl, and Clay had responded with words that still blistered Juliana's pride, even now. "I won't see you squandering good money," he'd written, "on shoes and schoolbooks for a pack of red-skinned orphans and strays."

A burning ache rose in Juliana's throat at the memory.

Clay would cease punishing her when she stopped teaching and married a man who met with his lofty approval, then and only then, and that was the unfortunate reality.

She'd been a fool to write to him that last time, all but begging for the funds she'd needed to get Joseph and Theresa safely home to North Dakota and look after the two little ones until proper homes could be found for them.

The situation was further complicated by the fact that Mr. Philbert, an agent of the Bureau of Indian Affairs and therefore Juliana's supervisor, believed the four pupils still in her charge had been sent back to their original school in Missoula, along with the older students. Sooner or later, making his rounds or by correspondence, Philbert, a diligent sort with no softness in him that Juliana could discern, would realize she'd not only disobeyed his orders, but lied to him, at least in part.

As an official representative of the United States government, the man could have her arrested and prosecuted for kidnapping, and consign Daisy and Billy-Moses to some new institution, far out of her reach, where they would probably be neglected, at best. Juliana knew, after working in a series of such places, all but bloodying her very soul in the effort to change things, that only the most dedicated reformers would bother to look beyond the color of their skin. And there were precious few of those.

To keep from thinking about Mr. Philbert and his inevitable wrath, Juliana turned her mind to the students she'd had to bid farewell to—Mary Rose, seventeen and soon to be entering Normal School herself; Ezekiel, sixteen, who wanted to finish his education and return to his tribe. Finally, there was Angelique, seventeen, like her cousin Mary Rose, sweet and unassuming and smitten with a boy she'd met while running an errand in Stillwater Springs one spring day.

Part Blackfoot and part white, Blue Johnston had visited several times, a handsome, engaging young man with a flashing white smile and the promise of a job herding cattle on a ranch outside of Missoula. Although Juliana had kept close watch on the couple and warned Angelique repeatedly about the perils of impulse, she'd had the other children to attend to, and the pair had strayed out of her sight more than a few times.

Privately, Juliana feared that Angelique and her beau would run away and get married as soon as they got the chance—and that chance had come a week before, when Angelique and the others had boarded the train to return to Missoula. Should that happen—perhaps it already had—Mr. Philbert would bluster and threaten dire consequences when he learned of it, all the while figuratively dusting his hands together, secretly relieved to have one less obligation.

Footsteps passed along the hallway, past her door, bringing Juliana out of her rueful reflections. Another door opened and then closed again, nearer, and then all was silent.

The house rested, and so, evidently, did Lincoln Creed.

Juliana could not.

Easing herself from between the sleeping children, after gently freeing the fabric of her nightgown from Billy-Moses's grasp, Juliana crawled out of bed.

The cold slammed against her body like the shock following an explosion; there was a small stove in the room, but it had not been lit.

Shivering, Juliana crossed to it, all but hopping, found matches and newspaper and kindling and larger chunks of pitchy wood resting tidily in a nearby basket. With numb fingers, she opened the stove door and laid a fire, set the newspaper and kindling ablaze, adjusted the damper.

The floor stung the soles of her bare feet, and the single window, though large, was opaque with curlicues and crystals of ice. A silvery glow indicated that the moon had come out from behind the snow-burdened clouds—perhaps the storm had stopped.

Juliana paced, making no sound, until the room began to warm up, and then fumbled in the pocket of her cloak for Clay's crumpled letter. Back at the mercantile, she'd been too overwrought to finish the missive. Now, wakeful in the house of a charitable stranger—but a stranger nevertheless—she smoothed the page with the flat of one hand, hungry for a word of kind affection.

Not wanting to light a lamp, lest she awaken the children resting so soundly in the feather bed, Juliana knelt near the fire, opened the stove door again and read by the flickering flames inside, welcoming the warmth.

Her gaze skimmed over the first few lines—she could have recited those from memory—and took in the rest.

> *You will be twenty-six years old on your next birthday, Juliana, and you are still unmarried. Nora and I are, of course, greatly concerned for your welfare, not to mention your reputation....*

Juliana had to stop herself by the summoning of inner forces from wadding the letter up again, casting it straight into the fire.

Clay had accepted the fact, he continued, in his usual brisk fashion, that his sister had consigned herself to a life of lonely and wasteful spinsterhood. She was creating a scandal, he maintained, by living away from home and family. What kind of example, he wondered, was she setting for Clara, her little niece?

He closed with what amounted to a command that she return to Denver and "live with modesty and circumspection" in her brother's home, where she belonged.

But there was no expression of fondness.

The letter was signed *Regards, C. Mitchell.*

"'C. Mitchell,'" Juliana whispered on a shaky breath. "Not 'Clay.' Not 'Your brother.' 'C. Mitchell.'"

With that, she folded the single page carefully, held it for a moment, and then tossed it into the stove. Watched, the heat drying her eyeballs until they burned, as orange flames curled the vellum, nibbled darkly at the edges and corners, and then consumed the last forlorn tatters of Juliana's hopes. There would be no reconciliation between her and Clay, no restoration of their old childhood camaraderie.

As much as she had loved the brother she remembered from long ago, as much as she loved him still, for surely he was still in there somewhere behind that rigid facade, she *could not* go home. Oh, she would have enjoyed getting to know little Clara and her brother, Simon. She had always been fond of Nora, a goodhearted if flighty woman who accepted her husband's absolute authority without apparent qualms. But Clay would treat her, Juliana, like a poor relation, doling out pennies for a packet of pins, lecturing and dictating her every move, staring her down if she dared to venture an opinion at the supper table.

No. She definitely could not go home, not under such circumstances. It would be the ultimate—and final—defeat, and the slow death of her spirit.

"Missy?" The lisp was Daisy's; the child could not say Juliana's whole name, and always addressed her thus. "Missy, are you there?"

"I'm here, sweetheart," Juliana confirmed quietly, closing the stove door and getting back to her feet. "I'm here."

The assurance was enough for Daisy; she turned onto her side, settled in with a tiny murmur of relief and sank into sleep again.

Even with the fire going, the room was still cold enough to numb Juliana's bones.

Having no other choice, she climbed back into bed and pulled the top sheet and faded quilts up to her chin, giving a little shiver.

Billy-Moses stirred beside her, took a new hold on her nightgown.

Daisy snuggled close, too.

Juliana stared up at the ceiling, watching the shadows dance, her heart and mind crowded with children again. At some point, she could send Joseph and Theresa home by train to their family in North Dakota.

But what of Daisy and Billy-Moses? They had nowhere to go, besides an orphanage or some other "school."

In her more optimistic moments, Juliana could convince herself that some kindly couple would be delighted to adopt these bright, beautiful children, would cherish and nurture them.

This was not an optimistic moment.

Poverty was rampant among Indians; many could not feed their own children, let alone take in the lost lambs, the "strays," as Clay and others like him referred to them.

A lone tear slipped down Juliana's right cheek, tickled its way over her temple and into her hair. She closed her eyes and waited, trying not to consider the future, and finally, fitfully, she slept.

THE COLD WAS BRITTLE; it had substance and heft.

Lincoln had carried in an armload of wood and laid kindling on the hearth of the big stone fireplace directly across from his too-big, too-empty four-poster bed that morning before dawn, the way he always did after the weather turned in the fall. He'd gotten a good blaze crackling in the little stove in Gracie's room, so she and Theresa would be snug—he'd seen children sicken and

die after taking a chill—but that night he didn't bother
to get his own fire going.

He stripped off his clothes and the long winter underwear beneath them, and plunged into bed naked, cursing under his breath at the smooth, icy bite of the linen
sheets. It was at night that he generally missed Beth
most, recalling her whispery laughter and the warmth of
her curled against him, the sweet, eager solace of their
lovemaking.

Tonight, it was different.

He couldn't stop thinking about Juliana: her new-
penny hair; her eyes, blue as wet ink pooling on the
whitest paper; the way she'd rested against his side,
under his coat, soft with the innocent abandon of sleep,
on the wagon ride home from town.

He reckoned that was why he wouldn't light a
fire. He was punishing himself for betraying Beth's
memory in a way that cut far deeper than relieving
his body with dance-hall girls in other towns. God Al-
mighty, he'd had to study the little gilt-framed picture
of his late wife on Gracie's night table earlier just to
reassemble her features in his mind. They'd scattered
like dry leaves in a high wind, the memory of Beth's
eyes and nose and the shape of her mouth, with his
first look at Juliana that afternoon, in the mercantile.

Beth would have understood about the loose
women.

Even a mail-order bride.

But he'd vowed, sitting beside this very bed, holding
Beth's hand in both his own, to love her, and no one else,
until they laid him out in the cemetery alongside her.

Lincoln's eyes stung as he remembered how brave she'd been. How she'd smiled at his earnest promise, sick as she was, and told him not to close his heart, for Gracie's sake and his own.

She hadn't meant it, of course. She'd read a lot of novels about love and chivalry and noble sacrifice, that was all. A woman of comparatively few flaws, at least as far as he was concerned, Beth had nonetheless been possessive at times, her jealousy flaring when he tipped his hat to any female under the age of sixty, or returned a smile.

He'd been faithful, besotted as he was, but Beth's wealthy father had kept a mistress while she was growing up, and her mother had withdrawn into bitter silence in protest, becoming an invalid by choice. Though the instances were rare, Beth had fretted and shed tears a time or two, certain that it was only a matter of time before Lincoln tired of her and wanted some conjugal variety.

He'd reassured her, of course, kissed away her tears, made love to her, sent away to cities like New York and San Francisco and Boston for small but expensive presents he hadn't been able to afford, what with beef prices bottoming out and his mother spending money as if she still had a rich husband, and his brother Wes running the ranch into near bankruptcy while he, Lincoln, was away at college.

No, he thought, with a shake of his head and a grim set to his mouth, his hands cupped behind his head as he lay still as fallen timber, waiting for the sheets to warm up. Beth hadn't meant what she'd said that day, only hours before she'd closed her eyes for the last time;

she'd merely been playing out a scene from one of those stories that made her sniffle until her face got puffy and her nose turned red. She'd believed, being so very young, that that was how a lady was supposed to die.

If it hadn't been for the seizing ache in the middle of his chest and the sting behind his eyes, Lincoln might have smiled to remember the earlier days of their marriage, when he'd come in from the barn or the range so many evenings and found his bride with a thick book clutched to her bosom and tears pouring down her cheeks.

"She died with a rose clasped between her teeth!" Beth had expounded once, evidently referring to the heroine of the novel she'd been reading by the front room fire.

His mother, darning socks in her rocking chair, wanting them both to know she disapproved of such nonsense, and saucy brides from Somewhere Else, had muttered something, shaken her head and then made a tsk-tsk sound.

"*Someone* had better start supper cooking," Cora Creed had huffed, rising and stalking off toward the kitchen.

Waited on by servants all her short life, Beth had never learned to cook, sew or even make up a bed. None of that had bothered Lincoln, though it troubled his mother plenty.

He had merely smiled, kissed Beth's overheated forehead and said something along the lines of "I hope she was careful not to bite down on the thorns. The lady in the book, I mean."

Beth had laughed then, and hit him playfully with the tome.

Now, alone in the bed where they'd conceived Gracie and two other children who hadn't survived long enough to draw even one breath, Lincoln thrust out a sigh and rubbed his eyes with a thumb and forefinger.

Morning would come around early, and the day ahead would be long, hard and cold. He and Tom and the few ranch hands wintering on the place would be hauling wagonloads of hay out to the range cattle, since the grass was buried under snow. They'd have to break the ice at the edge of the creek, too, so the cattle could drink.

He needed whatever sleep he could get.

Plainly, it wouldn't be much.

JULIANA HAD BEEN an early riser since the cradle, and she was up and dressed well before dawn.

Even so, when she wandered through the still-dark house toward the kitchen, there was a blaze burning in the hearth in what probably passed for a parlor in such a masculine home. The furniture was heavy and dark and spare, all hard leather and rough-hewn wood, the surfaces uncluttered with the usual knickknacks and vases and doilies and sewing baskets.

Perhaps Lincoln's mother—gone traveling, Gracie had said at supper, with marked relief—had packed away her things in preparation for a lengthy absence. As far as Juliana could tell, the woman had left no trace at all—even her room, where she and the children had passed the night, was unadorned.

Entering the kitchen, Juliana stepped into lantern-light and the warmth of the cookstove. Lincoln stood at a basin in front of a small mirror fixed to the wall, his face lathered with suds, shaving. He wore trousers and boots and a long-sleeved woolen undershirt, and suspenders that dangled in loose, manly loops at his sides.

He was decently clothed, but there was an intimacy in the early-morning quiet and the glow of the kerosene lamps that gave Juliana pause. She stopped on the threshold and drew in a sharp breath.

He smiled, rinsed his straight razor in the basin, ran it skillfully under his chin and along his neck. "Mornin'," he said.

Juliana recovered her inner composure, but barely. "Good morning," she replied, quite formally.

"Coffee's ready," Lincoln told her. "Help yourself. Cups are on the shelf in the pantry." He cocked a thumb toward a nearby door.

Juliana hurried in to get a cup, desperate to be busy. Came back with two, since that was the polite thing to do. She poured coffee for Lincoln, started to take it to him and was suddenly tongue-tied again, and flustered by it.

He chuckled, rinsed his face in the basin, reached for a towel and dried off. His ebony hair was rumpled, and glossy in the lamplight. "Thanks," he said, and walked over to take the steaming cup from her hand.

Tom entered while they were standing there, staring at each other, his bronzed skin polished with the cold. Behind him walked Joseph, carrying a bucket steaming with fresh milk.

Juliana smiled, feeling as though she'd been rescued from something intriguingly dangerous. "You're up early," she said to the boy. At the school, Joseph had been something of a layabout mornings, continually late for breakfast and yawning through the first class of the day.

"Tom needed help," Joseph said solemnly.

Juliana felt a pang, knowing why Joseph was so eager to be useful. He hoped to land a job on Stillwater Springs Ranch, earn enough money to get himself and Theresa home to North Dakota. With luck, the Bureau of Indian Affairs would leave them alone.

"We can always use another hand around here," Lincoln said.

Juliana shot him a glance. "Joseph has school today."

Some of the milk slopped over the edge of the bucket as Joseph set it down hard in the sink. A flush pounded along his fine cheekbones.

"School?" Lincoln asked.

Just then, Gracie burst in, dressed in a light woolen dress and high-button shoes and pulling Daisy behind her by one hand and Billy-Moses by the other. Both children stared at her as though they'd never seen such a wondrous creature, and most likely they hadn't.

"School?" Gracie chirped, her eyes enormous. "Where? When?"

Juliana smiled, rested her hands lightly on her hips. She hadn't bothered to put up her hair; it hung in a long braid over her shoulder. "Here," she said. "At the kitchen table, directly after breakfast."

Joseph groaned.

"Can I learn, too?" Gracie asked breathlessly. "Can I, please?"

"May I," Juliana corrected, ever the teacher. "And I don't see why you shouldn't join us."

"Will you teach me numbers?" Gracie prattled, her words fairly tumbling over one another in her eagerness. "I'm not very good with numbers. I can read, though. And I promise to sit very still and listen to everything you say and raise my hand when I want to speak—"

"Gracie," Lincoln interrupted.

Releasing Daisy and Billy-Moses, Gracie whirled on her father. "Oh, Papa," she blurted, "you're *not* going to say I can't, are you?"

Lincoln's smile was a little wan, and his gaze shifted briefly to Juliana before swinging back to Gracie's upturned face. "No," he said. "I'm not going to say you can't. It's just that Miss Mitchell will be moving on soon and I don't want you to be let down when she does."

The words shouldn't have shaken Juliana—they were quite true, after all, since she *would* be moving on soon, though the means she would employ to do that were still a mystery—but they did. She felt slightly breathless, the way she had the day Clay told her she was no longer welcome in the mansion on Pine Street.

Gracie's eyes brimmed with tears, and Juliana knew they were genuine. She longed to embrace the child, the way she would Daisy or Billy-Moses, if they ever cried. Which, being stoic little creatures, they didn't.

"I just want to *learn things* while I can, Papa," she said.

Tom broke into the conversation, pumping water at the sink. Washing up with a misshapen bar of yellow soap. "I'll get breakfast on the stove," he interjected. His gaze moved to Juliana's face. "We could use Joseph's help today, if you can spare him."

Joseph looked so hopeful that Juliana's throat tightened.

"I'll hear your reading lesson after supper," she relented.

Joseph's grin warmed her like sunshine. "I promise I'll do good," he said.

"Well," Juliana said. "You will do *well*, Joseph, not 'good'."

He nodded, clearly placating her.

When Juliana turned back to Gracie, she saw that the child was leaning against Lincoln's side, sniffling, her arms around his lean waist. The flow of tears had stopped.

"Saint Nicholas is going to bring me a dictionary for Christmas," Gracie announced. She looked up at her father. "Do you think he got my letter, Papa? He won't bring me a doll or anything like that, just because you already *have* a dictionary on your desk and he thinks I could use that instead of having one of my own? Yours is *old*—a lot of words aren't even in it."

Lincoln grinned, tugged lightly at one of Gracie's ringlets. "I'm sure Saint Nick got your letter, sweetheart," he said.

"Who's that?" Theresa asked, trailing into the room, hair unbrushed. Juliana wondered if Lincoln had heard her prayers, as he probably had Gracie's. Told her to sleep well.

"You don't know who Saint Nicholas is?" Gracie asked, astounded.

"We'll discuss him later," Juliana promised, "when we sit down for lessons after breakfast."

"I could recite," Gracie offered. "I know all about Saint Nicholas."

"Gracie," Lincoln said.

"Well, I *do*, Papa. I've read Mr. Moore's poem *dozens* of times."

"We'll have cornmeal mush," Tom decided aloud. "Maybe some sausage."

"What?" Lincoln asked.

"Breakfast," Tom explained with a slight grin. Then he turned to Joseph. "You know how to use a separator, boy?"

Joseph nodded. "We had a milk cow out at the school," he said. "For a while."

Separating the milk from the cream had always been Theresa's chore, since Joseph considered it "woman's work." Mary Rose and Angelique had taken turns churning the butter.

And then the cow had sickened and died, and Mr. Philbert hadn't requisitioned the government for another.

Sadness and frustration swept over Juliana, and it must have shown in her face, because, to her utter surprise, Lincoln laid a hand on her shoulder.

Something startling and fiery raced through her at his touch. She nearly flinched, and she saw by his expression that he'd noticed.

"Sit down," he said, watching with amusement in his dark eyes as she blushed with an oddly delicious mortification. "I'll get you some coffee."

CHAPTER THREE

THE SKY WAS A CLEAR, heart-piercing blue, and sunshine glittered on fields of snow rolling to the base of the foothills and crowning the trees. Creek water shimmered beneath sheets of ice, and the cattle, more than a hundred of them, milled and bawled, impatient for the first load of hay to hit the ground. Lincoln sat in the saddle, his horse restless beneath him, and pulled his hat down over his eyes against the dazzling glare.

He watched as Joseph climbed into the back of the sleigh—the snow was too deep out on the range for a wagon to pass—while Tom soothed the two enormous draft horses hitched to it.

Ben Gainer, a young ranch hand who'd stayed on for the winter because his wife, Rose-of-Sharon, was soon to be delivered of their first child, rode up alongside Lincoln on a spotted pony, a shovel in one hand.

"Best break up some of that ice on the creek," Gainer said.

Lincoln nodded, swung down from the saddle. It was there to be done, as his father used to say. When cattle weren't hungry, they were thirsty, and they weren't smart enough to eat snow or trample the ice with their hooves so they could get to the water beneath. He went to the sleigh, helped himself to one of the pickaxes Tom had brought along.

Wishing, as he sometimes did, that he'd chosen an easier life—Beth's father had offered him a partnership in his Boston law firm—Lincoln went to the creekside and began shattering ice an inch thick, two in some places.

If he'd stayed in Boston, he reflected, Beth might have lived, the two babies, too. Gracie would have been able to go to a real school, too.

Inwardly, Lincoln sighed. Left in Wes's incapable hands, the ranch would be gone by now, his mother displaced, Tom Dancingstar ripped up by the roots and left to wander in a world that not only underestimated him, but often scorned him, too. All because he was an Indian.

He'd been caught between the devil and the deep blue sea, Lincoln had, and if he'd made the wrong choice, there was no changing it now. The ranch wasn't making him rich, but he'd gotten it back in the black with a lot of hard work and Creed determination.

But what a price he'd paid.

Tom appeared beside him, toting another pickax. Sent Gainer and Joseph back to the hay barn, nearer the house, where the two remaining ranch hands, Art Bentley and Mike Falstaff, waited to load the sleigh up again.

"You look mighty grim this mornin'," Tom observed.

"Hard work," Lincoln said without looking at his friend.

"You've been working since you were nine. I don't think it's that."

Lincoln stopped to catch his breath, sighed. Cattle

nosed up behind him, scenting the water. "You going to insist on chatting?" he asked.

Tom chuckled. Cattle pushed past them to get to the creek, so they moved a little farther down the line, out of their way. "Something's thrown you, that's for sure. I reckon it's Miss Juliana Mitchell."

Lincoln felt a surge of touchy exasperation, which was unlike him. He started swinging the pickax again. "I might have had a thought or two where she's concerned," he admitted.

Tom laid a hand on his arm. "She needs a place to light. You need a wife and Gracie needs a mother. Why don't you just offer for Juliana and be done with it?"

A growl of frustration escaped Lincoln. He drove the pickax deep into the hard ice, felt satisfaction as the glaze splintered. "It's not that simple," he said in his own good time.

"Isn't it?" Tom asked.

"I'm paying you to work," Lincoln pointed out, humorless, "not spout advice for the lovelorn."

"Is that what you are?" Tom asked, and looking sidelong, Lincoln saw amusement dancing in the older man's eyes. "Lovelorn?"

"No, damn it," Lincoln snapped.

Tom was relentless. "You're a young man, Lincoln. You ought to have a woman. Gracie ought to have a mother, brothers and sisters. If you were willing to bring in a stranger from someplace else and put a wedding band on her finger, why not Juliana?"

"I was hoping for a governess or a housekeeper," Lincoln said. "Taking a wife was a last resort."

"All right, then," Tom persisted, "Juliana's a teacher.

She would make a fine governess. Maybe even a decent housekeeper."

"She won't want to stay out here on this ranch," Lincoln argued. "She's a city girl—you can see that by the way she moves, hear it in the way she talks."

"Beth was a city girl, and she liked the ranch fine."

It was all Lincoln could do not to fling the pickax so far and so hard that it would lodge in the snow on the other side of the creek. Tom sometimes went days without talking at all; now, all of a sudden, he was running off at the mouth like a lonely spinster at high tea. "Why? Why is this different, Lincoln? Because you think you could care about Juliana?"

Lincoln didn't answer because he couldn't. His throat felt raw, and a cow bumped him from behind, nearly sent him sprawling into the cold creek water. "I loved Beth," he said after a long time, because Tom would have kept at him until he gave some kind of answer.

Tom laid a hand on his shoulder. "I know that," he said. "But Beth is gone, and you're still here. You and Gracie. That child is lonesome, Lincoln—sometimes it hurts my heart just to look at her. And you're not doing much better."

"I'm doing fine. And there are worse things than being lonesome."

"Are there? You going to tell me you don't lie in there in that bed at night and wish there was a woman beside you?"

Again, Lincoln couldn't answer.

Mercifully, the talk-fest seemed to be over. Tom went back to work, another load of hay arrived, Joseph

and young Gainer threw it to the cattle and went back
for more.

Toward noon, satisfied that the stock would neither
starve nor perish of thirst, Lincoln sent the whole crew
back to have their midday meal in the bunkhouse kitchen
and then tend to other chores around the place, like split-
ting firewood and mending harnesses and mucking out
stalls in the barn. Winter work could be miserably hard,
but the season had its favorable side. There was a lot of
time for catching up on lost sleep and sitting around a
potbellied stove, swapping yarns.

Gainer, Lincoln knew, was always anxious about his
wife, fearing she'd run into some kind of baby trouble,
alone in the tiny cabin they shared, and he wouldn't be
there to help.

God knew, the possibility was real enough. Beth
might have bled to death with the first miscarriage if
Cora hadn't been around. She'd gone out onto the back
porch, Lincoln's mother had, and clanged at the iron
triangle with vigor until they'd heard the signal, out on
the range, and ridden for home.

What if Beth had been alone with Gracie, who was
only two at the time?

Lincoln stuck a foot into the stirrup and swung up
onto his horse's back. No sense in agonizing over something that was over and done with. He'd raced to town
for the doctor, but it had been Tom Dancingstar who'd
stopped Beth's bleeding. By the time Lincoln returned
with help, Cora had bathed and bundled the lifeless
baby, a boy.

Lincoln had sat in the rocking chair in the kitchen,
holding his son, and wept without shame until sunset

when he'd carried him out to the graveyard beyond the orchard, dug a tiny grave and laid the child to rest. Eighteen months later, Beth had given birth to a second daughter, stillborn.

He'd wept then, too, though not in front of his distraught wife. That time, Tom and Wes had done the burying, and more than a month had gone by before the circuit preacher stopped by to say prayers over the grave.

Turning his horse homeward, Lincoln set the memories aside, but they seemed to trail along in his wake like ghosts. Clouds gathered, black-gray in the eastern sky, bulging with snow.

Feeding the cattle would be harder tomorrow, cold work that would sting his hands, even inside heavy leather gloves, but mostly likely the creek wouldn't freeze again.

His heart seemed to travel on ahead of him, drawn to the light and warmth of the house. Drawn to Juliana.

Reaching the barn, he unsaddled his horse, rubbed the animal down with a wad of burlap and gave him a scoop of grain in the bottom of a wooden bucket. He was putting off going into the house, not because he didn't want to, though. No, he was savoring the prospect.

The first snowflakes began to fall, slow and fat, as he left the barn, and the sun was veiled, bringing on a premature twilight.

Lanterns shone in the kitchen windows, and Lincoln raised the collar of his coat, ducked his head against the wind and quickened his stride.

Gracie met him at the back door, her face as bright as any lantern, her eyes huge. "I'm learning the multiplication tables!" she fairly shouted. "And I gave a recitation about Saint Nicholas, too!"

Lincoln smiled, bent to kiss the top of Gracie's head, then eased her backward into the kitchen, out of the cold. The table was clear of the slates and books that had come out of Juliana's satchel that morning after breakfast was over, and she was at the stove, stirring last night's venison stew.

She turned her head, favored him with a shy smile, and it struck him that she was not just womanly, but beautiful. She made that faded calico dress of hers look like the finest velvet, and he wanted to touch her fiery hair.

Instead, he hung his hat on its peg, shrugged out of his coat and hung that, too. "School over for the day?"

She nodded. "We accomplished a lot," she said quietly.

Lincoln smiled down at Gracie again. "So I hear," he replied. "Where are the others?"

"Theresa's putting Daisy and Billy-Moses down for their naps," Juliana answered, seeming pleased that he'd asked. "Joseph is with Tom—they spotted a flock of wild turkeys and they're hoping to bring back a big one for Christmas dinner."

Christmas. He'd forgotten all about that, and it was coming up fast. Fortunately, he'd already bought Gracie's dictionary, and his mother had taken care of the rest. There was a stash of peppermint sticks, books, doll clothes and other gifts hidden away on the high shelf of Cora's wardrobe; she'd shown him the loot before she left on her trip, and admonished him not to forget to put up a tree.

As though reading his mind, Gracie tugged at his sleeve. "Are we getting a Christmas tree?"

Lincoln thought it was a foolish thing to cut down a living tree, minding its own business in some copse or forest, and he flat-out refused to allow any lighted candles in the branches. But he always gave in and hiked out into the woods with an ax, and nailed two chunks of wood crisscross for a stand, because it meant so much to his little girl. "Don't we always?" he countered.

"I thought you might change your mind this year," Gracie said. "You said it was a very *German* thing to do. What's German?"

It was Juliana, the schoolmarm, who answered. "Germany is a country, like the United States and Canada. People from Germany are…?"

"Germans!" Gracie cried in triumph.

"Very good," Juliana said, with pleasure growing in her eyes.

"Go take a nap," Lincoln told his daughter.

"Papa, I never take naps," Gracie reminded him. "I'm not a *baby.*"

"Neither are Daisy and Billy-Moses," Lincoln said. "Go."

Gracie turned to Juliana. "Is *Theresa* going to take a nap?"

At that moment, Theresa entered the kitchen, and it was apparent, by the sparkle of collusion in her eyes, that she'd heard at least part of the exchange. She held out a hand to Gracie. "Come," she said. "We'll just lie down for a while and rest. We don't have to sleep, and I'll read you a story."

"I'll read *you* a story," Gracie insisted.

Theresa smiled, nodded slightly.

Gracie could never resist any opportunity to show off her uncanny mastery of the written word. When she was barely three years old, Beth had taught her the alphabet, and after that, she'd been able to divine the mechanics of the reading process. It was as if the child had been *born* knowing how to make sense of books.

Lincoln felt a pang, thinking of Beth when he wanted so badly to be alone in that kitchen with Juliana, for whatever time Providence might allot them. It wasn't as if he meant to touch her, or "offer for her," the way Tom had suggested out there by the creek. She warmed him deep down, that was all. In places where the heat from the cookstove didn't reach.

When Gracie and Theresa were gone, though, he just stood there, mute as a stump.

"Wash up," Juliana told him, keeping her gaze averted. "You must be hungry."

He went to the sink, rolled up his sleeves, pumped some water and lathered his hands with soap. It was harsh stuff, fit to take the hide off, as his mother complained.

Juliana fetched a bowl and spoon, dished up stew for him. The task was ordinary enough, but it made Lincoln think about the conversation with Tom again.

He drew back his chair at the table, sat down. "Did you eat?" he asked, because he wanted Juliana to join him.

She nodded. "Coffee?"

"You don't have to wait on me, Juliana," he replied.

"Nonsense," she replied, bustling off, returning to the table with a steaming mug. "You've given us food and shelter, and I want to show my gratitude." A twinkle sparked in her eyes. "But I draw the line at polishing your boots, Mr. Creed."

"I guess you wouldn't be looking for a housekeeper's job," Lincoln said, and then wished he could bite off his tongue. Juliana Mitchell might have fallen on hard times, but she wasn't cut out to be a servant, even if she *had* poured him coffee and heated up last night's stew for lunch.

She sat down, though, and that was encouraging.

"Are you offering?" she asked, almost shyly.

Lincoln went still, his spoon midway between the bowl and his mouth. "Would you accept if I did?"

Juliana shifted in her chair. Folded her hands in her lap. "My brother would probably come here and drag me back to Denver by the hair if I did," she said, and she sounded almost rueful.

"Your brother?" *Yes, fool,* taunted an impatient voice in his head. *You know what a brother is. You have two of them yourself, three if you count poor Dawson, lying out there in the cemetery next to your pa.*

A fetching blush played on her cheekbones. Lincoln tried to imagine her scrubbing floors, beating rugs, ironing shirts and emptying chamber pots, and found it impossible. For all that her dress had seen better days, there was something innately aristocratic about this woman, something finely honed in the way she held herself, even sitting in a chair.

"Clay had enough trouble reconciling himself to my being a teacher," Juliana said after a few awkward moments during which she swallowed a lot. "So far he's left me alone, but he'd have a fit if I took to keeping house. Unless I was married—"

Her voice fell away, and the blush intensified. Now, Lincoln suspected, *she* was the one wanting to bite off her tongue.

"What if you were a governess?" he ventured, lowering the spoon back to his bowl even though he felt half-starved.

She shrugged both shoulders and looked miserable. "I suppose he'd see that as an improvement over teaching in an Indian School," she allowed.

Lincoln wanted to close his hand over hers and squeeze some comfort into her, but he didn't. "You do everything your brother tells you?" he asked, surprised.

"No," she said, meeting his eyes at last, trying to smile. He'd intended no criticism by his question, and to his great relief, she seemed to know that. "If that were so, I'd be a wealthy widow now, living in Denver."

Lincoln raised one eyebrow, waited.

She did some more blushing. "Clay wanted me to marry his business partner. I'd resigned myself to that, even though I was going to Normal School. But then my grandmother died and I'd graduated, and I realized I wanted to *use* what I'd learned."

There was more she wasn't saying, Lincoln knew that, but he didn't push. The situation seemed too fragile for that. Slowly, to give her a chance to recover a little, he looked down at his bowl, stuck his spoon into the stew and began to eat.

"This Clay yahoo wouldn't like your being a governess?" he asked carefully, when some time had passed.

She laughed softly, probably at the term *yahoo* applied to her no-doubt powerful brother. "Probably not."

"Why? Because he'd think it was beneath you?" Again, there was no scorn in the inquiry.

"No," Juliana said, with quiet bitterness. "He'd think it was beneath *him,* and he's already despairing of my reputation. To Clay, my teaching other people's children—especially *Indian* children—is tantamount to serving drinks in a saloon."

Again, Lincoln waited. Some process was unfolding, and it had to be let alone.

"It's starting to snow," Juliana said wistfully, her gaze turned to the window again.

"What will you do, then?" Lincoln asked. "After you leave here, I mean?"

She sighed. Met his gaze. "I don't know," she confessed.

"I guess we could get married," Lincoln said.

Juliana opened her mouth, closed it again.

Lincoln felt crimson heat climbing his neck, pulsing along the underside of his jawline. "You heard Fred Willand say it in the mercantile yesterday," he said, his voice raspy. "I've been advertising for a housekeeper or a governess, or both, for better than a year. Failing that, I'd settle for a wife."

Juliana began to laugh. Her eyes glistened with unshed tears, and she put a hand to her mouth to silence herself.

"I didn't mean 'settle,' exactly—"

"Yes, you did," Juliana said. Her look softened. "You loved Gracie's mother a lot, didn't you?"

"Yes," Lincoln answered readily.

"So much that you can't make room in your heart for another woman," Juliana speculated. "That's why you'd marry a stranger, someone answering a newspaper advertisement. Because you wouldn't have to care for that person."

She wasn't accusing him of anything; he knew that by her tone and her bearing. Most likely, the words stung the way they did because they were only too true.

"And that person wouldn't have to care for me," he replied.

"But you'd expect her to—to share your bed?"

"Sooner or later, yes," Lincoln said. "That's part of being a wife, isn't it?"

Juliana propped an elbow on the table, cupped her chin in her palm. They might have been discussing hog prices, she was so unruffled and matter-of-fact. "I suppose," she agreed.

Before things could go any further, Tom and Joseph banged in through the back door, their faces white-slashed with broad smiles.

"Christmas dinner's outside," Tom said. Then his glance traveled between Juliana and Lincoln, and he sobered a little.

Joseph, being so young, and buoyed by the pride of accomplishment, didn't notice that they'd interrupted something, he and Tom. "We got two turkeys," he announced proudly. "Tom's already gutted them, but we have to pluck them yet, and I might have to pick some buckshot out of the one I got."

Juliana winced.

Lincoln smiled. Pushed back his chair and stood, carrying his bowl and spoon to the sink.

"Better have some stew," he told Tom and the boy.

"And then I'll hear you read today's lesson," Juliana told Joseph.

The boy's face fell briefly, then he smiled again. A deal, he must have decided, was a deal. Juliana had allowed him to skip his schoolwork earlier so he could work with the men out on the range. Now she wanted her due.

"After I pluck the turkeys?"

"After you pluck the turkeys," Juliana conceded with a fond sigh. "And you're not bringing those poor dead creatures into the house to do it."

The command was downright wifely, and that pleased Lincoln, though he didn't let it show. The idea had taken root in his mind, and in Juliana's, too, and for now, that was enough.

Joseph's grin faltered a little. "Remember last Christmas, Miss Mitchell, when you tried to roast that turkey that farmer's wife gave us and it smoked so much that we had to open the doors and all the windows?"

"Thank you, Joseph," Juliana said mildly, "for that reminder."

Tom smiled at that.

Lincoln glanced at the windows, saw that the snow was coming down harder and faster. Through the flurries, he glimpsed his brother Wes riding up, leading a pack mule behind him, a huge pine tree bound to its back.

"I'll be damned," he muttered with a low, throaty chuckle, and headed for the back door, pausing just long enough to put on his coat.

Wes wore no hat, and snowflakes gathered in his

dark chestnut hair and fringed his eyelashes. His grin was as white as the snowy ground, and even from ten feet away, Lincoln could smell the whiskey and cigar smoke on him.

"Ma said she'd have my hide if I didn't make sure Gracie had a Christmas tree," Wes said cheerfully. "So here I am."

Lincoln laughed and shook his head. "Did you happen to credit that there's another blizzard coming on and it'll be pitch-dark by the time you get back to town?"

"I've got enough whiskey in me to prevent any possibility of freezing," Wes answered. He took a cheroot from the pocket of his scruffy coat, fitted at the waist like something a dandified gambler would wear, and clamped it between his perfect teeth. "Fact is, I might need a swallow or two before I head home, just the same."

Dismounting, Wes went back to the mule and began untying the ropes that secured the Christmas tree to the animal. The lush, piney fragrance his motions stirred reminded Lincoln of their boyhood. They hadn't been raised to believe in Saint Nicholas, but there had always been fresh green boughs all over the house, and modest presents waiting at their places at the breakfast table on Christmas morning.

"Are you just going to stand there," Wes grumped, grinning all the while, "or will you lend me a hand getting this tree into the house?"

"It's too wet to be in the house," Lincoln said, sounding a mite wifely himself. "We'll set it in the woodshed, let it dry off a little."

"Whatever you say, little brother," Wes replied affably,

even though he was six inches shorter than Lincoln and only two years older. "Fred Willand told me when I stopped off at the mercantile to see if you'd gotten any mail—you didn't—that you've got a woman out here. That pretty teacher from the Indian School."

Lincoln took hold of the sizable tree. It was a wonder the weight of the thing hadn't buckled that poor old mule's knees—he'd have to saw a good foot off the thing to stand it up in the front room. "Fred Willand," he said, through the boughs, "gossips like an old woman."

Wes laughed at that. "Hell," he said, "if it weren't for Fred, I wouldn't know what you were up to half the time. It's not as if you ever stop by the saloon or the newspaper office to flap your jaws."

"I don't have much time for flapping my jaws," Lincoln answered. In spite of nearly losing the ranch because of Wes's well-intentioned mismanagement, he'd always loved his brother. After Dawson's death, the old man had taken his grief out on his second son, since Micah, being the eldest, would have given as good as he got. Lincoln, taking Dawson's place as the youngest in the family, had stayed clear of his pa and taken to following Tom Dancingstar everywhere he went.

Wes looked up, his eyes serious now. "Ma's gone," he said. "I can feel the peace even from out here."

Their mother didn't approve of Wes's drinking, his poker playing and cigar smoking, or the woman he loved, and she made that clear every time she got the opportunity. So Wes stayed away from the ranch house when she was around.

Lincoln started for the woodshed, dragging the

massive tree behind him. "Go on inside and have some of Tom's venison stew," he called over one shoulder. "It's probably been a month since you've had a decent meal."

"I wouldn't miss a chance to drag my eyeballs over a good-looking woman," Wes responded.

Lincoln didn't dignify that with an answer, but it made him grin to himself just the same.

When he came out of the woodshed, he saw that Wes had left the horse and mule standing. Lincoln led them both into the barn, out of the icy wind, unsaddled the horse, fed and watered both creatures, and rubbed them down the way he'd done with his own mount earlier.

He'd been doing things his brother should have done for as long as he could remember, but he didn't mind, because Wes was always the one who showed up at the most unlikely times with the most unlikely gifts.

ALTHOUGH JULIANA PUT ON A GOOD show, she was shaken inside, and it wasn't just because Lincoln Creed had all but proposed marriage to her at his kitchen table a little while before. She might actually say yes, if he did, and that jarred her to the quick.

John Holden would have made a perfectly acceptable husband, despite his obnoxious daughters, but she'd refused him. Other men had tried to court her during the intervening years, too, though she'd discouraged them, as well. She'd always imagined that if she ever married, it would happen in a fit of wild, romantic passion. She'd be swept off her feet, overcome with desire.

Lincoln stirred something in her, something almost

primal—that was undeniable. But wild, romantic passion? No.

On the other hand, she knew he was kind, generous. That he worked hard, was an attentive father and didn't judge people by the culture they'd been born into. That he let his suspenders loop at his sides in the mornings while he shaved.

She smiled at the image, even as Tom introduced her to Weston Creed, and Gracie ran shrieking for joy into the kitchen, hurling herself into her laughing uncle's arms.

He swung her around. "Brought you a Christmas tree," he told her. "Your papa is putting it in the woodshed to dry off a little. What's Saint Nicholas going to bring you this year?"

Gracie paused at the question and her lower lip trembled. A troubled expression flickered across her perfect face.

"I hope he doesn't come," she confided, in a whisper that carried.

Weston looked genuinely puzzled, though Juliana suspected everything he said and did was exaggerated. "Why would you hope for a thing like that?"

"Because he doesn't know the others are here," she said, near tears. "And I don't want any presents if Billy-Moses and Daisy and Joseph and Theresa don't get some, too."

Juliana's heart melted and slid down the inside of her rib cage. If Lincoln *did* propose, she might just accept. She wasn't in love with him—but she adored his daughter.

CHAPTER FOUR

WHEN LINCOLN GOT BACK INSIDE the house, he found Wes standing in the middle of the kitchen, holding a dismayed Gracie in his arms.

"Well," Wes told his niece solemnly, "we'd better get word to Saint Nicholas right quick, then."

Shedding his coat, Lincoln raised an eyebrow.

"Christmas is only four days away," Gracie fretted. "And the train won't come through Stillwater Springs again until *next* week. So how can I write to him in time?"

Lincoln and Juliana exchanged looks: Lincoln's curious, Juliana's wistful.

"Papa," Gracie all but wailed, "could we send a telegraph to Saint Nicholas?"

"What?" Lincoln asked, mystified.

"He won't bring anything for the others, because he doesn't know they're here!" Gracie despaired.

Something shifted deep in Lincoln's heart, and it wasn't just because he was standing so close to Juliana that their shoulders nearly touched. When had he moved?

He thought of the gifts on the shelf in his mother's wardrobe, the box of watercolor paints he'd bought on impulse back at the mercantile the day before. "Oh, I already did that," he lied easily.

Gracie was not only generous, she was formidably bright. Her forehead creased as Wes set her gently on her feet. "When?" she asked skeptically.

"In town yesterday," Lincoln said. "Soon as I knew we were going to have company, I went straight to the telegraph office and sent the old fella a wire."

Gracie's eyes widened, while her busy mind weighed the logistics. Fortunately, she came down on the side of relief rather than reason, and Lincoln felt mildly guilty for deceiving her, pure motives or none.

She beamed. "Well," she said. "That's fine, then."

"'Course, he'll probably have to spread things a little thinner than usual," Lincoln added. "Saint Nicholas, I mean. Times are hard, remember."

Gracie was undaunted. "All I want is a dictionary," she said. "So I can learn all the words there are in the whole world."

Lincoln wanted to sweep her up into his arms, the way Wes had apparently done upon arrival, but he figured that would be laying things on a little thick, so he just replied quietly, "I'm proud of you, Gracie Creed."

Beside him, Juliana sniffled once, but when he looked, he saw that she was smiling. Her eyes glistened a little, though.

Seeing he was watching her, Juliana turned quickly and busied herself scraping the last of the stew from the kettle into a bowl and basically herding a clearly charmed Wes over to the table.

She didn't even make him wash up, which might have galled Lincoln a little, if he hadn't been so busy thinking what a fine daughter he and Beth had brought into the world.

Although Wes loved his woman, Kate, and to Lincoln's knowledge his brother hadn't been unfaithful from the day the two of them had taken up with each other, his amber-colored eyes trailed Juliana's every movement, danced with mischief whenever he met Lincoln's gaze.

He *knew,* damn it. Wes knew Juliana had his younger brother's insides in a tangle, and he was bound to rib him without mercy.

"You'd better spend the night," Lincoln said to his brother, even though, at the moment, that was about the last thing he wanted. "Snow's coming down hard."

Wes shook his head, shifted slightly so Gracie could plant herself on his knee. "I've gotta get back. Poker game."

It wasn't long before he'd finished his meal and said goodbye to Gracie. This, too, was like Wes—he'd been uncomfortable in the house since Dawson died. Once, he'd even confided privately that he half expected their murdered brother to tap him on the shoulder from behind.

Gracie went off in search of the other children, and Tom and Joseph were still outside plucking turkeys. Avoiding Juliana's eyes, just as he sensed she was avoiding his, Lincoln put his coat on again, followed Wes into the cold and walked alongside him toward the barn.

About midway, Wes chuckled and shook his head, then gave a low whistle. He hadn't even hesitated when his horse and mule weren't where he'd left them; he knew Lincoln would have attended to anything he'd left undone.

"What?" Lincoln asked, sounding peevish because he knew what the answer would be.

"You," Wes said happily, snow gathering on his hair and shoulders and eyelashes again. "Every time you looked at that schoolmarm, I thought I was going to have to roll your tongue up like a rug and shove it back in your mouth."

Lincoln felt his neck warm. He was half again too stubborn to honor Wes's good-natured taunt with a reply of any kind.

Wes laughed outright then, and slapped Lincoln hard on the back as they slogged heavily through the snow. "She's smitten with you, little brother," he went on. "I figured I'd better tell you that, since you can be a mite thickheaded when it comes to women."

"I suppose *you're* an expert?" Lincoln bit out, raising his collar again. Damn, it was colder than a well-digger's ass. If he could have willed green grass to sprout up right through the snow, he would have done it.

Wes laughed again. "If you don't believe me, just ask Kate," he said lightly.

Lincoln happened to like Kate, even if she was a "light-skirt," as his old-fashioned mother put it, but he wasn't about to put any questions to her, especially when it came to something that personal.

He was silent until they entered the barn, now nearly dark. Both of them knew every inch of the place, and neither of them hesitated to let their eyes adjust to the lack of light.

"Thanks," Lincoln said awkwardly. "For the tree, I mean."

Wes found his horse and opened the stall door, began saddling up. "That was for Gracie," he said. "You want me to stop by Willand's Mercantile and get some presents for those other kids?"

The offer touched Lincoln. "No," he said, his voice sounding gruff. "Ma laid in a good supply of stuff before she left. There'll be plenty to go around."

Wes nodded. "That's good," he said.

"I guess you must have seen Ma recently?" Lincoln ventured. Their mother was a sore spot between them; Lincoln accepted that she was a little on the irritating side, while Wes still seemed to think she ought to change anytime now. "I dropped her off at the depot myself, and there was no sign of you."

There was no humor in Wes's chuckle this time. "She sent Fred Willand's boy, Charlie, around to the newspaper office with a note. 'Course, I'd have lit a cigar with it if it hadn't been for Gracie."

Lincoln frowned. Just as their mother wasn't fixing to change, Wes wasn't, either. Both of them were waiting for the other to see the error of their ways and repent like a convert at a tent meeting, and that would happen on the proverbial cold day in hell. "You think it's wrong, letting Gracie believe in this Saint Nicholas fella?"

Wes lowered the stirrup, gave the saddle a yank to make sure it was secure, then swung up. "She's a child," he said. Lincoln couldn't make out his features in the shadows. "Children need to believe in things while they can. I'll leave the mule here for a day or two, if it's all the same to you."

Lincoln nodded, stepped forward, hoping in vain

for a better look at his brother's face, and took hold of the reins to stop Wes from riding out. "Do you believe in anything, Wes?" he asked, struck by how much the answer mattered to him.

Wes sighed. "I believe in Kate. I believe in five-card stud and whiskey and the sacred qualities of a good cigar. I believe in Gracie and—damn it, I must be sobering up—I believe in your good judgment, little brother. Use it. Don't let that schoolmarm get away."

"I've only known her since yesterday," Lincoln reasoned. He was always the one inclined to reason. Wes just did whatever seemed like a good idea at the time.

"Maybe that's long enough," Wes answered.

Lincoln let go of the reins.

Wes executed a jaunty salute, there in the shadows, and rode toward the door of the barn, ducking his head as he passed under it.

"Rub that horse down when you get back to town," Lincoln called after his brother. "Don't just leave him standing at the hitching post in front of the saloon."

Wes didn't answer; maybe he hadn't heard.

More likely, he'd heard fine. He just hadn't felt called upon to bother with a reply.

THE TURKEY CARCASSES HAD BEEN trussed with twine and tied to a high branch in a tree so they'd stay cold and the wolves and coyotes wouldn't get them. Looking out the window as she stood at the sink, Juliana watched the pale forms sway in the thickening snow and the purple gathering of twilight.

She was certain she would never be hungry again.

Behind her, seated at the table, Tom Dancingstar

puffed on a corncob pipe, making the air redolent with cherry-scented tobacco, while Joseph droned laboriously through the assigned three pages of a Charles Dickens novel. The other children had gathered in the front room near the fireplace; the last time Juliana had looked in on them, Theresa and Gracie were playing checkers, while Daisy examined one of Gracie's dolls and Billy-Moses stacked wooden alphabet blocks, knocked them over and stacked them again.

The afternoon had dragged on, and Juliana wondered when Lincoln would come back into the house, when they'd get a chance to talk alone again, whether or not she ought to attempt to start supper.

It wasn't that she didn't *want* to cook. She hadn't been allowed near the kitchen as a young girl—Cook hadn't wanted a child underfoot—and every school she'd taught at until Stillwater Springs had provided meals in a common dining room.

Now, resurrected by Joseph's account, the image of last Christmas's burned turkey rose in her mind. They'd managed to save some of it and eaten around the charred parts. After that, probably tired of oatmeal and boiled beans, the construction of which Juliana had been able to discern by pouring over an old cookery book, Theresa and Mary Rose had taken to preparing most of the meals.

A snapping sound made Juliana jump, turn quickly.

Joseph had closed the Dickens novel smartly. "Finished," he said. "Can— *May* I go out and help Tom with the chores?"

Juliana blinked. A fine teacher *she* was—for all she knew, Joseph might have been reading from the back of a medicine bottle instead of a book. She had no idea whether he'd stumbled over any of the words, or lost track of the flow of the narrative and had to begin again, the way he often did.

So she bluffed.

"Tell me what happened in the story," she said.

Joseph was ready. "This woman named Nancy got herself beat to death by that Bill Sykes fella."

He'd been reading from *Oliver Twist,* then.

"He was a bad'un," Tom remarked seriously. "That Sykes, I mean."

"He was indeed," Juliana agreed. "You may help with the chores, Joseph."

Tom sighed, rose to his feet. "You reckon you could start that story over from the first, next time you read?" he asked the boy. "I'd like to know what led up to a poor girl winding up in such a fix."

Joseph would have balked at the request had it come from Juliana. Since it came from Tom instead, he beamed and said, "Sure."

"When?" Tom asked, starting for the back door, bent on getting the chores done, his pipe caught between his teeth.

"Maybe after supper," Joseph answered.

Supper. Renewed anxiety rushed through Juliana.

And Tom gave his trademark chuckle. The man probably couldn't read, at least not well enough to tackle Dickens, but he soon proved he *could* read minds.

"I'll fry up some eggs when we're through in the barn," he told Juliana. "And Mrs. Creed put up some bear-meat preserves last fall—mighty good, mixed in with fried potatoes."

Bear-meat preserves? That sounded about as appetizing to Juliana as the naked turkeys dangling from the tree branch outside, but she managed not to make a face.

"You have enough to do," she said, with a bright confidence she most certainly didn't feel. "I can fry eggs."

"No, you can't," Joseph argued benignly. "Remember when…?"

"Joseph."

The boy shrugged both shoulders, and he and Tom let in a rush of cold air opening the door to go out.

The instant they were gone, Juliana hurried to the front room and beckoned to Theresa with a crooked finger.

Theresa obediently left her checker game and Gracie to approach.

"Quick," Juliana whispered, fraught with a strange urgency. "Come and show me how to fry eggs!"

WHEN LINCOLN CAME IN WITH an armload of firewood, he found Juliana and Theresa side by side in front of the stove, working away, and the kitchen smelled of savory things—eggs, potatoes frying in onions, some kind of meat. Gracie was busy setting the table.

His stomach grumbled. The venison stew had worn off a while ago.

"Where have you been, Papa?" Gracie asked, all but singing the words, and dancing to them, too. "Did you ride all the way to town with Uncle Wes so he wouldn't get lost in the snow?"

Lincoln smiled and shook his head no. "Wes's horse

knows the way home, even if your uncle doesn't," he said. Actually, he'd been in the Gainers' cabin, admiring the spindly little Christmas tree Ben had put up for his child-heavy wife and drinking weak coffee. And at once avoiding and anticipating his return to the house, to Juliana.

Gracie nodded sagely. "That's a good horse," she said.

Lincoln proceeded through the kitchen, then the front room, and along the hallway to Juliana's door. Tonight, he thought, entering with the wood and kindling, he wouldn't have to lie awake worrying that she and the little boy and girl were cold.

Oh, he'd probably lie awake, all right, but there would be something else on his mind.

He'd made a damn fool of himself, with all that talk about governesses and housekeepers and—he gulped at the recollection—taking a wife.

Unburdening himself of the wood, Lincoln bent to open the stove door. Methodically, he took up the short-handled broom and bucket reserved for the purpose and swept out the ashes. When that was done, he crouched, crumpling newspaper and arranging kindling. In an hour or so, the cold room would be comfortably warm.

"Lincoln?"

Startled, Lincoln turned his head, saw Juliana standing in the doorway, looking like a redheaded angel hiding wings under a threadbare dress. His heart shinnied up into the back of his throat and thumped there.

"Supper's ready," she said.

Another wifely statement. He liked the sound of it.

Smiled as he shut the stove door and rose to his full height to adjust the damper on the metal chimney. "Thanks," he said.

She lingered on the threshold, neither in nor out.

Lincoln enjoyed thinking how scandalized his mother would have been if she'd known. Straitlaced, she'd have had a hissy fit at the idea of the two of them standing within spitting distance of a bed—especially when that bed was her own. "Was there something else?"

Juliana swallowed, looked away, visibly forced herself to meet his gaze again. "About the presents—the children would understand. They aren't used to a fuss being made over Christmas, anyway, and—"

Lincoln smiled and went to his mother's massive wardrobe, opened the door. Gestured for Juliana to come to his side.

Reluctantly, she did so.

He pointed to the top shelf. Games. Dolls. Books. A set of jacks. A fancy comb-and-brush set. Enough candy to rot the teeth of every child in the state of Montana, twice over.

Seeing it all, Juliana widened her eyes.

"There's plenty," he said. "My brother Micah lives a long way from here, in Colorado, so Ma never sees his boys. Wes never married, and as far as we know, he's never fathered a child. That leaves Gracie, and Ma's been bent on spoiling her from the first."

Juliana stepped back, watched as Lincoln closed the wardrobe doors again. "You don't approve?"

"Of what?"

She went pink again. Fetchingly so. "Your mother, buying so many gifts for Gracie."

Lincoln considered, shook his head. "No," he said. "I guess I don't. But it doesn't seem to be hurting her any—Gracie, I mean—and anyhow, my mother is a force to be reckoned with. Most of the time, it's easier to just let her have her way."

Juliana moved closer to the stove, though whether the objective was to get warm or put some distance between the two of them, Lincoln didn't know. What she said next sideswiped him.

"The Bureau of Indian Affairs is probably going to put me in jail."

Lincoln's breath went shallow. "Why?"

"I was supposed to send these children to Missoula for placement in another school," Juliana said. "Joseph and Theresa have a family, a home, people who want them. Daisy and Billy-Moses will either be swept under some rug or placed in an orphanage. I couldn't bear it."

Lincoln went to her then, took a gentle hold on her shoulders. Tried to ignore the physical repercussions of touching her. "I'll pay the train fare to send Joseph and Theresa home," he said. "But how do you know the bureau won't just drag them out again?"

Gratitude registered in her face, and a degree of relief. "They won't bother," she said with sad confidence. "It would take too long and cost too much."

"The two little ones—they don't have anyone?"

"Just me," Juliana said. "I shouldn't have gotten attached to them—I was warned about that when I first started teaching—but I couldn't help it."

A solution occurred to Lincoln—after all, he was a lawyer—but even in the face of Juliana's despair, talking about it would be premature. His right hand rose of its own accord from her shoulder to her cheek. She did not resist his caress.

"After Christmas," he said, very quietly, "we'll find a way to straighten this out. In the meantime, we've got two turkeys, a tree—" he indicated the wardrobe with a motion of his head "—and enough presents to do Saint Nicholas proud. For now, set the rest aside."

She gazed up at him. "You are a remarkable man, Lincoln Creed. A remarkable man with a remarkable daughter."

Embarrassed pleasure suffused Lincoln. "I think we'd better go and have supper."

Juliana smiled. "I think we'd better," she agreed.

SUPPER WAS A BOISTEROUS AFFAIR with so many people gathered around the table, their faces bathed in lantern light and shadow. And to Juliana's surprise— she forced herself to try some, in order to set a good example for the children—the bear meat turned out to be delicious.

Tom and Joseph did the dishes, while Gracie sat in a rocking chair nearby, feet dangling high above the floor, reading competently from *Oliver Twist*.

Juliana, banking the fire in the cookstove for the night, stole a glance at Tom and noted that he was listening with close and solemn interest.

Gracie finally read herself to sleep—Billy-Moses and Daisy had long since succumbed, and Lincoln had carried them to bed, one in each arm—and Tom seemed so letdown that Joseph took the book gently from the little girl's hand and picked up where she'd left off.

Juliana hoisted Gracie out of the chair and felt a warm ache in her heart when the child's head came to rest on her shoulder.

She met Lincoln in the corridor leading to the bedrooms. She thought he might take Gracie from her, but he stepped aside instead, his face softening, and watched in silence as she carried his daughter to her bed. A lamp glowed on the nightstand, and Theresa, a pillow propped behind her, was reading one of Gracie's many books.

Juliana set Gracie on her feet, helped her out of her dress and into her nightgown.

Gracie, half awake and half asleep, murmured something and closed her eyes as Juliana tucked her in, kissed her forehead, and then Theresa's.

She took the book from Theresa's hands with a smile, and extinguished the lamp, aware all the while of Lincoln standing in the doorway, watching.

He stepped back again, to let her go by, and smiled when she shivered in the draft and hugged herself.

"I want to show you something," he said.

Curious, she allowed him to lead her to the end of the hallway, where he opened a door, stepped inside and lit a lamp, causing soft light to spill out at Juliana's feet. She hesitated, then followed, and drew in a breath when she saw a porcelain bathtub with a boiler above it, exuding the heat and scent of a wood fire.

Juliana hadn't enjoyed such a luxury since she'd left her grandmother's mansion in Denver. There, she'd taken gaslights and abundant hot water for granted. Since then, she'd survived on sponge baths and the occasional furtive dunk in a washtub.

"I mean to put in a commode and a sink come spring," Lincoln said, sounding shy. "They say we'll have electricity in Stillwater Springs in a few years."

Juliana was nearly overcome. She put a hand to her heart and rested one shoulder against the door frame.

He moved past her, their bodies brushing in the narrow doorway.

Heat pulsed at Juliana's core.

Without another word, Lincoln Creed left her to turn the spigots, find a towel and fetch her nightgown and wrapper from the toasty bedroom, where Daisy and Billy-Moses were already deeply asleep.

The bath was a wonder. A gift. Juliana sank into it, closed her eyes and marveled. When the water finally cooled, she climbed out, dried herself off and donned her nightclothes. A bar of light shone under the door to the room she supposed was Lincoln's, and if it wouldn't have been so brazen, she would have knocked lightly at that door, opened it far enough to say a quiet "Thank you."

Instead, she made her way back to the kitchen, walking softly.

Joseph was still reading from *Oliver Twist,* seated at the table now, and Tom was still listening, smoking his pipe and gazing into space as though seeing the story unfold before his eyes.

Without making a sound, Juliana retreated, smiling to herself.

That night, she slept soundly.

THE SNOW HAD STOPPED BY DAWN, but it reached Lincoln's knees as he made his way toward the barn. Even the draft horses would have a hard time getting through the stuff, but the cattle had to be fed, and that meant hitching up the sled and loading it with hay.

Lincoln thought of Wes, hoped his brother had made it safely home to the Diamond Buckle Saloon. There would be no finding out for a while, since the roads would be impassable.

He thought about Juliana, and how pleased she'd been when he'd shown her the bathtub. His mother had insisted on installing the thing, saying she was tired of heating water on the stove and bathing in the kitchen, ever fearful that some man would wander in and catch her in "the altogether."

At the time, he'd thought it was plain foolish, a waste of good money, but then Beth—destined to die in just a few short months—had pointed out that she'd had a bathtub of her very own back in Boston, and she missed it.

Lincoln had ridden to town the same day and placed an order at Willand's Mercantile. Weeks later, when the modern marvel arrived by train, shipped all the way from Denver in a crate big enough to house a grand piano, half the town had come out to the ranch to see it unloaded and set up in the smallest bedroom.

Husbands pulled Lincoln aside to complain; they were being hectored, they said. Now the wife wanted one of those infernal contraptions all her own.

He'd sympathized, and proffered that a bathtub with a boiler was a small price to pay for a peaceful household. Hell, it was worth the look of delighted disbelief he'd seen on Juliana's face when she saw it.

Guilt struck him again like the punch of a fist as

he entered the barn, lit a lantern to see by so the work would go more quickly. He'd bought that bathtub for *Beth,* not Juliana.

The cow began to snuffle and snort, wanting to be milked.

Lincoln soothed her with a scratch between the ears and gave her hay instead. Once he'd fed all the horses and Wes's mule, he undertook the arduous task of hauling water from the well to fill the troughs.

By the time he'd finished that, milked and started back toward the house, bucket in hand, it was snowing again.

For a moment, Lincoln felt weary to the core of his spirit. Ranching was always hard work, always a risk, but in weather like this, with cattle on the range, it could be downright brutal.

Finding Juliana in the kitchen, and the coffee brewed, he felt better.

Tom was nowhere around, though, and that was unusual enough to worry Lincoln. He was about to ask if Juliana had seen him when Tom came out of his room just off the kitchen, tucking his flour-sack shirt into his pants.

"Too much reading," he said. "That Oliver feller has me worried."

Lincoln chuckled, poured himself some coffee. "What's for breakfast?" he asked. "Gruel?"

Tom looked puzzled, but Juliana smiled. "How about oatmeal?" she suggested brightly.

"No gruel?" Lincoln teased.

She laughed. "You haven't tasted my oatmeal."

The gruel, he soon discovered, would have been an improvement.

Joseph, turning up rumpled at the table, made a face when he saw it. "Is there any of that bear hash left?" he asked, his tone plaintive.

Only Tom accepted a second bowl of oatmeal.

When the three men left the house, they met Ben Gainer in the yard, and he looked worried. His freckles stood out against his pale face and his brownish-red hair stuck out in spikes under his hat. "Rose-of-Sharon is feelin' poorly this morning," he said.

"You'd better stay with her, then," Tom said quietly.

"I told her she ought to let you come and see if the baby's on its way, but she said—" Ben fell silent, blushed miserably. Turned his eyes to the snowy terrain and looked even grimmer than before.

All of them knew what Rose-of-Sharon Gainer had said. She didn't want an Indian tending her, no matter how "poorly" she might feel.

"It's all right, Ben," Tom told the boy. "Things get bad, you send Joseph out to the range to fetch me."

Glumly, stamping his feet to get the circulation going, Ben nodded, his breath making puffs of steam in the air, like their own. "With all this snow, I don't see how I could get to town to bring back the doctor."

Joseph had turned to Tom. "Don't I get to go with you? Out to the range?"

"Mike can do that. You'll stay here and help Art load the sled with hay."

There was a protest brewing in the boy's face, but it soon dissolved. He sighed and went on toward the barn.

They hauled the first load of hay out to the range half an hour later, and found the cattle in clusters, instinctively sharing their warmth and blocking the wind as best they could. The air they exhaled rose over them like smoke from a chimney.

The creek was slushy, but it flowed.

They went back to the barn for another load of feed, and then another. Tom scanned the surrounding plain for wolf or coyote tracks, and found none.

They headed back and met a panicked Joseph, all but stuck in snow reaching to his midthighs and waving both arms.

Lincoln, driving the team while Tom rode behind him on the sled, felt a sinking sensation in the pit of his stomach.

The boy shouted something, but Lincoln couldn't make out the words. It didn't matter. Something was wrong, that was all he needed to know.

He drove the draft horses harder, and Tom scrambled off the sled and crow-hopped his way through the snow toward the boy.

CHAPTER FIVE

LINCOLN HEARD THE SCREAMS as he left the horses with Joseph to be unhitched, led to their stalls, rubbed down and fed. He followed Tom toward the cabin out by the bunkhouse, moving as fast as he could.

Glancing once toward the main house, he saw Gracie and Theresa standing at the window, both their faces pale with worry.

The cabin was only about eight by eight feet, so it was impossible to overlook the straining form in the center of the bed. Juliana was seated nearby, holding Rose-of-Sharon Gainer's hand and speaking softly, and the sight of her calmed Lincoln a little.

Nothing was going to calm Ben, though.

He paced at the foot of the bed, frenzied, shoving both hands through his hair every few steps. He looked like a wild man, some hermit from the high timber, baffled by his new surroundings.

"You go on over to the big house," Tom told the young husband firmly. "You'll be of no help to us here."

Ben set his jaw, glanced at his weeping, sweating wife, and looked as though he might throw a punch. Finally, though, he bent over Rose-of-Sharon, kissed her forehead and did as he'd been told, putting on his coat, passing Lincoln without a word or a look and closing the cabin door smartly behind him.

Lincoln, unsure of whether to stay or follow right on Ben's heels, stood just inside the door, turning his gaze to the pitiful little Christmas tree with its strands of colored yarn and awkwardly cut paper ornaments. Two packages, wrapped in brown paper and tied with coarse twine, lay bravely beneath it.

"Breathe very slowly, Rose-of-Sharon," he heard Juliana say, her voice soft and even, but underlaid with a tone of worry.

Lincoln slowed his own breathing, since the idea seemed like a good one.

"You'll be all right," Tom told the girl.

Rose-of-Sharon, a pretty thing with glossy brown hair, was well beyond fussing over letting an Indian attend her. "Is—is the doctor coming?" she asked, between long, low moans and ragged breaths it hurt to hear.

Lincoln thought of the snow, so deep now that the draft horses had had all they could do to get through it, plodding to and fro as they hauled hay to the cattle.

"Yes," Tom lied, rolling up his sleeves and inclining his head slightly in Juliana's direction. "He's on his way for sure."

An unspoken signal must have gone from Tom to Juliana. She nodded and raised the bedclothes.

The sheets and Rose-of-Sharon's nightgown were crimson.

Lincoln turned his back, busied himself building up the fire in the little stove that served for both cooking and heating the cabin. Because the chinking between the logs of the structure was good and the ceiling was low, the room would stay warm.

Rose-of-Sharon shrieked, and the sound scraped down Lincoln's insides like a claw. For a few moments, it was Beth lying in that bed, not Ben Gainer's child-bride.

He wondered again if he ought to leave, get out from underfoot the way Ben had, but something held him there. He'd go if Tom told him to; otherwise, he'd remain. Do what he could, which was probably precious little.

"Put some water on to heat," Tom said from the fraught void behind Lincoln. "Then go to the house for my medicine bag."

Lincoln nodded—no words would come out—found a kettle, went outside to pack it full of snow, since the water bucket was empty, and set it on the stove. He carried the bucket to the well next, worked to fill it, carried it back inside. Next, he made his way to the house, frustrated by the slow going, found all the kids and Ben gathered at the kitchen table, staring down at their hands.

For some reason, the sight left him stricken, unable to move for a few moments. When he managed to break the spell, he headed for Tom's room, really more of a lean-to, and grabbed the familiar buckskin pouch from its place under the narrow bed. Joseph's pallet, fashioned of folded quilts and blankets, lay crumpled against the inside wall.

Leaving the room, he nearly collided with Ben.

"Rose-of-Sharon?" Ben asked, his voice hoarse, his eyes hollow with quiet frenzy.

"Too soon to know," Lincoln said, and sidestepped past him.

"I'm going for the doctor," Ben said, following him to the back door.

Lincoln turned. "No," he said. "You'd never make it that far, and even if you did, old Doc Chaney wouldn't budge in this weather."

"My wife could die!"

Lincoln looked past him, his gaze connecting with Gracie's. She was white with terror, no doubt remembering Beth's passing, and he longed to go to her, assure her everything would be all right.

The problem was, it might not.

Lincoln laid a hand on Ben's shoulder. "Yes," he said gravely, because nothing but the stark truth would have done. "She could die. But there's no point in your freezing to death somewhere between here and Stillwater Springs, whether she does or not. Besides, if Rose-of-Sharon and the baby survive this, they'll need you."

Ben considered that, swallowed hard and gave a grudging nod.

Lincoln turned and bolted out the door, wading hard for the cabin, the long strap of Tom's medicine pouch pressing heavy into his shoulder.

JULIANA HAD NEVER, in the whole of her life, been so frightened. At the same time, she was oddly calm, as though another self had risen within her, pushed the schoolmarm aside and taken over.

The scene was nightmarish, with all that blood, and poor Rose-of-Sharon shrieking as though she were being torn apart from the inside.

When Lincoln returned with the bag Tom had sent him for, Tom took the bag, plundered it, solemn-faced, then brought out a smaller pouch with strange markings burned into it. His own hands covered in blood, he extended the pouch to Juliana and instructed her to put a pinch of the seeds under Rose-of-Sharon's tongue.

Trembling, she obeyed.

"Don't swallow," Tom told the girl. "It'll ease the pain some, in a few minutes, and then we'll see about getting that baby born."

"Am I going to die?" Rose-of-Sharon pleaded, her eyes ricocheting between Juliana and Tom. She looked so small and so young—no more than fifteen or thereabouts. It was only too common for girls of her station to marry at an early age. "Is my baby going to die?"

Tom spoke in the Indian way, some of his syllables flat. "No," he said, with such certainty that Juliana glanced up at him. She saw the determination in his face, at once placid and stalwart. "But this could take a while. You'll have to be as brave as you can."

Rose-of-Sharon bit down hard on her lower lip, nodded, her skin glistening with perspiration, her eyes catching Juliana's, begging. *Hold on tight,* they seemed to say. *Don't let me go.*

"I'm here," Juliana said, in the same tone she'd used when one of the children was sick or frightened in the night. She squeezed Rose-of-Sharon's small hand. "I'm right here, Rose-of-Sharon, and I'm not going anywhere."

The words, spoken so quietly, were at complete odds with her every instinct. Given her druthers, Juliana would have jumped up and run out into the snow, turning in blind, frantic circles, gasping at air and screaming until her throat was raw.

What was calming her?

Surely, it was necessity, at least in part. Tom's quiet confidence helped, too. In the main, though, it was knowing Lincoln was there, feeling his presence through the skin of her back, as surely as she felt the heat from the stove.

He seemed as strong and immovable as any of the mountains rising skyward in the distance.

Tom asked for a basin, once the water had been heated, and instructed Lincoln to prepare more. Juliana bathed Rose-of-Sharon, helped her into her spare nightgown, while Tom removed the soiled sheets, replacing them with a blanket.

And Rose-of-Sharon's travails continued.

Between keening screeches of pain, her body straining mightily, she rested, eyes closed, pale lips moving constantly in wordless prayer or protest.

The light shifted, dimmed, became shadow-laced.

Lincoln lit lanterns. Left the cabin again to make sure the children were all right and the barn chores got done.

Juliana, as preoccupied with tending to Rose-of-Sharon as she was, barely breathed until he came back.

It was well into the night when the crisis finally came; too exhausted to scream, Rose-of-Sharon convulsed instead, her eyes rolling back into her head, her back curved high off the mattress in an impossible arch.

The baby slipped from her then, a tiny, bluish creature, soundless and still.

Tom caught the little form in his cupped hands.

Was the child dead? Juliana waited to know, felt Lincoln waiting, too.

And then Tom smiled, grabbed up one of the discarded blankets and wrapped the baby in a clean corner of the cloth. "Welcome, little man," he said. "Welcome."

The infant boy squalled, such a small sound. So full of life and power.

Tears slipped down Juliana's cheeks.

Rose-of-Sharon, spent as she was, seemed lit from within, like a Madonna. She reached out for the baby, and Tom laid him gently in her arms.

"Get Ben," Rose-of-Sharon murmured. "Please get my Ben."

Juliana heard the door open as Lincoln rushed to do the girl's bidding, felt a rush of cold air, and shielded mother and child from the draft as best she could. Only minutes later, Lincoln returned with the new father.

Ben approached the bed slowly, a man enthralled, hardly daring to believe his own eyes.

"Come see," Rose-of-Sharon said, the last shreds of her strength going into her wobbly smile. "Come and see your son, Ben Gainer."

The room seemed to tilt all of the sudden, and the world went dark. Juliana was barely aware of being lifted out of her chair next to the bed, bundled tightly into her cloak, lifted into strong arms.

Lincoln's arms.

She felt his coat enfold her, too, the way it had in the wagon, on the way out from town. "I've got to stay," she managed to say, blinking against the blinding fatigue that had risen up around her between one moment and the next. "They'll need—"

"Hush," Lincoln said.

Even in the bitter cold, she felt only the warmth of him as he carried her through the snow and into the main house. A single lantern burned in the middle of the kitchen table, but the room was empty. What time was it?

"The children...?"

"Theresa put them to bed hours ago," Lincoln said, making no move to set her on her feet. Instead, he took her through the house, along the corridor, into a room several doors down from hers.

He laid her on the bed, covered her quickly with a quilt, tucked it in tightly around her.

The fatigue reached deep into her mind, into her very marrow. She tried to get a handhold on consciousness, but the strange darkness kept swallowing her down again.

She was aware of Lincoln moving about, now removing her shoes, now opening a bureau drawer.

"Lincoln?" she asked, scrambling back up the monster's throat only to be swallowed once more.

She knew when he left the room, knew when he came back, after what seemed like a long time, but could not have said which of her senses had alerted her to the leaving and the returning. She could not seem to fix on anything; she wasn't asleep, and yet she wasn't fully awake, either.

Lincoln was lifting her again, carrying her again, still cocooned in the quilt. When had she last felt so safe, so cared-for? Surely not since early childhood, when she'd had two loving parents and a brother.

"Where...?"

"Shh," he said.

The sound of running water and the misty caress of steam roused her a little. Lincoln stood her on her feet, supporting her with one arm, peeling away her clothes with the other hand.

He was *undressing* her.

But suddenly it seemed the most normal thing in the world for him to be doing. There was no fear in her, no resistance.

He helped her into the bathtub, and the warmth of the water, the soothing, blessed heat, encompassed her. Of course, she thought, drifting. She'd been soaked in poor Rose-of-Sharon's blood.

Her dress had surely been ruined, and she could not spare it.

Helpless tears welled in her eyes.

"My dress," she lamented in a despairing whisper. In that moment, she was grieving over so much more than the best of her three calico gowns. Her mother, her father. Grandmama and Clay. She had lost them all, and she could bear no more of such losing.

"There are other dresses," Lincoln told her, lifting her again, drying off her bare skin with soft swipes of a rough towel, pulling a nightgown on over her head. It felt soft and worn, and the scent—rosewater and talcum powder— was not her own.

Supporting her with one arm around her waist—*why was* she so weak?—he guided her out into the corridor again. Past the door to the room she'd been sharing with Billy-Moses and Daisy.

"The children," she protested.

"Theresa's with them," he told her.

He took her back to his room—a slight, wicked thrill

flickered through her at the realization—and put her into his bed.

She began to weep, with weariness and with relief, because, out in the little cabin, sorrow had drawn so near and then passed on. For now.

Lincoln sat down on the edge of the mattress. Kicked off his boots. In the next moment, he was under the covers with her, fully clothed, holding her close. Just then, Juliana knew only two things: she'd be ruined for sure, and she'd die if he let her go.

He did not let her go—several times during the night, she awakened, gradually growing more coherent, and felt his arms around her, felt his chest warm beneath her cheek.

When she opened her eyes the next time, all weariness gone, she found herself looking straight into Lincoln's face. By the thinning darkness, she knew dawn would be breaking soon.

"Since we just spent the night in the same bed," Lincoln said reasonably, as though they'd been discussing the subject for hours and now he was putting his foot down, "I think we'd better get married."

Juliana stared at him, her eyes widening until they hurt. "Married?"

He merely smiled.

She swallowed. "But—surely—"

The door creaked open. "Papa?" Gracie's voice chimed. "Theresa can't find Miss Mitchell and—"

Juliana wanted to pull the covers up over her head, hide, but it was too late. Gracie, fleet as a fairy, was beside the bed now.

"Oh," she said, in a tone of merry innocence, "*there* you are!"

"Gracie—" Lincoln began.

But she cut him off by shouting, "Theresa! I found Miss Mitchell! She's right here in Papa's bed!"

Juliana groaned.

Lincoln laughed. "Miss Mitchell has something to tell you, Gracie," he said.

"What?" Gracie asked curiously.

Juliana drew a very deep breath, let it out slowly. "Your father and I are getting married," she said.

"I'm going to have a mama?" Gracie enthused. "That's even better than a *dictionary!*"

"You go on back to bed now," Lincoln told his daughter.

She obeyed with surprising alacrity, fairly dancing through the shadows toward the door.

"That," Juliana told Lincoln, in a righteous whisper, "was a *very* underhanded thing to do."

He sat up, clothes rumpled, swung his legs over the side of the bed, then leaned to pull his boots back on. He was humming under his breath, a sound like muted laughter, or creek water burbling along under a spring sky.

"Soon as the snow melts off a little," he said, as though she hadn't spoken at all, "I'll send for somebody to marry us. Probably be the justice of the peace, since the circuit preacher only comes through when the spirit moves him."

She could have protested, but for some reason, she didn't.

Lincoln added wood to the hearth fire and got it

crackling again. "You might as well go back to sleep," he said. "Rest up a little."

Juliana lay there, the covers pulled up to her chin, and reviewed what had just happened. She'd accepted a proposal of marriage—of sorts. It was as unlike what she'd imagined, both as a girl and as a grown woman, as it could possibly have been.

It was all wrong.

It was wildly *un*romantic.

Why, then, did she feel this peculiar, taut-string excitement, this desire to sing?

Sleeping proved impossible. The children were up; she could hear their voices and footsteps. Besides, she was rested.

She must get dressed, do something with her hair, put on her cloak and go out to the cabin to look in on Rose-of-Sharon and the baby. Suppose the fire had gone out and they took a chill?

Rising, she realized that yesterday's calico, no doubt beyond salvaging anyhow, had disappeared. A pretty blue woolen frock with black piping lay across the foot of the bed—Lincoln's doing, she reflected with a blush. A garment his wife must have owned, since it did not look matronly enough to belong to his mother, as the oversize nightgown probably did.

For a moment, she considered her remaining dresses, both frayed at the seams and oft-mended, both worn threadbare. Both inadequate for winter weather.

She put on the lovely blue woolen, buttoned it up the front. Except at the bosom, where it was a little too tight, it fit remarkably well.

The children, she soon discovered, had assembled in

the kitchen. Seated around the table, they all stared at her as though she'd grown horns during the night. Lincoln was making breakfast—eggs and hotcakes—and Tom was just stepping through the back door, stomping snow off his boots.

Juliana forgot her embarrassment. "Rose-of-Sharon?" she asked, her breath catching. "How is she? How is the baby?"

Tom's smile flashed, bright as sunshine on snow. "She's just fine, and so is the little man," he said. "I don't reckon she'd mind some female company, though."

Juliana nodded, looking back at the children. "No lessons today," she said. With the exception of Gracie, they looked delighted. "And I expect you all to behave yourselves."

They all nodded solemnly, from Joseph right on down to Billy-Moses and Daisy. Their eyes were huge, though whether that was due to the blue dress or the fact that she'd spent the night in Lincoln Creed's bedroom and everyone in the household seemed to know it, she could not begin to say.

She looked about for her cloak, realized that it had probably been hopelessly stained, like her dress.

"Take my coat," Lincoln said.

Juliana hesitated, then lifted the long and surprisingly heavy black coat from its peg and put it on, nearly enveloped by it. With one hand, she held up the hem, so she wouldn't trip or drag the cloth on the ground.

She stepped outside into the first timorous light of day, and immediately noticed that the eaves were dripping. The snow was slushy beneath her feet.

Would Lincoln ride to town and fetch back the

justice of the peace, now that the weather was changing? A quivery, delicious dread overtook her as she hurried toward the Gainers' cabin. Light glowed in the single window, and smoke curled from the stovepipe chimney.

She *could* refuse to marry Lincoln, of course—even though she'd slept in his room, in his *bed,* nothing untoward had taken place. Why, he hadn't even kissed her.

She blushed furiously and walked faster, remembering the bath, trying to outdistance the recollection. He'd undressed her, seen her naked flesh, *washed* her. At the time, she had been too dazed by exhaustion and the delivery of Rose-of-Sharon's baby to protest. The experience hadn't seemed—well—*real.*

Now, however, she felt the slickness of the soap, the heat of the water, the tender touch of Lincoln's hand, just as if it were all happening right then. She quickened her steps again, but the sensations kept up with her.

It was a relief when Ben Gainer opened the cabin door to greet her, smiling from ear to ear.

"Rose-of-Sharon's been asking for you," he said.

Juliana hurried inside so the door could be closed against the soggy chill of the morning. A fire crackled in the stove, and the cabin was cozy, scented with fresh coffee and just-baked biscuits. Even the pitiful little Christmas tree had taken on a certain scruffy splendor. Rose-of-Sharon sat up in bed, pillows plumped behind her back, nursing her baby behind a draped blanket.

The girl's face shone with a light all her own, and Juliana felt a swift pang of pure envy.

Ben took Lincoln's coat from Juliana's shoulders and

told her to help herself to coffee and biscuits, explaining that Tom had done the baking.

"I'll be back as soon as we've fed those cattle," he added, putting on his own coat and hat and leaving the cabin.

Ravenous, Juliana poured coffee into a mug, took a steaming biscuit from the covered pan on top of the stove. She sat beside the bed, in last night's chair, while she ate.

When she'd finished nursing the baby, Rose-of-Sharon righted her nightgown and lowered the quilt to show Juliana her son. He was wrapped in a pretty crocheted blanket.

He seemed impossibly small, frighteningly delicate. His skin was very nearly translucent.

"Do you want to hold him?" Rose-of-Sharon asked when Juliana had finished the biscuit and brushed fallen crumbs from the skirt of the blue dress.

The only thing greater than Juliana's trepidation was her desire to take that baby into her arms. Carefully, she did so, her heart beating a little faster.

"My mama sent that blanket," Rose-of-Sharon said. "All the way from Cheyenne. Ben says he'll take me and the baby home to Wyoming for a visit come spring so we can show him off to the family."

The baby gave an infinitesimal hiccup. He weighed no more than a feather. "Have you given him a name?"

Rose-of-Sharon smiled. "I wanted to call him Benjamin, for his daddy, but Ben'll have none of it. Never liked the name much. So we picked one out of the Good Book—Joshua."

"Joshua," Juliana repeated softly. She pictured the

walls of Jericho tumbling down. "That's a fine, strong name."

"Joshua Thomas Gainer," Rose-of-Sharon said.

Juliana looked up.

"Yes," Rose-of-Sharon told her. "For Tom Dancing-star. Did Ben tell you I didn't want him looking after me, because it ain't proper for an Indian to tend a white woman?"

Juliana didn't speak. She did shake her head, though. Ben hadn't told her, and she was glad.

"If Joshua had been a girl," Rose-of-Sharon went on, more softly now, holding out her arms for the baby again, "I'd have chosen your name." She wrinkled her brow curiously, and Juliana, surrendering Joshua with some reluctance, thought of Angelique, wondered if she and Blue Johnston had gotten married. "What *is* your name, anyhow?"

She laughed. "Juliana."

"That's right pretty."

"Thank you. So is Rose-of-Sharon."

Rose-of-Sharon blushed a little. "I'm obliged to you," she said. "The hardest thing about having a baby was being so far from Mama—or at least that's what I thought until it started hurting."

Juliana smiled, tucked the blankets in more snugly around both Rose-of-Sharon and the baby. "You'll forget the pain with time," she said.

"I ain't yet," Rose-of-Sharon said devoutly, and with a little shudder for emphasis. She yawned, and her eyelids drooped a little. "I'm plum worn down to a nubbin," she added.

"Get some rest," Juliana urged gently.

"What if I roll over on Joshua while I'm sleeping?" Rose-of-Sharon fretted. "He's such a little thing."

"I'll make sure you don't," Juliana promised. There was no cradle, but she spotted a small chest of drawers in a corner of the cabin. Removing one drawer, she lined it with a folded quilt, set it next to the bed where Rose-of-Sharon could see and reach, and carefully placed the baby inside.

With no more quilts or blankets on hand, Juliana used several of Ben's heavy flannel shirts to cover little Joshua.

Satisfied that her baby was safe, Rose-of-Sharon slept.

Juliana sat quietly through the morning, her mood introspective.

At half past one that afternoon, the men returned, chilled and red-faced from the brisk wind, and Ben took over the care of his wife and son.

Juliana wore Lincoln's coat, and as they stood in front of the cabin door, he carefully did up the buttons, his gloved hands, smelling of hay, lingering on the collar, close against her face.

"Tom will ride to town and ask after the justice of the peace," he said, "if you're agreeable to that."

Juliana gazed up at him. She had not had time to fall in love with this man—he certainly hadn't swept her off her feet, not in the romantic sense, anyway—but she respected him. She *liked* him.

Was that enough?

It seemed that someone else spoke up in her place. "I'm agreeable," she said.

His smile was so sudden, so dazzling, that it nearly

knocked her back on her heels. "Good," he said huskily. "That's good."

A cloud crossed an inner sun. "This—this dress—"

"Beth's mother sent crates full of them, every so often," he told her, his eyes gentle, perceptive. "She never got around to wearing it."

Juliana absorbed that, nodded.

Lincoln took her hand. "Let's get that Christmas tree set up," he said with a laugh, "before Gracie pesters me into an early grave."

Minutes later, while Juliana and the children took boxes of delicate ornaments from the shelves of a small storage room off the parlor, Lincoln went to the woodshed to get the tree, Joseph right on his heels.

It was so big that it took both of them to wrestle it through the front door, its branches exuding the piney scent Juliana had always associated with Christmas.

Billy-Moses and Daisy stared at the tree in wonder, huddled so close together that their shoulders touched, and holding hands. Juliana remembered Mr. Philbert, and knew in a flash of certainty that he would come for them one day soon.

Tears filled her eyes.

She would be Mrs. Lincoln Creed by then, most likely, and with a husband to take her part, it wasn't likely she'd be arrested. Still, when Mr. Philbert took Daisy and Billy-Moses away, it would be as if he'd torn out her heart and dragged it, bruised and bouncing, down the road behind his departing buggy.

"Juliana?"

She looked up, surprised to see Lincoln standing directly in front of her.

He cupped her elbows in the palms of his hands, kissed her forehead. "Let them have Christmas," he said.

Either he was extremely perceptive, or he'd seen the worry in her face.

She nodded. Dashed at her eyes with the back of one hand.

It took all afternoon to festoon that Christmas tree, and what a magnificent sight it was, bedecked in ribbon garlands, delicate blown-glass ornaments of all shapes and colors, draped with shimmering strands of tinsel. Even Juliana, who had grown up in a Denver mansion with an even grander tree erected in her grandmother's library every December, was awestruck.

Tom appeared at dusk, while Lincoln was doing the chores in the barn. He carried a large white package under one arm.

Juliana, peeling potatoes and trying to think what else to prepare for supper, couldn't help looking past him to see if he'd brought the justice of the peace along.

She was both relieved and disappointed to see that he was alone.

He smiled, as though he'd read her thoughts again, and set the parcel on the counter. "Chickens," he said. "All cut up and ready to fry."

Mildly embarrassed, Juliana reported that she'd looked in on Rose-of-Sharon and little Joshua earlier, and they were doing well.

Moving to the sink to wash his hands, Tom nodded. Although, since his back was turned to her, and

Juliana couldn't be sure, she thought he was smiling to himself.

He brought lard and a big skillet from the pantry, set the pan to warming on the stove, then rolled the chicken parts in a bowl of flour. They worked in companionable silence, Juliana finishing up the potatoes and putting them on to boil.

The savory sizzle of frying chicken soon brought the children in from the front room, where they'd been admiring the Christmas tree.

"We'll need an extra place set at the table," Tom commented mildly, after Theresa had counted out plates and silverware for everyone. His dark eyes twinkled as Juliana turned to him. "For the circuit preacher. He's out in the barn with Lincoln."

Juliana nearly gasped aloud, and before she could think of a response, the back door opened and Lincoln came in, closely followed by a very large white-haired man in austere black clothes and a clerical collar.

The circuit preacher's eyes were a pale, merry blue, in startling contrast to his sober garments, and before Lincoln could make an introduction, he lumbered over to Juliana like a great, good-natured bear, one hand stuck out in greeting.

"This must be the bride!" he boomed.

Juliana's face flamed. She fidgeted, unable to meet Lincoln's gaze, and shook the reverend's hand.

Gracie piped up. "This morning when I went into Papa's room—"

Theresa put one palm over the child's mouth just in time.

The reverend turned to look at Tom, drawing in an appreciative breath. "Is that fried chicken I smell?"

Tom laughed, nodded.

"And me just in time for supper!" the reverend roared.

Just then, Daisy crept up beside the big man and tugged at the sleeve of his coat. "Are you Saint Nicholas?" she asked, almost breathless with her own daring.

The reverend bellowed out a great guffaw at that. Daisy started, but didn't retreat.

"Why, bless your heart, child," the preacher thundered, "nobody's ever mistaken this ole Bible-pounder for a saint!"

"That's Reverend Dettly, silly goose," Gracie informed Daisy solicitously. "Saint Nicholas always wears red."

"You'll spend the night, won't you, Reverend?" Lincoln asked, taking the preacher's coat. "It's dark out there, and mighty cold, even with the thaw."

"I reckon I'll burrow into a hay pile out in your barn, all right," Reverend Dettly said. "A belly full of ole Tom's chicken ought to keep me plenty warm."

"Surely we can offer you a bed," Juliana said shyly.

Reverend Dettly smiled down at her. "I won't be putting anybody out of their beds," he said. "If a stable was good enough for our Lord, it's sure as all get-out good enough for me."

CHAPTER SIX

Tom took plates out to the cabin for Ben and Rose-of-Sharon as soon as supper was ready. When he returned, everyone was already seated around the table, Reverend Dettly waiting patiently to offer up the blessing.

Juliana sat at Lincoln's right side, stomach jittering with fearful anticipation and hunger. Soon, she would be his *wife*. Mrs. Lincoln Creed. Would he expect her to share his bed that night, or would he give her time to get used to being married?

Did she *want* time to get used to it?

The reverend cleared his throat once Tom had joined them, held out his great pawlike hands and closed his eyes to deliver the longest and most exuberant blessing Juliana had ever heard. Behind closed eyelids, her head dutifully bowed, she imagined the gravy congealing, the mountainous piles of fried chicken going cold, and still the preacher went on, thanking God for everything he could think of, from seeds germinating in the earth under their blanket of snow, to the cattle on a thousand hills. When someone's stomach rumbled loudly and at length, Dettly laughed and shouted a joyful "Amen!"

"Thank God," Lincoln agreed.

Juliana elbowed him.

During that meal, it seemed there were two

Julianas—one seated next to Lincoln at the table, laughing and talking and enjoying the savory food, and one standing back a ways at the edge of the lantern light, wringing her hands and fretting.

"So," the reverend said, turning to Juliana when he'd eaten his third and apparently final helping of everything, "I'm told there's to be a wedding. I've known Lincoln here since he couldn't see over the top of a water trough, but I don't believe I've ever made the bride's acquaintance."

Juliana felt her cheeks warm, and it took some doing to meet that direct blue gaze, kindly but penetrating, too, head-on. She told him her name, though Tom had probably done that long since, and that she'd been the teacher at the Indian School until it closed down.

"You look good and sturdy," the preacher observed, as though she were a calf he might buy at a stock sale.

Juliana wasn't offended, but she *was* amused. "I have good teeth, too," she said with a twinkle.

Reverend Dettly laughed, but his eyes took on an expression of solemnity as he continued to regard her. "You're amenable to this, Miss Mitchell? Getting married is a serious thing, with eternal consequences. Mustn't be too hasty about it."

Was having no other viable choice the same as being amenable? Juliana didn't know. Her heart seemed to be getting bigger and bigger, sure to burst at any time, and it all but cut off the breath she needed to answer.

"I'm willing to marry Mr. Creed," she said. Even if she didn't get arrested, Mr. Philbert would probably see that she never taught in any school again. If she went home to Denver, it would be on Clay's terms, and she would essentially be a prisoner. She imagined herself growing more and more eccentric as the years passed, until she finally ended up wild-eyed and confined to the attic.

The thought made her shudder.

The children were unusually quiet. Juliana couldn't hear the big wall clock ticking, though she knew it was because she'd climbed up onto a stool and wound it herself earlier with a brass key.

"Very well," the reverend said, evidently satisfied, "let's get on with it, then." In remote areas like Stillwater Springs, Montana, where loneliness and hard work were the order of the day, he probably performed the marriage ceremony for all sorts of unromantic reasons.

Juliana cast a look up and down the table. "As soon as we've washed the dishes—"

"Hang the dishes," Lincoln said, taking her by the hand and pulling her to her feet. "Let's get this thing *done*." With that, he all but dragged her into the front room, the children and Tom following single file like goslings, Reverend Dettly bringing up the rear.

Lincoln stood with his back to the Christmas tree, Juliana at his side. Suddenly, it seemed to her that the whole scene was taking place under water, or inside one of those pretty crystal globes that produced snow flurries when they were shaken. Dettly pulled a small, oft-used prayer book from the pocket of his suit coat, cleared his throat ponderously.

Tom and Joseph were appointed as witnesses; Gracie insisted on being one, too.

The ceremony was amazingly brief; Juliana heard it all through a dull pounding in her ears, responded whenever Lincoln squeezed her hand. The reverend had to repeat himself a lot.

There were no rings and no flowers.

The dress Juliana wore belonged to someone else, and was too tight in the bodice.

For all that, she felt cautiously hopeful, if dazed, and perhaps even happy.

Reverend Dettly pronounced them man and wife, and that, Juliana thought, was that. Until Lincoln turned her to face him, cupped his hands on either side of her face and kissed her so soundly that she had to grasp at his shirt to keep herself from floating away.

When that kiss was over, Juliana stared up into her husband's face, confounded by all he'd made her feel. Fiery sparks leaped within her, and there was this odd sense of *expansion,* embarrassingly physical but going well beyond that into realms of mind and spirit she had never previously comprehended, let alone explored.

The earth shifted beneath her feet, heaven trembled above her.

She was different.

Everything was different.

Lincoln frowned slightly, looking puzzled and a little concerned. "Are you all right?" he asked.

She nodded. Shook her head. Sagged a little, as though she might swoon—she who had *never* swooned until last night, after helping with a difficult birth— causing Lincoln to slip an arm around her.

"Juliana?"

"I'm—we're—married," she said stupidly.

Lincoln's concern softened into a smile. "Yes," he said.

Gracie tugged at the skirt of Juliana's dress. "May I call you Mama now, please?" she asked.

Juliana's heart turned over; she glanced at Lincoln, but saw no urging, one way or the other, in his face. They were strangers to each other, she and Lincoln, and the decision to marry had been made out of expediency on Lincoln's part and desperation on her own. Suppose, in a month or a year, they found they could not tolerate each other? Gracie, thinking of Juliana as a mother, would be crushed.

Looking down into those hopeful eyes, though, Juliana knew she couldn't refuse. "Yes, darling," she said softly. "If you want to call me Mama, you may. But you had another mother—wasn't she 'Mama'?"

"Does a person only get one mama?" Gracie asked, looking worried.

Juliana was at a complete loss. She and Gracie both turned to Lincoln for an answer. He looked flummoxed.

Gracie took charge. "My first mama died," she said. "I loved her—she was pretty and she smelled nice—but she's gone. I won't see her again until I get to heaven, and that might be a long, long time from now. So I need another mama to get me through till then."

Juliana's eyes stung, but she smiled. She couldn't help it; Gracie had her thoroughly bewitched. "All right, then," she said, praying she would never have to let this trusting child down. "It's a bargain. I'll be the best mama I can."

Gracie wasn't finished. Placing her hands on her hips, she said, "Theresa told me that she and Joseph are going home to North Dakota as soon as they can raise the train fare. Couldn't Billy-Moses and Daisy stay here with us and be Creeds, too?"

Juliana closed her eyes.

"Go and help with the washing up," Lincoln told his daughter mildly.

"But you didn't *answer* me, Papa."

"Go."

She left, the reverend in tow, and Juliana and Lincoln were alone, as a married couple, for the first time. The tree sparkled behind Lincoln; a strand of tinsel caught in his hair. Without thinking, Juliana reached up to remove that thin silvery strip, draped it on the closest branch. Her touch was tender.

She'd done a fairly good job of setting aside her fears for the youngest of her charges, but now Gracie's question echoed in her heart like the peal of distant church bells. *Couldn't Billy-Moses and Daisy stay here with us and be Creeds, too?*

"What happens now?" she asked, unable to hold the words back any longer.

Lincoln put his arms around her waist loosely and drew her closer. Ducked his head to kiss the tip of her nose. "Now," he said throatily, "we take things slowly. I want you in my bed, Juliana Creed, I won't deny it. But I won't ask you for anything you're not ready to give—you have my word on that."

Juliana Creed. That was who she was now. It seemed remarkable, as though she'd lived all her life as one person and then suddenly turned into another. As she looked up at Lincoln, she wondered if what she felt—the crazy tangle of longing and sweet sorrow and myriad other things too new to be named—might be love.

Surely that was impossible. She had only known Lincoln for a few days—how could she have learned to love him in such a short period of time?

"I'm—I'm not sure when I'll be ready, Lincoln," she confessed. "I've never— I mean, John and I didn't— wouldn't have—"

He ran a hand lightly down the length of her braid, gave it a gentle tug. "We'll take our time, Juliana," he reiterated. A sparkle lit his brown eyes. "Not too *much* time, mind you."

A lovely shiver went through her, but then she remembered tales she'd heard other women relate, concerning intimate things that happened between a man and a woman, and frowned.

"What?" Lincoln asked. How he favored that one-word question. He was not one for long speeches, that was for sure.

Juliana flushed with tender misery. "Will it hurt?"

Gently, he ran the backs of his fingers along her cheek. "Maybe a little, the first time or two. But I'll be careful, Juliana. That's a promise."

She believed him. She might not know Lincoln Creed very well, but there *were* things she was sure of where he was concerned. Many men would have packed Gracie off to live with relatives after her mother died—Juliana's own father, for instance—or shipped her away to some distant boarding school, but he'd kept her at home. He clearly loved his daughter, but she wasn't spoiled. He'd brought a strange woman and four Indian children into his home, just because they'd needed someplace to go. He'd stood by, ready to do whatever he could to help, while a young wife gave birth to her first child amid screams and blood, and every morning, without fail, no matter how bitterly cold the weather, he rose before dawn and made sure the range cattle didn't go hungry.

Rising on tiptoe, she kissed his cheek, felt the stubble of a beard against her lips. "I'd better put Daisy and Billy-Moses to bed," she said. "Would you mind if I gave them a bath first?"

Lincoln smiled, touched her lower lip with the tip of one finger. "This is your house, too, Mrs. Creed. You don't have to ask permission to use the bathtub or anything else I own."

A niggle of worry snaked along the bottom of Juliana's stomach. "Speaking of Mrs. Creed," she said, after working up her courage, "what will your mother say when she finds out you've taken a wife?"

"I don't really care," Lincoln replied easily. "My guess is she'll be a little testy for a while, thinking I ought to have consulted her first, and then she'll get to know you better and come to like you. Anyhow, she won't be back from Phoenix for months—she hates the cold weather, and every year she threatens to stay there for good, since there's no 'culture' in Stillwater Springs, and she dreads being stuck out here on the ranch for weeks at a time. I think the only reason she comes back at all is because she's afraid Gracie will grow up to cuss, chew tobacco and wear pants if she's left with Tom and me for too long at a stretch."

Juliana smiled at the image of Gracie acting like a man. One thing was for certain; Gracie Creed would never be ordinary. "*I* think you and Tom have done a fine job making a home for that little girl."

He grinned, gave her braid one more tug. "I'll go

light a fire in the boiler and make sure there's water for a bath," he said. With that, he turned and walked away.

Juliana watched him until he'd vanished into the corridor on the other side of the front room, then took herself to the kitchen.

Tom and the reverend were doing up the dishes while Joseph read aloud from *Oliver Twist*. Theresa was wiping the table with a damp cloth while Gracie sat on the floor near the stove, entertaining Daisy and Billy-Moses with the alphabet blocks.

"That's your name," she said, lining up the blocks to spell *Daisy*.

Daisy stared at the letters in uncomprehending wonder. She was only three, after all. Gracie, with her bright hair and agile mind, must have seemed like a living oracle to her.

"Make *Bill*," Billy-Moses urged.

"It's time for your bath," Juliana interceded.

Daisy, who loved baths, was on her feet in a moment. Billy-Moses's small face took on an obstinate expression.

"I don't *want* a bath," he said, folding his arms.

Reverend Dettly turned from the sink, his big hands dripping with suds, smiling. It struck Juliana that his life was probably a very solitary one when he wasn't preaching, but traveling from place to place and sleeping in people's barns. No doubt he enjoyed evenings like this one, being around children and eating a home-cooked meal.

"This is not a question of what you want, Billy-Moses," Juliana said firmly. "You *are* going to have a bath, and then you are going to bed. Period."

"Are you going to sleep in Papa's room again tonight?" Gracie asked innocently. This time, Theresa hadn't been close enough to cover her mouth.

Juliana's face flamed, and she couldn't have looked at Reverend Dettly to save her very life. "Yes," she said, because there was nothing else *to* say.

Lincoln had to pump and carry water to fill the boiler over the bathtub, and then it had to heat. When it was finally ready, Juliana bathed Daisy first with Theresa's help, put her to bed and went in search of Billy-Moses.

By that time, Reverend Dettly had retired to the barn, and Tom and Joseph to their shared room off the kitchen. Only Lincoln was there, seated at the table, reading a newspaper.

"Have you seen...?" she began.

"He's hiding in the pantry behind the flour bin," Lincoln said, taking in his harried bride. The front of the marvelous blue dress was soaked from Daisy's happy splashing in the tub, and her hair was popping out of the braid like a frayed rope sprouting bristles.

"Oh, for heaven's sake," Juliana answered, starting in that direction. Normally, she was not easily exasperated, but the day had been a long and eventful one, and it wasn't over.

Lincoln leaned in his chair, caught hold of her hand and stopped her. Rising, he said, "I'll do it. Brew yourself up a cup of tea. Ma likes the stuff, and there's a tin of it around here somewhere."

Juliana sank into a chair.

"Bill," Lincoln said, approaching the pantry door.

"Quit fooling around, now. It's time to scrub you down a layer."

Billy-Moses appeared in the pantry doorway, still looking petulant. "*Joseph* didn't have to take a bath," he protested.

"Reckon he'll get around to it tomorrow sometime," Lincoln said easily. Then he bent, hooked Billy-Moses around the waist with one bent arm and carried him through the kitchen.

Billy-Moses squealed with a little boy's joy, kicking and squirming, and it was a sound Juliana had never heard him make before.

As soon as she was alone, Juliana folded her arms on the tabletop and rested her head on them.

Mr. Philbert would come, and soon. She could almost feel him bearing down on Stillwater Springs, on her, full of righteous wrath. How would she explain to Billy-Moses, only four, and Daisy, just three, that he would be taking them far away, handing them over to strangers? Would he even give her a *chance* to explain?

She stood slowly, crossed to the sink and pumped water into the teakettle, found the tin Lincoln had mentioned earlier and a yellow crockery pot. By the time the brew was ready, he'd returned to the kitchen, grinning, his shirtfront soaked with water.

"Bill's been bedded down," he said. "I've wrestled yearling calves with less fight in them."

Juliana smiled. Here, then, was the reason Billy-Moses hadn't asked Gracie to spell out his whole name with her alphabet blocks earlier that evening; he'd wanted "Bill." Because that was what Lincoln called him.

"Thank you," she said, warming her hands around her cup of tea.

Lincoln poured lukewarm coffee for himself, drew back his chair and sat down. With a slight nod of his head, he answered, "You're welcome, Mrs. Creed."

Once again, the name soothed her, and conversely that very fact made her uneasy. "Do you think the reverend will be warm enough in the barn?"

"He's bunking in between two bearskins, Juliana, and the animals put out a lot of body heat. The barn's warmer than the house a lot of the time."

Body heat. What an intriguing—and disturbing— term. She looked away, her tea forgotten.

And that was when Lincoln's hand, calloused by years of ranch work, came to rest on hers. "Maybe you ought to turn in for the night," he suggested.

She swallowed, nodded. Could not pull her hand out from under his, even—*especially*—when he began to stroke the backs of her knuckles with the rough pad of his thumb, setting her on fire inside.

Was this passion, this ache he aroused in her with the simplest touch of his hand?

Juliana was not prepared to find out.

"I'll be along in a while," Lincoln told her.

She stood.

He stood, too.

"Juliana?"

She met his gaze.

"Don't be afraid," he said.

How *not* to be afraid? She'd never experienced anything more daring than John's hand-patting and chaste pecks on the cheek during their brief and bland engagement.

She nodded and turned to leave.

LINCOLN HAD LOST INTEREST in the newspaper. The *Stillwater Springs Courier* came out once a week, if Wes got around to writing the articles and setting the type. As often as not, he didn't—but he was a good writer when he had something to say, and Lincoln usually enjoyed his brother's sly but often lethal wit. Hell, even some of the obituaries were funny, and the opinion pieces kept things stirred up around town.

With a sigh, Lincoln pushed the paper away and rose from his chair. He carried his cup and Juliana's to the sink and left them there, stood with his hands braced against the counter, staring out the window, looking past his own reflection and into the darkness.

Flakes of snow drifted down, and he wondered if they'd stick or melt away by morning.

He felt restless. He knew he wasn't tired enough to lie down beside Juliana and keep his hands to himself. He'd wanted a wife—someone to share his bed, bear him more children, provide the motherly affection Gracie craved—but not one who touched his heart. No, he had not planned on that part.

Resigned, he went to the door, took his hat and coat from their pegs and put them on. Quietly left the house.

He moved past the privy, past the Gainers' cabin, past the bunkhouse. The night air was cold, sweeping inside him somehow, scouring like a bitter wind.

He needed no lantern; even with the moon disappearing behind the clouds, enough light came through to illuminate the snow. Besides, he'd lived on this ranch all his life; he could have found any part of it with his eyes closed.

He reached the orchard—years ago, when they were boys, he and Micah and Wes and Dawson had helped to plant those apple and pear trees—then made his way, sure-footed, over ground he knew as well as the back of his own right hand.

Beyond the orchard was the little cluster of gravestones and markers where his father, his brother, the two lost babies—and Beth—were buried.

He didn't pause beside Josiah Creed's grave, walked right past Dawson's, too, even though he'd loved his brother.

Beth's resting place was marked with a stone angel, now cloaked in snow.

Lincoln brushed off the shoulders and the wings with one hand. He crouched, ran his right forearm across his face. How many times had he come here, said goodbye to Beth? Sooner or later, there always seemed to be something more that wanted saying.

And she wasn't even here.

Gracie believed her mother was in heaven.

Lincoln flat didn't know where dead people went, or if they went anywhere at all. Most likely, though, the journey ended in a pine box under six feet of dirt, but of course he wouldn't have said that to Gracie.

Graves weren't really for the folks who'd passed on, he supposed. They gave the ones left behind a place to go and remember, that was all.

"I got married today," he said, feeling foolish, but

needing to say the words all the same. They came out sounding gruff. "Her name is Juliana, and Gracie—Gracie wants to call her Mama."

A raspy chuckle escaped Lincoln then. If that grave had been some kind of passageway between this world and the next, Beth would have clawed her way right up out of it and given him what-for.

"I loved you," he went on, sober again. "I probably always will. But I've been too lonesome, Beth, and so has Gracie. I need somebody to wake up beside, somebody waiting when I come in off the range after a long day. I want Gracie to have a woman to look to so she doesn't grow up to smoke cigars like Ma says she will. I know you can't hear me, and wouldn't like what I've got to say if you could, but I still had to say it."

As he stood again, Lincoln wondered what he'd expected—an answer? Beth's ghost, absolving him of his promise to leave his heart buried with her?

The snap of a branch in the nearby orchard alerted him that someone was approaching—as it had probably been meant to do. He almost expected a specter, though he knew who had tracked him even before he saw Tom moving across the snowy ground toward him. If that old Indian hadn't wanted him to hear, he wouldn't have.

Lincoln waited, without speaking, as his friend drew nearer.

"She's not here, Lincoln," Tom said. "Beth is not here."

"Don't you think I know that?" Lincoln demanded, rubbing the back of his neck with one hand. "Where *is* she, Tom? With the Great Spirit? Or down in that hole in the ground?"

"Why are you doing this to yourself?" Tom asked reasonably. "Coming out here in the dark and the cold when you've got a pretty bride waiting back at the house? Is it because you didn't count on *feeling* anything for Juliana?"

"I think Juliana is beautiful," Lincoln said tersely. "I think she's smart and brave, and I want her. But that's *all* I feel, Tom. I loved my wife."

"Your wife is dead."

"So I hear."

Tight-jawed, eyes flashing, Tom reached out with a palm and shoved hard at Lincoln's chest, so he had to scramble to keep his footing. "Let Beth go," he almost growled. "Juliana doesn't deserve to go through what your mother did."

"What the hell is *that* supposed to mean?"

"It *means*, you damn fool, that your pa married your mother for pretty much the same reasons you married Juliana. He and Micah were alone after his first wife died, and he wanted to give the boy a mother. He never loved Cora, always mooning over his poor lost Mary, and your ma's life was a misery because of it."

Lincoln's mouth dropped open. He took a second or two to get his jaw hinged right so it would shut again. It was the first he'd heard of any of this, and that chafed at something raw inside him. It also explained why Cora couldn't keep the names of Micah's four sons straight, why she never visited them in Colorado or even wrote them letters. Maybe it even explained why Micah had lit out for another state the way he had and never looked back, as far as Lincoln could tell.

"Why tell me this now?" he asked bitterly, but his

mind was still reeling, still scrabbling for some kind of purchase. Micah was his father's son, but not his mother's? In that moment, he understood what folks meant when they said they'd had the rug pulled out from under them.

"Because you need to know it."

"I would have appreciated somebody's mentioning this before Micah left home for good," Lincoln said, fighting down the old hurt. "I looked up to him. I didn't even get to say goodbye. One day, he was just—gone."

"Micah didn't leave because things weren't good between him and Cora. He left because he'd always had leaving in him."

"And because his mother's folks lived in Colorado," Lincoln guessed.

"Yes," Tom said.

Lincoln thrust out a sigh, felt a letting-go inside him. "Well, I don't have to wonder what I did wrong anymore, I guess. Does Wes know all this?"

A nod. "He knows."

"Am I the only one who didn't?"

"Let it go, Lincoln. Wes is a little older. He overheard more, that's all."

"I suppose now you're going to tell me my ma was so lonesome, you had to comfort her, and I'm *your* son, not Josiah Creed's." For a brief moment, Lincoln held his breath, hoping it was true.

Tom clenched a fist, looked as though he might throw a punch. "If you were my son," he said, through his teeth, "I'd have claimed you a long time ago. No woman ever loved a man more than your ma loved Josiah Creed. She bore him three healthy boys and raised the one he brought with him when they married. When Dawson was killed, Josiah told her it was her fault, because it was one of her kin that pulled the trigger. To the day he died, he never had a kind word for her."

Lincoln closed his eyes for a long moment, let out the breath he hadn't realized he'd been holding. "But *you* loved my mother all these years, didn't you, Tom? That's why you stayed."

"I stayed because that's what I chose to do," Tom said coldly.

Lincoln started back toward the house, and Tom fell into step beside him.

They walked in silence with nothing more to say.

THERESA, BILLY-MOSES AND DAISY were sound asleep in Mrs. Creed's bed. Careful not to wake them, Juliana tucked the blankets in close and added wood to the fire in the stove.

She looked in on Gracie next, found her sleeping, too. Felt her heart seize with love for this child, the fruit of another woman's womb. It was a dangerous thing, caring so much, but it was too late. Just as it was with Daisy and Billy-Moses, Theresa and Joseph.

Juliana adjusted Gracie's covers and tiptoed out into the corridor.

In Lincoln's room, she lit a lamp. Slowly undressed, took her own nightgown from her satchel and put it on. After drawing a deep breath, she pulled back the covers and climbed into bed.

There, she waited.

Lincoln had promised to wait until she felt ready to give herself to him. That should have lessened her fears, but it didn't, because it wasn't the prospect of his love-making that frightened her most. It was her own desire to give herself up to him with total abandon.

He came in quietly, with the smell of the outdoors on his clothes—snow, pine, fresh, cold air. Feigning sleep, she watched through her eyelashes as he lowered one suspender, then the other.

"I know you're awake," he told her. "Most folks don't hold their breath when they're sleeping."

Juliana huffed out a sigh and opened her eyes.

After looking down at her for a long moment, he chuckled and reached to extinguish the lamp. "Move over, Mrs. Creed," he said. "I'm going to need more than an inch of that mattress."

Juliana scooted closer to the wall, her heart pounding. Lincoln was not going to force himself on her, she knew that if little else. He wouldn't touch her in any intimate way without her permission.

She ought to relax.

But she couldn't. What did married people say to each other at night when they got into bed?

He continued to undress. Dear God, did the man sleep naked? He didn't seem the sort to don a night-shirt.

She tried to take her thoughts in hand, but they wouldn't be governed. Instead, they scattered in every direction like startled chickens, squawking and flapping their wings.

Sure enough, she felt the bareness of his flesh, the hard warmth with its aura of chill.

He gave a long sigh. "Good night, Juliana," he said.

They both lay sleepless in the dark for a long time,

neither one speaking, careful not to brush against each other.

Juliana should have been relieved.

Instead, she bit her lower lip hard, and hoped he wouldn't hear her crying.

CHAPTER SEVEN

LINCOLN WAS ON THE RANGE the next morning, having bid the Reverend Dettly farewell, his muscles aching from a long night of self-restraint, wanting Juliana and not taking her, when Wes rode up, looking as rumpled and dissolute as ever. The cattle had been fed and Lincoln was there alone, he and his horse, just looking at the herd and wondering if those critters were worth all the grief they caused him.

"Came to get my mule," Wes said. "Tom told me you were out here."

There were bulging bundles tied where his saddlebags should have been. Gifts for Gracie and the other children, no doubt—Wes and Kate were always generous at Christmas and on birthdays, having no kids of their own.

Lincoln didn't say anything. Wes had known all along about Josiah's first wife, Micah's mother, and he'd never bothered to raise the subject. Now, after talking to Tom, he probably meant to make some kind of speech.

"A wire came for Miss Mitchell," Wes said, surprising him. "I thought I'd better bring it out here."

"She's not 'Miss Mitchell' anymore," Lincoln said, his tone flat and matter-of-fact. "I married her yesterday."

Wes gave a bark of pleased laughter at the news.

"So *that's* why I met the reverend on the road out from town this morning," he said. "Congratulations, you lucky son of a gun."

"Thanks." He gave the word a grudging note.

Wes pulled a yellow envelope from the inside pocket of his coat, squinting against the glare of sunshine on snow. Watched as Lincoln tucked away the telegram without looking at the face of it.

"It's from the Bureau of Indian Affairs, Lincoln," Wes said quietly.

Trouble, of course—telegrams rarely brought good news. Lincoln swallowed and braced himself for whatever was coming. He'd been enduring things for so long, toughing them out, that he'd learned to dig in whenever a problem appeared. "You'd damn well better not have read it," he said.

"I didn't have to," Wes answered easily. "The telegraph operator told me what it says. By now, half the town knows that that Indian Agent Philbert means to show up in Stillwater Springs some time before New Year's and stir up a ruckus. The new Mrs. Creed is out of a job for sure, but I don't suppose that matters now, anyhow, what with the wedding and all."

Even though he'd expected something like that, the knowledge buffeted Lincoln like a hard wind. Made him shift in the saddle. "What else?" he asked, still avoiding his brother's gaze.

"He's bound on taking the kids back to Missoula," Wes said.

Lincoln closed his eyes. Didn't speak.

He'd get Joseph and Theresa on their way back to North Dakota before Philbert showed up, no matter what he had to do. Take them to the train depot at Missoula if it came to that, and put them onboard himself. Juliana had prepared herself for that particular parting—it was best for them to be with their own folks—but things were different with the two little ones. Orphans, the both of them. Somewhere along the line, Juliana had taken to mothering Daisy and little Bill, and letting go would be a hard thing, for her and for them.

"Tom told you the family secret, I hear," Wes said, when Lincoln had been silent too long to suit him.

Lincoln turned his head then. Looked straight at his brother. "Why didn't *you* tell me, Wes?"

"Ma asked me not to," Wes replied with the solemnity of truth.

Still, Lincoln had to challenge him. "Since when are you so all-fired concerned with doing what Ma wants?"

Wes's smile was thin, and a little on the self-disparaging side. "I chopped down a Christmas tree and hauled it out here on a mule's back because she told me to, didn't I?"

"You did that for Gracie."

Wes sighed, stood in the stirrups for a moment, stretching his legs. "Mostly," he admitted gruffly. Then, after a long time, he added, "Things weren't always so sour between Ma and me, Lincoln. You remember how it was after Dawson died—she was half-mad with the sorrow. Doc Chaney had to dose her up with laudanum. I was pretty torn up myself—we all were—but I felt sorry for her. I wanted to do what I could to help, and God knew there wasn't much."

Lincoln took that in without speaking. He remembered how his ma used to howl with grief some nights, during those first weeks after the shooting, and how his pa had slammed out of the house when she did.

Saddle leather creaked as Wes fidgeted, leaning forward a little, looking earnest. "There was another reason I didn't tell you," he said, sounding reluctant and a little irritated.

"What was that?" Lincoln bit out, in no frame of mind to make things easy for his brother. Whatever Wes's reasons for keeping that secret, he, Lincoln, had had as much right to know as anybody.

"You tend to hold on to things you ought to let go of," Wes said, reining his horse around, toward the main house, looking back at Lincoln over one shoulder. "People, too."

"Beth." Lincoln sighed the name.

"Beth," Wes agreed. Another silence fell between them, lengthy and punctuated only by snorts and hoof-shuffling from their horses and the chatter of the passing creek. "Of the four of us, Lincoln, you're the most like Pa. Tougher than hell, and too smart for your own good or anybody else's. You've held on to this ground, just like he did, and made it pay, in good times and bad. But you take after the old man in a few other ways, too. If I hauled off and swung a shovel at your head—and I've wanted to more than once—it would be the shovel that fractured, not your skull."

"That was quite a sermon, Wes."

"Don't get out of your pew yet, because I'm not finished. Right now, because you're still young, that stubborn streak serves you pretty well—you probably think of it as 'determination.' Trouble is, over time, it might just harden into something a lot less admirable."

As much as Lincoln would have liked to disregard the warning, he couldn't. It made too much sense. He'd mourned Dawson in a normal way, but since Beth had died, he'd boarded over parts of himself, knowing it would hurt too much if he let himself care.

"What do you suggest I do?" he asked moderately, just to get it over with. Wes was going to tell him anyhow; he'd worked himself up into a pretty good lather since talking with Tom.

"You remember how different Pa was when we were little? How he'd haul one or another of us around on his shoulders, let us follow him practically every place he went? How he laughed all the time, even though he worked like a mule? Back then, he wouldn't have believed it if somebody had told him he'd wind up turning his back on all of us, but he did. You know why, Lincoln? Because he decided to go right on loving a dead woman, when he had a living, breathing one right in front of him. It took a while, but that decision—that one bone-headed decision—poisoned his mind, and eventually, it poisoned his soul, too." Wes paused for a few moments, remembering, maybe gathering more words. "Never mind Juliana. She's prettier than Ma was, and she's got a lot more spirit. She'll be all right, even if you're fool enough to keep your heart closed to her. But what about Gracie? She's already got a mind of her own, and she's only seven—what do you think she'll be like at sixteen? Or eighteen? She'll make a lot of choices along the way, and I guarantee you aren't going to like some of them. You're bound to butt heads—I suppose that's normal—but if you aren't careful, you might find yourself treating your daughter the same way Pa did us. Do you want that?"

Lincoln's throat had seized shut. He shook his head.

Wes had finally run down, having reeled out what he had to say. He nudged at his horse's sides with the heels of his boots and rode back toward the house to drop off the things stuffed into those bags tied behind his saddle and collect his mule.

Conscious of the telegram in his pocket, Lincoln waited awhile before following.

JULIANA WAS CROSSING THE YARD, returning from a brief visit to Rose-of-Sharon and baby Joshua, when she saw her brother-in-law leading his mule out of the barn. Tom, meanwhile, carried two burlap bags, stuffed full of something, toward the woodshed.

Because she liked Weston Creed, she changed course, smiling, and went to greet him.

His smile flashed, but his eyes were solemn, almost sad. "My brother," he said, "is a lucky man."

Juliana blushed. She wasn't used to compliments; schoolmarms didn't get a whole lot of them. "We've got two big turkeys for Christmas dinner," she told him, feeling self-conscious. "I hope you'll join us."

He slipped a loop of rope around the mule's neck and paused to look toward the house. "Is Kate welcome, too?" he asked. Without waiting for an answer, he moved to stand beside his horse and tied the other end of the rope loosely around the horn of the saddle.

"Of course," Juliana said.

"Do you know anything about her?" Weston asked, and while the inquiry sounded almost idle, Juliana knew it wasn't.

"I suppose she's your wife."

He chuckled, but it was a bitter sound, void of amusement. "Something like that," he said. "Kate owns the Diamond Buckle Saloon. She and I have been living in sin for some time now."

"Oh," Juliana said. She was intrigued at the prospect of meeting such a colorful personage, but perhaps she should have spoken to Lincoln before she'd issued the invitation.

"Yes," Weston said wryly. "Oh."

Juliana's cheeks stung with embarrassment. When she'd asked Lincoln for permission to bathe Daisy and Billy-Moses the night before, he'd said the ranch house was her home, too, and she didn't need his permission. She hoped that liberty extended to other things. "We'll sit down to dinner around two o'clock," she said. Since she wouldn't be roasting the turkeys, the hour was a mere guess. "But whatever time you and Kate arrive, we'll be glad to see you."

He rounded the horse to stand facing Juliana. His mouth, sensuous like Lincoln's, twitched at one corner. "You do realize, Mrs. Creed, that the roof will surely fall in, either the instant Kate sets foot over the threshold or when my mother finds out?"

Even without meeting the woman, Juliana was a little afraid of Cora Creed. Just the same, she wasn't one to let fear stop her from doing anything she thought was right. Raising her chin a notch, she replied, "I guess we'll have to take that chance."

Lincoln's brother chuckled again, but this time, it sounded real. "Brave words," he said. "But I think you might just mean them."

"I never say anything I don't mean, Mr. Creed."

"Call me Wes," he said, grinning now.

"Only if you agree to call me Juliana," she retorted.

He leaned in, kissed her forehead. "Welcome to my brother's life, Juliana," he told her. "God knows, he needs you."

Something made her look up then. She saw Lincoln approaching on horseback, a distant speck, moving slowly. Her heart quickened at the sight. "What makes you say that?" she asked Wes.

Wes sighed, and after glancing back over one shoulder, favored her with a sad smile. "He's lost a lot in his life. Beth, of course, and two babies. Pa and our brother Dawson. He's a good man, Lincoln is, but he's—well, he's mighty careful with his heart, as a general rule."

Juliana laid a hand to her chest; she had been too careful with her own heart, until Daisy and Billy-Moses and other special students had somehow gotten past the barriers.

Wes turned, stuck a foot in one stirrup and mounted the horse. After glancing in Lincoln's direction once more, he said, "I'll be going now. We've had a few words, my brother and I, and there will be more if I stay." He tapped at his horse's sides with the heels of his boots, tightened the rope to urge the mule into motion. "Unless there's another blizzard," he added, "Kate and I will be here Christmas Day."

Juliana smiled, though she was a little troubled by

talk of he and Lincoln "having words." "Come early," she said.

Wes nodded and started off, the mule balking at first, then trotting obediently along behind his horse.

Although it was sunny out, the weather was cold. Juliana huddled inside one of her mother-in-law's cloaks, hastily borrowed, and waited for her husband.

When he rode up to the barn, she approached, slowly at first, and then with faster steps.

The confession burst out of her. "I've asked Wes and Kate to come for Christmas dinner," she said, all on one breath.

He swung down from the saddle, stood looking at her with amusement on his mouth and sadness in his eyes, just as Wes had done. "Did he accept the invite?" he asked.

She took a breath, let it out and nodded quickly.

He laughed then, and hooked one stirrup over the saddle horn, so he could unbuckle the cinch. "Well, Mrs. Creed," he said, "you've succeeded where I failed, then. I've never been able to persuade Kate to set foot on this ranch, let alone sit down to Christmas dinner, and if she stays in town, so does Wes."

Juliana took a single step toward him, stopped herself, reading the set of his face. "Something is wrong," she said. "What is it?"

He went still for a long moment, then reached into his coat pocket and brought out a small yellow envelope.

Seeing it, Juliana felt her blood run cold. She was suddenly paralyzed.

Lincoln held out the envelope to her, and her hands

trembled as she accepted it. Fumbled as she tried to unseal the flap.

"Wes brought it out from town," Lincoln said.

Juliana began to shiver, finally shoving the telegram at Lincoln. "Please," she whispered. "Read it."

Lincoln tugged off his gloves, opened the envelope and studied the page inside. "It's from the Bureau of Indian Affairs," he said. From his tone, it was clear that he'd known that all along. "'Miss Mitchell. You are hereby—'" Lincoln paused, cleared his throat. "'You are hereby dismissed. I will be in Stillwater Springs by the first of January at the latest. At that time, you will surrender any remaining students now in your custody for placement in appropriate institutions.' It's signed 'R. Philbert.'"

Juliana stood absolutely still, though on the inside, she felt as though she were set to bolt in a dozen different directions.

Lincoln took hold of her shoulders, the telegram still in one hand, and steadied her. "Take a breath, Juliana," he ordered, his voice low.

She breathed. Once. Twice. A third time.

"Listen to me," Lincoln went on calmly. "We're going to handle this, you and I. Together."

Juliana's mind raced, but there was a painful clarity to her thoughts just the same. Mr. Philbert had effectively warned her by sending her a telegram announcing his intention to visit Stillwater Springs, which might mean he planned to come earlier, hoping to forestall any attempt she might make to flee with the children.

"Wh-what are we going to do?" she faltered.

"First, we've got to get Joseph and Theresa to

Missoula, put them on a train east. As for Daisy and Bill—well—I've been thinking about what Gracie said yesterday. Now that we're married, we could adopt them, and then they'd be Creeds. They could stay with us."

Juliana was grateful for his hold on her shoulders, because her knees wanted to buckle. "You'd do that?" she whispered, marveling. Surely there wasn't another man on the face of the earth quite like this one.

His eyes were shadowed by the brim of his hat, but she saw a quiet willingness in them even before he answered. "Yes."

"Why?"

"For them. For Gracie. Most of all, for you." Gently, he turned her toward the house. Spoke close to her right ear, his breath warm against her skin. "Go on inside before you catch your death in this cold. I'll be in as soon as I get this horse put up."

Juliana took a cautious step, found that her legs were still working.

Inside, the children, having finished the day's lessons, were pestering Tom to let them go out to play. Juliana gave her permission, with the stipulation that they must all bundle up as warmly as possible and not make noise near the Gainers' cabin because Rose-of-Sharon and the baby needed peace and quiet.

There was a flurry of coat-finding—Gracie was so excited, she could hardly stand still to let Juliana lay a woolen scarf over the top of her head and tie it beneath her chin. Tom found knitted caps for the other children, and they all raced for the front door.

Once they were gone, Tom asked straight out,

"You're pale as a new snow, Juliana. What's the matter? What's happened?"

Haltingly, she told him about Mr. Philbert's telegram.

His face hardened as he listened. "What did Lincoln have to say about that?"

"He wants to get Joseph and Theresa to the train in Missoula as soon as possible." She didn't mention the adoption; she still wasn't sure she'd actually heard Lincoln correctly, where that was concerned.

Tom nodded. "Missoula's half a day's ride from here, if the weather holds," he said. "If it doesn't, Philbert probably won't make it to town until the roads are clear."

Lincoln came in just then, looked from Juliana to Tom without speaking, took off his hat and coat and hung them up the way he always did. His expression remained grim.

"I'll take Joseph and Theresa to Missoula," Tom said. "Ride back to North Dakota with them to make sure they get there all right and folks are ready to take them in on the other end."

Sadness moved in Lincoln's face, but he nodded. Looking distracted, he said, "I'll be at my desk." Pausing in the doorway to the front room, he turned around. "You'll come back, won't you, Tom?" he asked.

Tom didn't smile. "I'll come back," he said very quietly.

Later, when the children had worn themselves out playing games in the front yard and returned to the house, bright-eyed and glowing from the cold, Juliana brewed up a batch of hot chocolate in a heavy cast-iron kettle and gave them each a cup. While they enjoyed the treat, she went in search of Lincoln.

He was where he'd said he'd be, seated at his desk in a corner of the front room, surrounded by thick books, all of them open. As she approached, he dipped a pen in a bottle of ink and wrote something on a sheet of paper.

Needing to be near him, she set a mug of hot chocolate beside him. "Thanks," he said.

Juliana's fingers flexed; she wanted to work the tight muscles in Lincoln's neck and shoulders, but refrained. Yes, he was her husband, but touching him, even in such an innocuous way, seemed too familiar. Even a little brazen.

Still, she could not bring herself to walk away, any more than she could have left a warm stove after walking through a blizzard.

"If you're going to linger, Juliana," he said mildly, without looking up from the paper and the books, "please sit down."

She moved to a nearby armchair, sat down on its edge, knotted her fingers together. And waited.

Lincoln finally sighed, shoved back his chair and turned to look at her. "Everything will be all right, Juliana," he said.

He didn't know Mr. Philbert. "Today," she ventured nervously, "out by the barn, I thought you said—"

He waited.

"I thought you said you would be willing to adopt Daisy and Billy-Moses."

Lincoln smiled. "I did say that, Juliana."

She gripped the arms of her chair. "How?"

"I'm a lawyer," he answered. He gestured toward the books on his desk. "I'm drawing up the papers right now."

"You didn't mention that. Being a lawyer, I mean."

"There are a lot of things I haven't gotten around to mentioning," Lincoln said reasonably. "I haven't had time."

She stood up, sat down again. "You could—you could get into trouble for sending Joseph and Theresa to North Dakota," she fretted.

"I'm no stranger to trouble," Lincoln told her. "In fact, I like a challenge."

"I need something to do," she confessed.

Lincoln opened a drawer in his desk, brought out a second bottle of ink and a pen. Gave her several sheets of paper. "Write to your brother," he said. "Tell him you're married now, and if he doesn't come here first, I'll be paying him a visit one day soon."

The thought of Clay and Lincoln standing face-to-face unnerved her a little, but she accepted the pen and ink and paper, and went back to the kitchen. Tom and Joseph were gone, and Theresa, Gracie, Daisy and Billy-Moses sat in a circle on the floor, playing with a tattered deck of cards.

She took a chair at the table, opened the ink bottle and awaited inspiration. After a quarter of an hour, all she'd written was "Dear Clay." Finally, out of frustration, she stopped trying to choose her words carefully, dipped the pen, and began.

As you have long wished me safely married, I am happy to inform you that yesterday, December

*22, I entered into matrimony with Mr. Lincoln
Creed, of Stillwater Springs, Montana—*

Juliana went on to describe Lincoln, Gracie, the house
and what she'd seen of the ranch. She extended sincere
felicitations for a happy Christmas and prosperous New
Year. Why, it would be 1911 soon. Where had the time
gone?

The letter filled three pages by the time she'd
finished.

She closed with "Sincerely, Juliana Mitchell Creed,"
and when the ink was dry, she carefully folded the letter,
her earlier trepidation having given way to relief. She
could not predict how Clay would respond to the missive, if he responded at all, but that took nothing away
from her sense of having turned some kind of corner,
found some new kind of freedom.

The rest of the day ground by slowly.

The younger children took naps without protest.

Theresa read quietly in the rocking chair, next to the
stove.

When she grew restless, Juliana avoided the front
room, where Lincoln was still working, and donned the
borrowed cloak and went to the Gainers' cabin again,
knocking lightly on the door. When Ben answered, whis-
pering that Rose-of-Sharon and the baby were asleep,
she smiled to cover her disappointment and promised
to come back later.

She visited the barn and spoke to the cow and all the
horses.

She went into the woodshed, planning to peek into

the two burlap bags Tom had left there, but the idea pricked at her conscience, so she dismissed it.

She was chilled, but too wrought up to return to the house.

Spotting the orchard nearby, Juliana headed in that direction. The trees were gnarled and bare-limbed, and she paused, laid a hand to a sturdy trunk. Late the following summer, there would be fruit. In the meantime, perhaps Tom would teach her to make preserves.

At first, glimpsing the stone angel out of the corner of her eye, Juliana thought she was seeing things. As she drew nearer, though, she realized she'd come upon a small cemetery.

The angel marked the final resting place of Bethany Allan Creed.

Juliana's throat tightened. Beth. Lincoln's first wife, Gracie's mother. Careful of her skirts—she was wearing the blue dress again—she dropped to her haunches. Brushed away a patch of snow, and the twigs and small stones beneath.

She couldn't have said why she felt compelled to do such a thing. "I'm going to take very good care of your little Gracie," she heard herself say. "She's so smart, and so pretty and so kind. I fell in love with her right away."

A breeze, neither warm nor cold, played in Juliana's hair. "I'll make you a promise, Beth, here and now. Gracie won't forget you, won't forget that you're her real mother."

Behind her, a twig snapped.

Startled, Juliana stood and, forgetting to lift her hem, spun around.

Lincoln stood at the edge of the orchard, wearing his round-brimmed hat and his long black coat. From that distance, she couldn't read his expression.

Feeling as though she'd been caught doing something wrong, Juliana didn't move or speak.

Lincoln came toward her slowly. Even when she could see his face clearly, she found no emotion there. No anger, but no smile, either.

"There are wolves out here sometimes, Juliana," he said. "In the summer, the bears like to raid the orchard. It isn't safe to wander too far from the house alone."

Juliana fought to speak, because her throat was still closed. "You must have loved your wife very much," she said, brushing the angel's wing with a light pass of her hand.

"Beth's father sent the marker," he said. "Nothing but the best for his daughter. Not that he bothered to come all the way out here to the wilds of Montana to pay his respects or meet his granddaughter."

Juliana didn't know what to say. And she probably couldn't have spoken, anyway. Despite Lincoln's lack of expression, the air felt charged with emotion.

"I did love Beth," he continued, when she held her tongue. "The strange thing is, if I met her today, for the first time, I mean, I'm not sure I'd do more than tip my hat."

Juliana reached out without thinking and touched his arm. Was relieved when he didn't pull away. "What do you mean?" she asked softly.

"I was a different man back then," he answered.

Although she was still puzzled, Juliana didn't ask for clarification. Instinct told her to listen instead.

"I wanted different things than I want now."

Juliana waited, her hand still resting on the sleeve of his coat.

He was quiet for a long time. When he broke the silence, his voice sounded hoarse. He told her about his father, his mother, his three brothers. He told her about going off to college in Boston, how homesick he'd been for the ranch and his family, about studying law and meeting Beth when he went to work in her father's firm.

He told her about Gracie's birth, and the two babies who hadn't lived—a boy and a girl. They'd never given them names, and now he wished they had, because then they'd have had identities, however brief.

Juliana didn't look away, though she would have liked to hide the tear that slipped down her right cheek.

Finally, he reached out, took her hand. Led her toward home.

Tom had made supper—bear-meat hash—and Juliana was surprised to find that she had an appetite. Most likely, it was all that fresh air.

She washed the dishes by herself that night, while Theresa got the three younger children ready for bed. Tom and Lincoln sat at the table with Joseph, making plans for the journey to North Dakota.

Juliana listened, knowing that the ache of missing Joseph and Theresa would be with her for a long, long time. They belonged with their family, though— shouldn't have been taken from them in the first place.

She finished the dishes, hung the dish towel up to dry.

Left the kitchen.

Gracie had climbed into bed with Daisy and Billy-Moses. Theresa sat cross-legged on the foot of the mattress, reading aloud from, of all things, the Sears, Roebuck catalog.

Juliana stood in the open doorway for a while, unnoticed, while the children listened raptly to descriptions of china platters, teacups and silverware. The words, she realized, didn't matter. It was the sound of another human voice that held their attention.

She slipped away. In Lincoln's room, she filled the china basin with fresh water from the matching pitcher and scrubbed her teeth with a brush and baking soda. She washed her face, unplaited her hair, brushed it thoroughly, and plaited it again.

Her nightgown felt chilly, so she draped it over the screen in front of the fireplace where a cheery blaze crackled. Lincoln must have lit the fire just before supper.

She unbuttoned the blue dress, stepped out of it. Took off her shoes and rolled her stockings down and off. Untied the laces of her petticoat and let the garment fall.

She was standing there, in just her camisole and bloomers, when the door opened and Lincoln came in.

He went still at the sight of her.

She imagined that the firelight behind her had turned her undergarments transparent, and that sent a rush of embarrassment through her, but she made no move to cover herself.

Lincoln started to back out of the room.

"Wait," Juliana said with dignity. "Don't go. Please."

He stepped over the threshold again, closed the door behind him. The conflict in his handsome face might have been comical, if she hadn't been so concerned with the pounding of her heart. He opened his mouth to speak, but when no sound came out, he closed it again.

"You asked me to tell you when I felt ready," she reminded him. Fingers trembling, she began untying the tiny ribbons that held her camisole together in front.

"And?" He rasped the word.

"I'm ready."

CHAPTER EIGHT

LEANING BACK AGAINST THE BEDROOM DOOR, Lincoln shook his head once and gave a raspy sigh. "I'm not so sure about that," he said. "Your being ready, I mean."

Was he rejecting her? Quickly, cheeks throbbing with heat, Juliana stopped untying the camisole ribbons and stood frozen in injured confusion. Without intending to, she allowed her deepest fear to escape. "Don't you— don't you want me, Lincoln?"

He blew out a breath. "Oh, I *want* you, all right," he said.

"Then, why…?"

"My brother said some things to me today that I need to think about," Lincoln explained calmly. "And, anyway, you've been through a lot lately. I won't have you doing this because you think you ought to, or because you want to get it over with."

"Get it over with?" She was astounded, but she probably sounded angry.

His powerful shoulders moved in a shruglike motion. "Making love can be painful for the woman the first time," he reminded her. "And it'll be more so, in a lot of other ways, if you're offering yourself to me for the wrong reasons."

He was such a—*lawyer,* building a case against what they both needed and wanted. "*What* wrong reasons?"

she demanded, careful to keep her voice down, so none of the children would overhear. Earlier, he'd found her visiting his first wife's grave. Did he think she was trying to exert some kind of *claim* on him, somehow supplant Beth's memory? Use her body to push the other woman out of his heart and mind?

Lincoln raised one eyebrow. "Well," he began, "you could be grateful, because I'm willing to adopt Daisy and Bill and raise them as our own."

Indignant, Juliana snatched her nightgown off the fireplace screen and pulled it on over her head, meaning to remove her undergarments later, when he was gone. As luck would have it, though, she got her arms tangled in the sleeves somehow and ended up flailing about like a chicken inside a burlap sack.

Lincoln laughed; she heard him come toward her, his footsteps easy on the plank floor.

She felt him righting the nightgown.

When he tugged it down so her head popped through the neck hole, his eyes were dancing.

"Don't you *dare* make fun of me!" Juliana sputtered.

He chuckled again, but there was something tender in the way he held her shoulders. "I wouldn't do that," he said.

As if she weren't humiliated enough already, hot tears sprang to her eyes.

"Listen," Lincoln said, after placing a light kiss on the top of her head. "Once we've made love, there will be no going back. It's got to be right."

She stared at him, aghast. *Once we've made love, there will be no going back.* Was he having second thoughts, thinking of annulling the marriage on the grounds that they had yet to consummate it?

"May I remind you, Mr. Creed, that getting married was *your* idea?"

"I'm well aware of that," he said affably.

"But now you want to make sure there's a way to *go back?*"

Surprise widened his eyes. "Hell, *that* isn't what I meant," he said.

Relief swept over Juliana, leaving her almost faint. She hoped to high heaven her reaction didn't show, because she'd made enough of a fool of herself as it was, behaving with such wanton abandon. "I practically *threw myself* at you," she fretted, "and you might as well have flung a bucket of cold water all over me!"

He sighed, yet again. "Oh," he said.

"Oh," Juliana repeated, in the same tone Wes had used when he'd repeated the word back to her that afternoon, in reference to Kate's reasons for avoiding the ranch.

Lincoln shoved a hand through his hair. "Maybe we ought to just start over—"

"Maybe," Juliana shot back, "you should go off by yourself and *think* about whatever it was that your brother said to you, out there on the range."

Something flickered in his eyes. "I believe I've come to terms with that," he said, and his voice sounded different. It was lower than before, and gruff in a way that made Juliana tingle in peculiar places. Her mouth went dry.

She waited for him to explain further, but, of course, he didn't, being a man and used to keeping his own counsel.

He raised his hands to the sides of her face, the way he'd done after the marriage ceremony, and then he kissed her.

The wedding kiss had rocked her, but this one was even more intense. He parted her lips and used his tongue, and the pleasure of that was so startling that Juliana would have cried out if her mouth hadn't been covered.

She slipped her arms around his neck and rose onto her tiptoes, caught up in her response like a leaf swept up into a whirlwind.

His tongue.

The way his body fit against hers.

The way her own expanded, ready to take him in.

All of it left her dazed, and when he finally stopped kissing her, he had to grab her shoulders again, because she swayed.

Blinking, she stared up at him.

"*That*, Mrs. Creed, should settle any question of whether I want you or not."

It had certainly settled the question of whether or not *she* wanted *him*. She most definitely did, and the consequences be damned.

"Then you'll make love to me?" she asked, brazen, flushed with desire.

"Inevitably," he answered, but he was releasing her shoulders, turning to leave the room. Only her pride, or what remained of it, kept her from scrambling after him, begging him not to leave.

"When?" she croaked.

He paused without turning to face her, and tilted his

head back, considering. "When it's right," he finally replied.

And then he was gone.

Juliana felt like some wild creature, caught and caged. She stood there trembling with rage and frustration for a few moments, then took up her brush, undid her braid and brushed her hair with long, furious strokes that left it crackling around her face like fire.

Once she'd regained her composure enough to risk leaving the room, she went to look in on the children. Billy-Moses, Daisy and Gracie lay curled against one another like puppies, sleeping soundly. Theresa was in Gracie's bed with her eyes closed.

Just as Juliana would have closed the door, though, the child spoke.

"Miss Mitchell—I mean, Mrs. Creed? Will you sit with me—just for a little while?"

Juliana approached the bed, sat down on its edge. Smoothed Theresa's dark hair with a motherly hand. "Sure," she said softly. "Is something bothering you?"

A stray moonbeam played over the girl's face, was gone again. "Joseph remembers the folks at home," she said. "I do, too, sort of, but mostly I remember going away and living in a lot of different schools."

Juliana simply waited.

"What if we get home, Joseph and me, and they can't keep us for some reason? Or don't want us after all?"

Juliana's heart ached. "You saw the letter they sent," she said gently. "They want you."

"But maybe somebody like Mr. Philbert will come and take us away again."

"I don't think that will happen," Juliana said.

Although unlikely, it *was* possible. "Tom is going with you, remember. He'll make sure you and Joseph get settled, and keep you safe all along the way."

"Folks might be mean to us. After all, Mr. Dancingstar is an Indian, too."

That, too, was possible. Juliana wished she could make the trip with the three of them, and stand guard over them, but of course she couldn't. Gracie and Daisy and Billy-Moses needed her—if Wes Creed could be believed, so did Lincoln. She had to face Mr. Philbert and settle things, once and for all, so she and Lincoln could go on with their lives.

"Don't worry, Theresa," she said. "That won't change anything. And Mr. Dancingstar *will* take care of you."

"I almost wish I could stay here with you, but I'd miss Joseph something fierce, and he might forget to practice his reading if I don't keep an eye on him."

Juliana blinked back tears. "Will you write to me when you get home? Tell me all about the trip, and what things are like in North Dakota?"

Theresa nodded and reached up with both arms for a hug.

She and Juliana clung together for a little while.

"Will you write me back?" Theresa asked finally, settling back onto her pillow. "Long, long letters?"

"Long, long letters," Juliana promised, choking back more tears. She leaned over, kissed the girl's smooth forehead. "Now, go to sleep, Theresa. Tomorrow is Christmas Eve."

"You don't think I believe all those stories about Saint Nicholas, do you?" Theresa asked in a whisper. "I'm twelve, you know. Besides, Joseph says it's all malarkey and I oughtn't to expect anything much."

With yet another pang, Juliana tucked the covers under Theresa's chin. "You mustn't stop hoping for things," she said. "Not ever. That's what keeps us all going."

"But Saint Nicholas *is* just a story?"

Juliana thought of the presents hidden in the top of Mrs. Creed's wardrobe. They were simple things, but seen through the eyes of these children, who'd never owned much of anything, they would gleam like Aladdin's treasure. "Yes," she admitted. "There was a real Saint Nicholas, once upon a time, and a lot of legends have grown up around his life, but they're just that, legends. Still, there *are* people in the world who have generous hearts."

Lincoln was one of them. Wes Creed was another. And, of course, Tom Dancingstar.

Theresa sighed, closed her eyes and settled into her dreams.

Juliana waited until she was sure the child was asleep, kissed her cheek and returned to the corridor.

She'd left the bedroom door open; now it was closed.

She stopped, put a hand to her throat before reaching to turn the knob.

The room was dark except for the flickering glow cast by the fireplace. Lincoln was already in bed, but sitting up with pillows behind his back. His chest was bare, she could tell, but his face was in shadow, making his expression impossible to read.

"I wondered if you'd come back to this room after our—discussion," he said.

"There is nowhere else to sleep," Juliana answered, and the formal tone she employed was at least partly an act. She wasn't angry with Lincoln, just confused. "Unless, of course, you'd prefer I retired to the barn like Reverend Dettly did."

Lincoln gave a snort. "The reverend is a man," he reminded her. "And despite being on a first-name basis with the Good Lord, he carries a gun in his saddlebags, right alongside his Bible."

Juliana folded her arms, keeping a stubborn distance from Lincoln Creed's bed, even though it was the very place she most wanted to be at that moment. "If you're going to be argumentative, perhaps *you* should sleep in the barn," she said, jutting out her chin. It was all bravado, and everything she said seemed to be coming out wrong—thinking one thing, saying quite another. What was the matter with her? "I was prepared to forgive you for your rudeness, Mr. Creed, but now I'm not so sure."

He chuckled, a low, rumbling sound, entirely masculine and not entirely polite. "That's very generous of you, *Mrs.* Creed," he answered. "Especially since I was trying to look out for your best interests, and if anybody ought to be apologizing around here, it's you."

"You were looking out for your own interests, not mine!" she whispered accusingly.

He patted the mattress. "Get into bed, Juliana. I'm tired and I won't be able to sleep with you standing there like you've got a ramrod stuck down the back of your nightgown."

Since her side of the bed was against the wall, she would have to crawl over him to get there, perhaps even straddling his limbs in the awkward effort. She wasn't *about* to do any such thing.

"Juliana," he repeated.

"The least you could do is get up and allow me to obey your *orders* with some semblance of dignity!"

He laughed then, though quietly. "You really want me to throw back the covers and stand up?" he teased. "Under the circumstances, that might be more than you bargained for."

Juliana reasoned that if she couldn't see Lincoln's face, he couldn't see *hers,* either, and that was a mercy, since she knew she was blushing again. It was the curse of redheaded women. "Oh, for heaven's sake!" she blurted, going to the side of the bed and scrambling over him, trying to keep her nightgown from riding up in the process.

Lincoln chortled at her predicament, and that made her want to pause long enough to pummel him with her fists. Once she'd crossed him, like some mountain range, she plopped down hard on her back and hugged her arms tightly across her chest, staring up at the ceiling.

He rolled onto his side, his face only inches from hers. "I'd like to propose a truce," he said. "I didn't mean to insult you, Juliana."

She didn't turn her head, but she did slant her eyes in his direction. "Do you apologize?"

Lincoln rose onto one elbow, cupping the side of his head in his palm. "Hell, no, I don't apologize. I didn't do anything wrong."

She turned away from him, onto her side.

He turned her back.

"All *right*," he growled. "I'm sorry."

"You are not!"

That was when he kissed her again. She struggled at first, out of pure obstinacy, but he just kissed her harder and more deeply, and she melted, driven by instincts that came from some uncontrollable part of her being. Plunged her fingers into his hair and kissed him right back.

She felt his manhood pressed against her thigh as he shifted on the mattress, and the sheer size of it caused her eyes to pop open in alarm, but then that strange, weighted heat suffused her again. She sank into helpless wanting.

"God help me," he murmured, almost tearing his mouth from hers.

Juliana ran her hands up and down his back, loving the feel of hard, warm muscle under her palms.

Lincoln let his forehead rest against hers. "Woman," he said, "if you don't stop doing that, I won't be responsible for my actions."

She raised her head, nibbled at his bare shoulder and then the side of his neck.

With a groan, Lincoln shifted again, poised above her now, resting on his forearms to keep from crushing her. "Juliana," he ground out, but if he'd been planning to say more, the words died in his throat.

He kissed her tenderly this time, tugging at her lower lip, wringing a soft moan from her. Then, with one hand, he caught hold of her nightgown and hauled it upward, past her thighs, past her waist, past her breasts—and then over her head.

Casting the gown aside, Lincoln sat back on his haunches, the covers falling away behind him.

He moved to straddle her now, his knees on either side of her hips. Firelight danced over her skin, and he seemed spellbound as he looked at her.

When he took her breasts gently into his hands and chafed the nipples with the sides of his thumbs, Juliana was lost, already transported far beyond the borders of common sense.

She couldn't bear too much waiting, not this first time, when she was in such terrible, wonderful suspense, and he seemed to know that.

He deftly dispensed with her undergarments, parted her legs, and she felt that most intimate part of him, pressed against her.

"You're sure, Juliana?" he whispered.

She nodded.

He eased inside her, in a long, slow stroke, and there *was* pain, but the pleasure was so much greater, a fiery friction, inflaming her more with every motion of their bodies, blazing like a little sun at her core. She clutched at Lincoln, gasping, rising to meet him, and he soothed her with gruff murmurings even as he drove her mad.

She was straining for something, wild with the need of it, and then it was upon her, and at the same time, it was as though she'd somehow escaped herself, given herself up entirely to sensation.

Her body dissolved first, and then her mind, and then their very souls seemed to collide. Lincoln covered her mouth with his own, muffling both their cries.

When it was over—it seemed to go on for an eternity, that melting and melding of so much more than their bodies—Lincoln collapsed beside her, gathered her in his arms. Propped his chin on the top of her head.

After a long time, he asked hoarsely, "Did it hurt?"

"Yes," she told him honestly. Surely he'd been aware of her responses, of the pleasure he'd given her. She felt transformed, even powerful.

"I'm sorry."

Juliana turned onto her side, facing him. Touched his cheek. "Don't be sorry, Lincoln," she said. "It was the most *wonderful* thing."

He chuckled, kissed her lightly. "Now will you go to sleep?"

She laughed. Kissed him back. "Now I will go to sleep," she conceded.

With his arms still around her, Lincoln soon drifted off, his breathing deep and slow, his flesh warm. Perfectly content, Juliana lay there in the fire-lit darkness, marveling at all she had not known before this night.

AFTER THE CATTLE HAD BEEN FED the next morning—the weather remained mild, though Lincoln felt a rancher's wariness and made good use of it while he could—he rode to town.

At the mercantile, he mailed Juliana's letter to her brother and bought presents—a wedding band for his wife, along with several ready-made dresses and a bright green woolen cloak with a hood. He chose coats for the four children, too, guessing at their sizes, and because he'd so often seen Theresa reading, he added a thick book to the pile. There were other things, as well—a stick horse with a yarn mane for little Bill, a music box for Daisy, good pipe tobacco for Tom and a few things for the Gainers and their new baby.

While Fred Willand was wrapping it all in tissue paper, Lincoln crossed to the newspaper office, found it locked up and made for the Diamond Buckle Saloon.

Since it was early in the day, and Christmas Eve to boot, there were no customers. Kate, with her too-blond hair and low-cut dress, sat at one of the card tables, drinking coffee.

"Lincoln!" she said, beaming, starting to rise.

He motioned for her to stay in her chair, joined her at the table after placing a brotherly kiss on her rouged cheek. Like Wes, Kate was something worse for wear, a little tattered around the edges, but there was a remarkably pretty woman under all that paint and pretense.

"Is my brother around?"

Kate made a face. "He was up late, skinning honest working people out of their wages at five-card stud," she said. "Then he decided to write a piece for the paper on how the Bureau of Indian Affairs does more harm than good. Last time I saw him, he was under the blankets, snoring for all he was worth."

Lincoln chuckled at that. Wes had always been more alive at night—daylight was something he tended to wait out, like a case of the grippe—while Lincoln, a born rancher, wrung all the use he could from the hours between sunrise and sunset. "My new bride tells me you and Wes will be at the home place for Christmas Day," he said.

Kate looked worried now, as though he'd forced her into a corner and started poking at her with a cue stick from the rack next to the pool table. "Wes shouldn't have said we'd come," she said, her voice small and sad. She looked down at her gold satin dress, and the cleavage bulging above and behind her bodice. "I don't have anything proper to wear."

Lincoln reached out, took her hand. She wore a lot of cheap rings, and a row of bracelets that made a clinking sound whenever she moved her arm. "Juliana is going to be mighty disappointed if you don't come," he told her. "Gracie, too. It doesn't matter what you wear, Kate."

"What do you know? You're a man."

He sighed. "All right, then. There are trunks full of dresses out at the ranch, up in the attic. Take your pick."

"Beth's dresses," Kate scoffed, but there was hope in her hazel-colored eyes. "Lincoln, she was a little bitty thing and you know it. I'd never fit into anything she wore."

That, Lincoln thought, was probably true. "How about something of Ma's, then?" he suggested.

Wes appeared on the stairway just then, shirt un-tucked, feet bare, hair rumpled from sleep. He plunged his hands through it a lot when he was composing one of his hide-blistering opinion pieces for the *Courier.*

He scowled at Lincoln, even as Kate gave a throaty little chuckle. "Wouldn't *that* stick under the old lady's saddle like a spiky burr?" Lincoln remarked.

"What the devil are *you* doing here?" Wes grumbled at Lincoln, reaching the table, hauling back a chair next to Kate and falling into it as heavily as a sack of feed thrown from the back of a wagon. He winced when he landed, and closed his eyes for a moment, probably suffering his just deserts after a night passed drinking, gambling and puffing on cigars.

"I came to tell you that you were right about what you said yesterday," Lincoln said, enjoying the visible impact this announcement had on Wes.

He opened his eyes, narrowed them suspiciously. Kate got up to head for the kitchen and fetch coffee for both of them. Lincoln could have done without, but Wes was plainly in dire need.

"Hold it," Wes ground out, grinning a little and working his right temple with the fingertips of one hand. "You just said I was *right*. Will you swear to it in front of witnesses?"

"Kate was a witness," Lincoln pointed out.

"I'm putting it on the front page. Two-inch headline. This is the biggest thing since McKinley's assassination, if not Honest Abe's."

Lincoln smiled, picked up a stray poker chip left behind after some previous game and turned it between his fingers. When he spoke, though, he looked serious, and he sounded that way, too. "I'm in love with Juliana, Wes," he confided. "And I'll be damned if I know how to tell her."

Wes leaned a little, laid a hand on Lincoln's shoulder, squeezed. "Same way you told Beth," he said quietly. "You just look her in the eye, open your mouth and say 'I love you.'"

Lincoln shifted uncomfortably in his chair, wishing Kate would come back with that coffee, even though he didn't want it, so the conversation might turn in some easier direction.

"You *did* tell Beth you loved her, didn't you?" Wes challenged, looking worried.

"I thought she knew it," Lincoln confessed. "By the things I did, I mean."

"Keeping a roof over her head? Buying her geegaws and putting food on the table? Sweet Jesus, Lincoln, you're even more of a lunkhead than I thought you were."

Kate returned, a mug of steaming coffee in each hand and a big smile on her face—he'd struck home with that suggestion that she wear one of his ma's dresses to Christmas dinner, evidently—but her arrival didn't change the course of the conversation the way Lincoln had hoped it would.

She set a cup in front of each of them, and Wes scooted back his chair, caught hold of her hand and tugged hard so she landed, giggling like a girl, on his lap.

"I love you, Katie-did," he said.

"So you claim," Kate joked, blushing right down to the neckline of her faded dress. "But you've yet to put a gold band on my finger, Weston Creed."

He feigned surprise. "You'd actually hitch yourself to a waster like me?"

"You know I would," Kate said softly, looking and sounding wistful now.

"Then the next time the reverend comes through, we'll throw a wedding."

Lincoln, though pleased, wished he was elsewhere. The trouble with Wes was, he had no idea what was appropriate and what wasn't, but he seemed to be sincere enough, all things considered.

"Is that a promise?" Kate asked cautiously.

"It's a promise," Wes replied, setting her on her feet again, swatting her once on the bottom for emphasis. That done, he pivoted on his chair seat to look straight at Lincoln. "See, little brother? That's how you tell a woman you love her."

Lincoln merely shook his head. He reckoned Fred had the presents wrapped by then, and he was eager to get back out to the ranch. After all, Christmas was coming, and this one was special.

He stood. "You might want to ride out with me," he told his brother. "Kate's going to borrow one of Ma's dresses, and she'll need time to take it in a little first."

Wes gave a guffaw of laughter that made Kate jump and got to his feet. "That," he said, "will be worth seeing. But I'll meet you at the ranch later on—I've got to put on boots and get my horse saddled, and I don't want to hold you up."

"See you there," Lincoln agreed with a nod. He was halfway home, with his sack of presents tied behind his saddle, when Wes rode up alongside him.

They'd didn't speak of serious things—there had been enough of that and it was almost Christmas—except when they reached the barn. Lincoln unsaddled his horse, Wes didn't.

"Are you really going to marry Kate?" Lincoln asked, half-afraid of the answer. She'd be mighty let down if Wes's proposal turned out to be a joke, and by Lincoln's reckoning, Kate had had more than her share of disappointments as it was.

"Didn't I say that I would?"

"You say a lot of things, Wes."

"This time, I mean it."

Lincoln nodded. "I hope so," he replied, and that was the end of the exchange.

Inside the house, Wes was greeted with an armload of Gracie, launching herself from the floor like a stone from a catapult, while the other kids hung back, looking stalwart and shy.

Wes noticed the way Juliana was glowing right away, and cast a sly look in Lincoln's direction before kissing her soundly on the forehead.

After that, the two brothers headed straight for their mother's bedroom and plundered the big mahogany wardrobe for a dress that would suit Kate without too much tucking and pinning. Flummoxed by the choices, they finally consulted Juliana, who chose a dusty-rose velvet day dress with a short jacket, pearl buttons and a nipped-in waist.

"Been a while since Ma could squeeze into *this*," Wes observed, holding the getup against his front as if he meant to try it on himself.

"It will look fine on Kate," Lincoln said drily. "Personally, I think you'd look better in blue."

Juliana took the dress from Wes, carried it to the kitchen and proceeded to fold it neatly and wrap it up in leftover brown paper, tying the parcel closed with thick twine.

Gracie, having worked out that her beloved uncle and Kate were coming out to the ranch to share in tomorrow's celebration, issued an invitation of her very own. "Come *early*," she pleaded, "because Papa probably won't let us see what Saint Nicholas brought until you get here."

Wes laughed, tugged at a lock of her hair. "Just what time is 'early'?" he asked. Of all the people in the world, Gracie was probably the only one he would have rolled out of the hay for. Lincoln had known him to sleep until four o'clock in the afternoon.

Gracie considered. "Six o'clock," she said.

Wes gave a comical groan.

"Uncle Wes," Gracie said firmly, "it's *Christmas*."

"You could come out tonight," Lincoln suggested carefully. "Sleep in your old room."

Behind his grin, Wes went solemn, no doubt remembering how it had been when their father was still alive, and testy as an old bear with ear mites.

"Bed's wide enough for you and Kate," Lincoln added. "Since you and Micah used to share it."

"Maybe," Wes said thoughtfully.

"Say yes," Gracie ordered, hands resting on her hips.

"Maybe," Wes repeated. He glanced sidelong at Lincoln, an unspoken reminder of the warning he'd given out on the range the day before, probably. Gracie definitely *did* have a mind of her own, and as she grew up, she'd be a handful.

Nothing much was said after that. Wes took the gown, wrapped in its brown paper, and left.

Lincoln went to work on the adoption petition he'd been drafting, and Juliana visited the Gainers. The kids, having been given the day off from their lessons because it was Christmas Eve, chased one another all over the front yard until Juliana rounded them up on the way back from the cabin and brewed up another batch of hot cocoa.

For the rest of the day, Lincoln had half his mind on the petition and half on Juliana. The way she moved. The way she hummed under her breath and looked like she was all lit up from the inside.

Mentally, he rehearsed the words he wanted to say. *I love you.*

By sunset, the children were all so excited—except for Joseph, who showed a manful disdain for the proceedings—they could barely sit still to eat supper.

New snow drifted past the windows, and for once, Lincoln didn't dread it.

The dishes were done, the fires were stoked for a cold night.

The kids were all in bed, asleep. Or so they wanted him to believe.

Just as Lincoln was about to extinguish the lanterns and join Juliana in their bed—he'd been looking forward to that all day—he heard a rig roll up outside.

He grinned, put on his coat and hat. There would be a wagon to unhitch, a team to put up in the barn.

Juliana appeared, still wearing her day dress, just as he was opening the door to go outside.

"Wes and Kate are here," he said.

Juliana beamed, as happy at the prospect of company as any country woman would be. "I'll start a pot of coffee."

CHAPTER NINE

CHRISTMAS MORNING was joyful chaos, the younger kids tearing into their packages and squealing with delight at the contents. Juliana watched them with a smile, as did Lincoln and Tom, Wes and Kate. Ben and Rose-of-Sharon had joined them for breakfast with the baby, and so had the other ranch hands.

Theresa opened her gifts slowly, while Joseph examined the first one—a set of watercolors Lincoln had given him—leaving the others unwrapped beside him on the floor.

Juliana, quietly happy, paused often to admire the gold wedding band Lincoln had given her late the night before in their bedroom. They'd made love afterward—Lincoln had taken his time pleasuring her, and the wonder of it still reverberated through her, when she let herself remember, like the aftershocks of an earthquake.

There had been no pain, only a little soreness afterward. Juliana had been as voracious as Lincoln, reveling in eager surrender, but that hadn't been the best part, nor had the ring.

When they'd gone to their room, after several hours spent visiting with Wes and his shy but delightful Kate around the kitchen table, Lincoln had sat her down on the edge of the bed, knelt before her and taken her hands into his.

He'd looked directly into her eyes, cleared his throat out of a nervousness she would always remember with tenderness, and said, "Juliana, I love you."

And she'd replied in kind. If she hadn't already loved him, that declaration, and the way he made it, would have sealed the matter for sure.

They were midway through dinner, Tom having roasted the two turkeys to perfection, when the inevitable happened.

A buggy appeared in the side yard beyond the kitchen windows, and Mr. Philbert drew back hard on the reins.

Juliana barely stifled a gasp.

Laughing at a raucous story Wes had just told, no one else had seen or heard the buggy's approach.

Lincoln, catching sight of the look on Juliana's face, turned in his chair and saw the small man alighting, righteous indignation apparent in his every move. "Is that him?" he asked.

Juliana nodded, afraid she'd burst into tears if she spoke.

Mr. Philbert had reached the back step. He pounded on the door, his fist still raised when Lincoln swung it open.

Everyone fell silent, and Daisy and Billy-Moses both rushed to Juliana and scrambled onto her lap, clinging to her.

The Indian agent wore an avidly righteous expression as he stepped past Lincoln, all his attention fastened on Juliana. Triumph sparked in his tiny eyes, behind the smudged lenses of his spectacles; he'd planned to arrive early all along, just as she'd feared, hoping to take her unawares, circumvent any steps she might take to avoid him. She *had* hoped to have Joseph and Theresa safely away from Stillwater Springs before he got there, but that was not to be.

Tom and Wes both slid back their chairs to stand.

Kate, sitting next to Theresa, slipped a protective arm around the girl's shoulders.

Philbert ignored them all, his gaze riveted on Juliana, trying to make her wilt. Jabbing an ink-stained index finger in her direction, he finally spoke. "I have half a mind to charge you with kidnapping!"

"Watch what you say to my wife," Lincoln said evenly.

Wes stepped in, exuding charm and hospitality. "Sit down," he told Mr. Philbert. "Have some of our Christmas dinner."

A silence fell. Clearly, Mr. Philbert had not expected the invitation.

Wes found a clean plate and silverware. Gave up his own chair so the unwanted guest would have a place to sit.

Looking baffled and taking in the spread of food with undisguised hunger, Mr. Philbert sat down.

Lincoln, after exchanging glances with Wes, returned to his own chair. Reached for Juliana's hand and squeezed it reassuringly.

Tom took Mr. Philbert's plate and filled it to overflowing with turkey, mashed potatoes, green beans and rolls still warm from the oven in the cookstove.

Mr. Philbert hesitated, and then, to Juliana's amazement, began to eat.

"My wife and I intend to adopt Daisy and Bill," Lincoln said after a few moments. "I've drawn up the papers, and I'll see that they're filed right after Christmas."

Both Daisy and Billy-Moses looked at Lincoln curiously, not understanding, but probably instinctively hopeful. Both of them adored Lincoln; he had a way of including them in the expansive warmth of his attention and affection without excluding Gracie.

Juliana held the little ones tightly in both arms.

His mouth full of mashed potatoes, Mr. Philbert couldn't answer.

Joseph spoke up. "I'm taking my sister home," he said. "And if you try to stop us, we'll just run off the first chance we get."

Mr. Philbert chewed, swallowed. He was red in the jowls, and his muttonchop whiskers bobbed. He waved a dismissive hand at Joseph. "Good riddance," he said. "I've got all the problems I need as it is."

Juliana's heart rose on a swell of relief, even though his attitude stung. Was that all *any* of the children whose lives and educations he oversaw were to him? Problems? Daisy and Billy-Moses huddled closer, and Gracie came to stand at her side, staring at Mr. Philbert.

"You have a big nose," the child remarked charitably.

"Gracie," Juliana said. "That will be enough."

"Well, he does. And it's purple on the end."

"Gracie," Lincoln admonished.

Gracie subsided, leaning against Juliana now. She

hadn't been deliberately rude; there was no meanness in her. She'd merely been making an observation.

Juliana shifted so she could wrap one arm around the little girl without sending Daisy toppling to the floor.

"Children," Mr. Philbert said with a long-suffering sigh. "They are such troublesome little creatures."

Juliana longed to refute that statement—there were a thousand things she wanted to say, but she held her tongue. It would not do to give the man a reason to dislike her even more than he already did.

"Nevertheless," he went on, taking clear and unflattering satisfaction in his power over all of them, "duty is duty. Adoption or none, I intend to take the little ones back to Missoula with me for the interim. I have to account for them, you know."

Tom's face turned hard, and he started to rise.

Wes, standing just behind him and to the side, having given up his chair to Mr. Philbert, laid a warning hand on Tom's shoulder.

"Now, why would you want to go to all the trouble to drag them all the way to Missoula?" Lincoln asked, with a sort of easy bewilderment. "They're fine right here, part of a family."

Mr. Philbert reddened again, stabbed his fork into a slice of turkey. "According to the storekeeper in town, you and Mr. Creed are married now. Is that true, Juliana?"

He'd spoken to Mr. Willand, Juliana concluded disconsolately. That was how he'd known about the marriage—the reverend had probably scattered the news far and wide—and where to find her and the children.

"It's true," Juliana said.

"Awfully convenient," Mr. Philbert remarked, with an unpleasant smile. "Wouldn't you agree?"

Gracie took issue. "Don't you talk to my mama in that tone of voice," she warned.

That time, neither Lincoln nor Juliana scolded her.

Mr. Philbert raised his eyebrows, took the time to fork in, chew and swallow more turkey before responding. The law was on his side, as far as Juliana knew. He had the upper hand, and he wasn't going to let anyone forget that.

Daisy, uncomprehending and frightened nonetheless, turned her face into Juliana's bodice and began to cry silently, her small shoulders trembling. Juliana kissed the top of her head, stroked her raven-black hair.

"I don't think I've ever seen an Indian cry before," Mr. Philbert mused, sparing no notice for the child's obvious grief and fear.

Tom started to his feet again; Wes stopped him by putting that same hand to his shoulder and pressing him back down.

"Daisy," Lincoln said to Mr. Philbert, his voice measured, the voice of a lawyer in court, "is a *child.* She's three years old. You're scaring her, and that's something that I won't tolerate for any reason."

"I have legal authority—"

"So do I," Lincoln broke in evenly. "This is my house. This is my ranch. And if you want to take these children anywhere, you're going to need a court order and half the United States Army to help you. *Do* you have a court order, Mr. Philbert?"

Mr. Philbert sputtered a little. "Well, no, but—"

"You'd better get one, then. Before you manage that,

I'll have been to Helena to file the petition and Daisy and Bill will be Creeds, as much my children in the eyes of the law as Gracie here."

Mr. Philbert considered that, gulped, then worked up a faltering smile and asked, "I don't suppose there's any pie?"

An hour later, having topped off his meal with two slices of mincemeat pie, the agent handed Juliana a bank draft covering her last month's salary, warned her that if she should ever apply for any teaching position, anywhere, she should not give his name as a reference.

And then, blessedly, he was gone.

TAKING NO CHANCES, LEST Mr. Philbert had a change of heart, Tom and Lincoln were up even earlier than usual the next morning. They hitched up the team and wagon while Juliana helped Joseph and Theresa pack for their journey. Once the two young people were on board a train east, with Tom to escort them, Lincoln would travel to Helena, stand before a judge and enter the petition to adopt Daisy and Billy-Moses.

Juliana was afraid to hope the Bureau of Indian Affairs would not step in. At the same time, something within her sang a silent, swelling song of jubilation.

Although she tried to keep up a good front, Juliana despaired as she watched Joseph and Theresa buttoning up the new coats Lincoln had given them for Christmas. They would miss her and the other children, she knew, but the joy of going home, of truly belonging somewhere, shone in their faces.

Juliana hugged both of them, one and then the other, but avoided looking through the window after they'd gone out, unable to watch as they got into the wagon. There would be letters, at least from Theresa, but considering the distance, it was unlikely that she would ever see them again. Eventually, their correspondence would slow, however good everyone's intentions were, and finally stop.

Gracie, standing at Juliana's side, took her hand. "Don't be sad, Mama," she said. "Please, don't be sad."

But Juliana couldn't help crying as she took Gracie into her arms.

Lincoln returned to the house to say goodbye. "I'll be back in a few days," he said. "Ben and the others will look after the cattle and the chores. If Philbert comes back here, send somebody to town to fetch Wes."

Juliana nodded, barely able to absorb any of it. The parting from Lincoln was, in some ways, the hardest thing of all.

He gave her a lingering kiss.

Then he, too, was gone.

Billy-Moses, who had sat quietly near the stove during all the farewells, stacking blocks, knocking them down and then stacking them again, suddenly hurtled toward the door, flinging himself at it, struggling with the latch and uttering long cries of angry sorrow. Juliana hurried to the child, knelt beside him, pulling him into her arms, stroking his hair, murmuring to him.

He wailed for Theresa, for Joseph, for Lincoln, sobbing out each name in turn, between shrieks of despair. Weeping herself, while Gracie and Daisy looked on with forlorn expressions, each clasping the other's hand, Juliana lifted Billy-Moses up and carried him to the rocking chair.

He was a long time quieting down, but Juliana rocked him, holding him tightly long after he'd stopped struggling. Eventually, he fell into a fitful sleep.

Gracie came to lean against the arm of the chair, her face earnest. "Doesn't Billy want to be my brother? Doesn't he want to be a Creed?"

Juliana, more composed by then, smiled and tilted her head so it rested against Gracie's. "Of course he does, sweetheart," she said very quietly. "He misses Joseph and Theresa, that's all. And your papa and Tom, too."

Gracie nodded solemnly, but quickly braced up. "Papa said he'd come back, and Papa always does what he says he's going to do."

"Yes," Juliana agreed, heartened. "He does."

The next day, Wes returned to the ranch, bringing a telegram from Lincoln, sent that morning from Missoula. Tom, Theresa and Joseph had boarded the train; they would be in North Dakota within the week.

To keep busy, Juliana divided her time between giving Gracie reading, spelling and arithmetic lessons at the kitchen table, visiting Rose-of-Sharon and the baby, and poring over a collection of old cookery books she'd found in a pantry cabinet.

Lincoln sent another telegram the following day when he reached Helena, promising that he'd be home soon.

Determined to use the waiting time constructively, Juliana bravely assembled the ingredients to bake a batch of corn bread, followed the directions to the letter, and almost set the kitchen on fire by putting too much wood in the stove.

On the third day, the previously mild weather turned nasty. Snow flew with such ferocity that, often, Juliana couldn't see the barn from the kitchen window, even in broad daylight. She knew that Lincoln planned to return to Missoula from Helena by rail, once he'd completed his business in the state capital, reclaim his wagon and team from a local livery stable and drive back to the ranch. With what appeared to be a blizzard brewing, Juliana was worried.

He could get lost in the storm, even freeze to death somewhere along the way.

In an effort to distract herself from this worry, Juliana carefully removed all the decorations from the Christmas tree, packing them away in their boxes. When Ben Gainer brought a bucket of milk to the back door that evening, shivering with cold even in his warm coat, Juliana made him come inside and drink hot coffee.

Somewhat restored after that, Ben dragged the big tree across the floor and out the front door. Later, it would be chopped up and burned.

The storm continued through the night, and snow was still coming down at a furious rate in the morning, drifting up against the sides of the house, high enough that if she'd been able to open a window, Juliana could have scooped the stuff up in her hands.

Ben brought more milk, and told Juliana he hoped the snow would let up soon, because he and the other two ranch hands were having a hard time getting the hay sled out to the range cattle, even with the big draft horses to pull it.

One question thudded in the back of Juliana's mind day and night like a drumbeat that never went silent.

Where was Lincoln?

She tried to be sensible. He'd probably had to stay in Missoula to wait out the storm, and sent another telegram informing her of that. Since the road between Stillwater Springs and the ranch was under at least three feet of snow, Wes wouldn't be able to bring her the message, like he had the others.

There was nothing to do but wait.

Juliana tried the corn bread recipe again, and even though it came out hard as a horseshoe, at least this time smoke didn't pour out of the oven. Soaked in warm milk, the stuff was actually edible.

The next day, Ben strung ropes from the house to the cabin and the cabin to the barn; it was the only way he could get from one place to the other without being lost in the blizzard. The draft horses knew the way to and from the cluster of trees where the herd had taken shelter; otherwise, the cattle would have gone hungry.

On the fifth night, Juliana lingered in the kitchen, long after the children had gone to sleep, watching the clock and waiting.

At first, she thought she'd imagined the sound at the back door, but then the latch jiggled. She fairly leaped out of her chair, hurried across the room and hauled open the door.

The icy wind was so strong that it made her bones ache, but she didn't care. Lincoln was standing on the back step, coated in ice and snow, seemingly unable to move.

Juliana cried out, used all her strength to pull him inside and managed to shut the door against the wind by leaning on it with the full weight of her body.

"Lincoln?"

He didn't speak, didn't move. How had he gotten home with the roads the way they were? Surely the team and wagon couldn't have passed through snow that deep—it would have reached to the tops of the wheels.

She had to pry his hat free of his head—it had frozen to his hair. Next, she peeled off the coat, tossed it aside.

She thought of tugging him nearer the stove, but she recalled reading about frostbite somewhere; it was important that he warm up slowly.

His clothes were stiff as laundry left to freeze on a clothesline. She ran for the bedrooms, snatching up all the blankets she could find that weren't already in use and hurried back to the kitchen.

Lincoln was still standing where she'd left him; his lips were blue, and his teeth had begun to chatter.

"Whiskey," he said in a raw whisper.

Juliana rushed into the pantry, found the bottle he kept on a high shelf. Pouring some into a cup, she raised it to his mouth, holding it patiently while he sipped.

A great shudder went through him, but he wasn't so stiff now, and some of the color returned to his face.

"Help me out of these clothes," he ground out. "My fingers aren't working."

She pulled off his gloves first, and was relieved to see no sign of frostbite. His toes could be affected, though, and even if they weren't, the specter of pneumonia loomed in that kitchen like a third presence.

She unbuttoned his shirt, helped him out of it, then pulled his woolen undershirt off over his head, too. She immediately wrapped him in one of the blankets. He managed to sit down in the chair she brought from the table, and she crouched to pull off his boots, strip away his socks.

His toes, like his fingers, were still intact, though he admitted he couldn't feel them.

He seemed so exhausted just from what they'd done so far that Juliana gave him another dose of whiskey before removing his trousers and tucking more blankets in around him.

"How did you get here?" she asked as he sat there shivering, a good distance from the stove. "My Lord, Lincoln, you must have been out in the weather for hours."

Remarkably, a grin tilted up one corner of his mouth. "I rode Wes's mule out from town," he answered slowly, groping for each word. "Good thing that critter can smell hay and a warm stall from a mile off."

"You rode Wes's mule?" If Juliana hadn't been so glad he was home, she would have been furious. "Lincoln Creed, are you insane? If you got as far as Stillwater Springs—and God knows how you managed that—you should have stayed there!"

"You're here," he said. "Gracie and Bill and Daisy are here. This is where I belong."

"You could have frozen to death! What good would that have done us?"

He didn't respond to that question. Instead, he said, "You'd better get some snow to pack around my feet and hands, or else I might lose a few fingers and toes."

The action was contrary to every instinct Juliana possessed, but she knew he was right. After bundling up, she took the milk bucket outside and filled it with snow.

Returning to the kitchen, she marveled that Lincoln had been able to travel in that weather, probably for hours, when she'd been chilled to her marrow by a few moments in the backyard.

The process of tending to Lincoln was slow and, for him, painful. It was after two in the morning when he told her there had been enough of the snow packs. She led him to their room, put him to bed like a child, piling blanket after blanket on top of him.

Still he shivered.

She built the hearth fire up until it roared.

Lying in the darkness, under all those blankets, he chuckled. "Juliana, no more wood," he said. "You'll set the house on fire."

There was nothing more she could do except put on her nightgown and join him. He trembled so hard that the whole bed frame shook, and his skin felt as cold as stone.

She huddled close to him, sharing the warmth of her own body, enduring the chill of his. When he finally slept, she could not, exhausted as she was, because she was so afraid of waking up to find him dead.

For most of the night, she kept her vigil. Then, too tired to keep her eyes open for another moment, she drifted off.

When she woke up, his hand was underneath her nightgown.

"There's one way you could warm me up," he said wickedly.

He was safe.
He was warm again, and well.
And Juliana gladly gave herself up to him.

EPILOGUE

June 1911

JULIANA CREED STOOD IN Willand's Mercantile, visibly pregnant and beaming as she read Theresa's most recent letter through for the second time before folding it carefully and tucking it into her handbag. She and Joseph had attended a small school on the reservation since their return to North Dakota, but now they would have the whole summer off. Joseph had a temporary job milking cows on a nearby farm, while Theresa would be helping her grandmother tend the garden.

Juliana looked around the store for her children.

Billy-Moses—now called just Bill or Billy most of the time, a precedent Lincoln had set—was examining a toy train carved out of wood, while Daisy and Gracie browsed through hair ribbons, ready-made dresses with ruffles, and storybooks.

With all of them accounted for, her mind turned to the men. Tom was at the blacksmith's, having a horse shod, and Lincoln had gone to the *Courier,* looking for Wes.

Marriage had changed Weston Creed. He was, as Lincoln put it, "damn near to becoming a respectable citizen." Remarkably, given the long estrangement between her and Wes, the elder Mrs. Creed had returned to Stillwater Springs for the wedding back in April. While she hadn't been happy about having a saloonkeeper for a daughter-in-law, she'd behaved with remarkable civility.

Cora had stayed long enough to size Juliana up, decided she'd do as a wife for Lincoln and a stepmother for Gracie, and then she'd announced that she was taking up permanent residence with her cousins in Phoenix. She was too old, she maintained, to keep going back and forth.

Although they'd been a little stiff with each other at first, Juliana had soon come to like her mother-in-law. While Cora had been cool to Kate, she *had* made the long journey home to attend the wedding. During her stay at the ranch, she'd treated Daisy and Billy as well as she had Gracie.

Before her departure, though, Cora and Juliana had agreed, in a spirit of goodwill, that one Creed woman per household was plenty.

When the little bell over the mercantile chimed, Juliana turned in the direction of the door, expecting to see Lincoln, or perhaps Tom.

Her heart missed a beat when she recognized Clay.

Their eyes met, but neither of them spoke.

Clay stood just over the threshold, handsome in his well-tailored suit. His hair was darker than Juliana's, more chestnut than red, but his eyes were the same shade of blue.

Watching her, he removed his very fashionable hat. "Juliana," he said gravely, with a slight nod.

"Clay," Juliana whispered. And then she ran to him, threw her arms around him.

Tentatively, he put his arms around her, too. After a stiff moment, he hugged her back. "You're looking well," he said, his voice gruff with emotion.

Juliana blushed, confounded by joy, pushing back far enough to look up into her brother's face. "When you didn't answer my letter, I thought—"

He smiled, glancing down at her protruding middle. "You did say you were married?" he teased.

She showed him her wedding ring. "How long have you been in town? The train came through three days ago."

"I've been staying at the Comstock Hotel, trying to work up the courage to hire a buggy over at the livery stable and drive out to the ranch to see you."

"Oh, Clay—surely you knew you'd be welcome."

"I *didn't* know," he replied. "According to my wife, I've been behaving like an ogre ever since you refused to marry John Holden, and I'm afraid Nora's right about that."

Juliana's eyes misted over. "I've missed you," she said.

He kissed her forehead. "I'd like to meet this husband of yours," he told her. "Your letter made him sound like a paragon."

The door opened again, and Lincoln was there.

Still tearful—tears came more easily with her pregnancy—Juliana moved to Lincoln's side. He put an arm around her, regarding Clay curiously and then with a grin of recognition.

"You must be Clay Mitchell," he said. "With eyes that color, you have to be related to Juliana."

Clay nodded in acknowledgment. "And you're Lincoln Creed," he replied.

"Papa!" Billy yelled, racing across the store to be hoisted into Lincoln's arms. Lincoln ruffled the boy's hair and laughed.

Clay's eyes widened momentarily, but then he smiled again.

"Daisy," Juliana called, "Gracie—come and meet your uncle Clay."

He charmed those two little girls by executing a gentlemanly bow. "Ladies," he said solemnly, making them giggle.

Still carrying Billy, Lincoln excused himself and went to the counter to speak to Fred Willand about their grocery order.

"You will come out to the ranch and stay with us for a few days, won't you, Clay?" Juliana asked quietly.

"I'd be glad to," Clay assured her.

On the way home, having collected his bag from the hotel, Clay rode on the wagon seat next to Juliana with Lincoln at the reins, while Gracie, Billy and Daisy bounced along in back like always, seated among crates of groceries.

"He doesn't seem so bad to me," Lincoln said much later, when he and Juliana had retired to their room for the night. They'd talked right through supper, the three of them, and for a couple of hours afterward.

"This is the Clay I knew before," Juliana said, choking up a little. The change in her brother seemed miraculous.

Sitting on the edge of the bed, Lincoln pulled off one boot and then the other. Juliana remembered the night he'd ridden a mule through three feet of snow, nearly losing his fingers and toes, if not his life.

"I've never had a sister," Lincoln said, "but I can imagine that if I did, I might have some pretty hard-headed opinions about what she should and shouldn't do."

Juliana stood in front of the mirror, brushing her hair. "We were so young when our mother died," she mused. She'd long since told Lincoln all about her family history, John Holden and his daughters, secretly studying to be a teacher when her grandmother believed she was in finishing school. "Clay's a little older, and I guess I expected him to be strong, maybe our grandmother did, too. But he was really a child, as scared and lost and hurt as I was. I hate to think what must have gone through his mind when our father left us at Grandmama's that day. Clay knew, even if I didn't, that Father wasn't coming back—and that meant he had to be a man from then on."

Lincoln came to stand behind her, bent his head to kiss her right ear. His hands caressed her round belly. "That corn bread you served at supper tonight was pretty good," he said.

She laughed. "It should have been," she replied. "I've been practicing for six months."

He took the brush from her hand, set it aside on the bureau, turned her around to face him. "Tom says you'll make a fine cook one of these days."

Juliana smiled. Tom had been giving her cookery lessons, and she was making progress. "He also says I try too hard." She slipped her arms around his middle and leaned against him. "What else can I do? I want to keep my husband happy."

Lincoln tasted her mouth, once, twice, a third time. "Your husband," he said, "is *very* happy."

She looked up at him. "I love you, Lincoln Creed. Just when I think I couldn't possibly love you more than I already do, something happens to prove me wrong."

"I love you, too," he replied, tracing the length of her cheek, and then her neck, with the lightest pass of his lips. He eased her toward the bed, still nibbling at her.

He put out the lamp.

"Lincoln, you're not listening to me," Juliana said, laughing a little, as delightfully nervous, in some ways, as she'd been on their wedding night.

He lowered her to the bed. "You're right," he said, kissing her again. "I'm not."

Already cherishing their unborn child, Lincoln was unspeakably tender as he caressed her belly and then slowly raised her nightgown, first to her knees, then her thighs, then her shoulders. With a groan of welcome, she raised her arms so he could slip the garment off over her head.

He kissed her distended stomach, his lips warm and faintly moist.

Juliana groaned again, rolled her eyes back in contentment and closed them, giving herself up to Lincoln, body, mind and spirit.

He loved the fullness of her breasts, kissed and nibbled at her taut nipples until she said his name in a ragged whisper.

Then he moved down along her breastbone, over her

middle, pausing at her abdomen before using his fingers to part the nest of curls at the juncture of her thighs. She whimpered as he stroked her with a slow, gentle motion of his hand, and although her eyes remained shut, she felt the dark burn of his gaze on her face. She knew he was silently asking her permission, and she nodded.

He made a sound that was wholly male, low in his throat.

In Lincoln's arms, Juliana had learned a sort of pleasure that she'd never imagined, and that night was no exception. Even before they'd conceived this child they both wanted so much, he'd always been careful, raising her to an explosive ecstasy and at the same time making her feel utterly safe.

For a time, he simply made slow circles with his fingers, and Juliana began to writhe in need and surrender, in triumph and exultation.

Her breath became shallow and rapid as he teased her. Then the first release came, shattering and sweet, leaving her shuddering. Knowing there would be more—much more—before the night was over, only increased her wanting.

Lincoln used his mouth on her next, and though it was scandalous, Juliana gloried in the intimacy of it, in the helplessness and the sheer power of the sensations he wrought in her, with every nibble, every flick of his tongue.

Again, she broke apart in a million fiery pieces, a primitive cry of satisfaction escaping her throat, but going no further than the thick log walls of their bedroom.

Only when Lincoln was certain he'd untied every

knot in Juliana's still-quivering body did he mount her, and ease into her depths with that heartrending tenderness she'd come to expect of him.

They rocked together, and she reached yet another pinnacle, softer and yet more intense than the others that had gone before. When Lincoln finally let himself go, Juliana finally opened her eyes, stroking his strong shoulders, his chest, his sides, her hands moving in ways that both soothed and inflamed.

Then he tensed upon her, and she felt life itself spill within her, the life that had brought their child into being, and Gracie, as well.

"I love you," Juliana whispered.

He sighed, kissed her cheek, her neck. Fell beside her. "And I love *you,* Juliana Creed."

IF JULIANA HAD YET TO MASTER cooking and housekeeping, she *had* learned to drive a buggy. On the morning of Clay's departure for Denver, she was the one who drove him to the depot in town.

"I've got eyes," Clay said, grinning, as they pulled up to await the train, "but I still need to hear you say it. Are you happy, Juliana?"

She kissed his cheek. "Ecstatic," she said, meaning it.

He reached into the inside pocket of his coat—his fine clothes made him stand out like the proverbial sore thumb in rustic Stillwater Springs—and brought out a thick envelope. Offered it to her.

In the distance, the train whistle shrilled.

Puzzled, Juliana looked at the envelope, then at Clay's face. "What...?"

"Your inheritance," Clay said. "These documents transfer full control to you. You're a rich woman, Juliana. Now that I've taken Lincoln Creed's measure, I know you'll be all right."

Stunned—it had been a long time since she'd given a thought to money—she accepted the papers. Then she beamed. "Now we can build a hay barn right on the range," she chimed in happy realization. "And the cattle will have somewhere to take shelter when the snows come."

Clay laughed. "Some women would want diamonds, or fine dresses."

The train chugged into view, and Juliana saddened a little at the sight, not willing to be parted from this brother she had loved for so long. "You'll come back when you can, won't you? And bring Nora and the children?"

He touched her cheek. "We'll be here," he said. "And you're welcome at our place anytime, Juliana. You and Lincoln and this brood of yours."

With that, he climbed down from the buggy, took his traveling case from under the seat. He looked up at her, winked, and then turned away, walking purposefully toward the depot.

Juliana waited until the train had pulled out before heading for home.

Lincoln was there, having minded the children while she was gone, and Ben and Rose-of-Sharon sat at the table, baby Joshua in his mother's arms. For all the difficulties of his birth, the infant was thriving.

Once the Gainers had left, Juliana took the envelope from her handbag and laid it on the table.

"What's this?" Lincoln asked.

"Open it," Juliana said lightly, "and read for yourself."

Lincoln hesitated, then did as he was told. His eyes widened as he read. "That's one hell of a lot of money," he said finally. "You are a wealthy woman, Juliana."

"*We* are wealthy," she clarified.

He grinned, and only then did she realize how tensely he'd held his shoulders while he read. Had he thought, for the briefest moment, that she'd leave him now that she was a woman of independent means?

She went to him, slipped her arms around his lean, hard waist. "I told Clay we'd be building a big hay barn out on the range, first thing."

Lincoln chuckled. "Speaking of the range, I'd better get out there. We've still got a few calves taking their time to get born."

Juliana began rolling up her sleeves. "I'll have supper ready when you get back," she said.

He gave a comical wince, and she slapped at him playfully.

Once he'd gone, Juliana took a deep breath. It was time to make another attempt at corn bread.

From the *Stillwater Springs Courier*:

September 18, 1911
This editor is proud to announce the
birth of a nephew,
Michael Thomas Creed.
Welcome.

* * * * *

**Don't miss this brand-new tale in
the McKettricks of Texas series from
New York Times and *USA TODAY* bestselling author**

LINDA LAEL MILLER

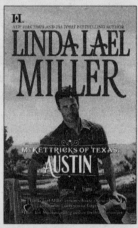

With his career abruptly over and his love life a mess, world
champion rodeo star Austin McKettrick has nowhere to go
when the hospital releases him. Except back home to Blue River,
Texas, to his overachieving brothers…and a sexy new nurse
who has her sights set on healing him—body and heart.

MCKETTRICKS OF TEXAS:

AUSTIN

Available now!

HQN™

We *are* romance™

www.HQNBooks.com

PHLLM446

New York Times and USA TODAY
Bestselling Author

DIANA PALMER

returns with two classic love stories in
a keepsake edition that will heat up your winter!

Lone Star Winter

Available now!

HQN™

We *are* romance™

www.HQNBooks.com

PHDP496

New York Times and **USA TODAY** bestselling author

SUSAN MALLERY

returns with a classic, sexy tale of small-town romance.

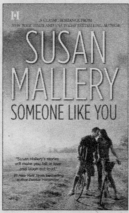

Jill Strathern left town for the big city and never looked back—until she returned home years later to run a small law practice. It turns out her childhood crush, Mac Kendrick, a burned-out LAPD cop, has also come back to sleepy Los Lobos, California...and neither can deny the sparks are still flying between them. But when mafia dons, social workers and angry exes start tangling up their lives, their romance might just get a little complicated....

SOMEONE LIKE YOU

Available now!

HQN™

We *are* romance™

www.HQNBooks.com

PHSM465